S0-AFN-908

CRITICS ARE RAVING ABOUT WINNIE GRIGGS AND *WHAT MATTERS MOST*

"A debut novel rarely comes together as perfectly as *What Matters Most*. . . . The story is well written, absorbing and, oh, so heart-warming. . . . This is a great start for an exceptional writer."

—*Romance Reviews Today*

"A quiet tale of faith and fortitude, [this] is one to warm the heart."

—*Romantic Times*

"Griggs creates likable characters in an engaging romantic conflict that will keep readers wide awake turning the pages and ignoring the lateness of the hour."

—*Crescent Blues Book Reviews*

"Ms. Griggs has given us a gentle read about strength, devotion, forgiveness and love. As matters of the heart go, this book is a must-read!"

—*Old Book Barn Gazette*

"*What Matters Most* is a heartwarming story. . . . I really enjoyed this book!"

—*The Romance Journal Reviews*

"Winnie Griggs's debut romance is sweet and emotional. . . . Solidly written with carefully drawn characters . . . *What Matters Most* is a charming first novel."

—*The Romance Reader*

A TELLING KISS

"Okay, now you give it a try."

Elthia froze. "What?"

"Your turn." Caleb tapped his cheek. "Just a little kiss, right here." When she hesitated, he raised an eyebrow. "What's the matter? Surely all this playacting isn't bothering you?"

"Oh, for goodness sake." She quickly leaned over and gave him a light peck.

Caleb shook his head. "Elthia darlin', you gotta do better. It needs to look like you want to kiss me. Let's try again. And remember, you're pretending to be a loving wife." He eyed her with a speculative gleam. "Of course, if you don't think you can remain unaffected . . . " He let a shrug finish his sentence.

Elthia glared. He was trying to manipulate her, to corner her into feeling she must prove herself. But even knowing this, she couldn't pass up the challenge. Tossing her head, she smiled. "Like this?" She lightly traced the side of his face with the back of her fingers as she leaned down to kiss him.

She lingered this time, but her I'll-show-*you* determination quickly changed to something softer. The sandpaper texture of his skin against her lips and the warmth of his breath stirring the hair next to her ear combined to set her pulse racing.

When she pulled away, her hand continued to stroke his jaw.

His cocky grin had disappeared.

Other *Leisure* books by Winnie Griggs:
WHAT MATTERS MOST

WINNIE GRIGGS

Something MORE

LEISURE BOOKS NEW YORK CITY

A LEISURE BOOK®

November 2001

Published by

Dorchester Publishing Co., Inc.
276 Fifth Avenue
New York, NY 10001

ISBN 0-8439-4934-1

Printed in the United States of America.

Visit us on the web at www.dorchesterpub.com.

To Connie, my talented critique partner and very dear friend.
Thank you for your enthusiasm, candor and generosity.
Thank you for seeing me as I really am and
remaining my friend in spite of it.
But most of all, thank you for always being there
when I need you.

Something More

Prologue

Harvestown, Indiana, 1872

Caleb crept downstairs, carefully avoiding the creaky third step. He wasn't supposed to be up, but this was important. Besides, he was six. That made him a big boy. Daddy said so. It was one of the last things he'd told Caleb before the accident.

Caleb's lip trembled, but he swiped the back of his hand across his nose and went on.

Reaching the bottom, he tiptoed across the hall and peeked into the dining room. Shadowy figures crowded the table. Dressed in black, they seemed strange, scary. Then he smelled Uncle Seth's pipe smoke, and with a blink of his tired eyes, the images settled into the familiar faces of his adult relatives.

Satisfied he was still safely among family, Caleb tiptoed to the parlor. He'd forgotten his pocketknife, and he just couldn't get to sleep until he knew for sure where it was.

He spied it on the bookshelf, just where he'd put it when Aunt Tabitha told him he couldn't bring such a thing to his father's funeral. No matter that it had been a birthday gift *from* his father. Sometimes grown-ups' rules made no sense.

With the treasured possession safely in his clutches, Caleb

retraced his steps, until he heard Grandfather's deep bass voice.

"It's agreed. We'll sell the farm and use the money to care for the young'uns. Now, who can provide a home to all six?"

Caleb froze and then eased back into the shadows. *They were gonna sell the farm! Their home!*

He chewed his lip. Maybe, if they were gonna live with one of the aunts and uncles, it wouldn't be so bad.

Caleb rubbed his thumb over the knobby-surfaced pocket-knife. Living with Aunt Tabitha and Uncle Seth might be fun. Then Sam and Philip would be like brothers instead of cousins. 'Course, living with Aunt Carol and Uncle Calvin wouldn't be so bad. Their young'uns were just babies, but they had horses.

For a while the only sounds were creaks and shuffling noises. Then Grandfather sighed. "I guess we'll have to split them up."

Caleb stiffened as the breath caught in his throat. *Split them up! No! It wasn't right. They needed—*

Aunt Tabitha's husky voice cut across his thoughts. "I'll take Annie. I love my boys, but I've always wanted a daughter."

"Any objections?" Grandfather asked. Then, "Very well; we'll put Annie in your care. Now, what about the others?"

Uncle Michael cleared his throat. "Twins should be together. Since we have the most room, Nora and I'll take Tommy and Timmy."

Aunt Carol, her soft voice just barely carrying to Caleb, spoke next. "Elizabeth can come with us. She's a sweet girl, and she'll be a help with the babies."

Caleb suddenly didn't feel like such a big boy. They were really doing it, splitting them up like a litter of puppies. Only he and Oren were left to claim, and then it would be done.

"I reckon we could take Oren too," Aunt Tabitha offered. "He and Sam get along like they hatched from the same clutch anyway."

Lucky Oren! Please, Aunt Tabitha, take me too.

Grandfather spoke again. "Now, that just leaves Caleb. George, Virgil, can one of you find a place for the boy?"

Silence. Caleb rubbed a trembling, sweaty hand on his nightshirt. Surely one of them would speak up.

Grandfather's voice was gruff when he finally broke the long silence. "Come now. Let's hear what you're thinking."

"Dorothy and I've been hitched less than a month." Caleb recognized Uncle Virgil's voice. "We need time to ourselves. Surely you can understand how we feel."

Then Uncle George spoke. "Father, you know as well as I do that I can't take the boy. I'm on board ship more than I'm home. There's no way I could take care of a child."

Grandfather huffed. "Well, then, who'll take on one more?"

Caleb inched closer so he could see into the room, anxiety overriding caution. Surely *someone* wanted him.

Aunt Carol cleared her throat. "What about Helen's sister?"

Grandfather Tanner reacted immediately. "Absolutely not! We Tanners take care of our own!"

"But we *are* taking care of our own," Uncle Michael interrupted. "We're taking in five of the children, and trying to find a good home for the sixth. I know Cora Fairfield is a spinster, but she's still young enough to keep up with a child."

Grandfather glared. "She lives in Texas. That'd be like sending Caleb into exile, parceling him off to a near stranger."

Aunt Nora took up the argument. "Father Tanner, shouldn't we at least talk to Cora? If something happened to Mike and me, God forbid, my brother'd want a say in what happened to our brood. Why, these are likely the only kin Cora has left."

The old man sat back. "Well, the idea just plumb don't sit right with me." He tugged on his beard, his expression as sour as if he'd bit on a green persimmon. Then he sighed. "You have a point about folks needing connection to their kin, though. I guess, if Cora truly wants Caleb, I won't deny her."

Caleb backed into the shadows again, hugging his knees tight against his chest. They were sending him away! Not just away from this house, but away from his brothers and sisters, away from his relatives, even away from Indiana.

Why didn't anyone want him?

Chapter One

Texas, 1892

"Whistling Oak," Mr. Farley announced as he yanked open the stagecoach door.

Left to stay seated or step out as she pleased, Elthia Sinclare pushed her glasses up on her nose. She was too relieved to have reached the end of this wretched, uncomfortable ride to concern herself with the driver's rudeness.

She picked up the basket that served as Poppy's carrier, tightened her hold on her parasol, and shifted forward. Moving to the door as if it were heaven's gate itself, she barely avoided a tumble when the coach lurched and then stilled again.

"Ooof!"

She turned to apologize to the passenger she'd inadvertently jabbed with her parasol. "Mr. Jenkins, I'm so—"

"Watch out!"

Elthia pivoted, this time carefully pointing her parasol toward the floor. "Oh dear, Miss Simms, I didn't mean—"

The matronly woman gave her a tight smile as she straightened her tipsily angled hat. "That's all right, dear. This *is* your stop, isn't it? You just go on now. Don't want to keep whoever's meeting you waiting."

"But—"

"No, really, just go on."

Elthia looked around. Several other passengers were nodding agreement. Really, this was the nicest group of people. Especially considering the fuss Poppy had made with his yipping eagerness to get to know the other passengers this past hour.

She gave them all a big smile, then stepped through the coach door, ready to begin her new life.

Feet finally planted firmly on the ground, Elthia took a deep breath of the dusty, pine-scented air, and arched her back. Not even cramped muscles could dampen her exhilaration.

She'd made it! Traveled all the way from Maryland to Texas on her own. Her family would be dumbfounded when they learned what she'd done. And even if they were angry, they'd never again be able to treat her as if she couldn't take care of herself.

She was determined to be the best governess the Tanners could have ever hoped to hire. In three months she would return home with glowing references, solid proof to present her father that he needn't rush out to find a husband to care for her.

Then she looked around and frowned.

Whistling Oak wasn't at all as she'd pictured it. Rather than a small town, it was a single weathered building set next to a horse pen and barn, stuck in the middle of nowhere. She hadn't expected to find the busy streets of Terrelmore, but she'd certainly expected to find more than pine trees and brush.

And where was Mr. Tanner? She was eager to start proving herself. The prospect thrilled her as nothing had for quite some time. Her brother was right; she'd spent too much time observing life and too little time participating. That all changed today.

On the heels of that thought, a heavily bearded ox of a man appeared from inside the station. Elthia's hands clenched on the handle of the basket as her heartbeat accelerated with a sickening lurch. Surely this wasn't—

When the rough-looking fellow moved to the front of the stage to help with the horses, she let out a little sigh of relief

and smiled at her own absurdity. This man couldn't possibly
have been Mr. Tanner. Mrs. Pembroke had described the Tanners as more genteel, more prosperous, than this lumbering
stage handler.

Poppy's yipping bark drew her attention back to the basket
in her arms. "I'm sorry," she told the handful of fluff. "You need
to stretch your legs too, don't you?"

She tucked the parasol under her arm and plucked a leash
from the basket. Clipping it to Poppy's collar, she rubbed her
cheek against his and set him on the ground.

When no one else appeared from inside the station, she
approached Mr. Farley, pointing the way with her parasol.
"Pardon me, but are you sure this is Whistling Oak?"

Hefting a trunk to his shoulder, the lanky driver paused and
eyed the parasol warily. "Yes, ma'am. See that ol' oak tree over
yonder with the hole in the middle? That's what gave this place
its name. Big wind blows through just right and you can hear
the whistling for nearly a mile."

She chewed on her lip, letting the parasol fall to her side.
"Oh. Well, perhaps Mr. Tanner is still inside."

Mr. Farley's scraggly mustache twitched. "Ain't no horses
hitched to the rail. Unless your friend walked, he ain't here."

"But Mr. Tanner was supposed to meet me." Elthia paused
when she heard the what-do-I-do-now tone in her voice. Panic
would never do. This was just one more obstacle to test her
mettle. She *could* handle this.

The driver spat on the ground between them. "Sorry your
friend's late." He nodded toward the bearded hulk helping
with the horses. "But Josiah'll look out for you while you wait.
Looks a mite rough, but you just don't pay that no mind. Josiah
wouldn't hurt a fly; leastways not without good reason."

Heavens! Surely Mr. Farley wouldn't leave before Mr. Tanner
arrived.

She followed him, struggling to keep up with his long-legged
stride. "But what if there's been a mix-up and Mr. Tanner
doesn't show up today? You can't just abandon me."

Mr. Farley set her trunk on the station porch and tilted his
hat back. "Sorry, lady, I can't sit around playing nursemaid 'til
your ride gets here. I've got other passengers to think about."

Her spine stiffened at the word *nursemaid*. One of the things she'd come here to prove was that she could handle things without the aid of her family.

Ignoring her, Mr. Farley marched back to the coach, hefted another trunk, then nearly dropped it as he turned to find her right behind him. Shooting her a thin-lipped grimace, he shifted his load and stepped around her. "Look, if you want to climb back in and go as far as Turtle Creek, the fare is two bits. But you need to make up your mind, 'cause once we've changed horses and I herd everyone back on board, I'll be on my way."

Elthia planted the tip of her parasol in the dust at her feet. She hadn't come this far only to give up at the first hint of trouble. "I'm staying," she announced.

Muttering darkly about schedules and females, Mr. Farley carried her last trunk to the station porch.

She pasted what she hoped was an unconcerned expression on her face. "Mr. Tanner will be coming from Foxberry. Can you tell me how far that is from here?"

He cut a quick glance at the dog as he pointed to his left. " 'Bout an hour's ride, more or less, that way."

Elthia raised a hand to shade her eyes and looked in the direction he'd pointed. A side road branched off, just past the infamous whistling oak.

Nothing stirred as far as she could see.

She tried another question. "Foxberry *is* a town, isn't it? I mean a *real* town, with stores and cafés and banks and such?"

Mr. Farley had moved to one of the watering troughs. Elthia watched as he pulled the faded bandanna from around his throat, dipped it in the water, and squeezed it out.

"It's a town all right," he answered as he wiped his neck. "But not a very big one. Leastways not by eastern standards."

The contempt in his voice told her quite plainly what he thought of "eastern standards." Feeling properly chastised, Elthia retreated and turned her attention back to Poppy.

Fifteen minutes later, the stage pulled away from the station, and still there was no sign of anyone from Foxberry. Elthia watched her link to civilization disappear around a bend in the road, taking much of her confidence with it.

She lifted Poppy, regaining a measure of courage from his warm, familiar presence. This *would* work out. Mr. Tanner was

17

running late, that was all. Nothing to be concerned about.

Besides, she *had* wanted a chance to test her self-sufficiency, to experience life outside her sheltered existence, and that was what she was getting. At least Mr. Josiah had gone back inside.

After a nervous glance at the open door, she gave in to the urge to get out of the blistering sunlight. She took a seat on one of the two rickety wooden chairs situated on the porch, not quite brave enough to enter the station proper.

With hands that trembled only slightly, Elthia removed Poppy's leash. Now that the stage was gone, it should be safe for him to run about and do a bit of exploring.

What if Mr. Tanner didn't come? She'd be stuck here with no one to turn to but the formidable-looking Mr. Josiah.

Elthia gave herself a mental shake. There was no point in dwelling on such things. Instead, she forced her thoughts to a less distressing topic—the position that awaited her.

According to Mrs. Pembroke, the Tanners had two daughters. When Mrs. Tanner fell ill, the couple decided to hire someone to help. They wanted more than a nursemaid, though. They wanted the girls to receive a basic education, to acquire eastern polish and to learn some of life's refinements.

The position had been just the sort Elthia was looking for. Knowing she herself didn't exhibit very much "New England polish," as her own governesses would attest, didn't bother her overmuch. She'd been around those who did all her life and knew she could play the part convincingly enough.

Elthia jumped as Poppy sprinted across the porch, yipping after a skittering lizard. Crossing her arms over her chest, she looked around at the unfamiliar landscape and shivered. Too bad she'd had to come all the way to Texas to accomplish her goal.

Mrs. Pembroke had promised her a traveling companion, a woman who'd signed a marriage contract. Unfortunately, there'd been a last-minute change, and Elthia had traveled alone after all.

She wondered now if the bride-to-be had gotten cold feet. Well, she was probably better off for it. A woman would have to be truly desperate to sign such a contract. Elthia shuddered as she imagined a hopeful young girl arriving at her new home to be confronted with someone like the intimidating Mr. Josiah.

After all, what kind of man would have to hire someone else to find a wife for him?

"So what's wrong with her?"

Caleb swiveled his head to look at Granny Picket, perched on the wagon seat beside him. "What do you mean?" He never slowed the horses, negotiating the dips and turns of the Hill Country road with practiced ease. Stopping to help Granny had already cost him valuable time. Surely the girl would wait for him. She had to. His whole plan depended on it.

Granny grabbed the seat as they hit a bump, then narrowed her eyes and continued without missing a beat. "A young lady from a fine back-East family leaves her home and kinfolk to travel all the way to Texas to marry a man she's never seen." She shook her head. "Bound to be something she's running from, some reason she ain't looking to get hitched to someone more like her."

Caleb kept his expression blank, letting the jingling of the harness and rattling of the wheels fill the silence. Pembroke Placement Agency had given him an explanation, all right. Miss Sinclare had taken this step to escape the gossip and pity of her friends in the face of her broken engagement. Seems she'd jilted her fiancé a week before the wedding, refusing to give a reason.

He gripped the reins tighter, but even with all the bouncing and swaying from the pace he was setting, Granny kept her hawklike eyes focused on him. He shrugged for her benefit. "The agency assures me Miss Sinclare has a sound reputation. She likes kids, and that's all that really matters to me."

"She likes young'uns, does she?" Granny poked his arm. "She been told you got six of 'em?"

Caleb nodded. "Yes, ma'am. I didn't hold anything back." She still looked unconvinced. "Look, Granny," he said, flicking the reins. "I figure, if she's running from something unpleasant in her life, that's her business. She's come here to start fresh, and I promised to see that she gets that chance."

Granny stared at him a second, then nodded, apparently satisfied to let the subject drop.

Caleb turned his attention back to the road, resisting the urge to give the reins another impatient flick. Miss Sinclare's tendency to turn tail and run rather than face up to her problems worried him. If she left with the stage because there was no one to meet her when she arrived, he wasn't sure what he'd do.

He felt another trickle of moisture roll down his back and knew the sweat wasn't totally due to the spring heat. He *had* to have a wife within three days or they'd take the kids from him.

No one was going to split up another family of Tanner kids, not if he could help it.

Ten minutes later, Granny had been safely delivered to her front door, and Caleb had Whistling Oak Station in sight. He leaned forward, trying to find some sign of how things stood.

A woman sat on the front porch, next to several trunks. It had to be Miss Sinclare. At least she'd waited.

He studied her as he neared. Yep, it was her all right. Sitting primly on the wooden chair, as if afraid to dirty her dress, she looked soft, like someone who'd never lifted a finger in her life except to crook it at someone. Her clothes were more appropriate for a tea party than a country kitchen. She even had a frilly parasol, more decorative than useful-looking. He sure hoped the rest of her wardrobe was more serviceable.

Spying the dirty smudges on his pants leg, he frowned. His efforts to wrestle Granny's horse out of the tangled harness and then clear the road of the crippled buckboard had done more than make him late. Instead of the smart, at-his-best appearance he'd wanted to present, he looked like he'd just come in from a day in the fields. Compared to her prissy, neat-as-a-pin image, it put him at a disadvantage, and that irritated the fire out of him.

Pulling up to the station, Caleb got a closer look at his intended. Generously freckled and bespectacled, she also had bold copper-colored hair. This girl would stand out in a crowd.

He hopped down and looped the reins over the hitching post, trying to wipe his mind of sour thoughts. After all, no matter what her life had been up to now, she'd come here to marry him, a step that probably hadn't been easy for her. He'd be willing to give her the benefit of the doubt, for the sake of the children.

Caleb forced a smile that he hoped appeared welcoming.

Elthia watched the stranger with the nut-brown hair take his wide-brimmed hat off and dust it against his leg as he climbed the three shallow steps. This couldn't be Mr. Tanner. The image Mrs. Pembroke's description had conjured up for her had been that of a fatherly businessman, a banker or shopkeeper perhaps.

This tall, lean man in work-stained clothes couldn't be but six or so years older than she, and he sure didn't look like he spent his days behind a desk or counter. That tanned skin and animal-like grace belonged to a man used to physical labor.

No, the Tanners must have sent someone in their place. After all, with Mrs. Tanner bedridden, Mr. Tanner no doubt wanted to stay close by to help with the children.

The man stepped up to greet her. "Excuse me, ma'am, do I have the pleasure of addressing Miss Sinclare?"

Elthia pushed her glasses up more firmly on her nose and smiled in relief. "Yes, sir. Did Mr. Tanner send you?"

His smile twisted. "You could say that. I *am* Mr. Tanner."

Heat rose in her cheeks. Good heavens! She'd just insulted her new employer. "Forgive me, sir."

She stood quickly and extended her hand. The reticule that had rested, forgotten, on her lap slid to the floor. He bent to retrieve it at the same time she did, and the parasol whacked him on the side of his head.

She straightened, appalled. "Oh, Mr. Tanner, I'm so sorry."

"No problem," he assured her through gritted teeth.

As he finished retrieving her bag, Elthia all but flung the lethally troublesome parasol on the chair behind her. She tried to paste an everything's-just-fine smile on her face as she turned back to him. "I do hope I didn't hurt you."

Then she stepped forward, studying his forehead to find some sign of a bump or bruise. And promptly caught her shoe on the hem of her dress. Horrified, Elthia helplessly pitched forward.

He caught her to him as she fell against his chest—a very firm, well-muscled chest.

21

Elthia shut her eyes, praying a hole would appear and swallow her up. She'd so wanted to make a good first impression, but she turned into a clumsy twit when she got nervous, and she was definitely nervous now. Too bad she wasn't the sort of woman who swooned. Oblivion would certainly be nice at a time like this.

Before she could apologize yet again, Poppy shot out from around the corner of the porch, yipping furiously and seemingly intent on taking a bite out of Mr. Tanner.

"What the—" He pushed her behind him, and his hand flew to his hip as if to reach for a weapon. Elthia was relieved to see he wasn't wearing one.

"Poppy, no!" She darted in front of him and scooped up her pet, cuddling the excited animal protectively against her bosom.

Mr. Tanner looked sorry he wasn't wearing the weapon he'd reached for. "What *is* that thing?"

Elthia drew herself up. "Poppy, sir, is not a *thing*. He's a Yorkshire terrier, a very intelligent animal. I apologize if he startled you, but he is highly protective of my person."

His autumn brown eyes narrowed. "An annoying little lapdog was not part of the bargain, Miss Sinclare. I have no use for critters who don't earn their keep."

She bristled at his continued unflattering descriptions of her precious pet. "I'm sorry you feel that way. But I made a thorough review of that contract before I signed it, and there was no mention of pets being disallowed. Mrs. Pembroke gave it as her opinion that his presence would not be a problem."

At his deepening frown, Elthia felt all her carefully made plans unravel, but she couldn't compromise on this issue.

"Besides," she continued, trying a persuasive smile, "I'll see to him myself, so he won't tax your time or resources."

When he still remained silent, she pushed her glasses up on her nose and took a deep breath. "I'm afraid, sir, that this is not a bargaining point. If you can't abide having Poppy in your home, then we'd best agree to dissolve our contract right now."

Mr. Tanner glared a moment longer. Finally he gave a curt nod. "Just keep him out of my way."

She allowed herself to breathe again. "Of course. You'll

hardly know he's about." Elthia didn't know what she'd have done if Mr. Tanner had called her bluff. She couldn't give up Poppy, but being sent home before she'd even left the station would have been a disaster, not to mention a humiliation.

Making a good impression seemed a lost cause now, though. Flashing her best conciliatory smile, she extended her hand. "Let's start over, shall we?"

Raising an eyebrow, he took her hand and gave a short bow before releasing it. "Welcome to Texas, Miss Sinclare."

"Thank you, sir." She ignored his sarcasm and pulled a sealed envelope from her handbag. "Mrs. Pembroke asked me to give this to you. I believe it's your copy of the contract."

He took the envelope, broke the seal, and began reading.

Elthia tried to maintain a dignified appearance. While he read through the papers, no doubt looking for some leverage to use against Poppy, she marshaled her thoughts, trying to focus on the positive aspects of her situation. After all, he wasn't in a position to be too choosy. According to Mrs. Pembroke, there hadn't been a rush of women eager to take this position.

She supposed it was because of the distance. Texas *was* a long way from Maryland. It had put her off at first too. But none of the other positions Mrs. Pembroke had available fit her needs. And, after all, it was only for three months.

Elthia straightened as Mr. Tanner looked up. He slowly re-folded the document, studying her in a way that reminded her of all her many flaws and inadequacies.

She tried not to let it rattle her. "Well, Mr. Tanner, it's been a very long journey. It'll be nice to have an opportunity to freshen up and meet everyone."

He nodded, taking her not-so-subtle hint. "Of course. Let me get your things loaded and we'll be all set."

Ten minutes later, he handed Elthia up onto the wagon seat. She placed Poppy's basket at her feet, carefully moving it as far from Mr. Tanner as possible.

Unfortunately, they'd barely started when Poppy propped his front paws on the edge of the basket and began barking excitedly. The horse tossed his head and skittishly broke stride.

Mr. Tanner took firmer hold of the reins. "Miss Sinclare," he said through clenched teeth, "will you kindly quiet down that four-legged hank of hair before he spooks the horse any more?"

Elthia reached down to soothe her pet. "Behave, Poppy," she scolded. "We don't want you startling the poor wee horsy."

He shot her a look that would wither an oak. "Poppy." His voice dripped disgust. "How did you come up with such a name?"

"His real name is Lord Popwell, but that seemed too pompous for such a playful creature. Poppy was a natural compromise."

He just shook his head and turned his gaze back to the horse.

A flash of color drew her attention to the trees lining the left side of the road. She watched as a blue jay hopped from one limb to the next before taking wing once more.

Everything here seemed a contrast of harshness and unexpected allure. The rugged landscape was home to beautiful wildflowers and colorful wildlife. The overbearing heat was tempered by soft breezes bearing scents of pine and sun-warmed wildflowers. The rugged man beside her who—

"I apologize for not meeting the stage."

Elthia blinked as his abrupt speech interrupted her wayward thoughts. Even though his words had been conciliatory, his tone was grudging.

He continued staring at the road. "It must have been awkward to arrive at a strange place with no one to meet you. I planned to arrive sooner, but I ran into some problems on the way."

Maybe he wasn't such a mannerless oaf after all. "Please don't concern yourself, sir. Poppy and I managed quite well."

This time he cut her a speculative look. "You don't strike me as a woman who would be drawn to the life I'm offering. In fact, you look like you're more used to being looked after than in looking after others. Are you sure you know what you're getting in to?"

She'd been wrong. He *was* a mannerless oaf after all.

Elthia raised her chin, reminding herself that he was her employer and she owed him a degree of deference. "I'm sorry my appearance doesn't inspire you with confidence, but I assure you, I do meet your stated requirements. I love children, all shapes and sizes. I'm confident I can build a warm, respectful relationship with yours. As for my credentials, I have a niece and nephew I watch over at times, and I taught a Sunday School class of young children for several years."

He snorted. "A Sunday School class! Are you really that naive, or do you just think I am? You're comparing a once-a-week gathering with a group of on-their-best-behavior young'uns to having total responsibility for the daily care of the active, prove-yourself-to-me kids you'll have in your charge here."

He spoke like two children was an unmanageable number. If she didn't know better, she'd think he was trying to scare her away. Why?

"The point I was trying to make, Mr. Tanner, is that I have experience working with children, and that I get along well with them. Those *were* the qualifications you stressed, remember?"

That wasn't idle boasting. She was truly confident of her capabilities where the Tanner daughters were concerned. She'd always been able to relate to and interact with children easily. It was the one thing at which she excelled.

Helping in the household *did* concern her, though. Mrs. Pembroke had assured her that the Tanners had a woman come in to help with the cooking and cleaning. But with Mrs. Tanner bedridden, she wanted to lend a hand where she could. The only domestic skill she possessed, however, was needlework. She hoped Mrs. Tanner would provide her with guidance on how to go about the other tasks.

But she wouldn't let Mr. Tanner see her insecurity. "I hope you're not having second thoughts, sir. There *is* the matter of our contract." Elthia couldn't believe her own audacity. Something about this man sparked a hint of rebelliousness in her.

"I'm perfectly aware of my obligations," he said stiffly. "I'm just making sure you're aware of yours." He raked a hand through his hair. "The kids have had to put up with a lot of changes in a short space of time. It hasn't been easy for them, and I won't let you play fruit-basket turnover with their lives."

Elthia's heart softened toward him just a little at his obvious concern for the children. His wife's illness must have been even harder on them than she'd realized.

He shot her another scowl.

"Once you enter that house," he said, "the kids need to be able to rely on your being there. I need to know you'll stick around and not run off at the first sign of trouble."

Elthia stiffened, then forced herself to relax. He couldn't possibly know the circumstances of her broken engagement. But did he have to be so insulting? She pitied poor Mrs. Tanner, and not just because the woman was bedridden.

A man as overbearing and judgmental as Mr. Tanner would make for an uncomfortable husband.

Chapter Two

Caleb glumly eyed the road, not sure if he was more irritated by the current turn of events or by his own reaction to them.

He gave the reins a flick. Damn! This was almost comic in its awkwardness.

But he wasn't laughing. Even given what Pembroke had told him, he still couldn't figure out why someone like Lady Privilege here would answer his posting. He had trouble believing she could be serious about making the kind of commitment he required. This whole scheme would fall apart if she couldn't get the kids to trust her, not to mention earn the approval of the adoption judge. He refused to even think about putting the kids through more upheaval after what they'd already suffered.

He studied her, perched primly on the wagon seat beside him. She was a mix of contradictions. While her pampered air and fancy clothes set her apart as a lady of means, there was also that awkwardness that made her seem little-girl vulnerable.

The bright copper-colored hair and liberal sprinkling of freckles across her nose and cheeks should have given her a schoolgirl appearance. The hair was pulled back into a prim bun, however, and her nose was crowned by a pair of spectacles that hid her eyes and gave her a bookish, schoolmarm look.

Then there were her lips, full and soft and shaped so that they seemed to hint at something neither school-girlish nor schoolmarmish. He might have enjoyed the challenge of finding out about that *something* if the situation had been different.

He snapped his gaze forward, shutting down that line of thought. He wasn't looking for any emotional entanglements, romantic or otherwise. He'd been down that road enough to know that it only led to disillusionment.

The blasted dog started his yipping again, allowing Caleb to refocus his irritation. It was an absurd-looking thing, all hair and vocal cords, and small enough to fit in his holster if he'd been wearing one. The animal's face hair was pulled back and gathered in a topknot on its head with a prissy blue bow.

All in all, a thoroughly useless critter. Its only function seemed to be decorative, like a piece of jewelry or a fancy muff.

And she'd chosen to draw the line over that mutt, to issue him a nose-in-the-air ultimatum over it. To his way of thinking, that provided surefire proof she was more than a little spoiled and clearly allowed to get her own way far too often.

Caleb gritted his teeth. It wasn't bad enough that he was having to make do with a parasol-toting, engagement-reneging, high-and-mighty Lady Privilege for a bride, but she had to add insult to injury by thumbing her nose at him with her lapdog.

She'd managed to get under his skin already, but he needed to rein in his dog-to-cat reaction before he let it jeopardize his whole plan. Good thing she'd obstinately ignored his fault-finding. 'Cause marrying her was his best hope right now of pulling this whole scheme off.

Heck, right now it was his only hope.

Not that he thought she'd have much to offer in the way of domestic or maternal skills. But even if she proved useless as a housekeeper, she'd be good to the kids. By God, he'd see to that.

A sudden cawing made her jump. Seems she wasn't as composed as she pretended. It was good to know the haughty miss had a human side, complete with a portion of female weaknesses.

He took a deep breath and tried again. "Look, you need to understand, this isn't a game. A lot depends on the right woman stepping in to provide the stability and guidance the kids need."

Caleb paused and deliberately narrowed his eyes. "To call a spade a spade, I don't intend to be part of some fool lark of yours. I know about you breaking your engagement, and it doesn't speak well of your ability to follow through on promises."

He ignored her indrawn breath. "Be warned: I *will* hold you to this contract. I won't have the kids made to feel abandoned or lacking in any way. There'll be no throwing up your hands and running back home to Daddy the moment things get difficult."

She was so easy to read. There was the guilty flash when he said "fool lark," then the pinched-lipped reaction to his mention of her broken engagement. And he'd swear her lips curved when he mentioned running home to Daddy.

What the heck did that signify?

Meeting his gaze, she tilted her chin up, though her face was slightly flushed. "The issues that came into play in the matter of my broken engagement had to do with a significant misalignment of expectations. I assure you that won't happen in this case. I discussed this arrangement at some length with Mrs. Pembroke and am confident I have a realistic understanding of what awaits me. I'm not sure what else I can say to convince you, sir."

She waved a hand in front of her face, shooing a honeybee that had come up to investigate. "My reasons for undertaking this are personal," she continued. "But I don't undertake the commitment lightly. You can rest assured that no matter what happens, I won't run out on the children. I give you my word I intend to live up to the full provisions of our contract."

She gave him a bright, placating smile. "I'm sorry I'm obviously not what you had in mind, but at the moment I seem to be all you have. It looks like we're stuck with each other."

Caleb nodded, feeling only a bit better about his soon-to-be bride. God knows she wouldn't have been high on his list of candidates if circumstances had been different, even with those intriguingly full lips of hers.

But that was beside the point now. "I'm glad to hear you say that. For better or worse, we *are* stuck with each other. I warn you, I won't settle for less than your full cooperation."

Her lips compressed and she gave a short nod as she no doubt swallowed some comment on his harsh words. Satisfied, he turned his attention back to the road. At least he'd let her know how he saw things. No point in sugarcoating the pill for her.

Ignoring the dust stirred up by the wagon, Elthia tried to study her employer without staring. It was mortifying to realize he knew of her broken engagement. She supposed it had been naive of her to assume Mrs. Pembroke would handle her file with extra tact because of the slight family bond they shared. After all, the woman had to maintain the integrity of her business.

Elthia pushed the glasses up on her nose, trying not to fidget. Actually, for all the time she'd spent discussing this position with Mrs. Pembroke, she now realized she'd learned very little about her employers. How had that happened? She was usually so meticulous in her research.

She'd made up a list of carefully thought-out questions and discussed every one of them with Mrs. Pembroke. She was only now realizing just how vague some of the answers had been. In fact, she'd learned much more about the children than their parents.

Elthia glanced sideways at her employer again. With his broad shoulders and autumn leaf eyes, he *was* rather attractive, if one was willing to overlook faults in personality and good manners—which she most definitely was not. His lean build and tough, callused hands were those of a laborer. And that firmly muscled chest she'd fallen against was—

She straightened, aghast at the turn her thoughts had taken. Good heavens, the man was her employer, and married no less.

"There's something you ought to know," he said, providing a welcome distraction. "We've been dealing with measles the past few days. It was rough going for a while, but it looks like they're on the mend now. Mrs. Johnston, one of the neighbors, has been helping out, but she'll be ready to go back to her own family now that you've arrived."

Remembering how ill her sister Julia's children had been last year, Elthia frowned. They'd come so close to losing little Jason. "I'll help in any way I can, of course. But Mr. Tanner, you should understand that I'm not qualified to act as a nurse."

He cut her a frowning sideways glance, as if she'd lived down to his expectations already. "Don't worry, they're over the worst of it. Doc Adams says they should be up and about in another day or so. It's just a matter of dealing with their fretting now. You *are* up to that, aren't you?"

She relaxed slightly. "Yes, of course."

His lips thinned and he snapped the reins again.

Elthia let the conversation die. Mr. Tanner obviously wasn't interested in small talk, and right now she didn't feel up to the task of navigating through his moods.

"Well, here we are."

Elthia drew her gaze away from the profusion of wildflowers she'd been studying and sat up straighter.

What was this? They turned up a dusty drive and she could see a large, white house set cozily in a tree-studded yard. There was a barn and barnyard nearby, along with some rustic, shed-like outbuildings scattered about. Everything seemed well tended, but they were in the middle of the countryside, with no neighbors in sight. Didn't Mr. Tanner live in town? As hard as she tried to recall just what she'd been told, she couldn't remember how much had been explained and how much she'd assumed.

She braced a hand firmly on the seat beside her. All right, so this position would be a bit more isolated than she'd thought. All the better for proving she could make it on her own.

Elthia studied the house more closely as they approached. Two storied and multigabled, it had slate blue shutters and was fronted by a roomy wrap-around porch, the steps of which were flagged by rose bushes. A far cry from the elegant colonnaded home with manicured lawns in which she'd grown up.

31

A buggy, hitched and ready to go, stood tied to the rail near the front porch. As Mr. Tanner pulled the wagon to a halt, the front door opened and a sturdily built, gray-haired woman stepped out. This must be the neighbor he'd mentioned earlier. Probably the same woman who did the cleaning and cooking for them.

Then Elthia frowned as she caught sight of two children watching from just inside the doorway. Both of the overall-clad urchins were boys. She'd understood the Tanners had only the two girls. Did these two belong to this neighbor woman?

"Mr. Tanner, I see she made it." The woman's words drew Elthia's attention away from the children.

"Yes, she did. Mrs. Johnston, I'd like you to meet Miss Elthia Sinclare." Mr. Tanner jumped nimbly down and moved around to help Elthia alight.

"Welcome to Foxberry, Miss Sinclare."

"Thank you. I'm looking forward to my stay here." Her remark, no more than a polite pleasantry, drew a startled look from Mrs. Johnston and a frown from Mr. Tanner.

Before she could find out why, the older woman turned to her employer. "I'll be heading back to my place. If you can keep them young'uns tied to their pallets for one more day, they'd be the better for it. But I don't envy you the doing of it."

Mrs. Johnston moved to her buggy as she spoke, but the two barefoot boys stayed where they were. So they weren't with Mrs. Johnston after all.

Mr. Tanner hurried to help his departing visitor climb up into her buggy. "I'm sorry if they gave you a hard time."

Mrs. Johnston's weathered face softened as she reached for the reins. "Don't let it worry you none. I remember what it was like to have a house full of young'uns at home. I'd rather see them up to mischief than ailing. Now, I set a pot of stew to simmering on the stove. That ought to take care of tonight's supper. Didn't want Miss Sinclare to worry herself with that sort of thing her first day here." She sent a smile Elthia's way, obviously expecting some sort of thank you.

Elthia blinked. Did Mrs. Johnston think she'd been hired to

cook? She looked to Mr. Tanner, expecting him to set her straight, but he met her gaze with a frown.

"That was very thoughtful of you, Mrs. Johnston," he said. "Miss Sinclare was just telling me how tired she was from her long journey. And your delicious stew is welcome, any time."

Mrs. Johnston looked from one to the other, obviously puzzled by the exchange. "Yes, well, think nothing of it."

Then she turned back to Elthia. "I'll leave you to settle in and meet your new family. Too bad this sickness had to hit just before your arrival. The young'uns won't be at their best, but I reckon it can't be helped. I guess you're about to prove to Mr. Tanner just how good a helpmeet you're going to be." With that, Mrs. Johnston flicked the reins and headed on her way.

New family? Helpmeet?

Elthia frowned at Mrs. Johnston's strange choice of words.

She watched as Mr. Tanner hefted the largest of her trunks up to his shoulder, and was impressed in spite of herself. The man was more powerful than he looked.

"Uncle Caleb, Josie's fretting again. You need to do something."

The belligerent-sounding statement came from the bigger of the two brown-haired boys on the porch. Elthia judged him to be about thirteen. So he was a nephew, not Mr. Tanner's son.

"Is Zoe with her?" Mr. Tanner asked, setting the trunk down on the porch for a moment.

"Yes, sir."

"Then she'll be all right for a little while. Now, I'd like you two to meet someone. Peter, this is Miss Sinclare."

"Miss Sinclare." The boy's voice sounded polite but not especially welcoming, and his expression remained guarded.

Assuming he was worried about his ailing playmates, Elthia smiled warmly. "Hello, Peter. I'm very glad to meet you."

"And this lad here is Alex."

Alex proved friendlier than his companion, giving Elthia a winning grin.

"Hello, Miss Sinclare. Welcome to Foxberry."

"Why, thank you, Alex. I'm sure I'm going to like it—Oh!" Elthia drew back slightly as she caught sight of two beady eyes and a furry muzzle peeking over Alex's shoulder.

33

Alex grinned again. "Sorry, ma'am. But there's no call to be scared. It's just Rip." He reached behind him, pulling forward a squirrel for Elthia's inspection. "See. You can pet him if you like. Rip won't hurt you, promise."

Before Elthia could say anything, Poppy popped his head out of the basket and began barking furiously. Rip skittered up Alex's arm, around to his back, and then down his leg. In a matter of seconds he'd shot off the porch and disappeared into the safety of a tall oak beside the house.

Worried she'd upset the boy by frightening off his pet, Elthia hurried to apologize. "Oh, Alex, I'm so sorry. I—"

"That's okay. I'm trying to get Rip to go back to the wild anyway, now that his foot's better." All the while the boy spoke, his gaze remained riveted on the basket in her arms, and more specifically on its occupant.

Elthia lifted Poppy so the child could get a better look. "Do you like dogs?"

Alex nodded, an expression of awe on his face. "Yes, ma'am. But I've never seen one like that before. Can I pet him?"

"Of course. In fact, he could use some exercise. Would you mind playing with him out here for a bit while I get settled in?"

"No, ma'am! I mean, I'd be glad to." The boy accepted the wiggling ball of fur, grinning with delight as Poppy got to know him better by licking his face.

Mr. Tanner shot Elthia a grimace, then turned back to the boys. "I'll need your help unloading Miss Sinclare's things from the buggy. Miss Sinclare, if you don't mind holding the door?"

Elthia moved past him and opened the screened door, holding it to let him pass through.

Following him inside, she looked around, eager to discover what her temporary new home looked like. She found herself in a roomy entry, warmly furnished with plain but well-crafted wooden pieces. The faint scent of linseed oil was almost masked by the tempting aroma of the simmering stew Mrs. Johnston had mentioned. The kitchen must be through one of the doors there on her right.

Still looking around, she caught the toe of her shoe on the braided rug that covered the plain wooden floor at the foot of the stairway. Grabbing the spindle-railed banister to keep from falling, she was grateful that Mr. Tanner was already climbing the stairs and missed this additional evidence of her clumsiness.

"We set up an infirmary downstairs," he said, nodding back toward an open door to her left. "I'll take you in and introduce you to the kids after you have a few minutes to freshen up."

The stairway led up to a *U*-shaped landing with six doors opening on to it, three on each side.

"Those doors there," he said, nodding to the left, "are the master bedroom, a linen closet, and the entrance to the attic stairs. The three on this side are the smaller bedrooms."

He moved toward the first of the smaller bedrooms, indicating she was to open the door. Setting her trunk just inside the room, he rolled his shoulders as he stood. "Just make yourself at home and I'll bring up the rest of your things."

Pausing inside the doorway, he turned back to her. "You do understand that you need to see to your things yourself? There'll be no maid along later to help you unpack."

Oh, this man was insufferable! She flashed him a smile through gritted teeth. "Don't worry, Mr. Tanner, I am perfectly capable of taking care of myself."

After he'd gone, she looked around. Her dressing room at home was larger than this. She set her reticule down on one of the two small beds, admiring the colorful, intricately pieced quilts that served as bedspreads.

A stout wooden chest guarded the space between the beds. She smiled when she saw the slingshot and rock collection scattered across the top. Mr. Tanner's nephews must have used this room until recently.

She removed her hat and moved to the mirrored dresser to check her hair. A vase of flowers, yellow roses like those on the bushes by the porch, sat proudly on a starched lace doily. She inhaled the scent, warmed by the feeling that someone had gone to this extra effort to make her feel welcome.

After patting a few stray hairs back into place, she turned toward the window to explore the view, but before she could cross the room, Peter and Alex arrived with the second of her trunks.

Winnie Griggs

"Oh, thank you, just set it down anywhere," she greeted them.

When they'd complied, Alex flashed her an engaging grin. "I put the leash on your dog, ma'am, and tied him to the porch so he won't run off. What kind is he?"

"A Yorkshire terrier. He came all the way from England."

Alex's eyes got a bit rounder. "Really? Are all dogs in England so tiny?"

Elthia laughed. "No. These just happen to be a naturally small breed."

She looked up as Mr. Tanner entered with more of her luggage, and added for his benefit, "Yorkies are quite intelligent and loyal animals. Once you gain their trust, they'll do anything in their power for you."

An audible sniff, almost a snort really, was her employer's inelegant response. "Come on, fellas," he said, waving the boys toward the door. "One more load ought to do it, and then we can leave Miss Sinclare to her unpacking."

Twenty minutes later, Elthia left her room, a few tools of the trade in hand. She hesitated a moment, eyeing the closed door to the master bedroom. Perhaps she should introduce herself to the lady of the house.

Then she decided against it. If Mrs. Tanner was sleeping or not feeling well, she probably wouldn't welcome the intrusion. No, she'd wait until Mr. Tanner was ready to introduce them.

Squaring her shoulders, she started down the stairs. It was time she began earning her keep.

As she reached the ground floor, Elthia could hear voices coming from the room Mr. Tanner had indicated earlier as the temporary infirmary. He laughed just then, a rich, warm sound that sent little tremors of gooseflesh chasing across her arms.

Shaking herself and pushing her glasses firmly up the bridge of her nose, Elthia smiled and stepped inside the room.

And stopped dead in her tracks.

She counted five children scattered across the large room, and the older boy, Peter, wasn't even present. What was Mr. Tanner thinking, taking on four extra children when he had a sick wife to see to? More importantly, did he expect the new governess to care for all of them?

*   *   *

Sensing her presence, Caleb looked up and stood, Josie snuggled securely on his left hip. He'd noticed the way Miss Sinclare interacted with Alex and Peter earlier, and felt some hope that he could make this work despite his earlier misgivings. If she was good with the kids, he could overlook her other faults.

But, seeing the censure in her expression as she looked around, the welcome on his lips cooled. Had the Tanners already failed to measure up to the exalted standards of Lady Privilege?

"Well, well, Miss Sinclare, ready to join us at last, I see. Come on in and I'll introduce you to everyone."

She flushed at his words, and pushed her glasses up on her nose. He was beginning to recognize the gesture as one of distress or determination.

"Of course." She offered an apologetic nod. "Sorry if I kept you waiting. I'm looking forward to meeting everyone."

He hefted the child in his arms. "This here's Josie, age five."

"Hello, Josie."

"I've been very sick," the little girl said solemnly. "I was all covered with red spots."

Caleb tweaked her nose. "Just like a ladybug, and twice as cute." Josie gave him a tickled grin and hugged his neck.

He patted the child's back, and was surprised to see Miss Sinclare's face soften. Maybe she really was as fond of children as she claimed.

His oldest niece moved to his side and held her arms out for Josie. "Come on, sweetie," she coaxed. "Let me rock you for a while."

Caleb nodded his head as he handed the toddler to her sister. "This is Zoe."

The older girl bobbed her head in Elthia's direction with a respectful "Hello, ma'am."

"She's twelve," Caleb continued. "And, like Alex and Peter, she's had the measles before so luckily didn't get sick this time. Zoe knows her way around the kitchen like a master, and you haven't lived until you've tried some of her buttermilk pie."

Miss Sinclare smiled at the girl. "I'm pleased to meet you Zoe. I look forward to sampling some of that pie soon."

Zoe gave a stiff smile, then turned toward the rocking chair.

Winnie Griggs

Caleb studied Zoe's closed expression, feeling a niggle of worry. He'd thought, given time, that she would recapture some of her joy and zest. But it'd been two months now, and she remained unnaturally solemn. Could Miss Sinclare make a difference?

He kept his voice light as he moved on. "Over there by the bookshelf is Alex. You met him earlier. As you no doubt noticed, Alex has a way with animals that's downright amazing. Hasn't met one yet he couldn't have eating out of his hands in a matter of minutes. He's a big help with the livestock. Alex knows quite a bit about caring for horses and can even milk the cows."

Alex grinned self-consciously. "Hello again, Miss Sinclare."

"Hello, Alex. Thank you for your help with my bags."

Caleb moved on again, this time indicating two boys sitting up on makeshift pallets.

"These two characters are Keith and Kevin. They're a double dose of six-year-old energy and curiosity. And they do everything together, even down to shedding their baby teeth."

"Theeeee," the boys confirmed, drawing their lips back to display identical gaps in their smiles.

His highfalutin' bride-to-be stooped to speak to them at eye level. "That's amazing. I'll have to really work on finding a way to tell you apart."

"Wha'cha holding?" Kevin asked, eyeing the books in her hand.

"These?" She held out the books as if only just remembering she carried them.

Both boys nodded.

"Just a couple of books. My father gave me these when I was a little girl. This first one has stories about knights and dragons and castles. And it has pictures too. Would you like to come over to the sofa and let me read some of it to you?"

The twins nodded, scrambling up to lead her to the sofa.

"Me too!" Josie slid from Zoe's lap. "I love stories."

"All right—Josie, is it? What about the rest of you? Would you like to hear a story with us?"

And, easy as that, Caleb found himself on the outside looking in, as the kids clamored around Miss Sinclare and her books.

Something More

Elthia spent the rest of the afternoon tending to the three fretful, attention-seeking youngsters. She held children, read to them, rocked them, fetched glasses of water, even sang to them. And somewhere along the way, lost her heart to them.

Mr. Tanner drifted in and out, checking up on her, she suspected, but he never tarried. She did wonder why there was no sign of his wife but assumed she was resting in her room.

Thinking about Mrs. Tanner and trying to picture what she must be like, Elthia found herself studying Josie. There was something about the girl that set her apart from the other Tanners. Where most of them had caramel-colored eyes and sandy or light brown hair, Josie possessed an almost exotic beauty, with her thick black hair and wide, slightly tilted green eyes.

Had she gotten those looks from her mother? If so, Mr. Tanner was blessed with a wife of rare beauty. Not a plain-Jane frump like herself.

Not that it made a bit of difference to her.

On the heels of that thought, Mr. Tanner escorted Dr. Adams into the room. As soon as the introductions were complete, she slipped outside for a welcome breath of fresh air.

Leaning on the porch rail, she inhaled the sweet scent of the blossoms from a nearby camellia bush. It was late afternoon, and the sun already hung low on the horizon. Alex appeared from around the corner of the house, Poppy at his heels.

The boy slid to a stop when he spied her. "I hope you don't mind, ma'am," he said with an urchinlike smile. "I gave your pooch some water and some scraps to eat."

Elthia returned his smile. "No, of course I don't mind. In fact, I'm grateful. And his name's Poppy, by the way."

"Poppy." The child rolled the name across his tongue, then smiled. "It suits him."

Moving to sit on the steps, Elthia smiled back. "I do believe Poppy's taken a shine to you."

Alex beamed. "I'm glad you brought him with you. Momma liked cats, so we never had a dog before."

Elthia wrinkled her forehead over his words as she watched him race with Poppy back the way he'd come.

Then she was distracted by the doctor's voice. He hadn't spent long with the patients. Which added to her suspicion that he'd come more out of curiosity about Mr. Tanner's new employee than to check on the children.

"No, don't bother to see me out," he was saying to someone inside. "You've got your hands full and I know my way." He pushed open the screen door just as Elthia rose to her feet.

"How are they?" she asked, dusting her skirts.

"Fine, fine. In fact, there's no reason you can't let them outside for a bit tomorrow. Don't let them overdo it, of course, but sunshine and fresh air will likely do them a world of good."

The doctor, short and rotund, put her in mind of a roly-poly clown doll she'd had as a child. Smiling at the whimsical comparison, she stepped aside for him to pass. "I'm sure the children will be glad to get out of the house."

Dr. Adams inclined his head. "Yes, well, I'd better be getting on now. It was a pleasure to meet you, Miss Sinclare. Not the best of introductions to your new family, but at least you can hope it'll go uphill from here."

Before Elthia could comment, he moved down the steps. "If you'll excuse me, it's time I got home to my supper." There was a twinkle in his eye as he looked back over his shoulder at her. "The wife is impatiently waiting for word on what Caleb's 'back-East' lady looks like and what sort of clothes she wears."

Elthia returned his smile, unable to take offense at his honest admission. Then, as she watched him climb into his buggy and turn his horse toward the road, something about his words made her uneasy, though she'd be hard-pressed to say just what.

Rubbing her arms against a sudden frissonlike chill, she turned back to see Zoe standing in the doorway.

"Uncle Caleb wants to know if you'd like to eat supper now."

"Why, thank you, I'd—" Elthia halted as the girl's words sunk in. "*Uncle* Caleb? I thought he was your father."

Zoe's face closed in a stony mask. "Uncle Caleb's *not* my father. I'm an orphan. We all are."

"Oh, I'm sorry. I—" Elthia was searching for words to comfort the child when the significance of what she'd said hit her. "*All* of you are orphans? You mean all six of you?"

Zoe nodded curtly. "Of course. Didn't you already know? It's why he sent for you."

Elthia's uneasiness grew more pronounced. What was going on? Was Mr. Tanner mad to have taken on such a responsibility with a sick wife to tend to? Or was this what had driven Mrs. Tanner to her sickbed? No wonder he'd been in such a hurry to secure help.

But why had he lied about the number of children and about his relationship to them? The Tanners didn't need someone to teach the children and provide polish. They needed a nursemaid, a mother hen to keep track of the baby chicks.

Zoe studied her as one would an irritatingly dense child. "Miss Sinclare, didn't you know Uncle Caleb only went looking for a wife because he got saddled with us and needed some help? He thinks you're going to be our mother."

Chapter Three

"Mr. Tanner, we need to talk."

The lying, scheming blackguard glanced up from his stooped position, a scowl of irritation on his face. Then his expression changed as something in her demeanor caught his attention.

"What's happened?" he asked, handing a glass of milk to one of the children as he stood.

Zoe slipped into the room behind her, but Elthia kept her gaze focused on Mr. Tanner. She stood stiffly, fighting the urge to back away as he approached. "Why did you bring me here?"

His scowl returned as he rubbed the back of his neck. "What do you mean? This is my home. Where else would I take you?"

"I'm talking about the role you expect me to fulfill." She watched him closely, looking for some sign of guilt or duplicity. "Mrs. Johnston called me your helpmeet and referred to you Tanners as my 'new family.' Just now, Dr. Adams did the same."

Elthia clasped her hands to prevent their trembling. Had this man lured her to his home under false pretenses? She was completely at his mercy here. The isolated location and the shadowy approach of dusk suddenly took on a sinister feel.

She had to remain calm, to think, to keep him from seeing her fear.

Mr. Tanner, however, looked more harried than threatening. Maybe Zoe had misread the situation. Dear God, please—

"I'm sorry that your role as a mail-order bride is public knowledge, if that's what this is all about. It's hard to keep secrets in a community like Foxberry."

"Mail-order bride!" Elthia almost choked on the words. Heaven help her, this nightmare kept getting more unbelievable.

His scowl returned. "Miss Sinclare, stop the hysterics, please. I know the kids' illness was unexpected, but surely—"

"There's been a mistake, a dreadful, terrible mistake."

His eyes narrowed. Then he looked at the children, who watched the grown-ups with wide-eyed interest. "Let's move this discussion to the kitchen, shall we?"

He nodded to the two older children. "Zoe and Peter, you help the others with their supper, please." Then he took Elthia's arm and all but pulled her out of the room.

As soon as they reached the kitchen, he released her, as if touching her was distasteful. His next words were all the more intimidating for their softness. "Backing out already? So much for all that talk about honoring commitments." His expression branded her as beneath contempt. "I should have known a pampered bit of high-class fluff wouldn't have a notion about honor or responsibility."

Elthia shook her head, confused and defensive. "No, no, you don't understand. I came here to fill the post of governess, not to be someone's mail-order bride."

The sound he made was suspiciously like a snort. "Foxberry has a great school. Why would I waste money on a governess?"

"But that's what you advertised for. I read the file myself." A spurt of anger momentarily replaced her fear. "How dare you misrepresent yourself in such a way! You took advantage of Pembroke and of me. It's vile and probably illegal. I have half a mind to find the local sheriff and have you arrested."

Mr. Tanner wasn't intimidated. "I *did not* misrepresent anything. I made it very clear to Pembroke exactly what I was looking for. If you paid any attention at all to my post, there's no way you could be confused about any of this."

She drew in a breath as he pointed a finger, stopping just short of poking her chest.

His frown turned contemptuous. "If this is some ploy to get out of the contract and still be able to hold your head up, don't bother. A weak, spoiled, characterless *lady* might be the last thing I want for the kids or myself, but I warned you earlier. I won't just cave in and make it easy on you. You're in this for good, whether you want to be or not."

"How dare you! Why, I—"

"I'd appreciate it if you'd keep your voice down," he interrupted. "There's no point in fretting the kids."

He straightened. "I don't have time for this posturing. If you're not going to help, at least stay out of the way. In the meantime, before you try that I-didn't-know-what-I-was-getting-into story again, you should reread that contract you signed."

Elthia watched him stalk out of the room. Slumping, she steadied herself with a hand to a chair. The long day and its emotional ups and downs had taken its toll. She suddenly felt too exhausted to think straight. Maybe her father was right. Maybe she *was* too helpless, too naïve, to make her own decisions.

How had this happened? Was Mr. Tanner a villain or had there been a terrible mix-up with the paperwork at the agency?

Paperwork!

Of course. He'd told her to reread the contract, and that's just what she'd do, and then force him to do the same. She wasn't her father's daughter for nothing. She'd read that sheet of paper very carefully before signing it. It was an employment contract for a temporary teaching assignment, nothing more.

Feeling her energy rebound, she hurried into the hall. Her copy lay somewhere in her luggage, but he still had the one she'd given him. "Mr. Tanner, just a minute please." Turning into the parlor, she ran smack into his rock-solid chest.

He placed his hands on both of her arms, steadying her before stepping back a pace. "Well, Miss Sinclare, what is it now?"

Elthia's cheeks heated, but she held on to what dignity she could. Pushing her glasses up on her nose, she kept her gaze locked on his as she held out a hand. "The contract, sir. I'd like to see your copy of it, if I may."

He raised an eyebrow. "And just what do you expect that to prove?" Then he scowled. "I warn you, don't try to tear it up."

She raised her chin. "Why would I want to tear it up? It's the proof I need to support my story. It states quite clearly that the position I accepted was that of governess."

"Does it now?"

Elthia frowned impatiently. "Yes, of course it does. You read it there at Whistling Oak. Surely you remember what it said. There was nothing at all vague about the terms."

"I agree, it spells things out in real plain language." He handed her the document and then leaned back against the wall.

Elthia, itching to rub the I'm-only-doing-this-to-humor-you expression from his face, glanced down at the document.

Then she blinked.

She read it twice. Where had *this* contract come from? It most definitely *was not* the document she'd read so carefully before signing. Someone had switched papers, but when and how? They'd hardly been out of her sight since she'd signed them.

It must have been Mr. Tanner. He'd somehow substituted the document she'd handed him for this one. Her gaze frantically turned to the bottom of the contract and she got another shock.

It couldn't be!

There was her name, penned in her own handwriting. Alongside it was the signature of Louella Pembroke. It must be a forgery, but it was such a good one even she couldn't tell the difference.

How *dare* he try to coerce her this way? She was Elthia Sinclare of the Terrelmore Sinclares. Her father would never allow him to get away with this. She shook the document under his nose. "How did you do this?"

"Do what?" He looked more puzzled than guilty.

"Forge my signature so perfectly. Did you trace it? And where's the real contract?"

His jaw tightened and his eyes narrowed at her accusation. "Don't you think you're carrying this charade a bit far?"

"Don't think you can intimidate me with that oh-so superior tone. I have my own copy of the contract."

She turned and marched upstairs. If he thought he could bully her with this elaborate act, he was *very* much mistaken. It took her a few minutes, but she finally located her copy in the larger of her trunks.

Marching back down the stairs, she found Mr. Tanner still standing where she'd left him, though now the lamps in the hall were lit against the encroaching darkness.

She waved the paper triumphantly. "*This* is the document I signed, not that substitute you're trying to fob off on me."

With the air of an adult humoring a child, the infuriating Mr. Tanner plucked it from her fingers, pulled the contract out of the sealed envelope, and looked it over quickly.

After reading it, he shrugged and handed it back to her. "I won't argue with you on that score. But I don't rightly see how it differs from the one I looked at earlier."

Her hands starting to tremble, Elthia took the contract and forced her eyes to focus on the print. He was right; it was identical to the one he'd handed her a few minutes earlier.

A very simple, very binding, marriage contract.

"No." Her voice seemed a strained whisper, even to her own ears. "It's not possible. That's not the paper I signed."

He reached out a hand. "Miss Sinclare, perhaps you'd better sit down."

"Don't touch me!" Elthia jerked her arm away from him. She had to get away, had to escape this nightmare. Turning, she bolted for the door, the sounds of Mr. Tanner's pursuit sending fingers of panic skittering up her spine.

She burst out onto the porch, stumbling to a stop, her waist pressed against the rail. Her heart thudded in her chest, but not loudly enough to mask the sound of boots stepping onto the porch behind her. She hugged a support post with one arm, refusing to turn and face him, but she didn't resume her flight.

There was really nowhere for her to go.

Alex, still playing with Poppy in the last of the fading light, looked up, startled by the adults' precipitous appearance. Elthia tried to smile reassuringly at the child but knew it was a miserable effort. Mr. Tanner rescued the situation, speaking to his nephew in a calm, everything's-okay tone. "Alex, why don't you take that irritatingly noisy skein of yarn out to the backyard? Miss Sinclare and I need to talk."

Alex scrambled up. "Yes, sir. Come on, Poppy." He shot Elthia a curious look, then headed around the corner of the house.

Elthia watched him go and felt the last vestige of her control start to slip away. There was a very real danger that she would collapse into sobbing hysteria any minute now.

If Mr. Tanner made the slightest move to touch or badger her, she would dissolve, she knew she would.

Caleb studied her brittle appearance. "Miss Sinclare."

He repeated her name, gentling his tone as if he were talking to Josie. Slowly she looked up, and he was surprised by the seemingly genuine panic in her eyes.

Hell, he wanted her to understand how serious he was, perhaps feel a little healthy fear, but not have her scared out of her wits.

"Look," he said, trying to be reasonable, "I might go along with your story that you didn't realize what you were getting into, if that makes this easier. But that doesn't change the fact that you signed that contract, and these kids need a mother."

She still stared at him as if afraid he would physically assault her at any minute.

Damn, he wasn't a monster. Why was she trying to make him feel like one? She must be bluffing. Obviously she'd changed her mind about wanting to marry him. But he had to find some way to bring her back around—he had to. He couldn't find another bride in just two days, and he couldn't risk having the kids taken from him to be scattered to who knows where.

Surely he could persuade her to stay. He hid a grimace as he realized he'd also have to help her salvage her pride over this bit of childish panic if he wanted her to be comfortable here.

He took a deep breath and flashed his best choirboy smile. "Why don't we go back inside and see if we can't figure out some way to untangle this mess?"

She blinked, as if his words had reassured her a bit. With

Winnie Griggs

visible effort, she gathered her dignity around her. "I agree, we need to talk this through logically. As long as we remain reasonable, we should be able to work something out." She attempted a smile. "But let's talk out here, shall we?"

Caleb nodded agreement. She was still wary of him, but some of the abject fear seemed to have eased.

Good.

He leaned back against the porch rail and folded his arms, careful to maintain enough distance so she wouldn't feel threatened. "Now, you said you thought you were coming here to take a post as governess, is that right?"

Her chin lifted a notch. "That *was* what I agreed to."

"What led you to believe that?"

She tucked a stray bit of hair behind her ear with not-quite-smooth movements. "When I went to Mrs. Pembroke, I made it clear I was looking for a temporary position as a teacher or governess. She presented your file among those that might meet my needs."

"Perhaps she included my file by mistake?"

Her lips curved haughtily. "I'm neither foolish nor unwitting. I read your file very carefully, along with the other files she presented. Everything in there indicated you were looking for a governess, not a wife."

Her superior tone got under his skin. So did those full pouty lips, but he couldn't afford to think about that right now. "As carefully as you read the contract you signed?"

She flushed again. "I tell you, the contract I read and signed was for a position as governess."

He let that pass. "If you read my file, then you must have seen the letters I sent to Pembroke."

She shook her head. "There were no letters in the file. Only the agency's notes."

Caleb frowned. What was she trying to say? "Miss Sinclare, do you honestly expect me to believe a reputable agency like Pembroke would stoop to trickery? It makes no sense." He waved a hand. "You obviously come from a well-to-do family, a family right in Pembroke's backyard. But I'm a stranger, a nobody to them, and it's a sure bet the fee they're going to make on this deal will be a drop in the bucket to them. There's

48

nothing here worth risking their reputation and a local family's wrath over."

Her lips compressed. "I didn't say it was deliberate," she said defensively. "It must have been a mistake."

Caleb gave himself a mental kick. If she wanted to pretend this was Pembroke's fault he should have let her so they could move on to working out a solution. He nodded, as if agreeing with her last bit of absurdity. "Could be."

As she relaxed, he remembered the way she'd held Josie on her lap as she read the story, remembered the way Josie had snuggled up to her so trustingly. What would his youngest niece feel if this new adult in her life disappeared as suddenly as she'd entered it? "Still," he added, "you did sign the contract."

Lady Privilege looked ready to stomp her foot at him. "This is preposterous. I tell you, there's been some kind of mistake."

Mistake or no mistake, he had to convince her to stay. "So how do you explain the contract? Are you saying now that you only glanced at it and assumed the rest?"

Her brows drew down at that. "I have more sense than that!"

Why was she so unwilling to admit she'd made a mistake? "You can't have it both ways, Miss Sinclare. We've already decided that Pembroke had nothing to gain by tricking you, and that I couldn't have switched the contract in your trunk. Either you didn't read the contract, or you've just got cold feet."

He tried a reassuring smile. "But don't worry, I won't hold either against you. Just tell me what I can do to make you comfortable enough to stay and go through with the wedding."

Her glare could have frosted a candle flame. "It is *so* kind of you not to hold my lying and reneging against me. Be assured, *nothing* you do could convince me to stay, much less marry you."

Lord, but her whole face glowed when she got riled. Her fire would provide a good example for Zoe, who seemed to keep too much of her feelings bottled up inside.

He raised a brow. "Isn't there? You seem to keep forgetting that I have your signature on this contract."

She raised her chin another notch, but he noted the rosy

tinge to her cheeks. "You, sir, are a vile-minded oaf, a piggish beast of a man. I will tell you once more, I came here in good faith to serve a three-month term as governess. There was never *any* indication that anything more would be required."

"I warn you, lady, you don't want to get into a name-calling contest with me." He took a deep breath. They were right back where they'd started.

If the fate of his nieces and nephews hadn't hung in the balance, he might have enjoyed the sparring. Her face was so expressive. It was fascinating to watch it reflect everything from fire-spitting anger to what-have-I-gotten-into flinching. All and all, he preferred the fire.

Taking a deep breath, she stabbed her glasses up on her nose. "Mr. Tanner, be reasonable. For heaven's sake, we never even met before this afternoon."

Caleb waved that aside. "Surely you've heard of arranged marriages?"

She grimaced. "Yes, of course. But that's different."

He shrugged away her weak rebuttal. "Not by much." Then he gave in to a bit of curiosity. "Tell me, even if you thought it was a governess job, why did you agree to come all the way to Foxberry? Surely there were suitable positions closer to home?"

Lady Privilege drew herself up again. "My reasons are personal and none of your concern."

He raised an eyebrow. She sure wasn't making it easy for him to feel sympathetic. "So you're running away from something."

She gritted her teeth. "I'm *not* running away."

"Did you give your family this governess story?"

She shifted uneasily. Obviously he'd struck a nerve. "This was my decision, and you'll deal with me, not my family."

Caleb shrugged, trying not to grin. "Very well. We'll get married day after tomorrow. It's already arranged."

Her expression took on an edge of desperation. "But I don't want to marry you."

She's just a spoiled socialite trying to renege on a promise, he reminded himself as her distress threatened to erode his determination. If only he could just wash his hands of the whole thing and send her on her way. But he couldn't.

The sudden hint of a tremble to those lips of hers stabbed at him, and he raked a hand through his hair. That lady-in-distress air succeeded in accomplishing what none of her words had. He couldn't go through with this.

Then an image of that scene from twenty-two years earlier flashed through his memory. But instead of himself sitting in the dark, listening at the dining room door, he saw Josie there. His failure to find a bride would likely condemn his niece to the same abandonment he'd faced.

No! He could not put an innocent through such a wrenching experience. Miss Sinclare would just have to abide by her agreement, even if she *had* changed her mind. He'd try to make it up to her, to do his best to see that she wasn't unhappy here.

Hardening himself against his reluctant bride-to-be's dismay, he met her gaze. "Irrelevant. Not wanting to live up to a commitment doesn't cancel the obligation."

Crossing her arms over her chest, Lady Privilege lifted her chin. Caleb swallowed his surprise as he was presented with this suddenly enhanced vision of her feminine curves.

Obviously unaware of his shift in focus, she switched tactics to stubborn defiance. "I won't do it."

He forced his gaze back up to her face. If she wanted to try a contest of wills, she'd soon find she'd met her match. He had a lot more at stake here than she did. "Just try backing out and I'll haul you up in front of the local sheriff and have you arrested for breach of contract."

"You are a mean-spirited, heartless man."

Caleb repressed the urge to respond in kind. She was beat and they both knew it. The sooner they settled this, the better. "Now that we've established just where we stand with each other, let's move on. We're stuck with this deal, for better or worse. Why don't you help me try to figure out how to make it better, rather than doing your darndest to make it worse?"

Elthia rubbed her temple. How did one reason with such an unmannered lout? "There has to be another way to settle this."

He pushed away from the rail and straightened. "You *will* marry me, Miss Sinclare. There'll be no last-minute reprieve. No matter what you may be used to, pouting and tantrums won't serve you out here. And I flat-out refuse to tolerate deceit. At least give some thought to the kids and their feelings."

She couldn't quite suppress a shiver. He really and truly meant to force her to do this.

"Now, it's been a long day." He offered his arm. "Maybe things'll look better to you in the morning."

In the morning?

Dear lord, she was here, in this house in the middle of nowhere, with six children and an arrogant stranger who wanted to force her to marry him.

Did he actually think she would get any sleep tonight?

Chapter Four

She stood there with a stiff back and a pale face, making no move to accept his arm. Caleb could almost read her thoughts as her gaze darted around the dusk-shadowed yard, searching for some means of escape.

Despite himself, a small measure of sympathy surfaced. It probably wasn't her fault she was so spoiled. He doubted she'd ever been taught to take responsibility for her actions.

He lowered his arm.

They stood that way for a long minute, until he finally broke the silence. "Come on into the kitchen," he said gently. "I don't believe you've eaten yet this evening."

Still she hesitated, and he forced a smile. "I promise not to pounce on you. Besides, you need to keep your strength up if you want to marshal your forces against me."

The don't-mess-with-me tilt of her chin let him know she didn't appreciate his attempt at humor, but she didn't resist when he took her arm and led her back into the house.

Caleb paused at the make-do infirmary. The sight of Zoe tucking Josie in delivered a forceful reminder of what he was fighting for. Moving back into the hall, he led his foot dragging bride-to-be into the kitchen.

He ladled up a bowl of the stew and placed it in front of

her. "Here you go, eat up. Looks like there's plenty more if that's not enough." He turned back to the stove to fix a bowl for himself, giving her time to pull herself together.

So what was the truth here? He couldn't believe she'd been duped. Which meant she'd either gotten cold feet or she'd made assumptions and signed blindly without checking her facts.

Whatever the case, he couldn't afford to care. Watching her with the kids had been eye opening. He had to admit, she was good with them, especially the little ones. She'd seemed . . . well, motherly, a trait that would be bound to impress an adoption judge. He might pull this situation out of the fire yet, if he could only manage to secure her cooperation.

He took a seat across the table, studying her. What he saw was a somewhat attractive, obviously pampered, seemingly confused miss, who, miracle of miracles, knew how to care for young'uns.

Not that he was fooled into thinking she was a working man's dream of a wife. No doubt Miss Sinclare was vain, spoiled, and expected the world to cater to her.

Right now, though, she looked tired and scared. He planned to take full advantage of the edge that gave him—after all, the kids' futures hung in the balance. But he didn't have to be heavy-handed. A high-strung filly responded better to a gentle touch.

He fought down his twinge of conscience by telling himself he was providing her with a chance to add meaning to her life, something Lady Privilege obviously needed. Even if she didn't appreciate that now, perhaps she would some day.

When she finally finished her meal, he put down his spoon and gave her his undivided attention. "Feeling better?"

She adjusted her glasses with a finger and eyed him suspiciously. "Yes, thank you."

"Good. Then first, let me say thanks for all you did for the kids this afternoon. I know they weren't at their best, but you kept the fretting down to a manageable level. I can tell the little ones are getting comfortable with you already."

Some of her stiffness eased. "I told you, I like children."

"Now, why don't you go on upstairs and get some sleep? The next few days are going to be busy for you."

The stiffness returned in spades. He'd seen broomsticks with more bend to them. Caleb offered up a silent prayer that she wouldn't bolt again. "Don't worry, you'll have the room to yourself. I plan to spend tonight downstairs, where I can keep an eye on the patients. But you can set the latch on your door if it'll help you sleep better."

Standing, he carried their dishes to the sink. "Is there anything you need before you turn in?"

"No." Then her head snapped up. "Oh, I almost forgot."

She left the room without another word. Caleb followed. Surely she wasn't going to try to run off?

Elthia could hear the sounds of restless children as she passed the parlor. Guiltily, she realized she'd barely spared a thought for them since she'd learned of this awful mix-up.

She stepped out onto the porch, relieved to find Poppy there, curled up in his basket. It was full night now and the only illumination came from the moon and the soft glow of lamplight from the windows. Elthia lifted the basket, raising it high enough for Poppy to sleepily lick her face.

"Poppy's sleeping in the room with me," she announced, and braced herself for an argument.

But Mr. Tanner only shrugged. "Just see that he doesn't tear anything up. And keep him away from me."

Head high, Elthia nodded and stepped past him into the hall. Spending an unchaperoned night under the roof of a bachelor placed her feet firmly on the path to social ruin, but she didn't have any other choice. It was night, and she was a complete stranger to this community. She'd shown him enough cowering, though. It was time she reasserted herself.

Elthia stopped by the parlor to tell the children good night, interrupting a whispered discussion among the three older children. From the guilty looks on their faces, she guessed she'd been the subject. Little Josie claimed her attention, sleepily clamoring for an introduction to Poppy. Keith and Kevin demanded a turn as well. As she tucked them back in, Elthia realized she could already see differences in the twins. Keith had a way of nodding his head to emphasize a point, and Kevin possessed an impish smile that was utterly charming.

55

With a pang, she mourned the fact that this hadn't turned out to be the governess role she'd hoped to fill. Even with the extra children, she'd have enjoyed working with this group. It was impossible now. No matter what Mr. Tanner thought, given the circumstances, she would not be staying more than the one night.

She turned, and found Mr. Tanner studying her from the doorway. He stepped back just enough to let her pass, and their arms brushed, sending an involuntary shiver through her.

Elthia forced herself to take the stairs with a dignified, ladylike tread, though the feel of his eyes boring into her back made her itch to scurry.

Reaching the relative safety of her allotted room, she set Poppy's basket down with not quite steady hands. She lit the bedside lamp while Poppy explored under the bed. Then she walked to the door, shut it, and very carefully set the latch.

Later that night, once the kids had settled down, Caleb sat on the porch, whittling by moonlight.

He'd had another letter from Annie yesterday, urging him to hold out on a wedding as long as possible. She and Liz were still trying to find another solution to the problem of a home for the kids. Both his sisters were appalled at the idea of him sending for a mail-order wife. Seems they still believed a body should marry for love. He was happy they'd found such matches for themselves, but it was not to be for him. This businesslike setup was more suited to his needs anyway.

And if he was willing to accept it, why couldn't his sisters? Besides, Judge Walters had promised to personally check on him by June first to make sure Caleb was complying with the conditions of their agreement. That didn't leave much wiggle room. Caleb sure as heck wasn't going to take a chance of the adoption judge getting the idea he wasn't taking this whole matter seriously.

He'd write Annie back first thing tomorrow and tell her it was too late to turn back. His bride had arrived, and he had no choice but to go through with his plan, for the sake of the kids.

Caleb blew the sawdust from his handiwork, then ran a thumb across it to test for splinters. Some of Caleb's earliest memories were of watching his father's large, callused hands turn a simple block of wood into a thing of beauty or amusement.

After Caleb had come to live with Aunt Cora, he'd sit on this very porch, take out the pocketknife his father had given him, and shave away at any stick or piece of wood he could find. He hadn't his father's skill in those days, but the feel of the knife and wood in his hands comforted him, as if it connected him in some way to the home he'd been forced to leave behind.

And when he sat here at night, he would, more often than not, look up at the stars and imagine his father up there, watching him. He poured out his soul to him in those early years, telling him all the things he couldn't say to anyone else, all his hurts and fears and dreams. And, somehow, when he needed it most, he found comfort and answers there in the stillness of the night.

If there was ever a time when he needed answers, it was now. If only he didn't have to be married so quickly. But Judge Walters had been quite firm.

Blast Lady Privilege! She'd taken one look at their little group and decided she was better off facing the music back home. She'd sounded so sincere, so impassioned when she'd spoken of being a "woman of her word" and of "living up to the full provisions of the contract" that he'd almost been suckered into believing her. More fool he.

But there was more than *his* future and happiness at stake, there was the welfare of the kids to consider. He wouldn't just quietly bow out and let her off the hook. He couldn't.

Caleb's hands stilled as he looked up to the heavens, brilliantly studded with thousands of stars.

Dad, if you're watching, you see how mixed-up everything's gotten. Forcing a woman into marriage against her will just doesn't sit right with me. Even if she is a spoiled-rotten, born-with-a-silver-spoon-in-her-mouth, nose-in-the-air priss, she did pitch in and help with the kids today, so I know there's a bit of good in her somewhere too. Besides, having to drag a woman to the altar is just plain hard on a man's pride.

But I've got the kids to think of now. If I don't hold Lady

Privilege to the contract she signed, I may lose them. How do I find a way to salvage this mess?

Caleb blinked as a falling star streaked across the heavens. Almost as if . . .

Shaking his head at his own fancifulness, he folded his knife and went inside to check on the kids. Shooting stars to the contrary, he didn't believe in foolish dreams anymore.

Elthia woke with a start. She hadn't intended to fall asleep. A quick glance toward the star-speckled windowpane, though, reassured her that it wasn't yet morning. She stretched, working the kinks out of her cramped muscles. The riding habit she'd donned earlier didn't make for comfortable sleeping attire.

Moving to the window, she noticed the faint lightening on the horizon that indicated the approach of dawn.

It was time! She had to make her move now or lose the chance. Her plan was simple. She would slip out to the barn and saddle one of Mr. Tanner's horses. Then she'd ride to Whistling Oak, where she hoped to find a stage headed east this morning. If not, she'd ride to Foxberry and send a telegram to the Pembroke Agency. Surely Mrs. Pembroke could do *something* to straighten out this mess. As a last resort, she'd send a telegram to her brother, asking him to rescue her.

She'd thrown a few necessities into a cloth bag last night. Elthia reached for it now, and with her other hand picked up Poppy. He'd have to travel in the bag; his basket was too bulky for her to manage on horseback.

She stealthily released the door latch. The resulting click sounded like canon fire to her ears. She held her breath, waiting for a sign that she'd disturbed someone's rest.

Poppy whined softly. Elthia stroked his head, whispering reassurances and begging him to be quiet. She opened the door, wincing at every creak and groan. Nothing stirred. There were no lights left burning upstairs, though Elthia could make out a soft glow coming from below.

Taking a deep breath, she made her way to the head of the stairs. Still nothing stirred. Keeping her hand moving reassuringly on Poppy's head, and praying that it would be enough to keep him quiet, she began the nerve-racking descent.

Finally, she reached the hall. The parlor was ahead and to her right, the door partially open. Those sweet children; what would they think when they found she'd left? She felt a pang as she remembered little Josie cooing at Poppy and telling him she'd play with him in the morning. She felt like she was betraying a trust, even though she'd made no promises. If only . . .

But she *couldn't* stay. Mr. Tanner asked too much of her. Silently Elthia apologized to the children for any confusion or hurt feelings her clandestine departure would cause.

She wanted very badly to peek inside, not only for a last look at the children, but also to reassure herself that Mr. Tanner was there, asleep among the children, that he wasn't lurking about somewhere, ready to pounce on her unawares. But that would be foolish, and she knew better than to tempt fate now.

Quietly she turned and headed for the kitchen. The one lamp left burning in the hall provided enough light for her to find her way. Once she reached the kitchen, though, it was a different matter. The light from the hall didn't reach into the room, nor did the faint light of the emerging dawn do more than betray the location of the door and windows.

She had to curb her urge to hurry, had to feel her way, inch by painstaking inch. But at last she reached the door. Again, the click of the opening door resounded like thunder in her ears.

She stood frozen for long, anxious seconds. When no one stormed out to stop her, she slipped outside and breathed a giddy sigh of relief. Elthia paused long enough to clip a leash on Poppy. It would be best to let him get a bit of exercise and take care of business before she cooped him back up in the bag for the ride to Whistling Oak.

Elthia stepped into the dark cavern that was the Tanners' barn and halted. She'd never been inside before and was reluctant to blindly venture farther.

It was warm in this part of the country, even at night. Her skin felt clammy, and beads of moisture trickled down her back.

After a few minutes, her eyes adjusted to the gloom enough

for her to make out nearby objects. There were horses in the first two stalls, and Elthia moved closer.

Disturbed by her presence, the animals whickered softly. Elthia moved to the stall of the smaller of the two. Speaking endearments, she stroked the mare's nose. Then, satisfied the animal was even-tempered, she looked around for a saddle.

Her heart jolted painfully when the rooster crowed nearby. The noise had obviously startled Poppy too, because the dog yipped defiantly. Shushing her pet, Elthia quickly reached for the tack once more, though her hands trembled slightly now.

It was getting lighter, and though that meant it was easier to see, it also meant the household would soon be stirring. If she was to make her getaway, she would need to move quickly.

"They hang horse thieves in these parts, you know."

Chapter Five

Caleb was quite pleased with the effect of his words, for all of about three seconds.

With a startled squeak, his reluctant bride-to-be whirled around, and the bit in her hand went flying. He raised a hand to protect his head, and only partially succeeded. His hand took the brunt of the assault, with a blow across the knuckles painful enough to draw an ungentlemanly oath from him.

Then her ridiculous excuse for a guard dog, apparently sensing that his mistress needed protection, launched full tilt at Caleb, attaching himself with growling tenacity to a pants leg.

Sucking on his bleeding fist, Caleb danced on one foot, kicking his other in a vain attempt to dislodge the evil-tempered hank of hair. The fact that he hadn't taken time to pull on his boots before he left the house didn't help matters any.

Miss Sinclare's nervously suppressed laughter brought him up short. She thought this was funny, did she? "If you care about this worthless animal," he said through clenched teeth, "you'll call him off right now. Because in about two seconds I'm gonna grab that pitchfork from over yonder to scrape him off."

Actually it was an idle threat. He wouldn't hurt such a puny critter, even an irritating, pint-sized nuisance like Poppy. But she took his words with almost insulting seriousness.

Sobering, she stretched a hand toward the rodent-sized mutt. "Come here, Poppy," she coaxed. Then, glancing sideways at him, her tone sweetened. "Let go, before you hurt the poor man."

Caleb's temper rose another notch as he registered the veiled mockery of her words. He was almost glad when the dog ignored her, and she had to come closer still.

With obvious trepidation, she stooped at his feet and took hold of the obstinate animal with both hands. When a gentle tug failed to dislodge her pet, Miss Sinclare's tone took on a sharper edge. "Poppy, you let go right now. If you get through to his leg, it'll likely give you indigestion."

The woman was obviously scared of him; it was evident in the slight tremor in her voice, and in the darting glances she sent him. Yet she continued to make verbal digs. It might be bluster, but a grudging admiration for her spunk tugged at him.

She gave a harder yank, and the contrary mutt finally let go. The proper Lady Privilege landed on her rump with a very unladylike thump. Caleb got a quick view of nicely turned calves before she scrambled to her feet, ignoring his outstretched hand.

With a have-it-your-way shrug, he lifted his foot to examine his pants leg, and didn't bother to hide his irritation. The annoyance was partly aimed at himself for the softening he'd felt just now. "I knew it. That furry gnat put a hole in my Levi's."

That observation didn't earn him any sympathy as she continued to soothe her dog with a defiant glare on her face.

Then her face blanched. "You're bleeding!" She set the dog down and approached him with none of her earlier wariness. "Here, let me have a look." She took his left hand, the one with the still-bleeding knuckles. Her teeth worried at her bottom lip as she examined his hand with a sure, delicate touch.

Caleb was caught off guard by her show of concern. How long had it been since anyone fussed over him? But it wasn't his well-being at stake, it was the kids'. He rallied his defenses against her gentle assault. "I'm pretty sure I'll live."

She reddened and dropped his hand as if it were a rattler,

but managed to summon a glare. "Well, it serves you right for sneaking up on me like that."

Caleb raised a brow. Surely she wasn't blaming him for this little farce? "You were stealing my horse!"

"I was *not* stealing it!"

At least she had the grace to blush. And a blush on this freckled redhead was a sight to see.

She lifted her chin another notch, as if denying the need for him to feel any sympathy. "I was just going to borrow it. I planned to pay Mr. Josiah to see that it was returned."

He crossed his arms. "The way I learned it, taking without asking is stealing. But maybe you were taught different. Like your signature on a contract isn't binding if you change your mind. And lying is okay if it gets you out of hot water."

"No! That's not true!" She took a deep breath. "All right. Maybe you're right about the horse. I guess you could argue I was stealing the use of it." She shook a finger at him. "But you left me no choice. You were going to force me to marry you."

Caleb winced as her accusation hit home. Put that way, it made him sound like a bully. But he couldn't back down. "I only insisted that you live up to your end of our bargain."

"I made no such bargain." She pushed her glasses up on her nose, obviously preparing for battle. "We were both under a bit of pressure yesterday. I hope you'll agree, now that we've had time to think things over, that under the circumstances our getting married is out of the question."

"That's not the way I see it."

The knuckles of her clasped hands whitened, and Caleb could see it took an effort for her to speak calmly. He found himself pulling for her, mentally applauding her rallying efforts. Why? And why did he itch to get her riled again, to see the spirited color climb back into her cheeks?

"I understand why you need a wife to help care for the children," she continued, "but surely you don't want someone you'd have to force. Let's assume that this is all some terrible mix-up, that you didn't lure me here under false pretenses."

He stiffened at the insult.

But she barreled on. "That being the case, I see why you'd be upset to have wasted so much time and money with nothing to show for it. So I'll agree to repay the money you've spent getting me here, and add a little extra for your trouble." She smiled at him, obviously pleased with her solution. "There, problem solved, and we can both get on with our lives."

Caleb felt some of his sympathy evaporate at this pointed reminder of her moneyed status. Didn't she understand what really mattered? He raised an eyebrow. "Do you always try to buy your way out of problems, rather than just face up to them?"

Her face reddened. "How dare you!"

He shrugged, eyeing her steadily. "Well, isn't that what you're proposing?"

A hunted expression clouded her face as she nibbled on her lip. "I can see how it might seem that way. But I'm willing to help in other ways too. I'll even stay on for a few days until you can make other arrangements for help with the children."

She flashed him a smile, as if it were all settled. "Then, when I get back to Terrelmore, I'll do everything in my power to expedite the search for just the right woman. I'll personally see that another mix-up like this doesn't happen." A wave of her hand dismissed the whole problem as a mere inconvenience. "Why, I imagine in less than a month we can have someone here, ready and willing to step into this household as Mrs. Caleb Tanner."

He set his jaw. "I don't have a month."

She looked down her nose at him, a good trick for someone nearly a foot shorter than he. "Come now, Mr. Tanner, I know this group must be a handful for you to manage on your own, but surely you can survive just a little longer."

Keeping a smile firmly pasted on his face, Caleb shook his head. "Today is May twenty-ninth. I have to be married before the first of June or I lose the kids."

That set her back. "But aren't you their legal guardian?"

"Not yet. Look, it's a long story. The important parts were in the file I sent Pembroke."

It was her turn to raise an eyebrow. "Not in the file I read. Under the circumstances, don't you think I have a right to hear the full story?"

She wanted to talk about *rights* after trying to sneak away, and steal his horse to boot? Damn, but Lady Privilege was some piece of work. He was getting plumb tired of her claims

of having been duped. "You want the whole story. All right."
He pointed to a pair of dusty crates behind her. "Sit."

She frowned at the makeshift bench and opened her mouth
as if to protest.

"I said sit." He barked the words this time. Did she never
just do as she was told?

Her mouth snapped shut and her eyes widened. Tipping up
her nose, she nodded and sat where he'd pointed.

Leaning against one of the stalls, Caleb folded his arms.
"Here's the information you'd already know if you bothered
to read the file. The kids are my nieces and nephews. Their
parents died in a fire about two months ago. I'm trying to work
things out so that I can legally adopt them."

Her expression softened for a moment, but then she straightened and eyed him levelly. "Very commendable. But that
doesn't explain the deadline you mentioned."

"I'm a bachelor, and I've been a bit of a drifter the last few
years. Not an ideal candidate for instant parenthood, especially not on this scale." He kept his jaw thrust forward. It
wasn't a very flattering picture of himself, but he'd be damned
if he'd act apologetic. "There were other relatives willing to
take some of the kids. So, when I first approached the judge
with my request to adopt, he wasn't sympathetic."

She frowned. "Mr. Tanner, noble as your desire is to take in
these children, if there were others equally as willing, don't
you think you're being a bit selfish?"

"Believe me, taking them in wasn't my first choice. I don't
know anything about being a father. I tried my da— . . . best
to find another solution. But I wasn't going to let them get split
up, and nobody wanted to take in the whole group." He
shrugged. "So I went to court and kept hammering away until
my relatives and the judge finally agreed to see things my way.
But I have to meet two conditions before the judge'll make it
official."

He raised a finger "First, I have to have a wife to help take
care of the kids. If I'm not married by June first, and to someone the judge approves of, I'll forfeit the kids." He paced away
from her. He had to make her see, make her understand. She
liked the kids already. If she realized what was at stake here,
she might be more willing to stay.

He raised another finger. "Second, I have to turn us into a real family. I have three months to do that. On September first, Judge Walters will look us over. If he thinks we fit his idea of a 'proper family,' then he'll sign the adoption papers. If not, the kids get split up, doled out to whatever relatives will take them." And that he absolutely would not allow.

She pursed her lips. "I sympathize with your predicament, sir. But that doesn't change our situation. I won't marry you."

He studied her until her pose lost some of its assurance. "You ran away from home rather than stand and face your problems, and you're trying to run away from here for the same reason. It's time you grew a bit of backbone, Miss Sinclare."

The next words fairly exploded from her. "You know *nothing* about my reasons for coming here. I did not run away from anything. I came here to prove something, not to hide."

"And just what are you trying to prove?"

Lady Privilege clamped her lips shut. "That doesn't matter now. I've botched things beyond repair. But you have to believe me, this is *not* the bargain I made with the placement agency."

Caleb decided to let the question of her reasons for coming here go for now. "Your bargain is with me, not Pembroke. They just served as my agent. And a commitment is a commitment, regardless of how careless you were in reviewing the terms."

"Mr. Tanner, please be reasonable."

"Miss Sinclare, being reasonable is a luxury I don't have right now. Let me spell it out: I would do just about anything to see that these kids don't get split up. If that means hauling you in front of the circuit judge to press my claim, I'll do it. And don't forget, I can add attempted horse theft to the charges now. One way or the other, you and I are going to get married."

"There's got to be another answer."

"If you can come up with something, I'm willing to listen."

Elthia searched her mind frantically for an answer, thinking out loud as she did. "Why does it have to be a wife? A live-in housekeeper could serve just as well. What if I help you find someone like that, someone willing to help raise the children?"

The infuriatingly stubborn Mr. Tanner shook his head. "I thought of that. Judge Walters didn't like the idea of hired help filling the role of mother. Said kids need more stability than that. Besides, even if the judge would agree to it, I couldn't afford to pay a full-time housekeeper/nursemaid. And if we got past all that, we still have the problem of time. I don't reckon I could find a good candidate for that role any faster than I could find a new bride."

Elthia, desperate now, pounced on that thought. "What if I stayed on as a governess for the next three months, just like I planned. You wouldn't even have to pay me."

Again he shook his head. "Like I said, the judge didn't like the idea of hired help raising the kids. He ruled I had to have a wife, someone with a personal interest in me and the kids, someone who'd stay around for their growing-up years, or no deal. And I'm not about to ruin my chances by trying to make him change his mind. Besides, I don't reckon he'd think it proper for a young lady to live here unless I was married to her."

She chewed her lip. How in the world would she ever get out of this mess? If only she could get word to her brother. Ry'd find a way to extricate her.

Mr. Tanner stuck a piece of straw between his teeth and propped one boot on the crate beside her. "Perhaps there is another way."

She looked up at him looming above her, waiting for him to explain. Even though the situation was impossible, even though he was being thoroughly unreasonable, she felt a spark of admiration for him. He really cared about those children. Though misguided, his efforts seemed honorably motivated. Had he really discovered an answer they could both live with?

He leaned an arm on his bent knee. "What if you were to marry me, but only temporarily."

Appalled, Elthia opened her mouth to protest, but before she could speak, he raised a hand.

"No, hear me out. All I need is a wife for the next three months or so, until the judge grants me permanent custody. What if we got married, but in name only? You would stay here as my wife, and help me care for the kids. Then, once they're legally mine, you and I can quietly get the marriage annulled."

"Annulled?"

He nodded. "Yes, of course. As long as you and I don't actually . . ." He paused and sent her a wicked grin. ". . . consummate the marriage, we should be able to arrange an annulment."

Elthia knew her face must be a flaming red, but she managed to choke out her outrage. "You can't seriously expect me to agree to such a plan."

"Have it your way." Again he flashed that wickedly suggestive grin, and she felt an odd fluttering in her stomach.

The piece of straw shifted from one corner of his mouth to the other. "If you prefer we treat this like a true marriage after the wedding, then I guess I'll be able to live with that."

"No!" She paused and took a deep breath. "You're deliberately twisting my words. This is blackmail!"

He shrugged. "Call it what you want. I warned you, I'll do what I have to to keep the family together. And I think that contract gives me a pretty strong case with the law. Of course, if you want to run home to Daddy and try to fight this, you can. But I promise I won't quietly cave in. You'll have one Texas-sized court battle on your hands."

Elthia frantically searched her mind for another option, one that would allow her to withdraw with her integrity whole. To run back home with such a scandal following her would verify her father's worst fears. He would be more determined than ever to find a husband to take charge of her.

But to agree to marriage to this stranger, even an in-name-only arrangement—could she go through with such a thing? Could she trust him to live up to the conditions?

"What about the children?" she demanded. "The judge had a valid point. It wouldn't be fair to them for me to engage their affections and then up and leave in a few months."

"I planned for you to stay, remember?" He raked a hand through his hair. "It can't be helped. And I'll still be here. Besides, it's not much different than if you'd come as governess like *you* planned. You would have 'engaged their affections' and then left after three months, wouldn't you?"

She had no answer for that.

He seemed a hard man, single-minded and inflexible when it came to getting his way. His motives, though, were noble. Not many men would take on what he had. And he seemed more focused on obtaining a mother for the children than a wife for himself.

Not that she thought she'd be much of a temptation to him. Heaven knows, she had years of evidence to convince her that men had no trouble resisting her limited charms.

She studied him, balancing his obstinance and lack of polish against the patience and sympathy he'd shown with the children. She couldn't really think of him as a bad man. Under different circumstances, she might have even been attracted to him. Those broad shoulders and that crooked smile held their own appeal. Even his strong-mindedness, if someone were to help him focus it properly, could be viewed as an admirable trait.

But then again, just what involvement had he had in the trickery that lured her here? Because she was beginning to believe this was more than just a mistake.

She squared her shoulders. Even if he created the father of all scandals, she didn't think he could force her to marry him, especially once her family rallied around. She'd sworn to see this adventure through without asking for help, but this was no longer the adventure she'd signed on for. And she wouldn't let a bit of foolish pride force her to throw away her future.

As if reading her thoughts, Mr. Tanner's expression lost some of its assurance. "You're the only chance left to keep the family together. The kids need you."

Her head shot up and she met his gaze. For a moment Elthia thought she glimpsed something vulnerable in his eyes. Then it was gone, and she could tell he already regretted his words.

But it didn't matter. He'd won, succeeded in snaring her with the only words that could have done the trick. Had it been merely happenstance, or had he somehow guessed that she longed to be needed, yearned for it with an almost physical ache?

Besides, what difference did it make if she married this man or someone of her father's choosing? At least here, she knew her money wasn't a factor, and she'd have the children on which to lavish her attention. And she could pretend this had been *her* choice.

Besides, he'd inadvertently handed her some leverage, some control over the situation. "You make a compelling case, sir."

Mr. Tanner's self-assured manner snapped back into place. There was no sign he'd ever doubted the outcome of their talk. "Then you agree to abide by the terms of the contract."

Elthia held up a hand. "First, I expect you to view this as a business partnership, not a marriage. I will agree to help you care for the children and do everything in my power to help you meet the expectations of the judge. In return I expect you to treat me with respect, to tolerate my pet, and to make it as easy as possible to obtain the annulment when the time comes."

She watched him nod his head, then narrowed her eyes. "The question is, how do I know I can trust you?"

He flashed an I've-got-the-upper-hand grin. "You'll just have to take my word for it."

She lifted her chin. "I'm afraid that's not good enough. I have no intention of getting myself mired deeper into your scheme. I want binding assurances that I can painlessly extricate myself from this partnership when the time comes."

His brow drew down in a frown, and Elthia was pleased to see his expression lose some of its cocksureness.

"What did you have in mind?"

"If I agree to this, we'll need to draw up another contract, one that spells out exactly what we are both committing to. I don't want any 'misunderstandings' this time around."

He shook his head. "Uh-uh. If a paper like that fell into the wrong hands, it could ruin my chances of adopting the kids."

She shrugged. It was a valid worry, but she would guard the good of the children as closely as he did. "No one need ever see it, unless you try to step over the line. Once the marriage is annulled, I'll hand it back over and you can tear the thing up."

"How do I know you won't use the document against me?"

She flashed her sweetest smile. "You'll just have to trust me."

His frown was fierce enough to make her lean away from him. "Lady, right now I wouldn't trust you any farther than I can toss my horse. But I don't have time to drag this out, so you'll get your contract. Rest assured I'll keep my end of our bargain."

The contemptuous look he shot her as he shifted forward reminded Elthia again that she was no prize catch. "But if you even think about betraying me, you'll regret it. Understand?"

He hadn't raised his voice. If anything, it had gotten softer. But the chill of his words sliced straight through her. She nodded, not trusting herself to speak.

"Good. Then we'll draw up that new contract today and the wedding will take place tomorrow, as planned. I expect you to put on a good front for the kids. They've been through enough without adding this to their list of worries. See that you do your level best to be a proper mother to them, at least until the judge makes a decision on the adoption. Agreed?"

Jaw clenched but head high, she nodded. "It seems the needs of the children are the only thing we *do* agree on, Mr. Tanner."

Elthia wasn't feeling particularly triumphant. What in the world had possessed her to let some softly uttered words convince her to agree to his ridiculous proposal? There were no signs of softness or vulnerability in him now.

"And speaking of the children . . ." He reached down to help her up. "It's time I went back in and checked on things."

After a slight hesitation, Elthia took his proffered hand.

Streaks of orange had already begun to fan out above the horizon as Caleb escorted her out of the barn. Despite his still-simmering anger, he again felt that unwanted tug of admiration for the surprisingly spirited Lady Privilege. True, she'd tried to buy her way out of this. But she was handling her defeat with more grace than he'd expected.

It was a good thing she hadn't realized that if he took her to court, he would be shooting himself in the foot. Even if he won, Judge Walters would never agree that such a marriage bargain was a legitimate response to his charge that Caleb find a mother for the kids. Caleb'd mentally held his breath as they sparred, afraid she'd discover that hole in his argument.

He squirmed, thinking of the way he'd manipulated her, using her sympathy for the kids as his trump card. But he couldn't afford to be soft, not with all he had at stake. There'd been steel in her expression. He'd almost seen the refusal form on her lips. He'd just done what needed to be done to win her over.

He had to be honest with himself, though. When he thought she'd turn him down, a pinprick of panic hammered its way up his spine. And not just because time was running out on him.

Even though she was a pampered, reneging, totally-unsuited-to-his-lifestyle miss, he wanted her. Something about Lady Privilege tugged at him, made him want to learn more about her, about what made her tick.

Not that he was attracted to her for himself. His interest stemmed from the relationship she was already building with the kids. She had grit, true, and it *was* fun to watch that nobody's-gonna-walk-all-over-me fire when she got riled. And she wasn't quite as prissy and schoolmarmish-looking now as he'd thought when he first spotted her. Still, she really wasn't his type.

Marriage to Lady Privilege—a not altogether unwelcome outcome. As long as he didn't make the mistake of letting his emotions get involved, it might be interesting to teach her some of the finer points of the simple life.

Chapter Six

"So tell me something more about the children." Elthia ignored the dew dampening her hem and held thoughts of her upcoming wedding at bay. Best to focus on the children.

He spread his hands. "What do you want to know?"

She studied the rosy horizon. "How did their parents die in a fire?"

Her would-be-groom looked at her curiously. "You really *didn't* read any of the details I sent Pembroke, did you?"

Here we go again. "The only thing in your file on the children," she said with exaggerated patience, "was a note about two girls, supposedly daughters of you and your wife."

He stopped in his tracks. "Wait a minute—you claim you were told I had a wife?"

"Yes, of course. I wouldn't have come out here otherwise. It wouldn't have been proper for me to take up residence with a single man, no matter how innocent the situation."

His brow furrowed. "And you didn't find it strange that there was no woman here to greet you when you arrived?"

Elthia could tell he found her story hard to swallow. Why did what he thought of her matter so much? "I was told your wife was an invalid." She shrugged. "I just assumed she was resting when I arrived, and I would meet her eventually."

"And what about the six kids? Didn't that raise your suspicions just a bit?"

Her chin tilted up. "Peter called you Uncle Caleb. I assumed that the boys were visiting nephews."

"That's an awful lot of assuming on your part."

"Well, I—"

He cut across her stammering response. "You thought I'd take in four visiting nephews when I had an invalid wife to see to and was looking for someone I could hire to help with my two girls."

He made her sound like a fool or a liar. Was that what he thought? "I'd just arrived," she said through gritted teeth. "It wasn't my place to question your lack of common sense."

Looking up at the sky, he shook his head.

She placed her hands on her hips. "Mr. Tanner, if we're going to make this arrangement work, you're going to have to stop questioning my story. I have no intention of spending the next three months listening to you cast clouds on either the honor of my intent or my understanding of the contract I signed."

His expression sobered. "All right, I'll give you that much. I won't say another word that hints at doubts on my part." Then he pointed a finger at her. "By the same token, you are not to give the kids or neighbors the slightest idea that you intended anything other than marriage when you arrived here. Agreed?"

Elthia noted that he hadn't said he believed her, only that he would stop voicing doubts. Fair enough. And the concession he asked for was to her advantage as much as his. Making this story common knowledge would only make her seem laughable. "Agreed."

Mr. Tanner leaned against the barnyard fence and, with a gesture, invited her to join him. "You asked about the accident. It was Tom and Carol's anniversary. They'd gone to the theater to celebrate. There was a fire—neither of them survived."

"How horrible!"

He nodded in grim agreement, then moved away to check the level of water in the nearby trough. She watched him in silence.

He returned to her side, propping a foot on the bottom

fence rail and resting his arms over the top. When he didn't say anything, Elthia resumed her probing. "Tell me a little about the children. What was their life like before the accident?"

"Well, let's see. Tom and Carol owned and operated a restaurant, and I believe the older kids helped out. Not because Tom couldn't afford to hire outside help," he assured her, "but we Tanners are very big on teaching the value of honest labor."

Elthia responded to his challenging look with a tight smile and a tilted chin. She refused to rise to his bait.

He grinned as if he'd read her thoughts. Pushing away from the fence, he indicated they were to move toward the house. "They lived in town and were prominent in the community."

Picking up a pebble, he sailed it across the yard. They watched Poppy bound away and sniff around in the grass for it. "The move to this place here in the country with nary a neighbor in sight was a bit of an adjustment for the kids."

Elthia pulled her gaze from Poppy and wrinkled her forehead. "So why did you move them? I mean, there's nothing really wrong with this place, but as you said, it *is* foreign to the children, and they're already facing painful changes in their lives."

His jaw tightened. "I had my reasons." Then he smiled crookedly. "I thought it best to give them a fresh start somewhere where they wouldn't be bothered by painful reminders."

Mr. Tanner's moods confused and intrigued her. But she was more comfortable focusing on the children. "What about Zoe? Has she always been such a solemn child?"

He glanced sideways at her, as if surprised she'd noticed such a thing. "Zoe is hard to read," he said, bending over to pluck a blade of grass. "She's always been a quiet one. But since her parents' death, she's lost her ability to smile."

There was frustration and worry in his voice. She felt another of those little tugs of sympathetic admiration for him.

Focus on the children. Keep probing. "Josie has a different look than the other children. Is there a reason for that?"

He nodded. "You sure picked up on a lot in the short time you've been here." He motioned for her to have a seat on the steps of the back porch. "Tom had a twin brother, Timothy, who worked on a merchant ship. Josie is Tim's daughter. Josie's mother, an Italian lady, died giving birth to Josie. Tim asked Tom and his wife to take care of Josie for him."

Elthia nodded. So that was what accounted for Josie's exotically different look. "How old was Josie at the time?"

Caleb shrugged. "About six months. She's been part of Tom's family ever since. When Tim died two years ago, the arrangement became permanent." He leaned back. "Any other questions?"

She nodded. "Peter seems a little, well, adversarial."

He shifted position and rubbed the back of his neck. "You noticed that, too, did you?"

"It's rather blatant."

His grimace seemed aimed inward. "It hasn't been easy for any of them. They've not only lost their parents, but as you just said, they've been uprooted from the places and people they know. Their world has been turned upside down and inside out."

He shoved a hand through his hair. "I'm afraid Peter's carrying a chip on his shoulder right now. He didn't want to move away from his friends and doesn't like country life."

She watched him squint at the emerging sun. Was he deliberately avoiding her gaze?

"Are you certain that's all it is? Have you asked him?"

He stood abruptly. "Miss Sinclare, I don't think you know enough to start questioning the way I'm handling the kids." The look he gave her could have frozen a lake. "Just stick to getting to know the kids for now, and figuring out how to take care of them and this house. That'll keep your hands plenty full."

And with that he opened the door and ushered her inside.

How *dare* he talk to her like that!

Elthia had to bite back the retort burning her tongue when she realized Zoe was in the kitchen.

Was this Mr. Tanner's idea of how their partnership was to go on? Well, if so, he had a big surprise in store. She was quite capable of thinking for herself. If she was going to take care of these children, then she was going to learn everything she could about them and what their needs were.

Zoe, stooping over the woodbin near the stove, glanced up in surprise. Her honey-brown hair was neatly braided, and a crisp apron protected her dress. There were no lingering traces of sleep in her expression. It would seem Zoe had been up for a while.

"Mornin', Zoe," Mr. Tanner greeted his niece, his voice losing the brittle edge of moments ago. "Here, let me help you."

"No thank you." Her tone was as stiff as her demeanor. "I can manage it."

"Of course you can." He reached over and plucked the sticks from her hands. "But I don't mind helping."

Elthia wondered at the expression she saw on Zoe's face, as if Mr. Tanner had deprived her of something she urgently needed.

But the girl caught her staring and immediately turned away. Grabbing a kettle, she moved to the sink. Her youthful arms worked the pump with fierce energy. Zoe was so capable, so self-reliant, so different from the pampered child Elthia herself had been at that age.

Mr. Tanner straightened and dusted his hands with a frown. "I told you it would be all right if you slept late this morning, Zoe. You don't have to keep trying to do it all any more."

The girl shrugged. "I figured everyone would still want breakfast at the regular time." Before Mr. Tanner could protest further, she changed the subject. "Do you think Josie and the twins will have their regular appetites back this morning?"

Mr. Tanner tightened his jaw, and Elthia felt a small twinge of sympathy. Zoe's defensiveness and stony reception of his concern would frustrate a saint. And Mr. Tanner was no saint.

She pushed her glasses up on her nose, ready to defuse the tension. She wasn't sure why Zoe should feel so defensive, but this wasn't the time for personal probing. So she focused on the girl's words rather than her attitude. "Surely you don't intend to cook breakfast for everyone all by yourself?"

Zoe stiffened, and her lips compressed.

Mr. Tanner rolled his eyes and speared Elthia with a just-what-I'd-expect-from-you frown. "There are no servants here. We all pull our own weight and pitch in to help get things

77

done. Zoe's been running the kitchen since we moved here, and doing a fine job of it."

Elthia felt herself redden, knowing her ill-conceived remark had earned her another black mark in Mr. Tanner's book. She could also tell he had no high expectations of her ability to help with the household chores.

And on that score she couldn't blame him. Zoe was obviously much more capable of the task than she herself was. Elthia'd been taught something about running a household, but only if that household came staffed with a full complement of servants.

However, the contract Mr. Tanner held required that she fulfill certain responsibilities to this family. It was time she started rolling up her sleeves and getting to it.

"I'm glad to hear you're such a good cook, Zoe, since I'm not. But I'd be glad to lend a hand. And maybe you can teach me something about cooking as we go."

The girl flashed her a superior look, as if she shared her uncle's evaluation. "No thank you. I can manage just fine."

Realizing she'd been dismissed, Elthia forced a smile. "Very well. I'll look in on our patients then." She turned and walked past both Zoe and Mr. Tanner.

She was looking for a way to make herself useful, to earn her keep, she assured herself. The fact that it would give her some time and distance away from Mr. Tanner was only a side benefit.

Elthia entered the still shadowy room to hear soft whimpering. Tiptoeing around sleeping children, Poppy prancing at her heels, she located the one who had awakened—Josie.

She knelt next to the child's pallet and stroked her raven's wing hair from her face. "What is it, sweetheart?"

The girl gave a watery sniff as she rubbed her eyes. "I had a bad dream."

Poppy propped his front paws on the edge of the blankets, tail wagging furiously as he tried to stretch his tongue out far enough to reach the child's cheek.

"Ooooh!" Josie squealed, her nightmare obviously forgotten. "You brought Poppy back. Can I hold him?"

"Of course." As Josie untangled herself from the covers and sat up, Elthia lifted the dog into the child's lap.

"I tell you what," she offered, noting the twins' restless stirrings. "Why don't I take you and Poppy out to the porch so we don't disturb the others? Would you like that?"

"Oh, yes. I haven't been outside in just days and days."

Elthia smiled at the child's earnest expression. "Well, then"—she wrapped both child and dog in the quilt from the makeshift bed—"let's remedy that right now, shall we?"

She carried the squirming handful outside and set it on the porch. Josie was still in her nightclothes, but it was already warm here in the emerging Texas sunshine. While the child and dog played, Elthia allowed herself to dwell on her situation for the first time since she'd agreed to Mr. Tanner's proposal.

How in heaven's name had she gone from vowing, just a few weeks ago, that she would never agree to an arranged marriage, to suddenly discovering that tomorrow was her wedding day? Not only was she obligated to marry a perfect stranger, but she had now assumed partial responsibility for the care of six children, the oldest of whom was only thirteen.

What would happen if—no, when—her family found out?

Julia would be shocked.

Her father would shake his head and announce that she'd made a royal mess of things once again.

Ry, studying her with that big-brother look, would simply ask if she wanted his help or merely his support. He was rarely judgmental and always ready to listen, *really* listen. Lord, but she missed her brother. She could use his counsel right now.

"What are you doing?" Zoe stepped out onto the porch, a fiercely accusing frown on her young face. "Josie shouldn't be out here; she's still sick."

Elthia blinked and pushed her glasses up on her nose. The child displayed an amazing amount of passion. "It's all right, Zoe. The doctor said yesterday that sunshine and fresh air would be good for them."

"You're not in charge here. You shouldn't have brought her outside without asking first."

Mr. Tanner stepped through the doorway, filling the opening with his presence. "Zoe, you apologize to Miss Sinclare."

"But she—"

He drew his brows down with an impressively parental air

79

of authority. "No buts. She's an adult, and she's going to be my wife soon. You'll treat her with the same respect you show me."

From the mutinous glare Zoe directed at her uncle, Elthia expected her to refuse. But at last, thinning her lips, she turned to Elthia. Staring at Elthia's chin, she made her forced apology. "I'm sorry, Miss Sinclare."

"Thank you, Zoe."

Josie tugged on Elthia's skirt. "Are you going to be my new mommy?"

"Well, I . . ." Elthia looked uncertainly toward Mr. Tanner.

But before either of them could answer the question, Zoe intervened. "Don't be ridiculous," she said, reaching down to pick up her little sister.

Then Zoe leveled another challenging glare at her uncle. "Our mother is dead, and no one's going to take her place, no matter what Uncle Caleb says."

Mr. Tanner's expression tightened.

Elthia stepped into the breach. "Of course, I won't be taking your mother's place, Zoe," she said, drawing the girl's gaze away from her uncle. "No one could ever do that."

She tried a placating smile. "I will be marrying your uncle, though, so that will make me your aunt."

Josie glanced at her uncle, then at Elthia. "My aunt too?"

Elthia beamed at the child, glad to have a reason to turn her attention elsewhere. "Of course."

"That's right, Josie." Mr. Tanner finally spoke up. "She'll be your Aunt Elthia. Won't you like that?"

Elthia checked. Her family and friends had long ago turned to the less formal appellation, "Elly." It had been a long time since anyone had used her given name. But she decided she liked the sound of it.

She was pleased to see Josie nod enthusiastically. Then the child met her gaze with a hopeful expression. "That means Poppy will be living here now too, doesn't it?"

So much for where she stood in the order of things. "Yes. Poppy and I are like fleece on a lamb; we just naturally go together."

Zoe hefted the child on her hip. "Come on, Josie. I'll get

you some breakfast." Without another word, she turned and reentered the house.

Elthia stooped to pick up the quilt. With a speculative look, Mr. Tanner took the far end and helped her fold it.

Their hands brushed against each other, and Elthia felt a shiver of awareness. His expression shifted, reminding her of a guard dog who'd just caught the scent of something dangerous.

She blinked, and the look was gone.

Elthia broke the silence, grasping for the first innocuous thing that popped into her head. "It seems the children don't share your dislike of Poppy."

He eyed her dispassionately. "They like to play with bugs and lizards too."

His dry remark drew a grin from her as he stepped aside to open the door. She was much more comfortable with this verbal sparring than with the undertones of a moment ago.

She shifted the blanket in her arms. "If you'll excuse me, I'll get Keith and Kevin up and ready for breakfast. I think we'll all eat at the table this morning."

Caleb watched his soon-to-be bride enter the parlor.

So far, so good. She seemed resigned now. But he wasn't about to relax his vigilance just yet. After the stunt she'd pulled this morning, he couldn't take any chances. Not that she was much good at sneaking around. He'd heard her and that nuisance mutt of hers as soon as she'd come down the stairs.

He'd wager she couldn't even have found her way back to Whistling Oak. And she had enough trouble controlling her dog while they were on the ground—how did she think she'd manage it on top of a horse? She'd probably have ended up tossed on her sweet little rump, lucky if only her dignity got injured.

Lord, but what had she been thinking? Did she really believe he wouldn't have come after her?

Chapter Seven

Elthia entered the kitchen, adjusting her steps to match those of Keith and Kevin. Poppy scampered at their heels.

Studying the bounty spread on the long trestle table, Elthia was amazed at what Zoe had accomplished in such a short time. The sturdy table was loaded down with platters of eggs, bacon, biscuits, and potatoes. She could also see butter, two kinds of jam, and a frothy pitcher of milk.

The children quickly slid into their places on one of the benches lining each side of the table. Mr. Tanner stood at the head and Elthia rather self-consciously took her place across from him at the foot. When she saw him frown at Poppy, though, she straightened and drew her shoulders back. Catching and holding his gaze, she patted her chair, calling the dog to heel.

His frown deepened, but he didn't say anything. Was he just humoring her until after the wedding? Would he be more vocal in his objections once he had her where he wanted her? It was the sort of tactic her father would use. Only time would tell.

Once she was seated, Mr. Tanner took his own seat and turned to his nephew. "Peter, would you lead us in the blessing?"

Elthia was startled when Josie and Kevin, the children seated to either side of her, reached for her hands. Then she noticed that everyone had joined hands around the table. She took firmer hold of the small, warm hands and then bowed her head with the rest of them as Peter solemnly asked a blessing over the meal.

She silently slipped in a prayer of her own. The thought of becoming mother to this brood, even if temporarily, was daunting. To be entrusted with the care of these precious little lives was a wondrous privilege and a fearful responsibility. She planned to give them the best she had. But would it be good enough?

When Peter finished, the whole group echoed his "Amen," then began to pass the platters. Elthia listened to the children's chatter as the meal progressed, watching them with fresh eyes as she tried to imagine what the next few months would be like.

Once the meal ended, Mr. Tanner stood. "I think our three patients could benefit from a bath and a change of clothes. Zoe, why don't you get the baths ready. Alex, you can round up their clothes. Afterward, come back here, 'cause you and Peter have kitchen duty this morning."

Then he turned to Elthia. "If you'll lend me a hand, I think the two of us should work on putting the parlor back to rights."

Elthia nodded, relieved. He wasn't going to relegate her to a mere spectator, but he wasn't going to assign her a chore that was clearly beyond her reach. Gathering bedding and moving a few items of furniture around were definitely tasks she could handle.

She followed him out of the kitchen. "What's first?" she asked as they stepped into the former infirmary.

"If you'll move the bedding, I'll set the furniture back in place. Just put the sheets and pillow slips in a pile in the hall to be added to the laundry. When we get through in here we'll take the quilts and pillows outside to air in the sunshine."

As Elthia dismantled the pallets, sorting the bedding into appropriate piles, she surreptitiously watched Mr. Tanner at work. For all his apparent boorishness, he was not a weak or lazy man. He moved the two sofas into place, facing each other. The sight of the bunched muscles in his arms as he worked sent a tiny fluttering through her body. She tried not to think about the fact that he was soon to be her husband.

Once she finished her task, she looked for something to do besides admire Mr. Tanner's masculine prowess. Noticing the room had a closed-in, musty smell, Elthia decided to let in some fresh air. She opened all the windows, inhaling deeply of the sun-warmed-meadow smell wafting in on the light breeze.

Pleased with her efforts, she turned around to look at the now transformed room and caught Mr. Tanner sliding his gaze away from her. Had he watched her as she'd watched him earlier? The thought set that stomach fluttering in motion again.

Mentally clamping down on such inappropriate responses, she tried focusing her thoughts elsewhere. As Mr. Tanner set a table beside a sofa, Elthia pictured herself seated there in the evenings. The children would gather around her, and she would tell stories or listen to them discuss the events of their day.

Finding her gaze lingering on Mr. Tanner again, she headed to the other side of the long room. Well-stocked bookshelves lined the wall on this end. Did that mean Mr. Tanner was a reader?

In front of the bookshelves sat an oval worktable surrounded by a half-dozen chairs, the perfect place for a child to work on homework or an adult to spread out paperwork.

Elthia drifted back to the center of the room, an open space that divided the parlor and study areas. The only furnishings here were a love seat and an end table.

Mr. Tanner crossed to the opposite side of the love seat. "Good idea," he said, nodding toward the open windows.

"Thank you." She felt inordinately pleased that he'd noted and appreciated her efforts.

He returned her smile, then waved toward the bedding. "If you're done looking, we can take those to the laundry room."

Elthia nodded, but paused as she spied a portrait of two young girls, both on the verge of womanhood, hanging above the fireplace. Intrigued, she stepped back to get a better view. Glancing over her shoulder, she found Mr. Tanner watching her. Would she ever get used to that speculative look?

Don't think about the upcoming wedding. "Do you mind if I ask who these women are?"

"Not at all. The younger one is my mother, the older is her sister, my Aunt Cora. I came here to live with Aunt Cora when my parents died. She passed on about four years ago."

"I'm sorry."

He shrugged, not offering any further insights.

Elthia gave in to the urge to pry a bit. After all, if she was going to marry the man, it behooved her to learn as much about him as possible. "Did you and your aunt live in this great big house all by yourselves?"

He nodded. "Yep. Aunt Cora had a lady from town come in to cook and clean five days a week, but she went home in the evenings." He looked at the portrait. "Aunt Cora never socialized much. Not that she was snooty. Guess you'd say she was a scholar. She called herself a botanist. Wrote articles for scientific journals and even wrote a book on the subject."

"Your aunt published works on botany?" He'd been raised by a maiden aunt? A maiden aunt who wrote scholarly works? Elthia's mind rebelled as she tried to fit this new bit of information in with what she already knew about Mr. Tanner.

He nodded again, rubbing his neck. "Uh-huh. Mostly on the native plants of northeast Texas." He pointed in the direction of the bookshelves. "Her book is there somewhere. Feel free to read it if you're interested in that sort of thing." He seemed uncomfortable, as if he'd revealed too much personal information.

"Thank you. I'll take you up on that." She pursed her lips at his offhand attitude. Obviously his aunt's accomplishments seemed unexciting to him.

Either unaware of her censure, or unconcerned by it, he gathered an armload of linens. "Come on. I'll show you where the laundry room is."

He led her past the kitchen. "You've already seen most of the downstairs, except for this." He pushed open a door. "My office. Actually, it's not much bigger than a large closet, but it's where I come to do paperwork. Feel free to use it if you need to work on correspondence or just need a bit of privacy."

Elthia stepped inside to look around at the neatly organized space. His offer was an unexpected concession. It *was* a small room, though, and felt even smaller with his presence looming behind her. She could feel his breath at her neck. Turning abruptly, she came face-to-face with the wall of his chest.

With a crooked smile and lightly drawled "Excuse me," he stepped aside to let her escape the room.

She moved ahead to the end of the hall, regaining her composure as he closed the office door and followed her. By the time he reached around to open the outer door for her, she was able to meet his gaze with a polite smile.

When she stepped onto the stoop, Elthia found an addition had been constructed at some point, adjoining this back wall.

Mr. Tanner knocked on the door, giving her a wait-until-you-see-this grin. "Aunt Cora added this on right after I moved in with her. She designed it herself and was mighty proud of it."

Elthia raised a brow in question as Zoe's voice called "Come in," from inside.

He threw the door open with a flourish. "You are now looking at the gaudiest combination bathhouse and laundry in the county."

Elthia blinked as she took in the opulence and startling colors. The floor was covered in bright turquoise-colored tile. A roomy pool of a bathtub was built into one corner of the room.

The tub was fashioned entirely of pink marble and fitted with ornate brass fixtures. *Large* was too weak a term to describe it. The dining-room table could fit inside, twice over. A pair of trifold screens, each brightly decorated in pink and turquoise, stood nearby. Elthia could easily picture such a bathing pool gracing a sultan's harem or some ancient Roman emperor's palace. But here, in this out-of-the-way corner of Texas? Even her own elegant home in Maryland had nothing to match it.

Zoe was bent over the tub, pouring steaming water from a large copper kettle. Elthia's glasses fogged, and she wiped them with her sleeve, impatient to see more. Shelves lined the wall near the tub. These held thick, soft-looking towels as well as an abundance of soaps, lotions, and bath salts. That must be where the faint floral and spicy fragrances were coming from. Elthia felt a sudden yearning to sprinkle that steaming tub with foaming bath salts and sink herself in the decadence of it all.

She cast a quick glance toward Mr. Tanner, and heat crept up her face at his knowing expression. Could he read her thoughts?

Tilting her chin defensively, she turned to examine the rest of the room. To her left, past the shelves, Josie sat on one of a pair of pink marble benches. Keith and Kevin stood nearby, studying something crawling across the floor, something Elthia refused to look at too closely.

A sudden squealing from Josie made her jump. She hid a grin as she realized the boys had apparently decided to gift their sister with the subject of their study.

Before she could say anything, Mr. Tanner intervened. "All right, boys, that's enough. Leave Josie alone."

The twins turned innocent, injured expressions his way. "But Uncle Caleb," one of them reasoned, "it's just an ol' beetle. It wouldn't hurt her. She's just being a baby."

Josie popped up from the bench and stood glowering at her tormentor. "You take that back, Keith Tanner. I'm *not* a baby."

Keith held out the beetle, waving it in her face. With another squeal, the girl retreated a couple of steps.

"That's enough, Keith. Josie's not being a baby. She just doesn't like beetles, is all. So stop teasing her."

Keith scuffed his toes against the floor. "Yes, sir."

Then Mr. Tanner turned to the other boy. "Kevin?"

The boy gave a quick nod. "Yes, sir."

Elthia was surprised by the ease with which Mr. Tanner dealt with the children's squabble. Then she hid a grin as Josie, from the safety of her uncle's back, stuck her tongue out at the boys.

A hissing sound captured her attention, and Elthia turned to see a second kettle resting on a cast-iron stove, steam escaping from its spout. How clever. Having the stove in here would not only be useful for heating water but would also keep the room toasty warm.

Having recovered somewhat from the shock of the gorgeous bathing area, Elthia turned her attention to the rest of the room. Near the door was a laundry tub, a large set of work sinks, and a very modern clothes wringer. A very efficient arrangement for doing laundry.

With transom windows lining the upper walls on three sides, the room was both well lighted and well ventilated.

She turned back to Mr. Tanner, still feeling slightly stunned. "Your aunt, the botanist scholar, designed this?"

He grinned. "Not what you'd expect to find in the home of a proper spinster lady, is it?" Without waiting for her answer, he dumped the linens near the washer. "Need any help, Zoe?"

The girl straightened, setting the now empty kettle down. "No, sir. The water's all ready for Josie." She moved to the screens, but her uncle was a step ahead of her.

In a matter of seconds he had the screens placed around the tub, affording the soon-to-be bather optimum privacy. Then, as Zoe ushered the younger girl behind the screen, he retrieved the kettle and moved to the sink to fill it. Setting the kettle on the stove, he called a good-bye to the children, took Elthia's arm, and escorted her out.

They lugged the pillows and colorful quilts outside to hang on the clothesline, working in silence for the most part. When they were done, Elthia moved to reenter the house, but Mr. Tanner stopped her. "Why don't I give you a tour of the place?"

Elthia wasn't fooled into thinking he wanted the pleasure of her company. He'd made it quite clear from the outset she wasn't the sort of woman he was apt to admire. And even though she'd caught him watching her several times this morning, she was sure it was prompted by curiosity more than anything else.

She supposed that also explained why he was deliberately trying to keep her by his side. He was probably curious about what sort of partner he'd saddled himself with. Or was he afraid she'd try to run away again if he let her out of his sight?

Not that it really mattered. It was a beautiful morning and she wasn't opposed to spending part of it in the sunshine.

He offered her his arm, and she took it. He flashed another of those crooked smiles, and she decided she'd have to be careful—the man had more charm than she'd first given him credit for.

"Thought you might enjoy getting a look at the barn and barnyard in full daylight."

Elthia decided his charm wouldn't be much of a problem after all. Tilting her chin, she chose not to dignify his ungentlemanly reminder with a response.

He took her around the barn and animal pens. She discovered the livestock included cows, horses, a mule, chickens, pigs, and rabbits. Elthia, who'd never been around farm animals much, did her best not to be obvious as she wrinkled her nose against the smells and watched her step in the barnyard. But she could tell she hadn't fooled her tour guide. What was worse, he seemed amused by her discomfiture. At least he refrained from comment.

Things went a little better in the carriage house. It was attached to the barn and housed garden tools as well as a buckboard and buggy. She noted with interest that everything was kept neat and well organized.

As they left the carriage house, Alex came up. Trapped in his hands was a feebly struggling, anxiously chirping bird.

Mr. Tanner's forehead furrowed. "What do we have here?"

Alex lifted his hands higher. "A robin. It's got a hurt wing and can't fly."

"Let me have a look." Mr. Tanner gently stretched the bird's wing, and was rewarded for his efforts by an almost successful peck on the hand. "Looks like it's been mauled. Probably let one of the barn cats get a bit too close."

Alex's brow furrowed. "Will it heal? Should I bandage it?"

"It should be okay in a few days." Mr. Tanner straightened. "And no, I don't think bandages would help. Just keep him out of harm's way until he can fly again. I suggest the bathhouse."

"Yes, sir." Alex gave his uncle a broad, relieved smile. "I'll get some old rags to make him a nest right now. And I'll find some bugs to feed him a couple times a day."

Elthia watched Mr. Tanner watch Alex walk away. It wasn't an act or even just a duty—he really *was* fond of the children.

As they moved back toward the house, she spied another outbuilding, tucked under the shade of an enormous oak.

"What's that?"

He didn't even glance in the direction she'd pointed, just kept walking toward the house. "Just my workshop."

There was something about his tone that caught her attention. Goodness, she didn't even know what he did for a living. She stopped, forcing him to halt also. "What sort of workshop?"

He rubbed the back of his neck, his expression saying

clearly that this wasn't something he wanted to talk about. "Woodworking."

She beamed at him. "You're an artisan! How fascinating."

But he shook his head and stuffed his hands into his pockets. "I make furniture, lady. Don't make me into anything fancy."

"Oh." Did he have to be so deliberately rude? But she was determined to learn more. "What kind of furniture do you make?"

He shrugged. "Whatnot tables, rockers, ladderback chairs. Whatever people will pay me for."

Was he embarrassed? Were his skills only so-so? She refused to be put off by his rudeness. She had a right to see how good a provider he'd be for the family. "Do you mind if I peek inside?"

His chin jutted out mulishly, and she was certain he intended to tell her no. What was he hiding? Was it truly a woodworking shed or something less innocent? She'd heard there were moonshiners in these parts. If he was involved in something like that, she'd better learn about it now.

She turned toward the building, pretending his permission was a given. "I envy you," she said, making conversation to forestall any protests. "It must be a source of pride to be able to craft beautiful, useful things from raw materials."

He followed her and she stiffened, feeling his belligerent glare prickling the back of her neck. But she didn't stop until she'd reached the door. She flinched as he reached past her to grab the knob, then tried to cover her start with a bright smile.

He stared at her for a long minute, and Elthia felt her pulse accelerate. He was going to refuse her. Why?

Then he shrugged, turned the knob, and threw the door open.

She took a deep breath and stepped past him, unsure of what she would find. The room smelled of sawdust, paint, and oils. It took a moment for her eyes to grow accustomed to the shadowy interior, but she could already tell it was just what he'd said, a woodcrafter's workroom. So why the melodramatics?

Just inside the door stood a simple ladderback rocking

chair. To her right she saw a long narrow table, the perfect size for an entryway. These were really quite good! So why his hesitation?

Then the other items in the room caught her attention, and Mr. Tanner's strange behavior was forgotten.

Rocking horses!

There were at least a dozen of them in various stages of construction, all of them different, all of them a child's delight. They ranged in size from one large enough to seat a child Peter's age to one small enough for a toddler to hold.

"Mr. Tanner, these are wonderful!"

Elthia walked farther into the workshop, drawn to touch the charming creations. She set one of the larger toys in motion, smiling at its smooth dipping and rising. Then she drifted to the workbench and lifted a smaller piece. It had been painted in spare but telling detail. He'd given the horse a playful expression, as if it invited the holder to join in its fun.

She could just hear her niece and nephew's delighted squeals upon being presented one of these. She looked around, noting other details to delight the eye and enchant the mind. An oddly quirked ear must must have taken exceptional talent to carve, and a long, feminine eyelash proclaimed one of the beasts a mare.

More than just routine woodcrafter's skill had gone into making these. She could see touches of whimsy and heart in them too. The person who'd crafted these toys understood children.

Mr. Tanner stood in the doorway, watching her with an unreadable expression. *This* man, this irascible, stubborn, have-his-own-way-at-all-costs man, made these wonderful toys?

He rubbed the back of his neck. "It's something I do to fill in between orders for the furniture pieces. A toy shop in St. Louis has a standing order for as many as I can turn out."

Elthia looked around her again. "I can see why. You're quite talented."

Suddenly, she felt better about the bargain she'd struck with him. After all, a man who would go to such trouble to see to the welfare of orphaned children, and one who made his living making children's toys, must have other admirable qualities as well.

*   *   *

Caleb made an excuse to hurry her out of his workshop. Darn nosy woman! He shouldn't have let her inside. The workshop was his private domain. And for someone who hadn't wanted anything to do with him a few hours ago, she sure was doing a lot of digging into his personal life. Hell, she was the one who insisted that their relationship be more of a business partnership than a marriage.

He refused to be moved by her enthusiastic appreciation of his work. And he definitely wasn't affected by the soft smile she'd flashed him as they left the workshop, no matter how much his traitorous body argued to the contrary. He didn't need her approval, just her cooperation.

Her job was to see to the kids, not him. The sooner she learned that, the better, for both of them.

Chapter Eight

By late afternoon, Elthia decided she'd been mistaken. Mr. Tanner obviously had *no* other redeeming qualities.

Nothing she'd done since leaving the workshop had met with his approval. She'd tried to help set the table for the noon meal, and he'd explained to her in exhausting detail just what she was doing wrong. How was she supposed to know the speckled blue mug was Josie's favorite, or that Keith and Kevin had to have identical settings? When she tried to help clean up, he'd hovered about, making her so nervous with his "helpful advice," she'd finally dropped a plate, breaking it into a dozen pieces.

Finally she excused herself to take a nap, just to get away from him for a while. Besides, due to her failed escape attempt, she hadn't gotten much sleep last night. She really *was* tired.

But sleep eluded her. After fifteen minutes of tossing and turning, she decided she'd spend her time doing something useful. Like drawing up that new contract for her and Mr. Tanner to sign.

A half dozen wasted pages later, Elthia had a draft she hoped would be acceptable to both parties. She read it over once more.

I, Caleb Tanner, enter into marriage with Elthia Sinclare for the sole purpose of providing a mother for the six children in my care. I agree that I will not exercise any privilege normally considered the right of a husband, other than that which she willingly grants to me. At such time as a final decision is reached on my petition to adopt the children, I will support Miss Sinclare's efforts to seek an annulment of this marriage.

Here she left space for his signature and a date. Then she continued with her half of the agreement.

I, Elthia Sinclare, enter into marriage with Caleb Tanner for the purpose of seeing to the welfare of the six children in his care. During the time I am partnered with Mr. Tanner, I will care for the children of his household as if I were their natural mother. I will not knowingly take any action that is contrary to their best interests. At such time as a final decision is reached on Mr. Tanner's petition to adopt the children, I will have fully executed my obligation and may seek an annulment with the expectation of Mr. Tanner's full cooperation and support.

Yes, that spelled it out quite clearly. Now, it was time to see if Mr. Tanner was willing to sign it as promised.

As Elthia stood, she was assailed by thoughts she'd held at bay all day, thoughts of this devil's bargain she'd made. What a miserable way to enter into marriage. Instead of hopes and dreams for a blissful future, they were going to walk down the aisle with plans to dissolve the union once they'd accomplished their noble but somewhat devious goal.

She was such a spineless ninny. If she planned to go along with this scheme, she should have had the courage to commit to a true marriage, not this shameful deception. But, aside from the fact that he was a stranger, something inside her rebelled at the thought of spending her life with a man who had settled on her because he had no other choice.

What would it be like to have a man desire her, feel passion and love for her? She'd thought for a while she had that with Baxter, but that dream had turned to ashes. Now it seemed she'd never know. Elthia held back her tears, fiercely chastising herself for indulging in such maudlin thoughts. After all, she'd come to terms with the specter of her old-maid future before she ever set foot in Texas.

Or at least she thought she had.

Regaining control, she drew back her shoulders and set out to find Mr. Tanner.

Caleb looked up from his workbench as he heard the kitchen door open and close. It was a sound he'd been listening for for the past hour. Through the open door of his workshop he could see Lady Privilege determinedly marching his way. Was she going to try to tell him again how impossible the whole situation was?

At least she wasn't making another break for it.

Caleb hastily gazed back down at his work as she drew near.

She stopped just outside the open door, knocking on the jamb. "Mr. Tanner, may I come in please? I need to speak to you."

He looked up as if just noticing her. "Of course." He set down his file and dusted off a chair for her. "Did you enjoy your nap?"

She sat, eyeing him as if wary of his solicitousness. "Actually, I spent most of my time working on this." She held up a piece of paper. "It's what I need to talk to you about."

Caleb's brows drew down. "If that's the contract again, I thought we'd already—"

"No, no." She raised a hand, cutting off his protests. "At least not the Pembroke contract."

Sitting again, Caleb frowned. "I'm not sure I understand."

She straightened, her cheeks turning rosy. "This morning, when I agreed to your proposal, I stipulated that we sign a new contract before we wed. I took the liberty of drafting it up myself. I'd like you to look it over and then sign it, please." She extended her arm stiffly, offering him the document.

Damn! He'd forgotten that little detail.

Caleb took the document and read it slowly, stalling for time. If he signed this and handed it back to her, she'd have a potent weapon to use against him. All she'd have to do was wave it under Judge Walters's nose, and his chances of adopting the kids would fly out the window. How far could he trust her?

He looked up, flashing her what he hoped was a friendly smile. "This all seems in order. But honestly, Miss Sinclare, do you really think it's necessary?"

She nodded firmly. "Oh, yes, Mr. Tanner, I think it's *quite* necessary. We agreed this would be a strictly business arrangement. That being so, I believe we should spell out the boundaries of our partnership in strictly business terms."

Caleb wasn't ready to completely trust her when he had so much riding on this. Was she planning something underhanded?

"Still," he pressed, "the whole point of this arrangement is to give me a fighting chance to adopt the kids. What if this document mysteriously came to the attention of the judge? It would quite nicely cut short your sentence as my wife."

"Mr. Tanner!"

Her affront seemed genuine enough, but he would be the last one to claim the ability to read a woman's mind. He smiled. "I thought we were leaving emotions out of this. I'm merely voicing a concern over your holding a trump card in our arrangement."

She compressed her lips, then nodded. "All right. But I have no intention of marrying you tomorrow unless you sign this. So, how do we make you feel less threatened by the arrangement?"

Caleb drew himself up. What was she implying? "See here, lady, I don't feel a bit threatened by you or this paper. I just want to make sure I don't hand you a noose to hang me with."

She raised a brow, as if to say he'd made her point for her.

Caleb's hand clenched tight enough to crumple the part of the document he held. Taking a deep breath, he deliberately relaxed his hold and handed the piece of paper back toward her. "Before I sign this thing, I want you to make one change."

She reached for the contract. "And that change *is?*"

He leaned forward, catching a whiff of the fresh flowery perfume she wore. The feminine scent seemed so at odds with the no-nonsense, businesslike manner she tried to project.

Ignoring the unwanted distraction, he released the paper. "Add something to the effect that, regardless of what happens, you won't work on an annulment before the three months are up."

Caleb could almost see her mind work as she sat back and pushed on her glasses. He couldn't help but admire her smarts, even if she did use them against him.

Finally, she nodded. "Very well, that seems acceptable. I'll make the change and then we can sign it later today."

"One more thing," he added. He was still chafing over her suggestion that he'd felt threatened by her.

She looked up suspiciously. "And that is?"

"Part of our bargain was that we'd make sure it looked like this arrangement is something we both want."

She nodded. "Yes. And I plan to do my part."

"Then we should drop the formalities. You call me Caleb, and I'll call you Elthia."

She shifted uneasily. "I suppose, when we're in public—"

He raised a hand, cutting off her words. "No. All the time. It needs to come naturally, like a habit."

Her lips thinned, but at last she nodded. "Very well."

He expected her to leave then, but she didn't. Instead she sat there, her gaze not quite meeting his. Absently, she brushed some sawdust and wood shavings from the table onto the floor. Then she fidgeted with one of his chisels.

What was bothering her now? "Well, Elthia," he said, emphasizing her name. "Is there anything else I can do for you?"

She took a deep breath and finally met his gaze again, though it seemed she forced herself. "I wanted to ask about the wedding, about what sort of plans you've made."

Caleb almost felt sorry for her. She'd no doubt had dreams of a big showy affair, with herself in a fairy-tale princess gown, standing next to a handsome, rich-boy groom, hundreds of guests to admire them, and a fancy reception afterwards. Of course, she'd had her chance at all that and thumbed her nose at it.

"The wedding will take place at the church in Foxberry tomorrow morning after the regular Sunday service. It'll be a short, simple ceremony."

There was no outward sign that this news had upset her.

"Will there be any guests?"

He leaned back in his chair. "I didn't send out engraved

invitations, but yes, I'm guessing there'll be a fair crowd. Weddings and funerals are big draws around here. A wedding with a stranger as the bride will definitely stir up some interest. I imagine just about everyone who can be there, will be."

She seemed to take the news fairly well. He might as well give her the rest of it. "After the ceremony, there'll be a reception on the church grounds in our honor. It'll give you a chance to meet the neighbors, and give them a chance to meet you. Granny Picket's organized some of the ladies to take care of everything, including providing a meal for the gathering."

"Granny Picket?"

"She's not my real granny. Her full name is Miss Odella Mae Picket, but just about everyone in these parts calls her Granny. She's upwards of sixty years old but still spry, and as sharp as they come. She's sort of the thread that holds this community together. Her word carries a lot of weight around here."

Later, after she'd gone, Caleb tried resuming his work on the chair leg he'd been shaping, but his mind wouldn't focus.

Would she really go through with it? All she had to do was stand in front of that church tomorrow and announce, before God and everyone, that she'd changed her mind, and there wouldn't be a thing he could do about it.

Somehow, though, he didn't think she'd let him down. No matter what her faults, he was learning Lady Privilege had grit and her own unique code of honor.

The next three months might prove a rocky road, but it was almost guaranteed to take him on an interesting journey.

The morning breeze ruffled the curtains as Elthia studied herself in the mirror.

This was her wedding day!

Even saying it out loud didn't make it seem any more real. She looked for the glow she always associated with brides. It wasn't there. But at least none of the turmoil she felt was apparent either. Except for the fact that her complexion was more pale than usual and her freckles stood out a bit brighter, she might have been preparing for nothing more than Sunday service.

She'd be walking down the aisle alone, without her father

there to give her away. None of her family was here to support her and wish her well. There'd been no time spent dreaming and planning. Rather than a fine gown of satin and lace, she was wearing one she'd brought along for church services.

And to think, less than a month ago she'd been appalled when her father announced his intention to select a husband for her. It had been right after she told him of her broken engagement.

She'd been relieved to find both her father and brother seated on the terrace that afternoon. It meant she'd only have to go through her announcement once. Taking a deep breath, she pasted a smile on her lips and joined them.

"Hello, Father." She bent to kiss his cheek, then smiled a greeting Ry's way. As she moved around the small table, she stubbed her toe on a chair but managed not to grimace.

"So how was the picnic, Elly?" her father asked. "And where's Baxter? Didn't he come in with you?"

"No." She took another deep breath. "I broke off my engagement with Baxter this afternoon."

Ry merely stared at her with that maddeningly perceptive gaze, but her father immediately began firing questions.

"You did what! Why? Did the two of you quarrel? Did he do something to upset you?"

"No, no, there was no quarrel. I just realized that I can't go through with it after all."

He frowned, tugging at his beard. "Just like that, after weeks of rhapsodizing over all Baxter's sterling qualities, you suddenly decide you don't want to marry him."

"Yes, sir. Just like that." Elthia poured herself a glass of lemonade from the pitcher on the table, pleased with the steadiness of her hands. Unfortunately, she knocked her glass over as she set the pitcher back down.

Ry quietly helped her sop up the spill. His look, though, told her that while he was holding his tongue now, he wouldn't let her off the hook indefinitely.

Her father waved an impatient hand, reclaiming her attention. "Oh, for heaven's sake, Elly, stop fidgeting and talk to me."

Elthia watched his expression soften as he quit tugging at his beard and merely stroked it. "Well, if your mind is made up, that's that. Truth to tell, I wasn't pleased with Baxter as a prospective son-in-law. There's a better man out there for you."

"Perhaps."

"No perhaps about it. In fact, I'll find him for you."

"But—"

"No arguments. I've let you have your own way in this long enough. You're twenty-one. It's high time you had a husband to look after you. Any number of men would be proud to wed a fine girl like you. Why, I'll have you married in no time."

She sputtered a protest, but he ignored it, patting her hand. "If you're worried about my finding the right sort of man, don't. I did all right by Julia. She may think she found Stephen on her own, but that's not entirely true."

"But I'm not Julia. There aren't men lined up, eager for you to pick them." Elthia regretted the self-pitying words immediately. She gave an inward groan as she saw Ry's gaze sharpen.

Her father, however, merely waved her words away. "Don't be silly. You're a biddable girl with a kind heart, and a Sinclare. Finding you the right man will be no trouble at all. As soon as I get back from this trip to Europe, I'll take care of it."

"No, Father, please." Elthia leaned forward, trying to make him understand. "I really don't want to get married if you have to coerce or bribe someone to have me."

He frowned and stood. "We'll have no more of that kind of talk. After you think on it, you'll see I'm right. Don't worry, I'll find someone who'll take good care of you."

Elthia slumped as her father exited the terrace. But she straightened as Ry stood, looming over her. "Okay Elly, let's have it. What *really* happened this afternoon?"

She traced circles on the table with a finger. "I told you. I just decided that Baxter and I don't suit after all."

His soul-searching gaze probed deeper. "What did Baxter say or do to drain the sparkle from your eyes?"

Dear lord, she loved her big brother dearly, but there were times when she wished he wasn't quite so observant. She couldn't, wouldn't relive the humiliation of that overheard conversation by repeating it, not even to Ry.

She tried a teasing smile. "Stop being melodramatic." But the tremble in her voice betrayed her. This was a mistake. She shouldn't have said anything while her feelings were still raw.

"Shall I rip his heart out and feed it to him for you?"

The contrast between his gentle tone and savage words drew a near-hysterical laugh from her. "Don't be ridiculous," she said, her voice barely quivering at all.

Ry drew her up and put an arm around her, and she reveled in his sympathy for a moment before she pushed him away, afraid she'd start crying. "Don't," she whispered.

Ry gave her shoulder a quick squeeze, then stepped back, propping a hip on the low terrace wall. "Father only wants what's best for you, you know."

Elthia nodded as she sat. "I know. But why should he think that involves finding me a husband?"

"What sort of alternatives do you have to offer him?"

She waved a hand. "Not every woman has to be married to be happy. Look at Aunt Lottie."

Her brother raised a challenging eyebrow. "Think about that a minute. I love Aunt Lottie—she's been wonderful to us since mother died—but is her sort of life what you want? Do you *want* to be someone who's forever dependent, forever on the fringes?"

Elthia shifted, searching her mind for another example. "There's Mrs. Pembroke. She has her own home and operates one of the most successful placement agencies in the area."

Ry pointed at her, schoolteacher fashion. "Mrs. Pembroke is a widow, not a spinster. Her husband started the agency and had it running smoothly before he died."

She thrust out her chin. "Are you saying a woman isn't capable of accomplishing such success on her own?"

"No, of course not. But it takes a woman used to making hard decisions and dealing with the consequences." The look he gave her was compassionate but firm. "You just don't have that kind of experience, Elly."

The words stung, but she was honest enough to admit the truth of it. When had she ever had to make a decision or perform a task that truly mattered? Other than her engagement to Baxter, that is, and look what a disaster *that* turned into.

"You're right." Elthia forced herself not to slump. All she wanted right now was to escape to her room and have a good cry.

Ry eyed her steadily. "Keep in mind I didn't say you couldn't learn, just that you're not experienced. The problem is, your interests and energies seem restricted to books and observation. To learn something well, there's no substitute for actually doing a task."

That conversation with Ry was what had spurred her to seek employment away from Terrelmore, to prove to herself and her family that she really could make her own way.

Now here she was, right where she'd started, heading straight into an arranged marriage.

She squared her shoulders. Even if Mr. Tanner wasn't what she dreamed of in a husband, he'd said he needed her. No one had ever said that to her before. Perhaps being needed was not so romantic as being loved, but it could be just as fulfilling.

Of course it could!

At least this had been her choice, in a manner of speaking. As far as her family would ever know, this was exactly what she'd set out to accomplish.

She checked her reflection once more. The queasy feeling in her stomach mocked her unruffled appearance. Grateful she'd only eaten a small breakfast, Elthia patted Poppy, then stood. She'd bathed him this morning, brushed his coat dry, and even tied a bright green ribbon on his topknot. Surely no one would object to having such a fine, well-behaved pet at the wedding.

This was it. She stepped into the hall and paused at the top of the stairs. Below her stood Mr. Tanner and the children, looking up at her with solemn, expectant expressions.

Her soon-to-be husband flashed a smile and climbed the stairs to join her. My, but he seemed a different man decked out in his Sunday best. With a short bow, he offered her his arm.

His gallantry eased some of her nervousness, made her feel, if not like a bride, at least like someone special.

Elthia smiled, determined to keep the mood light. "Why, Mr. Tanner sir, I had no idea you could be so gallant."

He gave her hand a light squeeze as he tucked it securely in the crook of his arm. Was he trying to reassure her?

"First names, remember?" he chided teasingly.

Her cheeks warmed and she knew the telltale flush that was

her bane was glowing brightly. "Oh, sorry. Caleb." She lifted her chin, rallying. "Thank you for the loan of your arm."

He gave her an approving smile. "You're welcome. We can't take any chances of your tumbling down the stairs, now can we?"

She drew back, prepared to take offense, but then saw his smile-with-me grin. Willing to be distracted, she sighed melodramatically. "Oh, dear, I'm afraid you've discovered my plan. I suppose I'll either have to find another way to break my leg or force myself to go through with the wedding after all."

He chuckled as they descended, but his smile died when she lifted Poppy's basket from the hall table. "Surely you don't mean to take that animal with us?"

"Of course." She kept her smile firmly in place, determined not to beg. *Dear Lord, please don't let him make a scene over this.*

"You'll have to leave him tied up outside. Dogs aren't allowed in church."

"I'm sure, if you back me up, the minister will make an exception. It's not like Poppy is some stray. He's clean, well behaved, and accustomed to being indoors." She lifted her chin a notch. "Besides, this is my wedding day. Brides are allowed a few concessions." She just *had* to convince him to let Poppy attend. He was the closest thing to family she had here.

Mr. Tanner shook his head, as if disgusted by the situation. "All right, but I won't have him standing up at the altar with us. You let one of the kids hold him during the ceremony."

Elthia released the breath she'd been holding for the past few seconds. "Of course. And thank you."

He grumbled away her thanks and opened the front door. "The buckboard's hitched and ready. It's time we headed for town."

As Elthia stepped out on the porch, Zoe touched her arm, claiming her attention. "Here, these are for you," the girl said, thrusting out a bouquet of flowers.

Elthia took the flowers, studying the mix with delight. The creamy camellias and yellow roses were no doubt plucked from the bushes here in the front yard. But there were other blossoms she didn't recognize, colorful, freshly picked wildflowers. "Oh, Zoe, these are lovely. Thank you so much."

Zoe shrugged. "Don't try to make something special out of this. I just figured a bride should have flowers, that's all."

Elthia smiled, not fooled by the girl's show of unconcern. "Still, it was very thoughtful of you, and I thank you."

Zoe nodded once and then hurried to climb into the buckboard.

Elthia took her seat beside her soon-to-be husband at the front of the wagon and faced straight ahead, to her future.

Caleb flicked the reins, setting the horse and wagon in motion. Well, it looked like she was actually going to go through with it. He hadn't been completely sure 'til now. In fact he'd slept in the parlor last night, just so he'd hear if she tried to slip out in the middle of the night again.

Her appearance at the top of the stairs had surprised him. That white and green gown softened her appearance considerably. It had also jabbed him with a reminder of the difference in their lifestyles. She'd looked like a princess, a princess plucked from her kingdom and left to make her way among strangers.

Her lost, vulnerable air made him feel like a bully. Giving in on the matter of her dog had saved his conscience some. But her overwhelming relief, as if she'd been braced for refusal, had pricked his sense of honor again.

Damn! He was caught between two belly-souring choices: either force an unwilling woman to marry him or let these kids get split up. Where was the honor in either of those options?

She angled her knees toward him as she turned to look at the kids. When she turned back, he caught her gaze with his. For one charged moment they seemed to share an understanding.

The feisty tilt of her chin and the no-regrets smile she flashed eased the tension from his shoulders. It was almost as if she was saying, *We're in this together.*

Impulsively, Caleb gave her hand a squeeze, releasing it as quickly as he'd taken it. Her startled expression was followed by a flood of color to her cheeks as she gave him a shy smile.

Could it be he'd ended up with exactly the right woman for the job after all?

Chapter Nine

Twenty minutes later Elthia saw the first outposts of the town. She watched with interest as they neared, skittishly avoiding thoughts of what they'd come here to do.

They turned onto a smaller track before they reached the town proper. The whitewashed church, its steeple pointing proudly skyward, perched on a gently sloping hill overlooking the town.

They'd deliberately arrived early. Mr. Tanner—Caleb—had said Reverend Hastings wanted a word with them before the ceremony. But Elthia counted fifteen people milling about already, setting up makeshift tables or visiting in small groups.

He'd barely helped her alight when a tall, severe-looking woman approached them. The gray-haired matron wore a faded brown and yellow dress topped by a bright blue shawl. On her feet were sturdy, mannish-looking boots, and she carried a hefty walking stick, though she didn't appear to be leaning on it much.

Elthia clutched her bouquet tighter, resisting the urge to step back. This army general of a woman studied her with eyes that didn't seem to miss much. It was hard to tell if she was pleased or not with what she saw.

"Welcome to Foxberry, Miss Sinclare. I'm Odella Picket, but

you can just call me Granny like everyone else."

This was Granny Picket? When Caleb told her Miss Picket was "the thread that held the community together," Elthia had pictured a societal arbiter, an elegant matriarch, not this eccentrically dressed, blunt woman with a voice as gruff as her manner.

Pasting a smile on her face, Elthia met the woman's gaze. "Thank you, ma'am. And please, call me Elthia."

"Well, Elthia, now that you've had a look at him and at us, you still planning to go through with marrying our Caleb?"

Elthia stiffened. This woman was direct to the point of rudeness. "Of course." She inhaled the sweet perfume of her bouquet before continuing. "In fact, since my arrival, Caleb and I have actually strengthened our commitment to make this work."

To Elthia's surprise, rather than take offense, Granny grinned. Thumping her stick on the ground, she turned to Caleb. "Hah! Her look tells me to mind my own business, but she's too much of a lady to say it out loud. Not too much of a lady to face me down, though. Seems you did all right after all, boy."

Granny turned back to Elthia. "We'll visit later." Then she made shooing movements. "Go on and see the reverend. I'll keep an eye on the young'uns. And Caleb," she added with a wink, "I suggest you go around back. Might save you getting stopped by all these nosy folks who can't wait to meet your bride."

Caleb returned her wink with a grin. "Yes, ma'am."

He tucked Elthia's arm in his and headed for the church. "Well, it looks like you passed muster with Granny."

Elthia still felt dazed from the encounter. "That's good?"

He grinned. "Oh, yes, that's very good. Believe me, she doesn't take to everyone. And with Granny on your side, you don't have to worry about the rest of the town." He slid her a sideways look. "That was fast thinking, by the way. You were able to answer her without having to lie."

She stopped in her tracks. How dare he! "I do not lie, not for you or anyone else. You'd do well to remember that."

He studied her as if to judge her seriousness. Then he gave her arm a little tug to get her moving again. "Duly noted."

Mollified, she executed a dignified nod and faced forward. As they walked, she grew increasingly aware of the touch of his hand on her arm, of his almost protective closeness. It was all for show, she told herself. Still, it was disconcerting to realize how reassuring, how right, it felt.

Looking around, she realized two things: One was that their little "discussion" hadn't gone unnoticed. Several people were watching with interest, though they turned away when they caught her looking back. And two was she was considerably overdressed by local standards. Though the gown she wore was by no means the finest she owned, its stiff, elegant folds far outshone the simple dresses worn by the other ladies present. In fact, *most* of the dresses she'd brought would have the same effect.

Just as Granny had suggested, Caleb led her to the back of the church where Reverend Hastings stood, ready to greet them. Elthia guessed he was about thirty, much younger than her pastor back home. He seemed more approachable as well. His serene, I'm-here-to-help-you demeanor both welcomed and offered comfort.

Once the introductions were complete, the compactly built man of God waved them to comfortable-looking chairs situated in front of his book-and-paper-cluttered desk. As they complied, he settled in the age-worn leather desk chair.

The reverend leaned forward, clasping his hands on top of his Bible. "Before performing a wedding, I like to talk to the couple, satisfy myself they're ready for the step they're about to take." Then he smiled. "Now, your situation is unusual, what with your not having met until two days ago. But, in some ways, that makes this talk more important than ever."

Elthia forced herself not to squirm. Heaven help her, Reverend Hastings was turning to address her first.

"Miss Sinclare, you've traveled a long way to marry Caleb, so I'll assume you did a lot of thinking about it first. But now that you're here and have seen the life you have to look forward to, you may find you have new doubts. So, before you actually make this commitment, I ask you to search your heart and be sure this is what you truly want. The vows you'll utter, to cherish, love, honor, and obey your husband, shouldn't be taken lightly."

Elthia's conscience balked, but she forced herself to face her interrogator squarely. "Reverend, I will not sit here and pretend I feel a love for Mr. Tanner that I do not. I only met him two days ago, hardly time enough to even get to know him."

She sensed the sudden tension in her soon-to-be husband. Hadn't he learned to trust her yet? Keeping her gaze on the reverend, she carefully chose her next words. "However, I did do some soul-searching before I left Maryland, and even more after I arrived here, and I'm convinced this is the right choice."

Caleb's gaze bored into her, but still she didn't turn to meet it. "Mr. Tanner and I have a mutual need, each for what the other can bring to this arrangement, and I think this will hold us together as firmly as any love match. That, and the fact that we are both committed to building a good life for the children."

Reverend Hastings nodded. "I see. Well, you certainly have a more pragmatic view of your upcoming marriage than most brides I've talked to." His tone conveyed neither censure nor approval.

He turned to Caleb. "And you? Making a home for your orphaned nieces and nephews as you have is certainly admirable. That's a heavy responsibility, and there's many who would have shied from it. But do you truly believe marrying a woman you barely know is the best thing for you and your family?"

She did turn to look at Caleb now. He met her look and gave her hand a light squeeze before turning back to the reverend. Was that to convey approval, or just for show?

"Yes, sir, I do. Elthia here has a fine way of saying things, and I guess I echo most of it. I've already learned she has a big heart when it comes to the kids. She's going to make them a fine mother. I think this marriage is going to work out even better than either of us thought it might a few days ago."

Elthia flashed him a smile, pleased by the compliments, even if they *were* only said for the reverend's benefit.

Reverend Hastings looked from one to the other of them, as if trying to probe for something left unsaid. But he finally smiled and stood. "Very well. It sounds like you are both sure of your decision. Let's take a few minutes to go over some of the whens and whats of the ceremony, and then we'll be all set."

An hour and a half later, Elthia stood next to Caleb, at the front of a church packed with strangers. There must have been a hundred folks present, more than the church had been designed to hold. The pews were uncomfortably full, with children perched on their mother's laps to make more room, and still a good dozen or so had to stand at the back.

Did all weddings draw so much attention in Foxberry, or only those that involved a mail-order bride?

Elthia was grateful she hadn't had to march up that aisle under the scrutiny of all those curious eyes. Reverend Hastings had suggested that she and Caleb sit in the front pew during the Sunday service. Once it was time for the wedding to begin, they'd simply stepped up to the pulpit from there.

The Tanner children sat in the front pew, along with Granny. Caleb had been true to his word: He'd talked to Reverend Hastings about Poppy, and while the reverend had reservations, Caleb had been quite persuasive. Poppy, tail wagging furiously, perched on Alex's lap.

How she wished Ry could be there too. She desperately needed her brother's counsel, his presence, as she took this step.

Then Elthia took herself to task. She was supposed to be proving she could stand on her own, make her way without her family's well-intentioned, confidence-robbing support. Looking for Ry's help now proved just how far she still had to go.

Firmly reminding herself that those orphaned children needed her, as did the stubborn man at her side to a lesser extent, she drew her shoulders back and lifted her head to face the reverend.

The ceremony passed in a blur until it was time for Elthia to pledge her troth. She handed the flowers to Zoe, then turned to face Caleb. He took her hands as Reverend Hastings read the vows.

Suddenly, the moment crystallized. Her pulse reacted to the tingling touch of his hands. Her gaze flew to his, captured by the reddish-brown warmth of his eyes. Her entire focus narrowed to his face and this moment. As she repeated her vows, she felt like an honest-to-goodness bride for the very first time.

Caleb noted the change in her immediately. The dazed look she'd had since they arrived at the church was gone. It was replaced by an intensity, a burst of something breathless and aware, something he couldn't quite define. He wished he could see her eyes, hidden by her thick glasses.

She recited her vows in a sure and unhesitating voice. There would be no reason for anyone in the church to believe she had any reservations about the marriage. Pleased and warmed by her graciousness, he gave her hand a squeeze of approval.

Then it was his turn. Repeating the vows that would bind them together, however temporarily, he slipped the ring he'd brought with him out of his pocket and onto her finger.

Her gaze shot from the ring to his face. Her surprise was obvious. Had she thought him unwilling to bear the expense, or just too uncaring to bother? Of course, this ring, a gold band unadorned by gemstones, wouldn't measure up to her standards. He wished he could have given her something finer, something to show he appreciated her honoring their agreement this way.

Just as Reverend Hastings pronounced them husband and wife, Poppy decided to join them at the altar. Jumping off Alex's lap, the dratted dog bounded up to them, yipping crazily and darting around Elthia's skirts.

There were smothered gasps and giggles from the congregation, but Caleb was surprised to see how composed his bride remained. Even the telltale pink coloring her cheeks seemed more a result of pleasure than embarrassment. Of course, she treated the little beast like it was family anyway.

He watched as she bent down and scooped up the dog, hugging it to her chest. Then she turned to him with a teasing smile. "I believe Poppy has given us his blessing. He apparently wants to be the first to congratulate us."

Granny Picket cackled from her front-row seat, stood and approached the newly married couple. "Caleb, you just wipe that scowl off your face. You got yourself a new bride, and that's something to smile about. Besides, you've just passed a test of sorts. A woman's pet won't accept you unless the woman has too."

Caleb cast a quick glance at Elthia in time to see her cheeks redden in earnest before she ducked her head, ostensibly to retrieve her flowers from Zoe. He suddenly felt a tad better about things—even the mutt.

Then they were swamped by friends and neighbors who wanted to wish them well and meet his bride.

From Elthia's perspective, the reception started out as a complete disaster. She and Caleb were separated early on. While he received the congratulations of his back-thumping friends, Granny demanded Elthia's arm. "Come along. It's time you met your new neighbors. And then we'll find you something to eat."

As Elthia looked at the sea of faces, she suddenly remembered everyone in this small community thought of her as a "mail-order bride," as someone who'd been forced to travel hundreds of miles to find a man desperate enough to marry her, sight unseen.

Only once before had she felt such acute humiliation, and that had been suffered in private. Imagining pity behind every cautious smile and speculative glance sent her way, Elthia's back stiffened, and she drew her flagging courage around her. She would get through this with what dignity she could muster.

They made slow progress. Granny stopped frequently to introduce her to townsfolk. The people were polite, welcoming her to the community and making small talk about the ceremony. Invariably, the ladies would remark on how lovely her gown was and ask questions about the latest fashions from back East.

Elthia answered as best she could, but fashion was something to which she'd never paid much attention. Her answers tended to be short, and she tried to redirect the conversation or move on whenever the subject came up.

Some of Elthia's tension eased as she spied a familiar face. "Dr. Adams, how nice to see you again."

The doctor doffed his hat. "Mrs. Tanner, good day to you. And Granny, you're looking as spry as usual."

Elthia started at the unfamiliar salutation. Goodness, she

was Mrs. Tanner now. Feeling an unexpected thrill of excitement at that thought, she stood straighter and sneaked a quick look toward Caleb, her husband.

Then the doctor reclaimed her attention. He turned to a petite, brown-haired woman with a warm smile standing next to him. "May I present my wife, Hannah."

"Mrs. Adams, how nice to meet you."

"You just call me Hannah, dear. Welcome to our community."

"Thank you. Foxberry seems to be a nice town."

"It is that," Mrs. Adams said with a smile. "The pace is probably a mite slower than what you're used to, but we like it that way. And we hope you'll grow to like it as well."

Elthia decided she liked the doctor's wife. Though she still wasn't comfortable calling the older woman by her first name. "Yes, ma'am, I'm sure I will."

Granny tugged on her arm. "Come along, Elthia; looks like the vittles are all spread out. Where's Caleb? The bride and groom have to serve themselves before anyone else will dig in."

As Granny searched the crowd for Caleb, Elthia's stomach rebelled at the thought of eating anything. Knowing she would be scrutinized by all these strangers didn't help matters a bit.

Why couldn't she and Caleb gather up the children and slip back to the house now that the wedding was over?

Elthia immediately squelched that thought. She would not turn and run like a coward. She'd faced scores of uncomfortable social situations in the past. This was just one more.

Odd how she'd grown to regard her intimidating husband as an ally, though; a safe harbor among these strangers. She actually wished it was he by her side instead of Granny right now.

Caleb finally found himself beside his bride again. He'd kept an eye on her since they'd separated, which had earned him a few teasing remarks and knowing grins.

But he wasn't mooning over his bride, he wanted to see how she reacted to his neighbors. And he didn't like what he saw. She held herself stiff, with a brittle smile that wouldn't fool an infant. Sure, this wasn't some fancy high-society gathering, but couldn't she at least pretend to enjoy herself?

She'd seemed to thaw a bit when she stopped to talk to Doc and his wife. But that pinched look was back now. Did she think a doctor was closer to her social equal than the simple farmers and merchants who surrounded them?

As Caleb took Elthia's arm, Granny excused herself and joined the reverend. Caleb kept the friendly smile planted firmly on his lips. "I've seen warmer smiles on a condemned man," he said, his voice pitched so that only she could hear him.

She started, biting her lip as she looked up. "Pardon me?"

"You heard me. These folks went to a lot of effort to set up this reception for you. The least you could do is pretend you appreciate it." He smiled and waved at his former school-teacher.

"But I do. It's just that—"

They'd reached the first of the tables, and Caleb shoved a plate in her hands. "I don't care what it is," he hissed through his smile, "just stop acting so blasted high and mighty."

She snapped her lips shut at that, and bright pink flooded her cheeks.

Mrs. Johnston, helping serve the food, stared at them with curiosity. Caleb knew she hadn't overheard the conversation, but the byplay must have been interesting.

Elthia shot him an angry have-it-your way look, just before she flashed a saucy smile, giggled, and tapped his arm. "Oh, Caleb," she teased, "you mustn't say such things here in public. What would these nice people think if they heard you?"

Was she batting her eyelashes at him behind those thick glasses? His ears grew warm as a couple of the men standing behind him let out guffaws.

She turned her ain't-it-all-wonderful expression on Mrs. Johnston. "It's *so* nice to see you again. This looks and smells delicious, just like the stew you left for my first Texas meal. It is just so generous of everyone to do this for Caleb and me."

Mrs. Johnston blinked at Elthia's seemingly artless words and gave her a warm smile. "It was our pleasure, Mrs. Tanner."

Elthia waved a hand. "Oh, please, call me Elthia. After all, we're neighbors now, aren't we?"

Then she turned to Caleb, still with that damned butter-wouldn't-melt-in-her-mouth smile. "Caleb, you dear, sweet

113

man, you're going to have to help me make my selections. There's just too much for me to choose from."

Before Caleb could say anything, she turned her face back toward Mrs. Johnston. "I'm certain it's all excellent, but I can't possibly have some of everything, can I? And Caleb's so good at making selections, don't you think?"

Caleb struggled to keep his smile in place as that remark earned him another snicker. He had to hand it to his bride; she sure had a sharp way with words when she got riled.

As they made their way along the line of tables, Elthia kept up her chatter. She managed to make her fulsome compliments sound sincere. And she never missed a chance to make him appear "such a dear, sweet man," very innocently done, of course.

By the time they'd filled their plates, Caleb was gritting his teeth so hard, his jaw ached. He steered her to a tree-shaded spot where Granny'd had a blanket spread for them earlier. "All right, lady, ease up on the sweetness-and-light act, will you?"

Elthia sat, balancing her plate on her lap, and lifted her chin. "You wanted me to appear happy with the town and with my husband," she said, waving at Dr. and Mrs. Adams as they strolled by. "Now smile, so folks don't think we're arguing."

Caleb jabbed his fork into a slice of ham and took a bite. Chewing with vicious energy, he waited until his temper was under control before he spoke. "Okay, maybe I *was* a little hard on you, but I don't want you looking down your nose at these folks."

She turned to glare at him. Then she looked at her plate, pushing the food around with her fork. "I wasn't looking down my nose at them, Mr. Know-it-all Tanner. But I'm sorry if it seemed that way. Let's call a truce, shall we?" Her eyes scanned the grounds. "Have you seen the children since the ceremony ended?"

Something in her tone worried him. Had he misinterpreted her earlier frowns? He kept forgetting how scary this must be for her. And she *had* done him proud through the wedding ceremony.

Promising himself he'd go easier on her, he allowed her to change the subject. "The boys are over there." He pointed to the left. Alex, Keith, and Kevin were playing a rowdy game of chase with some of the other boys from the area. Peter stood watching them, his back to a tree and his hands in his pockets.

"Josie's over there." He pointed to the church, where his niece sat on the ground with two other girls, playing with Poppy.

He caught the eye of a couple of men lounging by the steps. The pair grinned and saluted him, their knowing looks setting his teeth on edge. It was a good thing that they didn't know the truth, that there would be no wedding-night privileges for him. The thought of what he'd miss out on bothered him more at the moment than he'd thought it would.

She sure was pretty in her fancy gown, a shimmering flower in a field of new-cut grass. Despite the heat of the noonday sun she looked cool and crisp, every inch the lady.

"What about Zoe?" she asked, reclaiming his attention.

Caleb shrugged. "She's around somewhere. Don't worry, the adults all watch out for the kids. They'll be okay."

Nodding, she continued to toy with her food, and he realized she hadn't eaten anything. "It might not be fancy, but it's not poisoned, you know."

She threw him an annoyed frown. "Will you please stop trying to make me into a snob? I'm just not very hungry, that's all."

"That's not the point." He didn't like the second prickle of guilt her words conjured. Devil take it, she was just being too sensitive. He was careful, though, to moderate his tone as he continued. "You're going to insult these people if you don't eat something. It's their wedding gift to us."

She looked like she wanted to say more, but they were interrupted just then as three women approached.

Caleb stifled a groan as he recognized Foxberry's social elite, and the town's biggest gossips. "Good afternoon, ladies."

"Afternoon, Caleb. We haven't had an opportunity to meet your new bride yet and we wanted to welcome her to Foxberry." The speaker's sharp eyes stared at Elthia's dress with avid envy.

As Caleb helped Elthia rise he felt an urge to protect her. He balanced his plate in one hand and rested the other on the small of her back. "Elthia, this is Wilhemina Dawson. Her

115

husband owns Dawson's Mercantile. On her left is Faith Legate, wife of our banker. And this is Ida Starky, wife of Foxberry's mayor and owner of the smithy."

He shifted a tiny bit closer to her. "Ladies, this is my wife, Elthia Sinclare Tanner."

Elthia warily studied the ladies before her. They bore the look of a stern judge and jury, of the social variety.

Mrs. Dawson smiled brightly. "I hope there's nothing wrong with your food, my dear. I notice you haven't eaten much."

Elthia returned her smile with a brighter one. "Not at all. I've spent so much time looking around and asking questions that I haven't paused to eat. But it all looks and smells delicious."

"The yams are from Ida." Mrs. Dawson indicated the birdlike woman to her right. "I'm sure you'll find them quite tasty."

Ida Starky chimed in on cue. "And the corn relish is Wilhemina's. She's won blue ribbons at the county fair with it."

Elthia gamely took a bite of each, then heaped eloquent compliments on the ladies as to the fare's delectability.

Mrs. Dawson nodded. "Glad you like it. Now, don't you let us keep you from your meal. Just go on and eat while we chat."

Elthia tried to hold a smile as her stomach rebelled against the bites she'd already taken. She nibbled on a bit of bread.

Mrs. Dawson flashed another insincere smile. "We were all saying what a lovely ceremony it was, dear. I hope you weren't too upset when that darling dog of yours disrupted everything."

Elthia lowered her plate, trying to avoid the smells. It didn't work. "Not at all," she responded, trying to make it through the conversation by sheer willpower. "The ceremony was over anyway, and Poppy is like part of the family to me."

"How refreshing." But Mrs. Dawson's expression let everyone know she thought this was a decidedly odd attitude. Then she changed the subject. "Your gown is gorgeous. Is that—

"Excuse me." Elthia shoved her plate at Caleb. "I believe I need to see to one of the children." Leaving the women standing there with mouths agape, she marched toward her stepsons.

It was a poor excuse, and she'd undoubtedly pay for it later.

But she had to get away, had to find a bit of privacy before she embarrassed herself and Caleb. That line of trees just past where the boys were playing was her best bet.

Oh, dear God, please let her make it there in time.

"Elthia!"

She heard Caleb's call but didn't stop. No doubt he wanted to take her to task for running off, but it would have to wait. "I'll be back in a minute," she said without turning. "There's just something I need to take care of first."

Oh, Lord, even speaking threatened her control. The tree-line seemed to be getting farther away instead of closer. The dusty Texas heat had become unbearable. Surely that was the reason everything was shimmering out of focus.

She reached the edge of her goal just as Caleb caught up with her. He took her arm. "What's wrong? You took off like—"

He stopped as a moan escaped her. Taking a look at her face, he abruptly put his arm around her shoulder. "Come on." Swiftly but gently he led her into the blessed cover of the trees.

A second later she doubled over and emptied her stomach all over his boot.

Chapter Ten

Caleb held her head while a few additional spasms shook her, and then supported her as she straightened. He wanted to do more but wasn't quite sure what. "Feeling better now?"

She nodded, not meeting his gaze. "Yes. I'm sorry."

He gently shushed her and led her away from the smelly mess, tamping the toe of his boot on the ground as he went.

He hated that defeated slump to her shoulders. Better to have her riled at him than looking so miserable. "No need to apologize; you couldn't help it." He pulled out a handkerchief and dabbed at her mouth. "Why didn't you tell me you were sick?"

She took the cloth, and a touch of her fire returned. Wiping her face, she flashed him an exasperated look. "I *did* say I wasn't very hungry."

"And from that I'm supposed to figure out you're sick?" He shook his head at her makes-no-sense reasoning. "Why in blue blazes did you try to eat if your stomach wasn't up to it?"

"Why?" She stilled, looking at him as if he'd lost his mind. "Why?" she repeated in a louder tone, pushing her glasses up.

Caleb straightened warily. Oh boy, if riled was what he'd wanted, it looked like he was about to get it in spades.

She poked his chest. "After you gave me that lecture on how I was insulting the whole town?"

Another poke. "After those three very prominent citizens came up and admitted to having been personally responsible for half the items on my plate? What was I supposed to do?"

Poke. "Tell them I was so nervous about being the object of a whole town's curiosity that my stomach was doing flip-flops?"

Poke, poke. "Tell them that you'd made me so aware that I held the almighty Tanner family honor in my hands that even the thought of food made me queasy?"

She jabbed a finger at his chest one last time. "Is *that* what I was supposed to do?"

His back to a tree now, Caleb lifted his hands in surrender. "Okay, okay. Maybe I could have been a little more sympathetic to what you were going through."

Her anger evaporated, and she fidgeted with a tendril of hair that had fallen across her forehead. In the sudden silence Caleb could hear kids playing in the churchyard, but it only heightened the sense of being hidden, concealed by the canopy of trees.

She glanced up at him, her chin still tilted down. "I really messed up, didn't I? I'm afraid I didn't make a very good impression with those three ladies we were speaking to."

Caleb grinned and gave a dismissive wave. "Those old biddies? Don't give it another thought. You probably made their day, giving them something to talk about for the next week."

Elthia groaned, lifting her face. "That's not much comfort."

He laughed. "I told you, Granny's on your side, so don't worry." Her color was better, and she seemed to have regained her composure. "We should return to the grounds or we're really going to be the subject of some interesting gossip. If you're not up to socializing, though, we can make an excuse to leave."

She'd reddened at his reference to their disappearance. "No, I'm fine. There's no reason for us to leave right away. Just don't look for me to eat anything for a while."

He nodded, slipping off his soiled boot. "Let me clean this up. Is your dress all right?"

She examined her skirt. "Yes, I seem to have avoided that

much at least." She looked back up, chewing on her lip. "I'm sorry about your boot."

He shrugged. "Nothing a bit of dirt and a few leaves won't take care of. See, all better now." He stepped back into the boot and extended his arm. "Ready?"

Her chest rose prettily, but she managed a smile as she placed her hand on his arm.

Elthia felt more than a little self-conscious as she and Caleb walked out of the cover of the trees.

But her attention was immediately diverted by the simple fact that they stepped right into the middle of the boys' game of tag. One of the young sprinters barreled right into her. He was closely followed by a second boy—Keith, she thought—who finished the job of totally oversetting her. The end result was that all three of them ended up with their rumps on the ground.

Recovering from her momentary surprise, Elthia studied the boys, looking for signs of injury. "Are you two all right?"

Both of them nodded, and she was relieved to see their expressions were free of pain. Instead, both faces registered nothing more than a boy-are-we-in-trouble-now wariness.

Caleb knelt at her side, his expression reflecting a concern that warmed her. Behind him, she could see the other boys gathered around, studying them with avid interest.

"Are you all right?" he asked. "Does anything hurt?"

"Only my dignity. Would you help me up, please?"

Before he could comply, Poppy came racing up and took advantage of her seated position to jump on her lap. Her pet propped his front paws on her chest, vainly trying to stretch high enough to lick her face. She lifted the animal, giving him the access he wanted. "It's okay, Poppy, I'm fine, really."

She spied the irritated look Caleb shot at the dog and started laughing. And it felt so good to laugh, she kept it up.

Keith and his friend, looking hopeful that they'd escaped a dressing down, scrambled to their feet.

Caleb only shook his head in disgust. "If you're through playing with that wretched excuse for a dog, I'll help you up."

Noticing several of the adults had begun to gather around, Elthia smothered her laughter with a smile and extended her hand to Caleb. As she stood, she spied a tall, gingham-clad woman making her way purposefully toward their little gathering.

"Johnny Cooper," the woman said, confronting Keith's partner-in-crime. "What mischief have you been up to?"

"It was an accident, Ma, honest. I didn't see her."

"And why not? Weren't you looking where you were going?"

The boy hung his head and scuffed his foot in the dirt as the woman turned to Elthia.

"My apologies, Mrs. Tanner. I hope he didn't hurt you none."

Elthia waved a hand and smiled. "No need to apologize. No harm done. And it was as much my fault as his. I stepped right out in front of him."

Some of the stiffness eased from the woman, but she didn't return the smile. "Look what he's done to your beautiful dress."

Elthia looked at her skirt. Smudges of dirt decorated it now, and a small portion of the lace edging had torn. She smiled back at Johnny's mother. "Please don't give it another thought. It's nothing that a good washing and a needle and thread can't take care of. And I think maybe Poppy is responsible for some of this." She gave a little laugh. "Puppies and boys; they just naturally attract dirt and mischief."

Mrs. Cooper did return her smile this time. "I reckon that's the truth. It's good of you to be so understanding." She turned to her son. "Come on. It's time we got you some vittles."

Elthia turned back to Caleb. His look of approval surprised her, and sent a warm glow shimmering through her.

After that, she felt more at ease mingling with the crowd. Even when she and Caleb were separated again, she strolled around the churchyard on her own, stopping to chat here and there, thanking everyone she met for the reception.

Finding herself by the church steps, Elthia decided to slip inside to escape the hot Texas sun for a few minutes. What she wouldn't give right now for a touch of a cool ocean breeze, the kind that kept Terrelmore summers so pleasant.

But Elthia discovered she hadn't been the only one to seek refuge inside. Someone was playing the piano, very softly, very expertly. Elthia softly shut the door behind her, then got her second surprise. The piano player was Zoe.

Slipping into a pew near the front, Elthia had a clear view of the girl's profile. Zoe seemed immersed in the music, deaf to all but the beautiful sounds she created. There was a glow about her, a look of happiness that Elthia had never seen there before.

Why hadn't Caleb mentioned how talented his niece was? And did he have any idea how important music was to her?

When the piece was ended, Zoe sat with her head bowed for a moment; then, with a heartfelt sigh, she turned to rise. Spotting Elthia, she sat back with a thud.

"That was beautiful, Zoe," Elthia said with a smile. "You're quite talented."

Zoe shrugged and stood. "Thank you," she said offhandedly.

Elthia fell into step beside her as they moved toward the door. "Does your uncle know you play?"

Another shrug. "I suppose. But it's not important."

Elthia withheld additional comment. Caleb, however, would get the full benefit of her thoughts on the subject.

It was late afternoon when they finally returned to the Tanner home. Her home now.

After her conversation with Zoe, Elthia had discovered she was actually hungry. She discovered the plain country fare was quite delicious. Which was a good thing, because a heaping basket of food had been packed for them by their well-wishers. Enough to take care of supper tonight and lunch tomorrow.

As the children climbed out of the wagon, Caleb stopped Alex. "Hold on, son. What do you have there?"

Guiltily, Alex pulled a ball of fur from his shirt. It was a cat, gray brindled and just past kittenhood. Elthia's fingers itched to stroke the soft-looking creature.

"Her leg's hurt, Uncle Caleb."

Caleb leaned an elbow on the wagon, but his expression remained stern. "I thought we'd agreed to limit the stray critters you adopted to those that showed up on our doorstep."

Alex scuffed a toe in the dirt, facing his uncle earnestly. "Some of the other boys were poking at her and being mean. They might have hurt her more. I *had* to take her home with me."

Well, of course he'd had to. Surely Caleb saw that? Elthia stepped forward, ready to intervene, but then Caleb sighed.

"Now that you've got her here," he said, "I guess you can keep her. Another mouser for the barn, I suppose."

Elthia relaxed. This man just continued to surprise her.

Caleb turned to the other children. "Off with you. Your evening chores are waiting." As they scurried away, he turned to Elthia. "Well, Mrs. Tanner, what did you think of Foxberry?"

She gave him a rueful smile. "I'm not sure what sort of impression I made with your friends."

He shrugged. "I think you managed well enough. And you'll have lots of other chances."

Not the resounding reassurance she'd hoped for, but at least he didn't seem unduly upset with her. "Did you know Zoe could play the piano?" she asked, changing the subject.

He twisted his neck, as if easing stiff muscles. "I remember her mother was good at it. Probably taught her how."

"They would have had a piano in their home, then?"

Caleb nodded. "A small one. But it got sold, along with just about everything else. Tom'd built up some debts that needed paying off."

Elthia worried at her lower lip. Caleb apparently didn't realize how important music seemed to be to his niece. "That's a shame," she hinted, "because I think Zoe really misses it."

Caleb used his hat to shoo Poppy away from the horse. "If it means that much, maybe I can work something out by Christmas."

Christmas! That was six months away. Surely they could do something before—

"Now," he said, interrupting her thoughts, "I need to take care of the horse. Do you think you can move your things into my bedroom on your own, or do you want to wait 'til I can help you?"

All thoughts of Zoe and the piano fled. Had he tricked her? Had her trust been misplaced again?

Remain calm.

Take a deep breath.

She assumed her most haughty demeanor. "I believe we agreed that this would be a platonic arrangement, did we not?"

123

He frowned, as if suspecting *her* of some duplicity. "That's right. But you agreed to help me convince everyone that we have a normal marriage. And that means sharing a room." He leaned closer. "Remember that contract you insisted we both sign?"

Elthia abandoned hauteur for indignation. "Of course, I remember. I *wrote* it. There was nothing in there about sharing a room." She shivered, wondering if she'd find that contract mysteriously changed, just like the one from Pembroke.

He nodded. "It says you won't do anything contrary to the kids' best interest. Well, it sure as blue blazes wouldn't be in their best interest if folks got the idea we were only playing at being married, now would it?"

She shook her head, not quite sure how to argue with his logic. Instead, she addressed the heart of her concern. "You can't possibly be expecting me to share your bed."

His lips curled in a humorless smile. "Believe me, lady, nothing would happen if you did. There's a chaise longue in the room. You can sleep there if you don't trust me." Then his grin turned cocky. "Or maybe it's yourself you don't trust."

Elthia glared, but gathered her control before responding. She would *not* get into an emotional exchange with him. "It is not an issue of trust, sir, but of propriety. And yes, I will most certainly be taking advantage of the chaise."

He shrugged those broad shoulders again. "Suit yourself. It doesn't make me one bit of difference. Now, excuse me, I have work to do." With that he turned the horse toward the barn.

Elthia realized that, somehow, in the midst of that maddening conversation, she'd agreed to share his bedroom. Slowly she entered the house and climbed the stairs. It would be best if she took care of moving her things while he was occupied outside.

It was foolish to worry about amorous intentions on his part, she told herself bracingly. She was hardly the sort of woman men lusted after. And he'd made it plain from the beginning that not only was he more interested in a mother for the children than a wife for himself, but also that she was not the sort of woman for whom he held much admiration.

Somehow, those thoughts did very little to comfort her.

Gathering some miniatures of her family and a hatbox, Elthia marched across the hall to the master bedroom. She paused at the threshold, suddenly feeling like an intruder. Then, tilting her chin at an I-have-every-right angle, she opened the door.

Her gaze focused immediately on the bed. A four-poster, solidly built of polished mahogany, it looked wide enough to sleep four comfortably and was so tall, she'd probably need a short stool to climb into it.

Not that she harbored any intentions of ever doing so.

Quickly she turned away to survey the rest of the room. It was surprisingly large, almost as large as her bedroom in Maryland. But there were no soft carpets covering the planks of the floor, no velvet-lined window seat, no gilt-framed portrait of her mother gracing the fireplace mantel.

Instead of the delicate, feminine trappings of her room at home, these furnishings were built along the same solid, substantial lines as the bed.

Elthia set the hatbox down on the floor, set the other items on top of it, and went immediately to the chaise. She sat on it, running a hand across the velvety-soft fabric. She bounced a couple of times to test its sturdiness and was pleased with the results. It was large enough to accommodate her, with even a bit of room for moving in her sleep. Yes, this would do nicely.

She looked around again, trying to identify personal touches, things that would reveal the character of the man who lived here, the man she would share this room with for the next three months.

With a prickling of gooseflesh, she pushed that last thought aside.

There were surprisingly feminine touches in the room—the curtains with small yellow and green flowers, the daffodil yellow chenille bedspread, the delicate ivory china pitcher and basin on the washstand. These were no doubt left over from his Aunt Cora.

She had to look harder to find signs of Caleb's occupancy. There was a pair of boots on the hearth, a shirt thrown over the back of the desk chair. A lifelike figure of a wolf howled silently from the mantel. That was it. Few clues there, other than to reinforce her impression of how orderly he was.

Elthia moved to the wardrobe and opened it. Shirts and pants hung neatly to one side. More than half of the space sat empty, no doubt awaiting the arrival of her gowns. Impulsively, she fingered the sleeves of one of his shirts, and drew it up to her face. The cotton fabric was soft with wear, and she inhaled the clean, subtle fragrance of sunshine and soap.

She spied a wooden screen in a corner of the room, and moved closer. The polished wood, four-paneled device almost matched her in height. She looked from the screen to the chaise.

Yes, of course, it would be just the thing. But first she needed to get the rest of her belongings moved in.

Elthia recruited Peter and Alex to help her, and in no time at all had her belongings moved to her new sleeping quarters. Then she dismissed the boys to finish her unpacking in private.

Her dresses, hats, and shoes went into the wardrobe alongside Caleb's things. Her other articles of clothing fit neatly into the four empty drawers of the six-drawer highboy. She displayed her toiletries and jewelry case on the top of the dresser. Two of the miniatures found a home on a bedside table. The other miniature and an ormolu clock flanked the wolf on the mantel.

There, that should give the room a lady-in-residence feel. The rest of the unpacking could wait. There was something else she wanted to do right now. Rolling up her sleeves, Elthia set to work.

Fifteen minutes later, she stood back to survey the results. Dusk approached, but there was still enough light coming in the windows to see clearly. She'd shoved the chaise closer to the corner of the room, next to one of the four large windows. Near the head of her soon-to-be bed, she'd placed a small table she'd hauled from its place by the door. Some books she'd brought with her now graced its top. She'd find a lamp to add later. At the foot of the chaise sat one of her trunks. It now held the sheet and light blanket she'd appropriated from the linen closet.

And strategically placed between the chaise and the rest of the room was the blessedly solid wooden screen.

She smiled in satisfaction. The overall effect was to create a cozy little nook of a bedroom within a bedroom.

She could set the screen back against the wall during the day. The area would then appear innocent, just an inviting spot to while away a lazy afternoon with a book or a bit of sewing.

What could Caleb possibly find to object to in that?

Caleb climbed the stairs, all his senses on the alert for trouble—trouble of the Lady Privilege variety. She'd been upstairs for over an hour now. What in the world was she up to?

He reached for the knob and then paused, remembering it wasn't just his room now. Grimacing at the need, he knocked. But rather than a polite "Come in," a loud thud and bit-off exclamation answered him. Caleb swung the door open, his gaze sweeping the room for the source of the alarm.

Then he stopped in his tracks. Lady Privilege sat on the floor beside the bed. Her mouth gaped open in stunned surprise, her glasses were in imminent danger of slipping off her nose, several tendrils of hair had escaped her neat coiffure, and she clutched a pillow to her chest. But the sight that riveted his gaze was a bit lower. The hem of her skirt, with unladylike lack of constraint, caressed her knees, coyly displaying shapely ankles and calves to the appreciative gaze of her husband.

A moment later she'd yanked her wayward skirts down, glaring up at him with a flaming face.

Caleb recalled himself and moved quickly to help her up, though he couldn't quite control the twitch of his lips. "Are you okay?" he asked, reaching down a hand to her.

She pushed her glasses up before accepting his hand. "Yes, thank you."

His grin only widened at her obvious attempt to recover her dignity. "Were you trying out the bed to see what you'd be missing, or was it because you changed your mind?"

Lordy, if she tried to stand any straighter her backbone would likely snap.

"I was *not* trying out the bed." She bent to retrieve the pillow she'd dropped when he helped her up. When she faced him again, she seemed more composed but no less red-cheeked. "I'd merely taken this for use on my own bed, then climbed up on this monster to straighten the covers. I was on my way

127

down when you knocked." She shrugged. "It startled me and I lost my footing."

A picture of her up there among his pillows and blankets flashed across his mind. But in his vision she was recumbent and welcoming, eager for consummation of their vows. What did her eyes look like behind those glasses? How would her hair look, loose and mussed about her face and shoulders? How far did those freckles of hers go once you dipped below her neckline? The hungry surge those images evoked caught him off guard.

Then he gave himself a mental shake. Lust wasn't an emotion he normally let undermine his control. He'd just been too long without a woman, he assured himself. It had nothing to do with any attraction he might feel for this bespectacled puzzle of a female with the shapely legs.

He gave her a short bow, determined to keep things light between them. "My apologies for startling you."

She waved a hand, dismissing his apology as unnecessary, then moved across the room with the pillow.

Caleb frowned as he noticed the changes she'd made. "You've been busy." He moved to where he could see around the screen.

She looked over her shoulder with a breezy smile. "This is going to work out quite well, don't you think? It will give us both privacy without compromising the appearance that we are living in wedded bliss."

"Will it?" What the devil did she know about "wedded bliss"?

Nodding with an insincere, I'm-digging-in-my-heels smile, she tossed the pillow on the chaise and took hold of the screen. "I moved this here to see how it would look. During the day we'll set it against the wall, and the bed linens can go in my trunk."

He moved to help her with the heavy screen and was rewarded with an uncertain smile.

"See," she said when they'd finished. "It all looks perfectly innocent."

He stared at her rather than the corner of the room she'd made her own. "But we both know looks can be deceiving." He'd had his share of experience with angel-faced devils. So why did his instincts tell him that she was different, she could be trusted?

His wife tilted her freckled nose at him. "But that's what you want, isn't it? To deceive everyone into thinking we have a real marriage."

There was no answer for that. Then his gaze fell on the large basket resting on the floor beside the chaise. "No. Absolutely not. That mutt of yours will *not* sleep in my room."

"But he won't—"

"I don't care." He refused to let her little-girl-lost look deflect him, not this time. "I let him into my house, into my kitchen, even into my wedding, but I draw the line at my bedroom." He yanked the basket off the floor and handed it to her. "Find him someplace else to sleep."

She stared at him, chewing on her lip. "Where?"

Caleb was relieved she'd backed down. He didn't like acting the bully. But seeing that basket there had conjured up an image of her thinking she needed that pitiful excuse of a guard dog to protect her virtue. And he liked that thought even less.

He shrugged. "Set him in the kitchen. Or let him sleep in one of the kids' rooms. Just don't bring him in here."

She nodded, and he felt a twinge of conscience for putting the droop in her shoulder. "Come on," he said gruffly. "Zoe'll have supper set out for us by now."

Caleb climbed the stairs in the now quiet and darkened house. His only sources of illumination were the low-burning lamp on the downstairs hall table and the silvery moonlight filtering in through the window at the top of the landing.

There'd been a bit of a ruckus earlier when Elthia'd asked the children for ideas on where Poppy should sleep. The four youngest had all been very vocal in volunteering their rooms. It had finally been decided that the dog would alternate among them by weeks. The girls had won the draw for the first week. Caleb had been quite firm on the fact that the dog was to sleep in his basket, not on the beds.

The kids had been put to bed over an hour earlier. Tonight Elthia had done the honors. She sure had a way of getting them to settle down. The promise of a story or a lullaby, and they were under the covers and settled in in no time flat.

Elthia had turned in right after that. He'd stayed out on the porch, whittling. After the way he'd acted about her dog, the least he could do was give her privacy to get ready for bed.

The image of her shapely calves flashed through his mind, and he firmly squelched it. No point thinking of things like that. She wasn't interested in him, and he'd promised not to force any unwanted attentions her way.

He'd better check in on the kids one last time before he headed for his own bed. He cracked open the door to Keith and Kevin's room first, the room where Elthia had slept the last few nights. There were no traces of her in here now. The little-boy clutter of the twins had reclaimed it as their space.

The boys slept soundly, so he closed the door and moved on. Again, in Peter and Alex's room, the only sound was the even breathing of the sleepers. He stood a moment watching Peter. The lad looked so innocent, so boy-nearing-manhood vulnerable in his sleep. Quite a contrast to his surly disposition when awake.

Remembering how friendly and open the boy had been before his parents' death, Caleb felt a deep sense of frustration for his own failure to help Peter heal and move on. The insuppressible memory of the almost hero worship that Peter had once gifted him with added to Caleb's sense of loss.

Stuffing his hands into his pockets, Caleb moved to the girls' room. He frowned when he spied Poppy, curled up between Josie and Zoe. Then he shrugged. Moving Poppy now would likely result in that hairy flea trap waking the whole house. Better to just let it be for now. He'd talk to the girls in the morning.

Closing their door, he turned his steps toward his own room. As he had earlier, he paused with his hand on the knob. But this time he didn't knock. She'd had plenty of time to change into her nightclothes and climb into her makeshift bed. If she'd already gone to sleep he didn't want to risk waking her.

Easing the door open, he stepped inside. The lamp beside his bed had been left burning low, providing enough light to keep him from tripping over objects in the room. As he paused to let his eyes adjust, he heard the sound of her soft, even breathing.

So, she'd managed to drift off despite her nervousness. He

supposed it had a lot to do with the long day she'd had. Still, he felt deflated that she seemed to feel so . . . safe in his room.

Caleb undressed and put away his clothes without disturbing her slumber. After climbing into bed, he lay there, unable to sleep. He could smell a faint hint of the light floral scent she wore. The sound of her soft breathing taunted him. It seemed to whisper of her nearness while at the same time mocking his inability to bring her any closer. She was just across the room from him.

An unbridgeable distance.

He was married, by God, and he had a houseful of children. He was finally part of a large family again, something he remembered with longing from his earliest years. But it was all a sham. There was no closeness in this house, no trusting acceptance, none of that indescribable something more that had always been the essence of family to him.

The something more he hadn't felt since his father's death.

The something more that was still just out of his reach.

Chapter Eleven

Elthia awoke the next morning and sat straight up, looking around apprehensively. But she was alone. Caleb had already left. Or had he even been here?

Oh, yes, he'd been here. The wooden screen she'd so carefully placed to separate her corner from the rest of the room had been folded and set against the wall.

Had he paused to look down at her while she slept? That thought started an uncomfortable fluttering in her stomach.

Stop this foolishness, she chided herself. No man is going to look at your freckled face and garish hair with anything remotely resembling passion.

At least she knew now that he intended to honor their agreement. She hadn't felt quite so sure of that last night as she'd lain in the dark, waiting for him to enter their room.

She dropped her feet to the floor and glanced at the clock. It wasn't quite seven yet. Goodness, they rose early in this part of the country. Not that she was tired. This household also went to bed much earlier than was her habit.

Elthia entered the kitchen twenty minutes later to find Zoe busy at the stove. Josie sat on the floor playing with Poppy.

Elthia didn't make the mistake of asking Zoe if she could help this time. She'd been watching closely and had learned

132

a few things about how the kitchen was run. Giving the girls a breezy "Good morning," she went to the cupboard to get the dishes they would need for the table.

When Keith and Kevin came in carrying baskets of eggs, she appropriated the baskets and sent them off to wash their hands. After Zoe took what she needed, Elthia put the rest away in the larder and fetched the butter for the table.

Zoe removed her apron as Caleb entered with Alex and Peter. Elthia found she couldn't quite meet her husband's gaze. They hadn't shared a bed, but they'd shared a room, and he'd gazed at her as she slept this morning. It suddenly seemed an intensely intimate connection, one they'd repeat nightly for the next three months. A frisson shivered up her arm, and Elthia was very much afraid it had been spurred not by distress, but by anticipation.

She wasn't sure if she was relieved or upset when Caleb focused his attention on the children, treating her with no more than distracted politeness. As soon as the meal was over, he excused himself to return to his workshop, saying he'd gotten behind on his orders and needed to do some catching up.

The girls had kitchen duty today. Zoe cleared the table and counters while Elthia and Josie washed and dried dishes. Elthia watched the five-year-old working beside her, remembering herself at that age. The only chore she'd had was minding her manners and keeping her clothes clean. Not that Josie seemed bothered by having to lend a hand. In fact, she was humming, making a game of playing in the water as she rinsed the dishes.

Peter stuck his head in the room just as they were finishing. "Zoe, come on. There's work to do in the garden."

Elthia watched the older girl pluck her sunbonnet from a peg by the door. "I've always liked gardens. Why don't I join you?"

Zoe looked her up and down. "In that dress? You'd ruin it." She moved toward the door. "Why don't you stay with Josie?"

Elthia bit her lip as she watched the older children troop outside. She really didn't care if her dress got dirty or ended up with a few tears here or there. But Zoe was right; she needed to make changes to her wardrobe. The hows and whats would require a bit of thought, though. Sending away to her dressmaker back home would take too much time. Better if she went to a local shop, but did Foxberry have a clothing establishment?

Elthia drifted into the study, deciding to browse through the bookshelves. The reader in her had been itching to examine them since that morning she and Caleb had put the room back to rights. Josie pattered barefoot beside her but soon got bored and left to play outside. Elthia took her time, smiling as she recognized old favorites, thumbing through unfamiliar volumes.

Then she spied a large volume set on a bookstand in the corner of the room. It was a Bible, very old, and bound in padded leather. Was this Caleb's family Bible?

Opening it, she discovered the volume had not belonged to a Tanner, but instead to a family named Fairfield. The births, marriages, and deaths of several generations of these Fairfields had been meticulously recorded in the family history section.

Who were the Fairfields? Of course, that must be his Aunt Cora's family, and that of his mother. She looked at some of the later entries and found one for Cora Louise Fairfield, and next to it an entry for Helen Elizabeth Fairfield. These sisters had apparently been the last members of this branch of Fairfields.

Helen's marriage was recorded, as were the births of her children. Telling herself she had only a casual interest, Elthia scanned the list for Caleb's name. There he was, born June 15, 1866. So, he was twenty-six, only five years older than she. Yet he wore the air of a man several years older. Did that come naturally, or had something in his life forced it on him?

Then she looked at the date again. It also meant he had a birthday coming up in about two weeks. Now, what in heaven's name should she do with that bit of information?

Elthia stepped out of the bathhouse, tucking a damp tendril of hair behind her ear. It had seemed indolent of her to slip into that opulent bathing pool in the middle of the day, but she hadn't been able to resist. Besides, she didn't think anyone had noticed. Lunch was over, Caleb had returned to his workshop, and the children were either napping or lazing on the porch. It was too hot this time of day for even the children to work up much energy. The cool bath and scented salts had been marvelously refreshing. Maybe, when she returned to Terrelmore, she'd ask her father to add such a luxury to their own home.

Her steps faltered at this reminder of her father. Imagining how he would react when he learned of her unconventional marriage was beyond her powers of imagination.

Thankfully, he'd be out of the country for several weeks yet.

Clattering noises from the kitchen provided a welcome distraction from her thoughts. As Elthia pushed open the door, she blinked at the sight that greeted her. A wet and muddy Poppy raced around the room, leaving a trail of dirty paw prints over everything he touched. Josie and the twins were chasing him and in the process had knocked over a sack of a powdery substance, dusting the countertop and floor with a thick white coat.

"Oh my goodness!" Hoping to contain the mess, Elthia whirled around to shut the hall door. And slammed smack into Caleb's chest. His arms snapped around her, locking her in his embrace. The expression on his face set her stomach fluttering and her pulse racing.

When he released her and stepped back, she felt an unexpected twinge of disappointment.

With a scowl, he turned to survey the kitchen. "What the devil's going on in here?" he barked out.

Three little bodies froze and turned to face them. Elthia noticed that their clothes were damp and decorated with pasty patches of the spilled powder.

"We were trying to give Poppy a bath in the horse trough," Josie volunteered.

"He didn't like it none and jumped out," Kevin elaborated.

"And then he got *really* dirty," Keith chimed in. He finally had hold of the squirming ball of fur. "We tried to throw him back in, but he's hard to catch when he don't want to be."

Caleb turned and pinned her with a frown. "Sounds like that furry gnat of yours caused all this mess."

Elthia stiffened. His accusation wasn't fair and certainly wasn't exactly true. But the other children had arrived by this time, and she refused to argue with him in front of the them.

"You just go on back to whatever it was you were doing,"

she told him. "The children and I will take care of this mess." With that, she turned her back on him.

"Zoe, you take these three to the bathhouse and help them wash up. Alex, go along and get Poppy cleaned up as well. And make sure you keep the door closed until he's dry," she warned.

Then she turned to Peter. "I'll start on the counters. While I'm doing that, please fetch a mop and bucket."

By the time she glanced back at the door, Caleb was gone. Good riddance.

Elthia surveyed the mess, chewing her lip. She'd never done any serious housework, but surely this wouldn't be too difficult.

Peter was gone for quite some time. In fact, Elthia was beginning to wonder if he was going to return at all when he finally stepped through the open doorway.

"Here's the mop and bucket. I filled the bucket with water, so it's all ready for you." He tilted his head, studying her doubtfully. "Are you sure you know how to do this? Maybe I should just fetch Zoe to take care of it."

Elthia stiffened. His tone had been an uncanny imitation of Caleb's when he was questioning her ability to follow through. "That won't be necessary. I'm sure I can handle it." *I hope.*

Peter shrugged, and set a can down beside the bucket. "Suit yourself. This is the cleaning solution you'll need." At her questioning look he rolled his eyes and elaborated. "Just spread it around on the floor over the mess first, then mop."

Elthia swiped the back of a hand across her cheek. "Thanks. You can run along now." She'd rather not have any witnesses as she tried to teach herself the fine art of mopping a kitchen.

Peter's look told her that she hadn't fooled him, but he left without another word. She picked up the can of cleaning solution and looked around at the mess—unappealing blobs of mud and flour everywhere. If it would truly make the job easier, there was no point in being stingy. With a chore like this, it was probably better to have too much soap than not enough.

Elthia started near the counter where some of the messiest clumps lay, and tipped the can. Hmm, it was awfully thick. She carefully drizzled the solution around the room, concentrating on the muddy paw prints.

Setting the can aside, she picked up the mop.

All right, what now?

Drawing on vague memories of watching a maid at work, Elthia dipped the mop in the bucket, then pulled it out and slapped it on the floor. She jumped as beads of water flew everywhere.

Recovering, Elthia gave the mop a halfhearted push into a heavy tracing of the cleaning solution. Then she frowned. Something was wrong. Instead of aiding her in cutting through the dirt, the cleaning solution was only making things worse, turning the whole area she was mopping into a gooey mess.

What was she doing wrong? Maybe there wasn't enough water on her mop. She dipped it in the bucket and pulled it out, allowing water to slosh on the floor. Again she pushed the mop over the area in front of her, and again received the same results.

Perhaps she just needed to try harder. Elthia took firmer hold of the mop handle and shoved it across the floor. With a startled squeak, she lost her footing on the wet floor.

She lay flat on her back a moment, too stunned to move. Her first thought was that she was glad Caleb and the children hadn't witnessed her latest attack of clumsiness. Her second thought was that she should have waited on that bath.

Gingerly she sat up, relieved to find she didn't seem to be seriously hurt. When she lifted her palm from the floor, globs of goo clung to her hand. She rubbed some of the nasty stuff between her fingers and then cautiously sniffed it.

This was no cleaning solution!

From the smell and feel of it, it was almost surely molasses. And her whole back was half covered in it, including her hair.

Her head shot up at the sound of the front door opening and Josie speaking to someone. "Uncle Caleb's out in his workshed, but Aunt Elthia's in the kitchen. Come on, I'll show you."

There was no time to try to scramble to her feet, much less hide. Josie threw open the door to reveal that she'd been talking to an older gentleman Elthia had never met before. But even from her poor vantage point, it was obvious this distinguished-looking man was a person of some importance.

Both stared at her in wide-eyed astonishment. Then Josie

brought a hand to her mouth, trying to hide her giggles. Elthia closed her eyes. This situation just couldn't get any worse.

A second later she realized she'd been wrong. The screen door flew open and Caleb stood looking at her with brows drawn down. "What the devil is going on in here now?"

Then he glanced across the room and stiffened, looking like he'd just taken a punch to the stomach. "Judge Walters!"

She'd been very, *very* wrong.

Chapter Twelve

Caleb helped Elthia up. Why in the world had he let her take charge of this mess? It was clear she didn't know her way around a mop and bucket. But he'd never imagined she would make matters worse. Was that molasses she'd spread on the floor?

"Are you okay?" he asked as she came to her feet.

She nodded with a weak smile. "Yes, just a bit shaken up."

He frowned, noting a bit of blood on her arm. "You're hurt!"

"It's only a scratch. I'm fine." Then she turned to the judge. "I hope you'll forgive the mess, sir. I'm afraid I'm still trying to learn a bit about how to do housework."

Caleb groaned inwardly at her artless confession. He mentally kicked himself. Why hadn't he realized the old fox would come a day early, just to catch them off guard?

But the judge gave her a gallant smile. The gray-haired gentleman sketched a bow, hat to his chest. "It's I who should apologize, madam, for arriving unexpectedly. I'm Judge Loomis Walters, and you must be Caleb's new wife."

She gave a ladylike curtsy, surprisingly graceful given her current state. "Yes, sir. I'm Elthia Tanner." Then a dimple appeared as she flashed the judge a smile. "I'm pleased to meet you, though I wish it had been under less messy circumstances."

Elthia turned to Caleb. "Why don't you escort our guest to the parlor and visit with him while I clean up a bit?"

Caleb blinked, surprised by her poise. "Of course," he agreed absently. How could she appear so composed, standing there with her hair all matted and her skirts soaked with the same gooey substance that covered the floor?

She handed him a rag. "Here; make sure you wipe your shoes before you step into the hall."

He caught the piece of cloth she'd tossed, still confused by her unruffled air. What had happened to her clumsy tendencies? "Do you want me to send Zoe in to help you?"

"That won't be necessary." She turned toward the back door, where Peter stood just inside the room. "I believe Peter here will be able to give me all the help I need," she said. "Won't you, Peter?"

Caleb saw their gazes lock, and a message flash between them. To his surprise, Peter nodded and picked up the mop.

Was something going on here? But he didn't have time to sort it all out now. He had to settle Judge Walters in the parlor and try to convince him that, regardless of what he'd just witnessed, Elthia really *was* going to be a good mother to the children.

After Caleb escorted the judge out of the room, Elthia turned to Peter, who was industriously pushing the mop across the floor.

She could tell from the quick, apprehensive glance he shot her way that he was expecting an angry dressing down.

"You seem to be having more luck with that thing than I was," she said mildly. "You'll have to teach me your trick."

He met her gaze, his surprise evident. Then he turned back to his work. "There's no trick. It just takes a lot of water and a lot of muscle."

"And a bit of cleaning solution?" She moved past him toward the sink, picking up a clean rag to wipe the blood from her arm.

He paused and slowly looked up. "I never meant for you to get hurt, honest."

"I know." She believed him. Peter might have wanted to

cause her a bit of mischief, but he wasn't malicious. "Don't worry, it really *is* just a scratch. I didn't even know it was there until your uncle brought it to my attention."

He nodded and resumed mopping. "You gonna tell him?"

Elthia could hear the wariness beneath his attempted nonchalance. "This is something for you and me to settle between us. I don't see any reason to involve your uncle."

He nodded without looking up, but she noted that some of the tension eased from his shoulders.

"Now, if I can trust you to finish up in here, I need to change clothes and get myself cleaned up. Oh, would you ask Zoe to brew some tea for our guest when she has a minute?"

Fifteen minutes later Elthia felt fit to join Caleb and their visitor. Her hair was still damp, but she'd twisted it into a prim bun on the back of her head, and it looked passable enough.

She stopped in the kitchen first. Peter was nowhere to be seen, but the room was spotless. Elthia nodded in satisfaction, then squared her shoulders and turned to the parlor.

This was it, the reason Caleb had been so determined to marry her. For the sake of the Tanner family—*her* family now—she had to help convince Judge Walters that he would have no cause to regret handing these children over to Caleb.

She now truly did believe the temperamental Texan would be an excellent guardian for the children. Beneath his rough exterior, his dedication to their well-being was clearly evident.

Telling herself that this was no different than playing hostess to her father's business associates, Elthia pasted a friendly smile on her face and entered the parlor.

"Judge Walters," she said, extending her hand as he and Caleb stood. "My apologies for the poor welcome I extended earlier. I trust Caleb has made up for my lapse." The tea service was on the table between the sofas and each man had a cup in hand.

The judge set his down and bowed over her hand. "No need to apologize. You clearly had pressing matters to attend to."

She smiled as she sat on the sofa beside Caleb, across from the judge. The men took their own seats, Caleb with a guarded expression, the judge with a curious one.

Regardless of what Caleb expected from her, she'd already decided it would do no good to pretend a competence she didn't have. He'd have to let her handle things in her own way.

She lifted a hand in disclaimer. "What a diplomat you are, sir. In case Caleb's been too much of a gentleman to tell on me, I must confess that I am a novice when it comes to housework."

Caleb placed a hand on her dress at the knee. While the gesture might have appeared affectionate, the light squeeze he gave with it wasn't. "My wife is being a bit too modest. She—"

"Caleb, please, there's no need to spare my feelings." She patted his hand, ignoring his warning look as she turned back to the judge. "I can't tell you how supportive he and the children have been. They are all helping me learn my new role, each in their own way."

The judge raised a brow. "And that incident in the kitchen?"

Again Caleb jumped in to respond before she could. "She was trying to clean up a mess the kids and the dog made."

Elthia laughed. "You should have seen the children chasing that dog around the room. Then I'm afraid I made matters worse. I mistook a tin of molasses for cleaning solution." She sensed Caleb's stiffening beside her. "But my father always said, the lessons we learn best are the ones experience teaches us."

The judge nodded. "Sounds like a sensible man. Now then, Mrs. Tanner, I can tell from your accent that you're not from around these parts. Do you mind if I ask where you call home?"

So, the inquisition was moving on to her background. She pushed her glasses up and sat a bit straighter. "My home is now here, of course. But if you're asking where I come from, I was born and raised in Maryland, in a town called Terrelmore."

The judge tugged gently on his beard. "Maryland. That's a far piece from Texas, and in more than just distance. I imagine you must get a bit homesick now and again."

She lifted a hand. "I miss my Maryland family, naturally, but there's been so much to do and learn since I arrived here, I haven't had much time to dwell on it."

"I understand you and Caleb met only a few days before

the wedding." Her inquisitor flashed a sympathetic smile. "You've had a lot of adjustments to make in a short period of time."

Elthia leaned over to pour herself a cup of tea. "I imagine all new brides face the need to make some adjustments to their lifestyle when they first get married."

"But not all new brides face what you have." He watched her closely, as if trying to read every nuance of her expression. "Six children and a husband are a lot to take on all at once."

She paused in the act of pouring her tea. "Yes, it is. But I love children. And these six are already very dear to me."

She finished pouring her tea, unsettled by the expression on the judge's face. Did he think she was insincere? Lifting the teapot, she smiled. "May I refill your cups, gentlemen?"

"Not for me, thanks." Caleb's stiffness was reflected in his voice. Had he seen the same flicker of disbelief in the judge's expression, or was he just afraid she'd spill something?

The judge passed her his cup, one hand raised again to stroke his beard. "I'll take you up on the offer."

Elthia poured carefully, feeling Caleb's taut watchfulness. She wished he'd just relax. He was making her nervous.

She filled the cup without incident, then lifted it to pass to the judge. But somehow, in the process of exchanging it from her hand to his, the cup slipped, crashing to the table. Tea spattered as the fine porcelain broke into four large pieces.

Elthia and Caleb sprang to their feet at the same time.

She grabbed a napkin and began dabbing at the mess, horrified by what she'd done. "Oh, Judge Walters, I'm so sorry."

"As much my fault as yours." The judge frowned as he dabbed at his pants with his own napkin, but his tone remained polite. "No harm done. I believe I escaped with just a drop or two."

"Here, let me do that." Caleb's voice was controlled, but she saw the look-what-you've-done-now exasperation in his gaze.

Elthia relinquished the napkin and lifted the tray, which had captured most of the spill. "I'll take this to the kitchen." She was fleeing like a coward, but she needed time to regain her composure.

Just before she reached the doorway, Josie entered the parlor, big teardrops trickling down her apple cheeks. Elthia im-

143

mediately knelt in front of the girl, setting the tray on the floor. "Josie, what is it, baby, what happened?" She set one hand gently on Josie's shoulder and pushed a lock of hair from the girl's forehead with her other.

The girl gave a hiccuping sob before she answered. "I got a big ol' sticker stuck in my finger and it *hurts.*"

Elthia felt a surge of relief that it wasn't more serious but kept her expression solemn. "Oh, my! Let me have a look."

The girl placed her hand in Elthia's palm. Elthia gently examined the injured finger. She could see the small sliver of wood, lodged firmly in the pad of the grubby, child-pudgy finger. "You're right, that *is* a big ol' sticker. How brave you are!"

Josie's eyes got a bit rounder. "I am?"

Elthia nodded. "Of course. Now, would it be all right if I try to pull it out for you? I promise to be *very* careful."

The little girl nodded, her expression a mixture of trust and fearful anticipation.

Elthia took a deep breath, then with her fingernails, grasped the protruding end of the sliver and drew it out. "There we go."

Josie studied the offending bit of wood, then beamed up at Elthia. "Thank you, Aunt 'thia."

Elthia returned her smile, feeling a lump form in her throat. Josie's acceptance of her was a sweet, priceless gift. Clearing her throat, she tapped the girl's nose. "You're welcome. Now let's wash that finger and make sure we got it all, shall we?"

Caleb smiled. He'd lay odds that Elthia had forgotten her embarrassment and her audience until she reached for the tray.

He caught the judge watching Elthia's exit with a thoughtful expression on his face. Had he noticed her easy way with Josie? Had he seen the concern and motherliness in her actions? Surely that would make up for what she lacked in other areas?

The judge met Caleb's glance just then and set his napkin down. "Do you mind if we go outside and sit on the porch? It's a fine day, and I'd welcome a chance to enjoy it up close."

Caleb nodded. "You go on out and I'll join you in a minute. I just want to let Elthia know where we've disappeared to."

Caleb entered the kitchen to find Josie sitting on the counter, examining Elthia's watch brooch. Elthia stood in front of her, studying the now dirt-free wounded finger.

"How are you ladies doing in here?"

They both looked up, and Caleb frowned as Elthia's smile faltered. Then Josie claimed his attention. "Look, Uncle Caleb, isn't it pretty? And it ticks, just like Poppa's pocket watch."

Caleb drew closer, pretending to examine the expensive-looking bit of jewelry. "Very nice. But how's your finger?"

Josie shrugged as Elthia released her hand. "All better now, see? Aunt 'thia says I'm very brave."

"And so you are." Caleb lifted the girl, gave her a squeeze, and set her feet on the floor. "Now, give Aunt Elthia her watch and you can go back out and play."

Josie handed Elthia the watch and raced on out the back door, calling for Poppy.

Caleb watched Elthia try to pin the watch back on her bodice. She seemed to be having trouble with the clasp.

Finally he took it from her. "Here, let me."

He heard her quick intake of breath as he slipped the pin through the cloth of her bodice. Acutely conscious of the curve of her breast beneath his not-quite steady hand, Caleb took his time with the task.

The color climbed in her cheeks as he stood there, lightly fingering the gem-studded trinket. What would her skin feel like? Would she recoil from the touch of his callused hands?

He inhaled the light floral scent that was uniquely hers and suddenly had to work to keep his breathing normal. Could she hear the pounding of his pulse, feel the heat that seemed to be generated by the closeness of their bodies?

He looked at those tempting, teasingly full lips of hers and wondered what they'd taste like. He leaned closer.

Abruptly she stepped back, her expression confused and wary. "Thank you," she stammered, avoiding his gaze.

Hell, what was he doing? He lifted his head, trying to pull off a cocky smile so she wouldn't guess how affected he'd been. She wanted their relationship to remain strictly businesslike, he reminded himself. It was what he wanted too. Wasn't it?

"Looks like you got a spot of tea on your dress," he said, breaking the awkward silence.

She glanced at the spot on her skirt, then smiled wryly. "Learning to run this household is proving hard on my wardrobe."

Caleb, whose pulse had almost slowed to normal, was surprised by her light tone. Had she been less affected by what had just happened than he'd been, or was she just better at hiding it?

She picked up a rag and dabbed at the spot. "I'm sorry I acted so clumsy in front of Judge Walters."

He shrugged, no longer as irritated as he'd been earlier. "No point getting upset over what you can't change. I'm sure the judge won't throw out my adoption petition just because you spilled a little tea on him." At least he hoped not.

Caleb took the rag from her and set it back on the counter. Then he offered his arm. "Come on. He's out on the porch waiting for us to join him. Don't want to leave him at the mercy of the kids and that dog of yours for too long."

An hour later Elthia was relieved to be waving good-bye to the judge. She wasn't sure what sort of impression she'd made, or where his feelings stood as far as awarding Caleb custody of the children. As he'd stepped off the porch, he promised to pay another visit "in a month or so," just to see how they were doing.

While not unkind, the older gentleman was both intelligent and perceptive. He had a way of looking at you with his stern, piercing eyes, as if he could see your deepest secrets. At one point, when he'd heard her maiden name, he'd speared her with one of those sharp looks. "Sinclare? From Maryland, did you say?"

Elthia had hurriedly tried to stem his speculation. She wanted to stand or fall on who *she* was, not on who her father was. "It's a common name where I come from," she said quickly. "There's even a wealthy branch near the coast. You might have heard of them. I believe they deal in imports or some such."

The judge nodded. "Yes. I think Rupert Sinclare is the head of the family there, isn't he?"

Elthia tried not to react to her father's name, giving a small shrug as she smiled. "That sounds right." Then she turned the topic with a reference to one of the children. Luckily, Caleb had seemed oblivious to the nuances of the conversation.

With a sigh, Elthia entered the house. As Caleb had said, there was no point worrying over what couldn't be changed. Right now, she needed to get to the kitchen, or Zoe would cook supper without her. Elthia was determined to acquire some culinary skills, even if it meant hovering at Zoe's elbow and just plain getting in her way. She didn't want to usurp Zoe's position if the girl truly enjoyed her work, but she wanted to be prepared to step in when and if Zoe ever decided to be a young girl again.

And she planned to see that that happened soon. Zoe was much too solemn and industrious for a twelve-year-old.

Watching Zoe, and assisting where she could, Elthia found she had trouble concentrating on the task at hand. Her thoughts kept returning to that earlier interlude with Caleb in this very room.

Having his work-roughened hands on her bodice had spawned forbidden thoughts of how those hands might feel on her skin. Watching his fingers play across her timepiece had raised tingly gooseflesh on her arms. The intensity of his gaze as he leaned forward had mesmerized her, started a fluttering in her chest.

Would he really have kissed her if she hadn't stepped back? Would she have resisted if he'd tried?

Of course she would have! This was only a temporary partnership. Neither of them wanted to turn it into a real marriage.

But the edgy, unsettled feeling she'd had since Caleb reached down to pin on her watch whispered to her that she was wrong.

By the next morning, Elthia had decided how she would handle her wardrobe problems. After breakfast, she marched upstairs, Josie trailing along behind her. Opening the wardrobe, she surveyed her gowns and pulled out the four most extravagant.

Next she looked over her bonnets and found two of them with which she was quite willing to part. Josie volunteered to carry these to the bed for her, and Elthia hid a grin as she watched the little girl try on the flower-bedecked creations.

Elthia turned back to study her three pairs of walking shoes and four pairs of fine dress slippers. She picked up one pair of each and handed them to her chapeaued helper.

There, that should be enough. She sent Josie to fetch a sheet for her and then they bundled it all up.

Elthia dragged her bundle down the stairs and then left it in the kitchen while she went in search of Caleb.

Caleb looked up as she entered his workshop, then straightened as he noted her determined expression. "Is there something I can do for you?"

She nodded. "I plan to visit Granny Picket this morning. I can drive the buggy myself if you'll give me directions."

She was up to something, he could see it in her too-innocent expression. "What're you going out there for?"

Shrugging, she traced a circle in the sawdust on the table. "Just visiting. I thought I'd try being neighborly."

Lady Privilege visiting the less fortunate? No, that wasn't fair. She was probably just at loose ends.

He nodded. "Take Peter with you. He knows the way." Then he stood. "I'll get the buggy hitched for you."

She waved him back down. "No, no, you're busy. I'm sure Peter and Alex will be able to help me." Then, before he could ask any more questions, she turned and hastily made her exit.

The feeling that she was up to something, that there was more to this than "being neighborly," grew as he watched her call to Peter. The feeling intensified a few minutes later as he caught a glimpse of her tossing a large bundle into the buggy.

Surely she wasn't running away; not now, after they'd come this far? He wanted to trust her, to give her the benefit of the doubt, but there was too much at stake. He moved to the doorway.

She spied him as she settled in the buggy, and her expression froze. Then she waved and flashed a dazzling smile. How could anyone look so damn guilty and innocent at the same time?

Caleb stepped out of his workshop. He had no idea what he was going to say, just that he had to stop her from leaving.

Then an excited yipping off to his left stopped him.

Turning, he saw Josie and that mosquito-sized mutt playing tag. The tension eased from his muscles and his heartbeat slowed to normal. Regardless of what mischief she was up to, Lady Privilege would be back. He knew her well enough by now to know she would never leave without her pet.

Elthia breathed a sigh of relief as the buggy turned onto the road. She wasn't ready to discuss her plan with Caleb yet, not until she was sure Granny Picket would help her.

Peter looked over his shoulder at the bundle she'd thrown in the back and then at her. "You running away?"

She turned to face him fully, realizing they were almost of a height. "No, of course not. I'm part of this family now."

"But you didn't want to be. *He* made you." Peter brushed his ready-for-scissors, sandy-brown hair off his forehead.

How much did the boy really know? "What makes you say that?"

Peter shot her a scornful look. "I got eyes and ears. Anyone who saw you that first night could tell you'd changed your mind. You found out what Uncle Caleb was *really* like, didn't you? You looked like a cornered rabbit facing a hungry fox."

Elthia tried not to squirm at his unflattering description of her that first night. She should focus on Peter, not her own pride. "Actually, you're only partly right. I did get pretty upset that night. You see, I'd just found out your Uncle Caleb and I had different understandings of why I was here. And I suppose our discussion was a little heated at first. We didn't handle it in a very grown-up fashion, did we?"

He maintained a stony silence, refusing to return her smile.

She pushed her glasses up on her nose and tried again. "But we did work it out. He didn't force me to do anything. If I hadn't wanted to marry him, all I would have had to do was say so in front of all those people, and he'd have had to let me go."

The trees along the roadside gave way to hilly pasture land as the silence stretched out. Elthia tried another approach. "I know losing your parents hurt a lot. I *know* that, because even though I still have my father, my mother died when I was only ten." That did earn her a sympathetic glance. She smiled and pressed her point. "You need to give your Uncle Caleb a chance. He does love you and your brothers and sisters very much."

Peter's snort eloquently conveyed his disbelief.

Elthia frowned. Her intuition told her that his belligerence hid some hurt other than the loss of his parents. What was really bothering him? "You don't seem to believe your uncle has your best interests at heart. Why else would he have taken you in?"

"Uncle Caleb doesn't really want us. Aunt Annie and Aunt Lizzie talked him into it. I guess they didn't want us either."

Elthia remembered Caleb saying he'd tried his hardest to find another solution. "But the thing is, Peter, he *did* take you in when it came down to it. Surely that shows he cares."

Peter shrugged, unconvinced. The wagon hit a bump, jostling them, but still he held himself rigid. A minute later he cut her a sideways glance. "So what was this misunderstanding between you two about? Did he forget to tell you about all us kids?"

Elthia was aghast that he would think such a thing. Did he really feel so unwanted? "No, of course not. In fact, one thing we do agree on is how much we want to make a good home for you all." She shifted, trying to figure out how much to say. "The subject of our disagreement is a personal matter, but the important thing is, we have it all worked out now."

Peter snorted again. "Most likely *he* worked it out and you had to go along. Just like—" His words halted abruptly.

"Just like what?"

"It doesn't matter." His face closed again and he pointed to a narrow, rutted road that forked to the left. "Turn here. Granny's house is a little piece down this way."

Chapter Thirteen

They arrived at Granny's rough-hewn log house to find her on the front porch, shelling peas. The shawl she wore today was an alarmingly bright shade of purple.

Granny set her bowl aside and grasped her cane when she spotted them. "Hi there, Elthia, Peter. Good to see you."

Elthia climbed down and reached back to lift out her bulky bundle. For the first time she wondered how Granny would view her unorthodox request. Would she be intrigued? Or would she be put off? Well, it was too late to worry about that now.

"Thank you, Granny. I'm afraid this isn't entirely a social call. I've come to ask for your help."

Granny's eyes lit with curiosity as she studied the bundle. "You just tell me what you need and I'll see what I can do. Why don't you come inside and let me pour you a cup of my homemade apple cider."

Elthia smiled. "That sounds wonderful."

Granny turned to Peter, who lounged against the buggy, hands in his pockets. "You're welcome to come inside too."

But Peter shook his head. "No, thank you, ma'am. I'll just stay out here with the buggy."

151

Winnie Griggs

At least the refusal had been polite. Elthia touched his arm in acknowledgment, then followed Granny.

The house was quite small. A creaky front door swung into an open area, divided almost evenly between a kitchen/dining space and a parlor. Elthia spied a closed doorway in the far wall that undoubtedly led to a bedroom.

Granny waved her to the parlor, where Elthia placed her bundle on one end of the faded sofa, then sat on the other end. Granny handed her a cup of the amber-colored drink and took a seat in a rocking chair facing her.

Elthia took a sip of the cider, enjoying its tangy sharpness. "Thank you, Granny. This is quite good."

Granny nodded and set her own empty cup on a small side table. "So, what is it you want my help with? Got some mischief brewing, have you?" She leaned forward eagerly, as if she relished the idea of getting involved in a bit of mischief.

Elthia smiled. "Not mischief, precisely. My problem is, I'm afraid I've discovered I didn't pack the right kind of clothing for life here. Most of my things are too showy or too delicate to allow me to be very active."

Granny cocked her head, studying the dress Elthia wore. "If your other things are anything like what you've got on today, I reckon I'd have to agree." She looked disappointed. "If you're asking me to stitch you some new clothes, though, I'm afraid I'll have to warn you that my handiwork is only passable at best."

Elthia shook her head. "No, no, I wouldn't dream of imposing on you to such a degree. What I have in mind is something that I hope will be a bit more fun." She stood and unwrapped her bundle. "I want you to work out a trade for me."

Granny's eyes lit up as she moved to Elthia's side. "What did you have in mind?" she asked, fingering the gowns.

"Since you're more familiar with the people of Foxberry than I am, I hoped you could find a lady about my size who would be willing to trade some of her clothes for these. I don't care about color or style, just so the dresses are suitable for working about the house or playing with the children."

She looked up hopefully. "What do you think?"

Granny nodded. "We won't have trouble finding gals willing to trade. You're a mite slimmer and shorter than most, so that'll narrow the choices some. But I think we'll still be able to spread it out over several ladies. Now, how many garments do you want in exchange for yours? I wouldn't think you'd have any trouble getting two or three apiece for each."

"I think a one-for-one trade would be best." Sharing from her ample wardrobe felt right. She was embarrassed by how little thought she'd given to her material advantages in the past.

Granny wrinkled her nose, then shrugged. "Your choice. Leave this with me and I'll take care of it. I should be able to bring your new clothes to you in a day or two." Her gaze fell on the hats Elthia had brought. Lifting one, she fingered the silk roses adorning the brim. "My, but ain't this a beauty."

"It's yours," Elthia said impulsively. "You can take it as commission for working out the swaps for me."

Granny protested, but Elthia held firm and convinced the not-too-reluctant woman to accept the offer. Delighted with her new possession, Granny tried it on, preening for Elthia's benefit.

A few minutes later, Elthia glanced out the window, checking on Peter. The boy now sat on the porch steps, intently whittling on a stick of wood. So, he had some interests besides sulking. And surely this hobby, regardless of the level of Peter's talent, was common ground for Caleb to use in reaching out to the boy.

By the time the ladies stepped outside, the knife and wood were nowhere in sight. Instead, Peter leaned against the porch rail, hands stuffed in his pockets.

As they climbed into the buggy, she thanked Granny again for her willingness to help. Wryly, she figured she was probably the first bride in history who deliberately set out to wear *less* attractive clothes in order to please her husband. She just hoped Caleb appreciated her efforts.

When they pulled the buggy to a halt at home, Alex ran up to greet them. "Come see what me and Uncle Caleb made."

The excited boy led them to the back of the barn. "Look," he said as they rounded the corner, "aren't they great?"

The object of his enthusiasm was a series of five large cages built against the back wall of the barn. The wire and wood pens seemed almost complete; in fact one already housed the cat Alex had brought back with him from town.

"It's for my critters," the boy added unnecessarily. "So I'll have a place to keep 'em safe when they need doctoring."

Caleb stood on a ladder nearby, nailing something to the barn above the cages. He paused long enough to greet them. "Welcome back. Did you have a nice visit with Granny?"

Elthia could tell he was still curious about her purpose. Unless he asked, though, she'd wait until she saw what Granny came up with before enlightening him. "Yes, I did. And Peter was good company on the ride over and back."

Alex was proudly pointing out the features of the cages to Peter. "See the latch Uncle Caleb and I fashioned? I'll bet not even a 'coon could get out of here less'en I wanted him to."

Elthia glanced back up at Caleb. "I thought you didn't like his taking in so many strays?"

Caleb shrugged. "Stopping him from adopting strays would be like asking a river to run backwards. I figure I might as well fix up a few pens so he can keep the nuisances out of the way."

Elthia wasn't fooled. He might grouse about all the animals Alex took in, but he didn't really begrudge the boy his passion.

How had someone as warm and giving around children as Caleb Tanner gone so long without starting a family of his own?

As she turned to leave them, a tiny, not-to-be-subdued voice inside her whispered how lucky a woman would be to have him as the father of her children.

That evening, after the children were all down for the night, Elthia felt too restless to go to bed. She headed downstairs with the vaguely formed intention of searching the bookshelves for something to read.

Instead, she found herself at the front door. Almost before she knew it, she'd stepped out onto the porch, where Caleb sat on one of the steps, whittling by the light of the nearly full moon. The lock of hair dangling over his brow gave him a younger, less assured look. Would he welcome her intrusion?

His hands stilled as he looked up. He studied her face for a long moment, then nodded a greeting and focused back on his work.

Elthia crossed her arms over her chest and looked out over the front yard. "The children are tucked in for the night."

He nodded without looking up. "That's good."

She should go back inside. He obviously wanted to be alone.

She took a step closer to him. "Do you think Judge Walters's visit yesterday helped or hurt your case?"

He shrugged, still concentrating on his task. "Hard to say. The old codger doesn't give much away. But all in all, I think we still have a fair chance with him."

"That's good." She rubbed her arms and took another step.

Still not looking at her, Caleb shifted position, opening the way for her to sit next to him on the step if she wanted to.

She decided she did.

Angling her knees so she could watch him work, she took great care to make sure no part of them touched. That edgy awareness she'd felt yesterday in the kitchen was back, only it seemed intensified now by the velvety shadows of the moonlit night.

He, on the other hand, seemed barely aware of her presence.

Elthia tried to focus on his hands, tried to discern what he was creating with his knife and piece of wood. It looked like a pipe or whistle of some sort. A toy for one of the children?

She dropped her hands to hug her knees. "Did you know Peter likes to whittle?"

He did look up at that. "*Liked* to whittle, you mean. Back before his folks died, he'd ask for lessons whenever I'd visit. He seems to have lost interest lately."

Elthia shook her head. "I don't think so. I saw him working with a knife and a piece of wood at Granny Picket's this morning. But by the time I came out of the house he had it put away."

She saw his jaw tighten and a flash of emotion flit across his face before he lowered his head.

"There's another thing you should know," she said hesitantly.

He glanced up again, meeting her gaze. Then he looked toward the road. "If you're going to tell me Peter doesn't like me much, don't bother. I've already figured that out."

155

His words were gruff, almost uncaring, but Elthia's heart softened. Instinctively she knew Peter's rejection had hurt him. "Peter thinks you don't want him, don't want any of them."

His head swung back to face her. "What in the world would give him a dang fool idea like that? I'm working my ta—I'm doing everything I can to keep these kids with me."

Elthia placed a reassuring hand on his arm. "I know that, and I think a part of Peter sees it as well. But for some reason he thinks your sisters forced you to take them in, that you'd give them up in a minute if someone else offered."

Caleb groaned. "He must have heard part of my conversation with Annie." His knuckles whitened on the knife handle. "The *last* thing I wanted to do was make any of them feel unwanted."

Elthia was surprised by the strength of his self-reproach. "You had no way of knowing what Peter overheard or how he'd react. But now that you *do* know, maybe the two of you can find a way to work it out."

"Thanks for telling me." Caleb's tone was even, but as he resumed whittling, his knife attacked the wood with a passion that was all the more unsettling for the tight control he applied.

Elthia stood, deciding he needed time alone. She wondered if he even heard her good-night as she headed inside.

As soon as the door closed behind her, Caleb ceased his work. The small whistle he'd been carving snapped in his hand, and he flung it out into the darkness.

How could he have been so damned blind?

He'd only thought Peter was having a tough time adjusting to his parents' deaths. He should have known what the boy was going through. Hadn't *he* lived with similar feelings for years after his own parents' deaths?

The knowledge that he'd been responsible for making Peter feel unwanted made him want to howl in frustration.

Made him want to drive his fist through something.

Made him want to beg the boy to forgive him.

He couldn't do any of that. But maybe, as Elthia had said, he could help make it right, now that he knew what was wrong.

Elthia.

156

How in the world had she managed to unearth this source of Peter's pain in just a few short days when he hadn't gotten anywhere near it in two months? How could a woman who seemed so out of place here, seemed such a disaster in the making, have turned out to be just what this family needed to make it whole?

And what would it do to this family when she left in three months' time? The kids would be devastated all over again.

Of course, he would miss her too. Getting her riled was the most fun he'd had in ages. Must be that red hair of hers. An unbidden thought of what life would it be like if they truly had a till-death-do-us-part marriage brought a smile to his lips.

Not that he really *needed* her. After all, with six children to raise, he wouldn't be lonely. Anyway, it didn't matter what he wanted. It hadn't mattered to anyone in a long time.

No, he wasn't thinking about his own druthers. It was for the sake of the kids that he couldn't let her go.

He had to find some way to change her mind.

But what would be a strong enough motive for her to stay? She was mighty fond of the kids, but was that enough? If this had been that governess job she talked about, she'd have left after three months. It wasn't like they were her own flesh and blood.

He went very still as his mind jumped to the next logical thought. If there *were* a child of her own flesh and blood, *that* would be something to hold her here.

He hadn't been as unaware of her glances and awareness as he'd pretended. If tonight was any indication, seducing her wouldn't be a trial for either of them. Not that he planned to force anything on her. Any steps they took down the path toward a physical relationship would be by mutual consent.

His conscience twinged, but he resolutely ignored it. After all, she was a big girl; she'd even been engaged once.

He stood and dusted the shavings from his pants.

Despite his carefully detached reasoning, a heady bolt of anticipation flashed through him. A satisfied smile curved his lips as he considered carrying out the seduction of his wife.

Granny Picket arrived two days later bearing an armful of clothing. Elthia had just stepped out on the porch to greet her when Caleb appeared from around the corner of the house.

Elthia watched as he strode forward to relieve Granny of her burden. "Here, let me take that for you."

The visitor gifted him with a haughty frown. "No need to treat me like a helpless old woman, boy."

Caleb shot her a cheeky grin as he took the clothing. "Not an old woman, Granny, but a lady."

Elthia hid a grin as Granny cackled and gave him a coy smile. Was the old woman actually flirting with him?

Granny spied her. "Howdy, Elthia. I did like you wanted. Made some pretty good trades, if I do say so." She looked over her shoulder. "Don't dawdle, boy. Bring those on into the house so I can show your wife what I brung her."

Caleb sent Elthia a questioning look, but she just smiled and turned to open the door. The three of them trooped to the parlor, where Caleb dumped his load on a sofa. "Would one of you like to explain to me what's going on here?"

Elthia tilted up her chin to compensate for her feeling of sheepishness. "I asked Granny to find a couple of ladies willing to trade some of their clothes for some of mine."

Caleb frowned. "You didn't need to trade your things. If you wanted new clothes, I could've bought them for you."

Before Elthia could respond, Granny spoke up. "Smart girl, your wife. There are now at least four women in Foxberry who think kindly of her. And now she won't be showing everybody up when she goes to church on Sunday."

His demeanor remained stiff for just a moment; then he flashed a crooked smile. "You're right; my wife is a smart lady." He gave them a short bow. "Appears I'm no longer needed here. You ladies have a nice visit. I have work to do."

As Elthia helped Granny spread the dresses and accessories over the two sofas, she wondered if she'd inadvertently hurt Caleb's pride. It was so hard to read him.

Granny stepped back and swept her cane over the display of clothing. "Well, there they are. What do you think?"

Elthia studied the five dresses, pleased with what she saw. They were all in very good shape, two of them looking brand-new. They were simple, with none of the fancy ruffles and trims of the gowns she'd given in exchange. But the colors were crisp and the fabric much more durable. These would serve her purpose nicely.

"Thank you, Granny. These are just what I was looking for."

"And see here." Granny pointed to three bonnets spread on one end of the sofa. "You can use these for working outside."

Elthia lifted them one at a time. The first was a wide-brimmed affair of woven straw. The other two were poke-fronted cloth sunbonnets.

Granny reclaimed her attention, pointing to the floor near the sofa. "These are yours too."

These were two pairs of sturdy, mannish-looking lace-up shoes. They looked heavy and decidedly uncomfortable, but Elthia figured they would probably be more sensible for trekking across the open countryside than the shoes she'd brought with her.

"Granny, I don't know how to thank you. This is so much more than I expected."

Placing both hands on her cane, Granny gave a self-satisfied smile. "Glad I could help." Then she pointed to an empty spot on one end of the sofa. "Mind if I sit for a spell?"

"No, of course not." Elthia moved the dresses to make more room. "Can I get you some tea or coffee?"

"No thanky, gal. Just sit here and visit for a spell." Granny looked around as Elthia took her seat. "I always liked this room. Has a real welcoming feel to it."

"You've been here often?"

Granny glanced at the portrait on the far wall. "I used to pop in now and again, when Cora was alive. I haven't been here since she died, though, nigh on four years ago."

Elthia leaned forward, her interest piqued. "You knew Caleb's Aunt Cora?"

Granny nodded. "Yep. Cora was a fine woman. God fearing, kindhearted, and smart as a whip at book learnin'. Too bad she didn't know anything about how to raise a child."

Elthia straightened, prepared to be outraged on Caleb's behalf. "What do you mean?"

The older woman waved a hand. "Oh, she didn't mistreat him. Cora kept him fed and decently dressed and saw that he had proper schoolin'." She looked back up at the portrait. "But she was more at home with her books and her writing than

159

with folks." The look she gave Elthia was full of meaning. "Cora wasn't one for hugging or holding. There was no doubt she loved the boy; she just didn't do much to show it."

Caleb's brusqueness, his I-don't-need-anyone's-help attitude, made more sense now. No wonder he seemed to keep everyone at arm's length. "How old was Caleb when he came to live here?"

Granny gave a regretful sigh. "Six."

So young! Elthia's breath caught in sympathy for the lonely little boy of all those years ago.

"His momma died a year earlier," Granny continued. "When his daddy died, the kids got split up. Caleb wound up here in Texas with Cora."

No wonder he was so determined, so passionate about keeping the children together. Then the significance of Granny's words hit her. "You said here in Texas. Where did he come from?"

"Up Indiana way." Then Granny abruptly changed the subject. "Caleb didn't tell you about Suzannah, did he?"

Elthia, still dwelling on the way Caleb's life had been turned upside down at such an early age, merely shook her head.

"I thought not." Granny leaned forward, folding both hands on top of her cane. "Well, he'll no doubt call me an old busybody for speaking of her to you, but I think you need to know."

Elthia knew it wasn't right for her to sit here listening to gossip about her husband, but she couldn't quite work up the resolve to put an end to it. "Who is Suzannah?"

"She was the girl Caleb was engaged to marry six years ago."

Elthia felt a jolt of something uncomfortably like jealousy. "What happened?"

"Suzannah was a beautiful girl with shining blue eyes and a face pretty enough to shame the angels. She had spirit and zest and a knack for making a body feel good to just be around her. All the lads were after her, but she set her sights on Caleb. Problem was, Caleb wanted to settle down and raise a family, and Suzannah wanted to see the world. 'Course, being young, they figured they could work it out between 'em."

Elthia shifted in her seat, suddenly feeling dowdy and dispirited. Was that the kind of woman Caleb preferred? No won-

der he hadn't been overjoyed that he'd ended up with her.

"And did they?" Elthia asked.

The older woman suddenly looked every bit of her age. "The day before the wedding, Caleb got a note from Suzannah explaining that she loved him, but she just couldn't spend the rest of her life in Foxberry. She'd run off with a tinker who'd been passing through town and who promised to show her the world."

Dear God, how could a woman who claimed to love him have done such a thing? "That faithless hussy!"

Granny nodded. "And a coward to boot, slinking off in the night like she did." She sighed. "Strange thing was, after she left, Caleb turned into just the kind of man she'd wanted him to be. He left Foxberry. Started going from town to town, wherever he could find carpentry work. He didn't settle back down in one place again until he found out those kids needed him."

Using her cane for leverage, Granny stood. "I'd best be getting back home." She pointed the cane at Elthia. "People have been walking away from Caleb most of his life, one way or t'other. Sure glad he's got you and the kids to count on now."

Elthia's stomach clenched in guilt. Her leaving in three months wasn't the same kind of thing, her mind protested. It wouldn't be a shock or a surprise. It was what he wanted too.

So why did she still feel so wretched?

After Granny left, Elthia carried her new clothes upstairs. As she put them away, she couldn't stop thinking about what Granny had told her. The thought of a six-year-old boy, newly orphaned, without a lap to cuddle up in, without someone to kiss away his childhood hurts, without loving arms to comfort him when he felt sad, brought a lump to her throat.

What a lonely childhood that must have been.

The fact that he might have been heartbroken over the desertion of his fiancée, that Suzannah might have been the love of his life, she refused to think about at all.

Chapter Fourteen

Caleb put a hand to his back as he straightened. He'd spent the past hour painting the final two pieces in his current order. The extra effort he'd made these past few days had paid off. He ought to be ready to take it all to town by Friday, right on schedule. Not bad, considering all that had happened recently.

As he cleaned his brushes, he mulled over Elthia's unorthodox plan to get herself a new wardrobe. He'd had the impression she had money of her own, but maybe he'd been wrong. Had she been afraid to ask him to buy clothes for her, or just too proud?

He had vague memories of his father giving his mother money periodically. Pin money, they'd called it. Should he do the same for Elthia? He sure as heck couldn't go on having her trade her things to his neighbors for necessities *he* should be providing.

He just wished she'd come to him to start with.

"Hello."

As if his thoughts had conjured her up, Caleb looked up to see Elthia standing in the doorway. She was wearing one of the dresses Granny'd brought, and he was surprised by the change it wrought. Gone was the high-class socialite. She'd been replaced by a shy-faced, small-town girl. There was something about her expression, a softness that hadn't been there before.

He most definitely approved.

"I hope I'm not interrupting your work." She fidgeted with a fold in her skirt, as if uncertain of her appearance. "Zoe made some lemonade, and I thought you might like a glass."

"Thanks. Come on in." Now, what had sparked that friendly gesture? Not that he minded—it was a promising turn of events.

"I'm just getting my brushes and tools put away." He pointed a brush. "That one of the frocks Granny brought?"

"Uh-huh." She fanned out one side of her skirt. "What do you think?"

He thought she must not have looked in the mirror if she was worried about her appearance. The pale green shade complimented her, and the simple style gave her a whole-some, fresh-faced look. She didn't seem so out of place here anymore. And the bodice, while acceptably modest, fit just a hair snugger than her other dresses had. Oh, yes, he liked it just fine. "Looks nice."

She rewarded his faint praise with a smile. "Thank you."

As he put away his tools, she placed the lemonade on the worktable beside him. Then she wandered farther into the room, setting one of the larger rocking horses in motion with her hand.

Caleb searched his mind for some way to take advantage of her mood. If he wanted to make real progress on his scheme to seduce her, he'd have to get her alone occasionally. Sure, he could do *some* teasing and flirting even with the kids around; already had, in fact. Casual touches and meaningful looks, handled properly, could do a lot to get her in the right frame of mind.

But serious sparking required privacy.

Then he hit on it. "How'd you like to take a walk with me? There's a spot back in the woods that was a favorite of mine when I was a boy." When she hesitated, he added, "And there's some things we need to work out before the judge's next visit. Might be best if we talk somewhere where the kids won't overhear."

She met his gaze, then gave a nod. "Of course."

He flashed her a broad smile. "Just give me a minute or two to get cleaned up."

She nodded, and they moved toward the house. Things were falling into place rather nicely. Thirty minutes away from the kids should give him plenty of time to set his plan in motion.

"Have a seat," he said, pointing to the bench outside the bathhouse. "I won't be long."

Whistling a jaunty tune as he stood at the laundry sink, Caleb scrubbed the resins and grime from his hands and arms. Getting a good look at his work-stained shirt in the mirror, he stripped it off and gave his upper body a quick sink bath.

When he stepped back outside, he was smugly gratified by the wide-eyed, impressed glance she gave his bare chest. "Just give me another minute to grab a fresh shirt and I'll be ready."

Elthia met his gaze, red flooding her cheeks as she nodded.

Resuming his whistling, he climbed the stairs two at a time. When he returned, she seemed composed once more.

He offered her his arm. "Shall we?"

Nodding again, she ignored his arm and stepped into the yard.

Well, the afternoon was early yet. "This way." He pointed toward a tree line west of the house. "I told Zoe and Peter we were going for a walk. They'll keep an eye on the others."

They hadn't gotten far when Poppy bounded up to join them. Elthia stooped to give the mutt a scratch behind the ears, and Caleb frowned over this annoying development. At least when she straightened, she left the dog down on the ground.

"You wanted to talk to me about the judge's next visit," she prompted, breaking the silence.

"Yes. I'm afraid it's my fault we weren't ready for his first visit." She stumbled over something in the grass, and he grabbed her arm to steady her. "Careful. It's rough going here." He casually tucked her hand in the crook of his arm. It felt warm and soft and *right* there. "Now, where were we?"

She cast him a suspicious look but left her hand where he'd placed it. "You were saying it was all your fault."

He grinned. "That's right. The judge showed up a day earlier than I'd reckoned on, but I still shouldn't have put off telling you what to expect until the last minute."

She nodded agreement and then wobbled again as her toe caught on a chunk of rusty-looking iron ore half buried in the ground.

He steadied her, pulling her a tad closer to his side as they resumed their walk. He caught a whiff of her scent, a fragrance sweeter than the wildflowers they were walking past. "There's no point in dwelling on what's past," he continued, jerking his focus back to his purpose. "This first visit was just to check that I'd gotten married by the deadline he'd set. The next visit, he's likely to want to dig a bit deeper."

She worried her bottom lip. "Dig deeper?"

Caleb nodded. "Well, sure. He's gonna want to see if our marriage is working out and how we're doing with the kids. The judge takes his job *very* seriously." He ignored the four-legged tumbleweed trying to tangle up his feet. He wanted her focus on him, not on defending her mutt.

"I see." She pushed her glasses up higher on the bridge of her nose. "So how do we go about setting his mind at ease?"

They reached the tree line. The change from the heat of the sun's glare to the relative cool of the dappled shade was very welcome. The cloak of privacy was an added bonus.

Caleb tilted his head, pretending to consider her question. "We shouldn't have trouble convincing him we can and want to take care of the kids. He seems more than halfway to believing that already." He paused, rubbing the back of his neck. "The happily married part, though, that may take a bit more work."

Her suspicious look returned full force. "What do you mean?"

He tamped down the stab of guilt for the way he was leading her on. After all, he was doing this for the kids. "Well, now, if he wanted to learn how we get along, he'd likely question the kids and our neighbors about how we act when we're together."

Her chin thrust out at a haughty angle. "There's nothing wrong with the way we act when we're together."

Caleb shrugged. "Not if we wanted to convince him we were brother and sister. But that's not what we're after, is it?"

She yanked her arm away and rounded on him. "What do you mean? This is supposed to be a business arrangement, remember?"

"Of course, and I'm not suggesting anything different." He reclaimed her arm and started walking again. "Come on. The spot I want to show you is just a little ways ahead."

Elthia knew he was up to something; she just wasn't sure what. She'd go along a bit longer, both down this trail and in this conversation, just to see where they led. But if he planned to try any hanky-panky, she'd set him straight soon enough.

The quickening of her pulse was solely due to the exertion of the walk, not anticipation.

A few moments later the path ended at the rock-strewn banks of a gurgling stream. There were several large rocks embedded in the channel, and the water danced its way past them with a musically pleasing sound.

"How lovely."

Caleb shook his head, reaching for her hand. "Oh, this isn't what I wanted to show you. Come on, it's just a little farther."

He drew her along the creek bank, chivalrously lifting branches out of the way and helping her over fallen logs. Elthia was so busy watching her steps, it wasn't until he stopped and stepped aside that she became aware of her surroundings again.

Then she caught her breath. It was beautiful! The stream emptied into a large pool, a place of almost magical aspect. Willows bowed at the water's edge, the tips of their ropelike branches brushing the glassy surface. Wildflowers bloomed everywhere, filling the air with perfume and using an errant breeze to flirt with the honeybees paying them court.

Over to her left, a trio of turtles sunned themselves on a half-submerged log. Poppy broke through the underbrush just then, and his barking sent them all diving into the cover of the water.

"Well, what do you think?"

Caleb's question drew her gaze back to him, and she smiled. "It's wonderful. I can't believe such a precious bit of paradise is just a few minutes' walk from the house."

He nodded. "I know." He took her arm and began walking

along the edge of the pool. "When I was a kid, I used to spend a lot of time in these woods. This pool became my own private swimming hole in the summertime."

Elthia felt both envy and sympathy. This would be a great place for a child to play. But it would have been more fun if he'd had someone to share it with. Had he ever brought Suzannah here?

He halted in front of a large stone formation that jutted out into the water. But when he made as if to climb up on it, she held back. The boulders looked wet in spots, and she wasn't sure she could keep her footing, especially in these cloddish shoes.

"Come on," he urged. "The part that looks out over the water makes a great perch. We can sit there and rest a spell."

"I don't know. These really aren't climbing shoes."

"I promise not to let you fall. Trust me."

She met his gaze and slowly nodded. "All right. But let me take these shoes off. I think I can climb better in my bare feet." She sat on an outcropping from the natural pier.

Elthia bent over to unlace her shoe, but Caleb was quicker. He took her foot in his hands. "Here, let me do that."

She leaned back, studying his bent head. Would she ever understand him? Earlier, she'd suspected him of some very adult scheming. But his pride in this place, his eagerness to show it off, put her in mind of a boastful little boy. Every time she decided he was one thing, he changed to something else.

He set her shoes aside, and she drew in a sharp breath as his hands skimmed up her right calf to just below the knee.

Shaking loose from her surprise-induced paralysis, not to mention the prickling gooseflesh, Elthia yanked her skirts down, forcing his hands away. "Just *what* do you think you're doing?"

He sat back on his heels. "Why, just helping you off with your stockings."

Though his expression would have shamed a choirboy, he no longer reminded her of an innocent youth, boastful or otherwise. "No, thank you. I'll take care of my stockings myself."

He held his hands up, palms outward. "Of course."

She quickly slipped off her stockings, trying to regain her composure as she did so. But her traitorous memory kept replaying the shivery feel of his hands on her leg.

As she stood, he held out a hand. "Ready?"

Still distrustful of his just-being-helpful smile, she allowed him to take her hand and help her climb up the rock.

Once they reached the top, he led her to the far edge. "This was my favorite diving spot," he said, looking over the edge.

She followed his gaze, peering into the blue-green depths. The bottom dropped off deeply here. She imagined a fearless boy taking a running start; then, as he flew off the edge, tucking his legs, grabbing his knees, and landing a split second later with a satisfying splash. In her youth, she'd watched Ry perform that stunt dozens of times. But Caleb would have had no audience to applaud his efforts, or to yell indignantly when his splash was more generous than expected.

He took her elbow. "Let's sit and rest our feet a spell."

Letting their legs dangle over the edge, they sat in companionable silence. The lapping of the water, the buzz of the insects, and the occasional trill of a bird were the only sounds.

Caleb leaned back, bracing himself with his muscle-corded arms, his face raised to the sun. Her hand itched to reach up and brush back the lock of hair that had fallen across his brow.

She straightened abruptly, appalled at the direction of her thoughts. Time to refocus on the supposed reason for this walk.

"You say you're concerned about our ability to convince folks we're happily married. As long as we remain civil, even friendly to each other, I don't see that anyone'll be able to find fault."

Caleb shook his head. "You don't understand. Judge Walters just has to get a whiff of something not seeming quite right, and he has the power to whisk the kids away from me."

She tucked a tendril behind her ear. "So what do you suggest we do? Act like love-struck adolescents when we're in public?"

He grinned. "We don't have to go that far. All I'm saying is, we should act a bit more *married* when we're around others. I can put my arm around you once in a while, or give you a peck on the cheek. You can give me a hug, or fuss with my shirt collar. You know, the little things married folk do for each other."

"I don't—"

"Remember, I said *act* like a married couple. We'll know it's not real. Or don't you think you can pull it off?"

Perversely, his reminder that their marriage was a sham stung rather than reassured her. "Of course I can 'pull it off.' That's not—"

"Good. Let's try it."

"What?" Surely he didn't mean—

"I'll put my arm around your waist and give you a kiss. Just a quick one, mind you, the kind you give when you're not alone, but you can't resist the urge to show a bit of affection."

"But I—"

He held up a hand. "No, really, I think that would be best. Trying one of those deep, passionate kisses that you feel all the way down to your toes would be overdoing it. 'Cause you only do those in private, and after all, we're just doing this to convince our audience we're happily married."

"Will you *please* let me finish a sentence?"

He held up his hand. "Sorry. What did you want to say?"

Elthia took a deep breath. His words had conjured up images she was trying hard to suppress. "I'm not sure this is such a good idea. We *did* agree to keep this arrangement business-like."

He nodded slowly. "I see. You don't trust yourself to be able to keep the actions and the emotions separate. I hadn't realized that would be a problem for you."

Elthia drew herself up, irritated by his condescending tone. Did he consider himself irresistible? Did he think she had no emotional control? "Of course I can keep them separate."

He looked skeptical now. "Are you sure? I can't have you falling for me. We have an agreement, remember?"

Oh, he was insufferable. How could she have ever felt sympathy for him? "Don't worry," she said through gritted teeth. "There's absolutely no danger of my falling for you."

He shrugged. "Well, okay, if you're sure. Let's give it a try." He slipped his arm around her waist and drew her closer.

Elthia's pulse jumped and she stiffened.

He touched a finger lightly to her chin. "You've got to relax and pretend to enjoy this if we're going to fool anyone."

She nodded, swallowed hard, and then tried to relax.

He gave her an approving smile. "Better, but I can see we'll have to get a bit more practice in before you're entirely comfortable. Now, lean against me."

Reminding herself they were only acting, she fitted herself more snugly to his side. She was acutely aware of his closeness, of his hand at her waist, of the lingering scent of paint and something disturbingly masculine that clung to him. Deep inside her, a butterfly woke and began to flutter its wings.

Caleb, however, seemed as unaffected as he'd claimed he'd be. There was nothing at all distracted or soft about him. "No, no," he chided. "Don't lean on me like a broom propped against a wall. *Pretend* you like me, that you can't wait to get me alone so we can cuddle proper."

"Mr. Tanner, really!" Was he laughing at her?

"Like I said, we'll just have to get in some practice to get comfortable with it." He raised a brow. "Now, are you up to trying a kiss? Just a little one?"

She felt that butterfly flutter again, but she did her best to ignore it. It was time to take the offensive. "If I didn't know better, I'd say you were trying to take advantage of me."

Her accusation only served to earn her a frown. "For goodness sake, I'm only talking about a peck on the cheek."

She suddenly felt foolishly prudish. "Very well."

"That's good," he said. "You sit just like that, pretending you're nervous or upset, and I'll try to coax a smile from you." He leaned over, using his fingers to turn her face.

The kiss he gave her was just as he'd promised, no more than a peck on the cheek. It was the caress of his warm breath on her skin, the gentle stroking of his finger against her jaw, that caused her to draw in her breath.

Chapter Fifteen

Elthia placed a hand on his arm, whether for support or to hold him near, she wasn't sure. He didn't pull back immediately.

"If that doesn't work," he said, his voice huskier, more seductive, "I could move from your cheek to the tip of your nose, like this." The butterfly inside her started moving faster now.

He did pull back this time, shifting and drawing up one knee.

She blinked, trying to figure out what had just happened to her. It was several seconds before she could meet his gaze.

He waved a hand. "You see? We should be able to handle such tame displays without becoming affected."

She pushed her glasses up and returned his smile with a nod, praying he wouldn't detect the slight tremble in her hands.

"Okay, now you give it a try."

She froze. "What?"

"Your turn." He tapped his cheek. "Just a little peck, right here." When she hesitated, he raised a brow. "What's the matter? Surely all this playacting isn't bothering you?"

"No, of course not."

"Well, then." He tapped his cheek again.

"Oh, for goodness sake." She quickly leaned over and placed a light peck on his proffered cheek.

Caleb shook his head. "Elthia darlin', you gotta do better. It needs to look like you *want* to kiss me. Let's try again. And remember, you're pretending to be a loving wife."

Enough was enough. "You must think me an absolute simpleton. I know not all married people are so demonstrative in public."

"True, but not all married folk are trying to convince the rest of the world what an ideal match they are." He eyed her with a speculative gleam. "Of course, if you don't think you can remain unaffected . . ." He let a shrug finish his sentence.

Elthia glared. In the momentary silence, she heard the lap of the water, could hear a bird trill in a nearby tree.

Pressing her palms to the rough stone, she shifted. He was trying to manipulate her, of course, to corner her into feeling she must prove herself.

But even knowing this, she couldn't pass up his challenge. Tossing her head, she smiled. "Like this?" She lightly traced the side of his face with the back of her fingers as she leaned down to plant a kiss on his cheek.

She lingered this time, but her I'll-show-*you* determination quickly changed to something softer, warmer. The sandpaper texture of his cheek against her lips, the firm, supple feel of his skin under her fingers, the warmth of his breath stirring the hair next to her ear, combined to set her pulse racing.

The poor little butterfly was frantic now.

When she pulled away, her hand continued to stroke his jawline, almost of its own accord.

His cocky grin had disappeared. He lifted a hand to brush some hair away from her face. "You know," he said, his voice thrumming through her, "sometimes, when we're home and only have the kids around, we might want to try a real kiss. Just to add a touch of realism to our act, you understand."

Elthia nodded, unable to speak. The butterfly changed into a hummingbird.

"Good girl." Slowly he lowered his head.

Her eyes closed just before his lips met hers, and she felt her senses come alive with anticipation, straining toward something she wouldn't let herself identify.

172

* * *

Caleb ignored his mind's screaming urge to fully taste those luscious lips. His hand snaked behind her, and his thumb stroked her nape. Her shivery response heightened his awareness of her as an utterly desirable, sweetly feminine creation.

It took every bit of his control to just brush her lips with his and then pull back. If he wasn't careful, his plan would backfire. He wasn't supposed to be the one getting aroused.

Her eyes flew open, and he was pleased to see a flash of frustrated disappointment mingle with her surprise. "There," he said, forcing a lightness to his smile he didn't feel. "You seem to be getting the hang of this. Nothing to it, just like I said." He watched her struggle to regain her composure. It was all he could do not to preen in satisfaction.

"Yes, well, time to go." She moved to stand and he assisted her, letting his hand linger at her waist an extra heartbeat or two.

He took her elbow to guide her across the rocky pier. What would she do if he pulled her to him and gave her a *real* kiss, the kind he knew they both were itching for right now?

Whoa there, he chided himself. The plan was to leave her wanting more, not give her an excuse for righteous indignation.

When she sat to pull on her footwear, he didn't offer to help. Not that he couldn't have handled it, he assured himself. But there was no point in overplaying his hand.

He plucked a blade of grass and stuck the stem in his mouth. Stuffing his hands in his pockets, he leaned against a pecan tree. Doing his best to maintain a bored expression, he tried to ignore the bit of leg she exposed as she pulled on her footwear.

Poppy rejoined them, abandoning whatever smell he'd been following the past few minutes. Elthia gave the mutt's head a vigorous rubbing behind the ears, then stood.

Caleb straightened. "Ready?"

She nodded. "Just lead the way."

They backtracked along the creek, single file, until they met the trail again. Caleb offered her his arm then. He could feel the tension in her, could sense the churning of her thoughts, could see the edgy glances she sent his way.

173

So far, so good. He only hoped he didn't look as unsettled as he felt. His lips greedily craved another taste of hers. His hands itched for one more brush against her soft cheek. His arms longed for a chance to pull her tight against him. But the stakes were too high to risk scaring her with his passion now. He had to wait until she was not only ready, but achingly eager.

So Caleb clamped down harder on his control. Maybe a bit of conversation was what they needed right now. "Tell me a little about your family." It had been a casual question, but her defensive, stiff-backed reaction sharpened his interest.

"What do you want to know?"

He shrugged, trying to put her at ease. "I'm not after any Sinclare family secrets. You got a passel of brothers and sisters? You the oldest, the youngest, or somewhere in the middle? Your parents living? You know, that sort of thing."

She relaxed. "Well, I don't have a 'passel' of siblings. I have one brother and one sister, both older than me."

So she was the baby of the family. No surprise there.

"Julia is the oldest," she continued, "and quite a beauty. My brother Ry is also my best friend. He's intelligent and understanding and nonjudgmental." She shot him a look that silently added, *unlike you*.

Then she turned her gaze back to the trail. "As for my parents, Mother died when I was ten. Father is still alive, though. He's a businessman and is away from home a lot."

What wasn't she telling him? "Tell me about your life back East. What would a typical day be like for you?"

She shifted uneasily. "I'm sure my typical day would be quite boring to a man such as yourself." She didn't give him time to ask more questions, turning the talk instead to a discussion about the oppressively hot climate in Texas.

What was there in her background that she didn't want him to know about?

Elthia plopped down on the chaise and pulled off the irksome footwear. Turning her left shoe upside down, she caught the pea-sized rock that had caused her such misery on the walk home. But not for anything would she have stopped and asked

Caleb to assist her. His touch was something she both longed for and dreaded.

How could this be possible? Even at the height of her attraction to Baxter, she'd felt none of the sensations Caleb had elicited this afternoon.

She shouldn't have been attracted to Caleb Tanner. He wasn't classically educated, though he did seem intelligent. He wasn't Prince-Charming handsome, though his rugged, lean-muscled looks had somehow grown on her. He didn't respond to logic or reason; in fact he was stubborn, opinionated, and convinced he knew best in most everything. But he cared for those children, and he made his living crafting whimsical rocking horses.

Elthia tossed the shoe across the room. She absolutely *refused* to become emotionally involved with Caleb. Especially since he seemed quite willing and able to treat this all like a game.

She recalled the feel of that kiss he'd given her, and again it sent a little thrill through her that she couldn't quite suppress. She began to hum softly as she glided across the room to retrieve her mistreated shoe.

After supper, Caleb spent some time working on his books. When he stepped out on the porch later, whittling knife in hand, he found the whole family gathered there.

Elthia sat on the gently swaying porch swing with Alex beside her. She smiled a greeting his way, then returned to whatever conversation she and Alex had been having.

Beside the swing he spied his Aunt Cora's sewing basket. This afternoon Keith had ripped a button from the shirt he was wearing. Before anyone else could offer, Elthia had announced that sewing was one chore she could handle. Not only had she taken care of Keith's button, she'd told all of the kids to bring her any of their clothing that needed repair.

He'd wondered at the time if she knew what she was letting herself in for. But she'd seemed pleased when they'd taken her up on her offer and handed her a pile of shirts and dresses.

His attention caught by a low growling, Caleb turned to the other side of the swing. Josie sat cross-legged on the floor, playing tug-of-war with Poppy and a bit of rag.

175

Keith and Kevin knelt on the hard-packed ground at the foot of the steps, shooting marbles.

Zoe was plucking old blooms from the rosebushes. That girl didn't seem to know how to play, or even how to just sit and do nothing.

Peter, predictably, stood apart from the others, leaning against a support post and watching the twins.

Caleb reached for one of the scraps of wood he kept handy for his nightly sessions. "It's getting on to bedtime. Time you headed inside to clean up and get tucked in."

He smiled at the grumbling that greeted his words. "Okay, a few more minutes, but then it's off with you, and no arguments."

Josie abandoned her game with the dog and stood. "Aunt 'thia," she said, "would you tell us a story?"

Elthia lifted Josie onto her lap. "Of course, sweetie."

Alex shifted forward. "Want me to fetch your book for you?"

She shook her head. "I can tell you a story without a book."

Josie gave her a wistful look. "Can you tell one with a beautiful princess in it?"

Elthia nodded.

From Caleb's feet, Kevin snorted. "Princesses are sissy stuff. What about an evil witch or a big ol' dragon?"

Elthia nodded again. "But of course. A really good story will always have a nasty villain in it." She settled Josie more comfortably in her lap. "Now, let's see, where do we begin?"

Caleb watched her slip an arm around Josie as the little girl snuggled closer. What a pretty picture they made. He could almost imagine she was the real mother of these kids.

There was no denying her love for little ones. Watching her like this, he could tell himself that if his plan succeeded, and he got her with child, she would welcome the situation rather than feel trapped. Please God, let that be true.

"Once upon a time," she began, "in a faraway land, there was a kingdom called Tannerhaven. Tannerhaven was ruled by King Noble, a wise and just man who had six children. Now it happens a good fairy had gifted each royal child with a special talent."

She met Caleb's gaze for just a moment, a hesitant expression on her face. Then she smiled and looked back at the kids.

"The first born was Prince Justice. Since he would one day be king, he was given two gifts, courage and artistry. Next came Princess Lyrical, who was given the gift of music. The third child, Prince Pippin, was gifted with the ability to converse with animals. Prince Hijinx and Prince Jester came next. They were given the ability to read each other's thoughts. Finally came Princess Honeybee, who was given the gift of persuasion."

Caleb smiled as he listened to Elthia place each of the kids in her story. She went on to describe grand adventures, fighting dragons, rescuing innocents, embarking on heroic quests, and in each of these, she found a way to show how the princes and princesses used their talents to work together and achieve victory.

When she'd happily resolved the fourth adventure, Caleb stood. "I believe that's enough for one night."

Elthia silenced their protests with a smile. "Your uncle's right. It's getting late. I can tell you more about the adventures of Tannerhaven's royal family another day." She kissed Josie on the forehead, then set her down on the floor.

As she stood, Caleb came closer and put an arm around her waist. "Got one of those for me?" he asked.

He felt her slight stiffening and thought for a moment she might refuse. Then her gaze met his and her expression signaled acceptance of her role. "Of course." She turned fully toward him, as if at home in his embrace. Then, with a teasing smile, she placed her hands on his chest and gave his cheek a peck.

"Nothing to it." The words were pitched so that only he could hear. As she stepped back, her hand lingered on his chest, then slid slowly away in a gesture that caused his pulse to jump.

She turned, took Josie's hand, and escorted the kids inside.

Caleb sat on the steps and picked up his chunk of wood. Rubbing a thumb across the smooth-grained surface, he wished instead it was the soft, satiny texture of her skin. Recalling the faint blush that had warmed her cheeks, he wondered just how far the sprinkle of freckles that dusted her neck extended. What would it be like to loosen the buttons on her bodice and trace their path with his lips, one sweet inch at a time?

With a frustrated growl, he pitched his carving and stood. Raking a hand through his hair, he wondered why on God's green earth he was so tied in knots over someone like Lady Privilege. She wasn't beautiful, and she sure as hell wasn't biddable.

But she'd sure gotten under his skin.

He kicked at a pebble, wondering what he'd set himself up for. Circling the house with long, edgy strides, he headed for his Aunt Cora's marble-tiled folly.

No way was he going up to that bedroom until he'd plunged his traitorous body into a tub of cold bathwater.

"Now, you're sure you can handle this?"

Elthia frowned at her inquisitor. Irritation was a safer emotion than the unsettling attraction she'd felt since that walk two days earlier. "I told you, I've driven buggies since I was ten." She lifted the reins. "Now, do you want to lead or shall I?"

Caleb stepped back, his expression still reflecting doubt. But he didn't question her further. "Unless you want to eat dust all the way to town, it'd probably be best if you lead," he said. "Zoe can help you with directions if you don't remember the way."

"I think I can manage." Good grief, how much of a henwit did he think she was? When they'd traveled to town for the wedding it had been almost a straight shot.

"Well, I guess we'd better get started." Caleb moved to the buckboard. He tugged on one of the ropes securing the crated furniture he and the boys had loaded earlier, then climbed onto the seat next to the twins. "Remember," he called out, "we'll be taking it slow. Try not to get too far ahead of us."

She rolled her eyes at him, then turned to Alex and Peter, who were seated in the back of the wagon with the crates. "You boys be careful back there, all right?"

Smiling when she discovered herself to now be the one on the receiving end of long-suffering looks, she turned to the girls seated in the buggy with her. "Ready, ladies?"

At their nods, she turned the horse toward town.

Something More

Yesterday, Caleb had asked if there were any supplies she needed him to pick up when he made his delivery run to town. Elthia had immediately announced that they were all going along.

She was, in fact, quite pleased. She'd been trying to find an excuse to go to town. There was something she wanted to purchase, and she couldn't ask Caleb to do it for her.

Elthia had cudgeled her brain for ideas on a birthday gift for Caleb. Problem was, even if she knew what he might need or like, she had no idea what merchandise the local shops carried.

She'd finally hit on something yesterday while mending one of Zoe's pinafores. She'd make him a shirt. The more she thought on the idea, the more she liked it. Not only was she familiar enough with his wardrobe to know he didn't have an overabundance of shirts, she liked the idea of giving him a gift she made herself. She just had to buy the cloth without him seeing.

As Elthia stared at the dusty road, she wondered why it was so important to her that she make this birthday celebration into something extra special for Caleb.

Caleb watched the buggy up ahead with a frown. What was she up to now? Since yesterday, Elthia'd been walking around with an I-know-something-you-don't air. It made him decidedly uneasy.

Still, he couldn't fault her for much else. He had to admit, once she agreed on something, she didn't hold back. She'd thrown herself into their playacting without visible reservation. They'd made a nightly ritual of the goodnight kiss, for the kids' benefit, of course. And when he'd mentioned that perhaps he shouldn't always be the one to initiate it, she surprised him by greeting him with a good-morning kiss at breakfast today.

She'd even stopped jumping every time he touched her.

Well, not *every* time, he remembered with a grin. Yesterday he'd reached over to close a curtain and "accidentally" brushed an arm across her chest. She stepped back so quickly, she almost tripped over her own feet, and she hadn't been able to meet his gaze for an hour after without blushing clean up to her hairline.

Yep, one thing Elthia wasn't was a cold fish. Perhaps tonight he'd try putting a little more heat into their good-night kiss. Lord knows, he'd been wanting to anyway.

And maybe tonight he wouldn't wait until she had time to fall asleep before he climbed up the stairs to their room.

Chapter Sixteen

Elthia sat on the porch swing, enjoying the evening breeze as the soft murmur of the children's conversation flowed around her.

Her gaze turned to Caleb, as it had so often lately. During the trip to town today, she'd found the perfect piece of fabric. She was itching to get started, but she'd have to wait for times when he was in his workshop if she wanted to keep it a surprise.

Would he appreciate her efforts?

His brow furrowed just then, and he paused, looking up at Peter. "Something's not quite right about this carving, but I can't put my finger on it. What do you think?"

Elthia pushed her glasses up. He'd been doing quite a bit of that lately, asking the boy's opinion and quietly complimenting him on some well-done piece of work.

Peter only shrugged. Elthia studied him, realizing his I-don't-care attitude wasn't quite as firm as before. There were cracks showing, signs that he was softening just the tiniest bit.

Caleb blew on the pipe whistle and a weak, sour note sounded. Leaning back, he shook his head. "Hear that? Maybe it's a flaw in the wood. Here, take a look."

Elthia thought Peter would refuse. Then he snatched it and

began a meticulous examination. Finally he looked up with a smug expression. "I see the problem. You haven't cleared this hole. There's a sliver under the lip here that needs to come out."

Caleb's frown deepened. "You sure about that?"

Peter handed it back to him. "Have a look for yourself."

Caleb studied the hole in question. "Well, I'll be; I think you're right." After some delicate maneuvering with his knife, Caleb put the pipe to his lip again. This time a clear, true note sounded. "Much better. Thanks."

Peter gave a stiff nod, his expression a mix of suspicion and pride. Elthia felt a stirring of hope. It would take time, but there was a chance now that Caleb could win his nephew over.

Caleb tossed the whistle to Josie, who'd been standing a little distance away. "Here you go, sweet pea, this one's for you. Just make sure you don't go blowing it in the house."

Beneath his stern facade, he was so generous to the children. Did they truly understand what he was doing for them?

She stilled as a flash of inspiration struck.

Of course! She and the children could plan a celebration for Caleb's birthday. It would give them a chance to give something back to him, and him a chance to see how much they cared.

Caleb brushed the wood shavings off his leg as he stood.

Elthia, realizing she'd been staring at his hands, stood as well. "All right, children, time to get ready for bed."

She turned at Caleb's approach, anticipating the ritual kiss. Last night, when she kissed his cheek, he brushed her neck with his fingers, raising gooseflesh all the way down to her toes.

Would he do it again? Did she want him to?

When she met his gaze, there was a look in his eyes, an intensity that reminded her of a banked fire, one that could burst into flames at any moment. She faltered for just a second, then closed her eyes against that look, and raised her face.

But instead of the sandpapery texture of his cheek, her lips met something infinitely softer, infinitely more sensuous. Her eyes flew open as his arms snaked around her back. The embrace was far from confining. He held her tenderly, as if she were a precious treasure he needed to support but was afraid to crush.

His mouth teased hers, nibbling, caressing, tasting. Heaven help her, it was wonderful, exhilarating. Then she heard a little-boy snort and a disgustedly uttered "Grown-ups."

Pulling back from the kiss but not the embrace, she blinked and looked around. The kids were staring at them with looks ranging from Josie's romantic mooning to the twins' disgust.

She chanced a glance Caleb's way, though she didn't dare meet his gaze, and was gratified that he seemed as bemused as she felt. Stepping away, she stumbled and recovered all in a heartbeat, then flashed a bright smile. "Well, good night, then."

Turning quickly to the children, she made shooing motions. "Come along, inside with all of you." Time to put distance between herself and her tempting, but very temporary, husband.

For the next several minutes, she helped the younger ones change clothes and wash their faces. Then she went from room to room, tucking them in and listening to their prayers. But tonight her attention wasn't entirely focused on the children. Her mind kept replaying that kiss and her unexpectedly heated response to it.

By the time she retired to her bedroom, she was ready to admit to herself that she hadn't wanted it to end. If they'd been alone, how far would that kiss have taken them?

As Elthia stepped behind the screen, her thoughts circled back to the kiss. She'd never known a man's touch could evoke such feelings. There'd been a promise in that kiss, a promise of richer and more wonderful sensations to come. And she wanted those sensations, those feelings.

As a married woman, she had a right to them.

Problem was, she wasn't truly married because she hadn't made an until-death-do-us-part commitment to him.

She brushed out her unruly mop of hair, wondering how she'd come to this point after little more than a week of knowing him. She hadn't even liked him much for the first couple of days.

She set down the brush and started toward her bed. Then

she froze in her tracks as the door opened and Caleb stepped inside.

Caleb felt an immediate, gut-clenching reaction to the sight of her. He'd expected to catch her still awake, but not still up. The vision she presented, garbed in that virginal white gown, with her wonderful river of wavy red hair tumbling over her shoulder, was unexpectedly arousing. She stood frozen, but he saw the pulse jump in her throat, and felt his own mimic it. The lamp behind her silhouetted her figure through her gown.

That kiss they'd shared on the porch was still fresh in his mind. Teasing at that tempting lower lip of hers had been every bit as satisfying as he'd imagined it would be. On the other hand, the fact that she'd been so responsive, so pliant in his arms, had been wholly unexpected. How would she feel about a repeat, here in the privacy of their bedroom?

Caleb clamped down on his control, trying to appear at ease. "Sorry if I startled you. I decided I'd turn in early tonight."

She came out of her trance, pulling her shoulders back as if to face a firing squad. Caleb tried not to gulp as her movements outlined her firm, sweetly rounded breasts beneath the gown.

"Of course." She turned, moving quickly to her alcove. "This is your room as well. I was just about to turn in myself."

He drew a deep breath as she stepped behind the screen. Now it was time to make her as aware of him as he was of her.

She turned her lamp down, but there was still the light from his. He undressed, making as much noise as possible. He wanted her to picture in her mind exactly what he was doing.

When he stripped to his drawers, he moved to the desk, a spot that would give her a clear view of him, if she cared to look. The sound of her quickly indrawn breath told him she had.

She didn't say anything, though if the prickling sensation at his back was any indication, she stared at him for the full two minutes he stood there rummaging through his papers. Satisfied that he'd given her something to think about, perhaps even squirm over, he headed back to bed, whistling softly.

Fifteen minutes later he smiled as he heard her plump her pillow for the dozenth time. "Having trouble sleeping?"

There was a moment of utter silence, and then a heavily breathed sigh. "Yes. Sorry if I'm keeping you awake."

He grinned but kept his voice merely neighborly. "That's all right. Hope there's not something bothering you."

"No, not really. Just having trouble settling down."

"Oh, that's too bad." Then he had a wicked inspiration. "You know, I give a pretty good back rub if you think that'd help."

"No, that's all right, thank you."

His grin broadened. He hadn't really thought she'd take him up on it, but now she'd have something else to think about. "Suit yourself. Just thought I'd offer." He sat up and threw his feet over the side, making sure she could hear him.

"What are you doing?"

Was that a hint of panic in her voice? "Thought I'd see if I could talk you into joining me for a slice of that apple pie from supper. It might cure your restlessness. What do you think?"

He held his breath, unsure of her response. What would it be like to have her want to stay with him, without coercion or tricks? The flash of longing for such a trusting, accepting relationship stabbed through him with an almost physical pain.

It had been so very long . . .

Hearing her feet hit the floor, he shook off his moment of weakness.

"All right," she said. "Just give me a minute."

A flash of velvet appeared from the other side of the screen and then withdrew. Caleb smiled. He'd wondered how long it would take her to realize the situation.

"Caleb?" she called hesitantly.

"Yes?"

"Do you . . . I mean, are you . . . well . . ."

He took pity and interrupted her stammering question. "I've put my shirt and pants back on, if that's what you're wondering."

When she stepped out from behind the screen, she was primly covered, neck to toe, in a tightly belted pale blue robe. It contrasted nicely with the beet-red color of her cheeks.

He'd deliberately not buttoned his shirt. After her first startled glance, though, she apparently decided to ignore his highly informal manner of dress.

Smiling, he stepped to the door. As he opened it, he bent in a theatrical bow, his hand sweeping the air in front of him. "After you, milady."

Taking her cue from him, she gave a regal nod, tilted her chin haughtily, and swept from the room with a swish of her robe.

He took time to admire the sway of her hips as she passed. Then he joined her at the head of the stairs. Finger to his lips, he pointed to the kids' rooms and offered her his arm.

Once in the kitchen, he lit a lamp while she served the pie.

Caleb took a seat next to her and they ate in silence for a while. But there was nothing companionable about that silence. He was acutely aware of her presence, of her every move and every breath. He could tell she felt something too. It was there in the effort she made not to meet his gaze, in the control she exerted over her movements, and in the tension that stretched between them with such intensity you could almost touch it.

She gave in to the need to break the silence first. "I think you're doing a very good thing with Peter."

He paused, his fork halfway to his mouth. "What?"

She met his gaze now, giving him a soft caress of a smile. "The way you're drawing him out. Like tonight; you didn't really need his help figuring out the problem with that pipe, did you?"

Caleb shrugged and finished his bite before answering. Damn, but she was perceptive. "Peter's a good kid, and he's got a lot of woodworking talent. I'd hate to see all that go to waste just 'cause he's mad at me about something."

She pinned him with an I'm-not-gonna-let-you-off-the-hook-that-easy look. "It's more than just tonight. The past few days I've heard you ask his opinion—with a convincing man-to-man tone, I might add—on everything from the garden to the livestock."

Caleb shifted in his seat. Looks like he hadn't been as subtle as he'd hoped. "You're reading more into things than are there."

He shoved his now-empty plate away. He hadn't brought

her down here to discuss the kids. "That was just what I needed."

She pushed her dish away as well, though she'd only eaten half her slice. "Me too. But I'm full now." She rose and reached for his plate. "You go on back to bed. I'll clean up."

He stood as well. "I'm not the least bit tired. I'll help with these, and then what do you say we sit on the porch a spell?"

She turned away, moving toward the sink. "I don't know. Perhaps we shouldn't—"

He stepped up behind her, so close his breath stirred the hair at her neck. "Shouldn't what?"

She started, rattling the plates. Then she set them down and turned to face him. "Shouldn't be together under the stars, when I want so much for you to kiss me again the way you did earlier."

Startled by her directness, Caleb froze. Damn those glasses of hers. Just once he'd like to gaze directly into her eyes.

But as he studied her face, noting the mixture of fear and anticipation, vulnerability and courage, he forgot everything but the tiny seed of tenderness that was taking root in his heart.

He raised a hand to brush the hair back from her temple. "But we're not under the stars right now."

The gruffness of his voice sent little tingles of sensation shooting through Elthia's chest. She looked into his eyes and saw the color deepen, saw his expression soften into something both warm and hungry. It was a hunger her soul echoed.

Surely, *surely* a kiss, no matter how passionate, would not compromise her ability to leave him when the time came. And she wanted it, *needed it,* so much.

"No, we're not," she agreed, placing a hand on his chest.

It was all the encouragement he seemed to need. This time, when his lips met hers, there was nothing tentative or polite about it. Instead there was an urgency, a passionate explorativeness that excited her, that made her greedy for more.

Her hands slipped inside his shirt until the firm muscles of his back were beneath her fingers. Mercy, but he felt so good, so wonderfully masculine. Her hands could not keep still.

When his mouth urged hers to open for him, she didn't hesitate. When his tongue slipped inside to taste her, she paused for only a startled second before she welcomed him and began to imitate his movements.

Deep inside her, a sweet, tender ache formed. It seemed to drive her deeper into his arms, as if only closer contact with him could satisfy it.

When his mouth left hers, she moaned a protest, but he was only switching the direction of his passionate assault. The kisses and tastes he rained on her neck, the nipping and nuzzling to her ear, were nearly as heady to her as his kisses had been.

Elthia wasn't sure she could remain standing much longer. Her bones had suddenly turned to jelly. His kisses returned to her lips, and she leaned back, clutching his shirt for support.

Her fervor surprised even her. She heard a groan escape him, and then his hand slipped inside her robe and begin to gently massage her breast through the thin fabric of her gown.

Sensations flooded through her in a flash that left her breathless. Never had she felt anything like it, or even dreamed it possible. It rocked her back on her heels, and she bumped her back against the counter, jostling the plates she'd placed there.

They pulled apart and stood facing each other for an eternity of seconds, both breathing heavily. Finally she turned away, reaching for the dishes with unsteady hands. "I can take care of these. There's no need for you to help."

She heard him draw in a deep breath behind her. "If you're sure, I think I'll go outside for a spell." She heard the wry smile in his voice when he continued, "Don't wait up for me."

After he left, Elthia leaned against the counter, trying to regain her balance. The kiss on the porch had been tame compared to this. What had he called it by the pool? *A deep, passionate kiss that you feel all the way down to your toes.* Yes, that described it. Not only had she felt it down to her toes, but it had stirred sensations in other, more intimate areas as well.

She was very afraid she'd been wrong in her earlier thinking. What had happened tonight would most definitely complicate matters when it came time for her to leave.

A few minutes later Elthia would have sworn she heard the door to the bathhouse open.

*　　*　　*

Elthia stuck out her lower lip and blew a troublesome lock of hair from her forehead. Caleb's birthday was tomorrow and she still had to finish his shirt before the sun rose in the morning.

Helping the children, especially the younger ones, figure out what they could make Caleb for his birthday, and then helping them get it done, had put her behind on her own project. But that was all done now. Peter was mounting Zoe's sampler and Josie's drawing in frames he'd made, and then they could wrap everything up and hide it away until morning.

Elthia smiled as she heard a whoop of victory from outside. Keith and Kevin were keeping Caleb occupied with a game of horseshoes, and from the sounds of it, the boys had just scored.

Here in the kitchen, Josie and Poppy stood lookout at the door. Peter, Zoe, and Alex were debating whether Caleb would prefer ham or fried chicken for his birthday meal.

Planning the party had been good for the children, especially Peter. Elthia was pleased that his surliness had disappeared, to be replaced by enthusiasm and youthful energy.

"Let that go!"

Elthia jumped at Peter's command, then realized it was aimed at Poppy.

The dog was dragging one of the birthday banners across the kitchen floor. Josie made a dive for the animal and succeeded in grabbing hold of him. "Bad doggie!" she exclaimed, pulling the corner of the feedsack from the dog's mouth.

Zoe took it from her. "Oh, no, it's ruined!"

"Here, let me look." Elthia took the maligned bit of cloth and spread it out on the table. Earlier, she had taken pictures and birthday-greeting signs the children made and pinned them to feedsacks. They planned to hang these around the kitchen while Caleb was in his workshop tomorrow morning.

"It's not so bad," she said after a quick look. "There's a hole in the corner, but it's so small nobody'll notice. And only one picture is torn. We can make another and fix it right up."

She turned to Peter. "While I clean this section, would you go up to my room and get my box of art supplies? It's in the trunk at the foot of my b—at the foot of the chaise."

When Peter returned with the requested box, Elthia was still

189

blotting the corner of the cloth dry. She offered him a quick smile of thanks and then turned back to her work.

"Who'd like to draw us a new picture?" she asked without looking up. She was surprised when it was Zoe and not Peter who volunteered. He'd been her most enthusiastic artist this week.

She looked up as she heard the door open and saw Peter's retreating back. Surely he wasn't upset just because Zoe'd beat him to the punch? No, he was probably just ready to get outside for a bit. They'd been in here ever since returning from church.

Elthia asked Zoe and Alex to finish the banner upstairs so they wouldn't run the risk of discovery. Then she headed for the parlor. She pulled out the shirt she was making Caleb and held it up, studying her work with a critical eye.

Even given her interruptions, making this shirt was taking longer than expected. But she was taking extra care that the stitches were precise, the seams straight, the collar sharply pointed. It would be as perfect as she could possibly make it.

Actually, there wasn't much left to do. She had to attach the cuffs and the sleeves and it would be done.

She tried to picture it on him. With his broad shoulders, he should fill it out quite well. The color, the crisp blue of the wide Texas skies, would look good on him. Would he appreciate her efforts? Would it lead to another of those delicious kisses?

This past week had been so wonderful. The Tanner family had touched her in so many little ways, had worked their way into the very center of her heart. It was getting harder and harder for her to think about leaving.

And not just because lately those good-night kisses had left her aching for something more. Even without the sensual daydreams he sent her way, she was coming to believe Caleb was the man who could make her happy, fulfilled.

How would he react if she told him that she'd decided to stay? If he agreed, would it be because he wanted *her,* or just someone to be a mother to the children?

It seemed she wanted it all now.

"Oh."

Elthia looked up to see Peter in the parlor doorway. "Yes?"

"Sorry, didn't know you were in here."

Was something the matter? That glower was back, and so was the negligent slump to his shoulders.

Elthia bundled her work and tucked it beneath some mending in the sewing basket. "Come on in, you're not bothering me. I just wanted to take a look and see how much work I had left on this."

Peter drifted across the room toward the bookshelves.

Elthia studied his back. "Is something the matter, Peter?"

The boy picked up whatever he'd come after and stuffed it in his pocket. "Nothing worth talking about," he answered stiffly.

Elthia wrinkled her brow. "But surely—"

Peter's hands balled into fists at his sides. "I *told* you, I'm *fine*. Just leave me alone." With that he fled the room.

Dismayed, Elthia wondered what had caused him to react so angrily. She'd have to ask Caleb. Perhaps he'd noticed something happen to Peter outside. But right now she had to take advantage of Caleb's absence to finish preparations for tomorrow. No party would be complete without a cake.

When she entered the kitchen, Elthia looked out into the backyard. Caleb and Keith were now ranged against Alex and Kevin in the game of horseshoes. Elthia chewed on her lip as she noticed Peter was nowhere to be seen.

It looked like she'd have the kitchen to herself, though, for just a little longer.

Elthia pulled out a book of recipes she'd found earlier. She debated about whether or not to call Zoe down, just to look over her shoulder while she worked, but then decided against it. She wanted to do this on her own. And with such detailed directions to follow, how hard could it be?

Elthia set to work. It would be nice to be able to brag on having made the cake herself. As she gathered and mixed the specified ingredients, she found herself puzzled by a few of the instructions. But she used her ingenuity to plow her way through, and finally was able to pour the batter into a pan and slip it into the oven.

There! The hard part was over. Nothing to it, really. All she had to do now was keep an eye on it so it didn't overcook.

Basking in the glow of her newfound confidence, Elthia decided that she should be a little firmer with Zoe about taking over some of the kitchen duties from her.

Humming, she began to clean up the mess she'd made.

Chapter Seventeen

Alex shifted his weight from one foot to the other. "It's awfully flat," he said doubtfully.

Kevin wrinkled his nose. "It smells funny."

Keith poked at it with a finger. "It's hard as a rock."

Josie gave Elthia a pleading look. "Do we have to eat it?"

Elthia looked at the children, who in turn were studying the lump that lined the bottom of the cake pan. She herself avoided looking at it. Her last glance had almost reduced her to tears.

"No, Josie," she answered the apprehensive child. "I don't believe even Poppy would eat any of this one."

Alex cocked an eyebrow at her. "Want me to get Zoe?"

Elthia swallowed her pride and nodded meekly. "Yes, please." Then she turned to the twins. "You boys keep an eye on your uncle's office. Let me know if he comes out any time soon."

When Zoe stepped into the kitchen, she joined the group gathered around the counter. After a moment she said, without looking up, "You're supposed to use flour, not cornmeal."

Elthia winced. She thought she *had* used flour.

"Don't worry," the girl announced. "There's still plenty of time. I'll make us a really special one using some strawberry preserves." She cast Elthia an apologetic look as she said this.

Miserably realizing this twelve-year-old actually felt sorry for her, Elthia nodded. "Come on," she said to the others. "Let's get rid of this mess and give Zoe room to work."

The house was utterly quiet. Elthia sat alone in the parlor, trying to finish Caleb's birthday present.

After putting the children to bed, she'd told Caleb she planned to stay up a while. Thankfully, he'd gone to bed almost immediately. That was an hour ago. She'd restarted work on one seam three times. But all she had left now was the buttons.

All in all, it hadn't been one of her better days. Peter had turned surly again, she'd failed miserably at her first venture into baking, and now this late-night session with the shirt.

She was so tired, she was having trouble concentrating. The fact that it was so muggy and oppressive wasn't helping her any. Placing the buttons just so had become an onerous chore.

At last! She picked up her scissors. A snip of the thread and she could go up to bed.

No! Elthia stared in horror at what she'd just done. It wasn't possible, not after all the work she'd put into this.

But there it was. The slash in the sleeve leered at her, glaring proof that she'd failed at yet one more thing.

Tears trickled down her cheeks. Sobs clogged her throat, threatening to erupt in loud, pitiful wails. She had to get out of the house before she woke someone.

Elthia jerked to her feet. She moved through the hall as quietly as she could, but haste drove her more than caution.

It was time to admit the truth. No amount of resolve could change the fact that she was a complete failure as a homemaker and wife. She'd been fooling herself to think she'd fit in here.

And, dear God, the fact that she could lose this newfound family hurt much more than the thought of going home in disgrace. Somehow, over the past weeks, her goal had shifted from proving her independence to proving herself a good wife and mother.

Grabbing a lamp from the kitchen, she headed for the barn as if it were a sanctuary. Her personal demon ran alongside her. Nothing she put her hand to worked as she intended, it mocked. The Tanners . . . Caleb . . . deserved so much better than this.

Halfway across the backyard, she stumbled and fell to her knees. Doggedly she stood and resumed her flight. She wouldn't loose the choking flood of emotions until she was safely inside.

Caleb rolled over for about the twentieth time in as many minutes. He hadn't gotten a lick of sleep since he'd come up here. Seemed he'd grown used to falling asleep to the sound of Elthia's soft breathing, to the feel of her presence in the room.

Besides, there'd been something about the way she was acting when she talked about staying up for a while, something that didn't quite ring true. It was nagging at him, and he'd been looking for an excuse to go down and check on her.

The sound of someone leaving the house, though, brought his feet to the floor in a heartbeat. He shot to the window, where he caught sight of Elthia stumbling her way to the barn.

Something was wrong.

He snagged a pair of pants and tugged them on as he crossed the room. His shirt and boots were left behind.

He descended the stairs two at a time, raking a hand through his hair. What was wrong? Had he done something to upset her?

As he strode to the barn, a sprinkling of rain baptized his shoulder, but it was the sound of muffled sobs, not the drizzle, that drove him to sprint the last few yards.

He paused in the barn's wide entryway just long enough to get his bearings. Her lamp hung on a hook by the door and bravely guarded a small circle against the encroaching shadows. At the edge of this circle, Elthia lay against a pile of straw, head buried in the crook of her arm, shoulders shaking with each sob.

Caleb sat and pulled her close, rocking her gently on his lap. Each sob drove a thorn into his soul. He wished there was a dragon to slay, like in one of her stories, an evil villain he could vanquish, to bring a smile back to her face.

Guilt clawed at him. Was she so unhappy here?

Elthia kept crying, her face buried in her hands, as if oblivious to his presence. Slowly, as he rubbed her back and murmured reassurances, the sobs lessened. Finally, with a watery hiccup, she quieted and her hands lowered, fidgeting with a bit of cloth she held.

"Feeling better?" He moved his hand up to stroke her hair.

She nodded. "I'm sorry," she whispered.

"Care to talk about it?"

She shook her head.

Caleb couldn't let it go. He tucked a lock of hair behind her ear and realized she wasn't wearing her glasses. "Is it something one of the kids did?" *Look up,* he silently begged. *Let me see your eyes.*

Again she shook her head.

He braced himself, asking the question he feared for her to answer. "Is it something *I* did?"

Her head shot around at that. "Oh, no! Please don't think that. It's just me."

He barely had time to register relief that he hadn't been to blame when he found himself facing the most beautiful pair of eyes he'd ever seen in his life.

Dear God, her glasses had been guarding precious jewels. He'd never seen such a pure, deep violet color before. Even swollen from crying, they were lovely, enchanting, mesmerizing.

Without her glasses, she seemed younger, softer, vulnerable. The temptation to stroke the tear trails from her cheeks and to kiss the distress from those sweet lips almost overwhelmed him. With a superhuman effort, he pulled his thoughts back to the question of her distress. "What do you mean, it's just you?"

She looked down again, and he mourned the lost view of her eyes. "I'm a failure as a homemaker."

That was the absolute last thing Caleb had expected to hear. "Nonsense. I think you're doing quite well."

She glanced up quickly, and he again felt the tingling effect of those devastatingly beautiful eyes. Her expression registered surprised gratitude before her face clouded and she lowered her eyes again. "That only speaks to how low your expectations really were. I can't even follow directions in a recipe book. I tried baking a cake, and not even Poppy would touch the results."

He smiled at the top of her head, feeling an unaccustomed tenderness. Who would have thought Lady Privilege would try so hard to fit in? "You're being too hard on yourself. Just give it time. Besides, you can't claim to have no skills at all. You've been keeping all of our clothes mended. No one can complain about your needlework skills."

The words he'd intended to bring her comfort instead drew a moan and a fresh flow of tears. He watched helplessly as she buried her face in the piece of cloth she held. "Elthia, sweetheart, whatever I said, I'm sorry. Please don't cry."

"I *am* a complete failure." She jerked her head up and pulled back. She held up the piece of cloth, stretching it between her hands and shaking it with a firm snap.

It was a man's shirt, but not one of his.

"Look," she demanded. "Just look at this. Is *this* the work of someone who can claim to have needlework skills?"

Confused by her vehemence, Caleb studied the shirt. She held it by the shoulders, and other than it being badly wrinkled, he could find nothing wrong. "I'm not sure I understand. Did you make it? If so, it seems perfectly all right—"

"All right?" The volume of her voice rose a notch. She grabbed one of the sleeves and shoved it closer to his face. "Does *this* look all right to you?"

He saw it then, the gaping cut in the fabric. But surely that wasn't such a tragedy. Why the flood of tears?

She pulled the shirt back and stared at it forlornly. "I don't even have enough fabric to make a new sleeve."

He gave her shoulder a little squeeze. "I assume you bought this cloth at the dry goods store when we were in town on Friday."

She nodded.

"Well then, next time we go to town we'll just get some more. Then you can fix it and no one will ever know the difference."

She shook her head. "That'll be too late."

"Too late for what?"

She looked up at him, and he could see the tears form again.

"I found out your birthday is tomorrow. The cake and this shirt were supposed to be my gifts to you."

A shaft of something akin to both pain and pleasure sliced through him. His birthday! No one had made a fuss over the event since his parents died. He'd ceased to even mark the day.

And she was upset because she'd spoiled his gift? The fact that she'd cared to do anything at all, that she'd put forth a real effort to do something so personal for him, was a far more precious gift than any material item. How could he make her see that, how could he change her tears back to smiles?

He took the shirt and held it up. He heard a soft gasp, and from the corner of his eyes saw her eyes widen as she glanced at his chest. Had she only just noticed it was bare?

Hiding a smile at her flattering display of attention, he continued to study the shirt. "You made this for me?" he asked. "Mind if I try it on?"

Her gaze shot back to his face. "It's ruined. Why bother?"

He shook his head at her with a smile, reluctantly sliding her from his lap as he stood. "Now, now, it's my gift. Let me be the judge of whether or not it's ruined."

She scrambled to her feet as he donned the shirt, wringing her hands and chewing on her lip. To his dismay, she retrieved her glasses and once again hid the violet beauty of her eyes.

"Well, now," he said, fastening the first few buttons, "it's a fine fit. How'd you manage that without taking measurements?"

She waved dismissively. "I just copied from one of your other shirts." She reached a hand out as if to stop him from going any further with the buttons, then dropped it again. "Please, you don't have to try to make me feel better."

"Look at this," he said, crossing his arms over his chest. "Don't think I own another shirt that fits so well. And see." He started rolling up his sleeves. "When I wear it like this, that little ol' slit don't matter at all."

His words only seemed to stoke the fire of her temper. "Stop it!" she demanded, her hands fisted at her sides. "I'm not a little girl to be soothed by a pat on the head. I won't stand here and listen to your condescending remarks." She spun on her heel and stalked away.

Surprise kept Caleb frozen for a moment; then he shot after her. The rain had quickened while they'd been otherwise occupied. She seemed oblivious to it, though. She'd already marched several paces outside when he caught up to her.

Grabbing her elbow, he spun her around. "What do you think you're doing? Come back to the barn before we both get soaked."

For a moment he thought she'd resist, but then she nodded and allowed him to lead her back into the barn. They stopped just inside the soft circle of light, and Caleb turned to face her, putting his hands on her shoulders.

They were both wet, and her clothes clung to her like a second skin. His body hardened at the sight of her, but he forced himself to keep his desire in check.

He held silent until she finally met his gaze. "I wasn't trying to be condescending. I truly do appreciate the gift."

The stubborn doubt remained in her stony expression. Caleb sighed. There was only one way to make her believe him.

He held her gaze prisoner while he exposed a piece of his past to her as matter-of-factly as he could. "I came to live with Aunt Cora when I was six. This is the first time, since that happened, that anyone has taken notice of my birthday."

Her expression softened immediately. "Oh, Caleb," she whispered, her hand reaching out to touch his chest.

The pressure of her hand burned through his wet shirt, as if they touched flesh to flesh. He nearly groaned at the image that thought conjured. "You see," he said, desperately trying to focus on *her* needs, "this shirt *is* special. It means someone cared enough to make me feel important, if only for a day."

She removed her hand from his chest, lifting it to stroke his cheek. "You are special. How could you think otherwise?"

Caleb lost his struggle to remain detached as tenderness and warmth washed over him. He captured her hand, moving it to his lips. Holding her gaze, he worshiped her palm with kisses, tasting greedily of her warm flesh. All thought of control, of contracts, of coolly planned schemes, evaporated. There was only this warm, giving woman and his desire to please her.

Her breath quickened as a delicate shiver shook her.

"Oooh!" Her drawn-out, breathy exclamation thrummed through him.

Caleb drew her into his arms, and she came willingly, lifting her face for the kiss he was all too eager to give her. As soon as their lips touched, the passion ignited. It was like the other kiss they'd shared, but hotter, greedier. The feel of her breasts rubbing against him through their wet clothing drove him crazy, made his fingers itch to caress them.

His hands glided up her sides until he touched the curve of her breasts. His thumbs began a gentle, circling massage as his lips nuzzled her ear, tasted the hollow of her throat.

Her hands were busy with their own explorations. He'd only fastened two buttons of his shirt, and now she slipped her hands inside, combing the hairs on his chest with her fingers.

Caleb groaned and moved his mouth back to hers. Almost of their own accord, his fingers began to loosen the buttons of her bodice. She was so sweet, so responsive, so damned desirable.

The wet fabric slowed him, but at last he reached her waist. His hands slipped inside, massaging the lusciously soft mounds with his palms. She wore a chemise, but the silky fabric was nearly as damp as her dress, and provided no barrier whatsoever.

She squirmed and arched her back. A moment later she was moaning into his mouth.

Unable to bear it any longer, Caleb leaned back and got his first glimpse of the treasures his hands already knew intimately. Her wet chemise clung to her like a lover's kiss. The rosy, pebbled peaks drew his mouth with the pull of a siren's song.

Lowering his head, he began to suckle, gently at first, then with increasing urgency. While his mouth and tongue laved the right breast, his hand paid homage to the left.

The breathless sounds coming from her deepened, grew frenzied. He felt her legs buckle, and without removing his lips from her rosy crest, he lifted her, carrying her to the pile of straw she'd watered with her tears earlier.

Impatient with even so flimsy an obstacle as her chemise, he drew down her dress until the bodice flared around her waist. Then he drew the undergarment over her head. Elthia raised no objections. In fact, she lifted her arms to assist him.

Could she want him half as much as he wanted her? The idea staggered him, stole the breath from his lungs.

Then he looked up and came face-to-face with her utter and complete trust in him. And that was his undoing.

He couldn't do it, couldn't take advantage of her innocence and awakening passion to trap her. She deserved better. She deserved to make this decision freely, not in the throes of untried passion.

He captured her hands between his, then leaned his forehead against hers, trying to steady his breathing.

"What's the matter?" Her voice projected uncertainty, doubt.

"Elthia, you're not thinking straight right now." Damn, she was so aroused and willing, and he was so ready he ached. Calling a halt now was the hardest thing he'd ever had to do.

Pulling a bit of straw from her hair, he let his gaze follow his hand rather than look at her kiss-swollen face. "You were upset earlier and then we kissed, and then . . . well, we got carried away. I don't think you realize where it was all leading."

She cupped his chin. "I know exactly where it was leading. And you don't have to worry about my regretting it later." Then she bit her lip as color heated her cheeks again. She had the stricken, vulnerable look of a child who'd just been told her kitten died. "Unless *you* don't want . . . Oh!" Scrambling up to her knees, she tried ineffectually to pull up her dress.

Caleb stilled her with a hand on her shoulder. How could she believe he didn't desire her? Tilting her chin, he forced her to look at him. "I want to, very much."

She searched his face, but he could see doubt in her eyes.

Didn't she know how desirable she was? He couldn't let her believe he'd rejected her. "Elthia, I do want you. But you don't have to take just my word for it." He took her hand, and before she could realize what he was about, he moved it down until she could feel the evidence of his arousal.

Her eyes widened behind her glasses. She stole a guilty glance downward, trying to pull her hand away. But he held her fast. "That's the power you have, sweetheart. The sight of you, the feel of you, the scent of you, combine to set my body on fire, to make me desire you as I've never desired another woman."

She raised her eyes again. The dawning confidence he saw there pleased him, made him feel as if he'd given her a gift. But it was still so fragile, could so easily be destroyed, he knew he had to choose his next words carefully.

He raised her hand and placed a gentle kiss on her knuckles. "If you're really ready, nothing would please me more than to show you the pleasure and passion a man and woman can share." She shivered as he stroked her face. "*Are* you really ready?"

"Oh, yes." Her breathy response was barely audible.

His lips drew up in a crooked smile. "I'm glad. Now, let's get rid of these." He removed her glasses and set them aside. "I want to see your eyes when I kiss you."

Elthia watched his eyes darken as he bent to deliver the promised kiss, and she shivered in anticipation. He wanted her! He truly wanted her! The surety of that knowledge overwhelmed her, infused her with joy and a budding sense of her own power.

Was it too much to hope that from the seeds of his desire, love could someday grow? That perhaps, with careful nurturing, it could blossom into something warm and wonderful and lasting?

As their lips met, her breasts rubbed against his shirt, and heat flared again. Impatiently, she slid her hands up to loosen his buttons. She wanted, *needed,* to feel his flesh against hers.

As soon as she'd finished, Caleb shrugged out of the shirt and pulled her full against him with a groan. Elthia's arms snaked around him, her hands beginning a thorough exploration of every inch of his back. Merciful heavens, but he felt so *good.*

When his mouth moved back to her breast she arched, giving him access to as much of her as he would take. Somehow, while he lavished her upper body with attention, he unfastened the buttons of her dress below her waist. In a swift, fluid motion, he lifted her hips and swept her dress and undergarments away from her. She lay bared to him, clad only in her stockings and shoes.

When he sat on his knees to look at her, she felt a shyness, an awkwardness that hadn't been there until now. It was shadowy here on the edge of the lamp's circle, but not fully dark.

Instinctively, she moved her arms to shield herself, but he stopped her. "Don't, please. Let me look at you."

Elthia paused, her movements stilled more by his look and tone than his words. Slowly she leaned back, trying to relax.

He ran a finger down her side in a movement that raised the gooseflesh on her arms and legs. "You are so very beautiful."

She made a sharp movement, halting his words. Why did he have to offer platitudes? "No, you don't have to—"

He put a finger to her lips. "I know I don't *have* to. But it happens to be true. You are a sweetly proportioned, seductively violet-eyed, spicily freckled bit of loveliness."

His words started a fluttering inside her, uncurling something warm and yearning from the depths of her soul. She reached for him, pulling him back to her.

He gave her another of those toe-curling kisses, then kissed the tip of her nose and eyed her sternly. "Stop distracting me, lady. I'm not through undressing you. And I *never* leave a job half done." With a wicked grin, he tugged her leg onto his lap.

First Caleb slipped her shoe off, then his hand slid up her leg. Reaching her garter, he tickled her leg with the ribbon, then untied it and slowly began to roll down her stocking. He followed its path with hot, lingering kisses. When he finished, he began the process all over again on the other leg. By the time he was through she was breathless and squirming and aching for something she couldn't quite name but knew he could give her.

His hands skimmed up her legs to her hips, then up her sides, until they paused at the swell of her breasts. "Now," he said, staring into her eyes with mock-seriousness, his thumbs tracing swirls on her skin. "Now, I'll let you distract me again."

He rained kisses on her—on her face, on her neck, on her chest. His hands were everywhere, stroking, massaging, tweaking. And she was equally frenzied, wanting to explore every inch of him, wanting to experience every sensation he could offer her.

Her hands encountered his waistband and, frustrated with part of him being hidden from her, she began to fumble with the buttons. As soon as she was done, Caleb slipped the last of his clothing off. Her palm slipped down his side to stroke his hip, reveling in the feel of its muscular smoothness.

Then Elthia's hand nudged the velvety-tipped evidence of his arousal and snapped back as if burned. Curiosity got the better of her, though, and she let her fingers inch back, measuring his length with feather-light touches.

Oh, my! The heat rose in her face; the fluttering in her stomach increased tempo.

Caleb's groan caught her by surprise, startling her into snatching her hand back once more.

"Not yet, sweetheart. Not unless you want this to end quickly." He captured her lips again as his fingers moved to the nest of curls at the junction of her thighs. When his hand moved lower she stiffened, squeezing her legs together.

"Relax, sweetheart. Trust me." His words, whispered into her mouth, were almost a plea.

Slowly she forced herself to do as he asked, and within seconds it was no longer forced. His fingers were doing marvelous, magical things to her. The waves of sensation flooding through her were unlike anything she'd ever felt before.

"Yes, yes." Caleb nuzzled her ear. "Let it sweep over you. You're so warm, so sweet. You're ready, aren't you, sweetheart?"

When he stopped, she cried out. There had to be more, had to be some kind of release from this screaming urge to find . . . find whatever it was he'd headed her toward. She would burst any minute now with the wanting of it.

Caleb answered her unspoken plea. "I know, I know. Just trust me a little longer." He settled himself between her thighs. Again his hand sent her on an upward spiral to the heavens, and again he paused before she'd reached her goal. But this time, before she could even groan, he replaced his hand with that part of him designed to give her the release she sought.

Slowly he eased in and out, stilling her when she tried to accept more of him. Finally, capturing her mouth with his, he drove deep into her, searing her with a burning pain that caused her to cry out.

"I'm sorry." He held himself perfectly still with an effort she could actually see. "I promise it'll be better in just a moment, and it won't ever hurt like that again."

And he was right. After a moment the pain eased, to be replaced by a rising urgency to try the wings of her passion, to complete this journey to the heavens. She moved against him. It was all the encouragement Caleb needed. He began to move within her again, slowly at first. But she was too impatient for that. She picked up the movements of this intimate dance from him and then increased its tempo.

Heaven help her, the pressure was building inside her to an unbelievable extent. She was surely going to shatter at any moment. And then—it happened.

Her whole body, starting at a point deep inside, spasmed, contracted in upon itself, and then exploded into a million burning, throbbing stars.

From somewhere far away, she heard Caleb's exultant yell as he joined her in repopulating the night sky.

Chapter Eighteen

Caleb smiled as a wisp of red hair tickled his chin. A horse nickered, and Elthia shifted, curling deeper into his embrace.

He tightened his arms around her, feeling fiercely possessive. He reveled in her closeness, in the way she snuggled against him like a contented kitten. They fit together perfectly, as if they had been made for each other.

He'd suspected she had a passionate nature, but even so he'd been surprised at the extent of it. The mixture of her sweet innocence, her awakening passion, her eagerness to both give and take, had brought him to heights he'd never scaled before.

Caleb wanted to shout from the barn roof. She might even now harbor the seed of his child, their child. The thought banked a sweet warmth in his chest.

The joy surging through him slowly gave way to a nagging sense of guilt. His seduction scheme hadn't entered his thoughts tonight, but the end result was the same. He'd taken the gift she'd given him and twisted it to his own purpose.

Squirming, he pushed that unwelcome thought aside. What they'd shared had been glorious, shattering, and mutually desired. He would do everything in his power to see that she was happy.

Everything short of loving her. He'd made that mistake once too often in his life. He wouldn't give his heart away and risk having it discarded again.

Something told him she wouldn't be happy with less.

The devil on his shoulder taunted him, niggled at him, wouldn't leave him be. *You poor fool,* it whispered, *now you'll never know if she would have chosen to stay on her own, would have chosen you over the life she left behind.*

Elthia stirred, roused from her drowsy contentment by the sudden absence of the arms that had cradled her, of the body that had shared its warmth with her.

Rolling over, she saw Caleb sitting with his back to her, reaching for his pants. Pulling a piece of straw from her hair, she eyed the muscled plane of his back, admiring his masculine grace. What they'd shared tonight had been wonderful, glorious, soul-stirring. And no small part of it had been the knowledge that she'd given as much pleasure as she'd received.

Unable to resist the temptation, she raised a hand and delicately traced his spine with her finger. His muscles contracted, and she reveled again in the firm, vital feel of him. Her body tingled in anticipation as she waited for him to turn and sweep her up in his arms again.

He looked over his shoulder with a smile. "The rain stopped. We'd better head for the house before it starts back up." He faced forward again, shaking at his pants and then pulling them on.

Elthia drew her hand back. Even without her glasses she could see there'd been no special warmth in his expression, no hint of remembered embraces. Instead, his smile had seemed forced, overbright.

Suddenly unwilling to have him turn again and see her naked, she grabbed her glasses and clothes and drew them on with frantic, fumbling fingers.

What had happened? She knew she wasn't the only one who'd experienced heart-melting passion. She could still hear the echo of his exultant yell as he found release, could still feel his fervent endearments tickle her neck.

As she forced the last button into place, he stood. Glancing up, she saw him lift the lamp from the hook by the entrance.

He met her gaze, that hatefully polite smile still in place. "Ready?"

Nodding, she picked up her shoes and stockings. She could walk to the house barefoot. He was obviously in a hurry.

They walked toward the house, side by side, mere inches of space and countless miles of vibrating silence separating them. He set the lantern down in the kitchen and turned to face her.

"Elthia." A world of emotion colored his whispered invoking of her name. So much so that she couldn't sort it all out.

"Yes?" Her lover was back for the moment. It was there in the curve of his lips, in the tender way he looked at her, in the touch of his hand as he removed a bit of straw from her hair.

Whatever he'd wanted to say, however, was left unsaid. She watched the polite stranger return to chase the words away. But it was too late. She knew now that he was still there, just overshadowed by his I-*will*-maintain-control twin. But why?

Had she fallen short as a lover? Was Baxter right, was her money the only thing she really had to offer a man—or in Caleb's case, her ability to care for his children? Dear God, how could the most glorious experience of her life have been so quickly followed by this low heart-tide?

"You go on up to bed." He planted a chaste kiss on her forehead. "I need to take care of a few things in my office."

Refusing to let him see how hurt she was by his dismissal, Elthia nodded and left him. Feeling his gaze follow her, she kept her head up until she'd closed the bedroom door behind her.

Caleb watched her climb the stairs, then jammed his hands in his pockets. Damn! He'd botched that good and proper. At this rate he'd be lucky to even keep her here the full three months.

What was wrong with him? She'd been warm and sweet and willing. If he'd used a little more finesse, he could have spent the whole night holding her, stroking her, making love to her. Just thinking about it was getting him hard all over again.

He stalked to his office, unlocked a cabinet next to his desk, and pulled out a bottle of whiskey. He wasn't much of a drinker, but there were times when a drink was definitely in order. And this was sure as hell one of them.

He gulped a swallow, grimacing as it burned its way down his throat. Setting the glass on the desk, he stared at it moodily, turning it in circles between his fingers.

Problem was, he not only wanted her to stay, he wanted her to *want* to stay. Not for the kids, not even because she might be pregnant, but for him.

So what if he couldn't offer love? They'd both been engaged before, so they both knew how fleeting an emotion that was. He could offer her something more stable; friendship and security.

With a frustrated growl, he took another drink, wondering if he could ever heal the hurt he'd caused Elthia.

Whack! Whack!

Elthia coughed as dust puffed out from the rug hanging on the line. Undeterred, she swung the beater again, landing another solid wallop. She was glad the rain had finally let up. The rug-beating chore was turning out to be very, very satisfying.

He wanted to pretend last night had never happened, did he? Well, let him. *Whack!*

He wanted to prove there were no tender emotions involved in their relationship. *Whack!* That he had no need for her outside the one the judge imposed. Then so be it. *Whack!*

She wasn't fooled a bit. She'd seen desire and, yes, *need* in his eyes. Mr. I-don't-need-anybody Tanner hadn't been controlled or aloof when he'd held her in the shadow-filled barn. And *that's* what he was having trouble facing. Well, too bad. *Whack!*

Did he think she'd be looking for declarations of love? That she'd turn into a clinging vine. *Whack!*

Well, she hoped his pride was sufficient company to warm him at night, because if he thought he could treat her so cavalierly and then expect her to climb into his bed again he could just—

"Whoa, now. Are you trying to beat that rug into a rag?"

Elthia halted in mid-swing, startled by Caleb's sudden appearance. She'd been so lost in her thoughts, she hadn't noticed him crossing the yard from his workshop.

Recovering, she tossed her head and completed her aborted swing. "Just making sure I do a good job," she said sweetly.

"Here, let me have that." He plucked the beater from her hand. "Your face is all flushed. You look like you could use a break."

She stepped back a few paces, watching him work. Despite still being *very* irritated with him, she couldn't help but admire the play of his muscles, the effortless strength of his swing.

His gaze slid to hers and then quickly away. "The birthday party was . . . well . . . anyway, I wanted to thank you for doing it."

Elthia thawed as he stumbled over the thank you. "You're welcome. But the children did most of the work."

He slid her another sideways glance. "But you put them up to it. And I saw your hand in the gifts they made. Thanks."

Elthia smiled, pleased by his praise. The party had been a success, marred only slightly by Peter's surliness. Caleb had made a big show of opening his presents and exclaiming over the contents. Each of the homemade items had found a place of honor in his office, workshop, or bedroom.

He was making it difficult for her to stay angry with him.

But they still needed to talk. "Caleb, I—"

Poppy bounded up from around the corner, his normally silky fur wet and muddy. No doubt he'd been exploring the mud puddles that decorated the yard after last night's rain. He made a beeline straight for Elthia with tail-wagging eagerness.

She stiffened and held out a warning hand. "No! Stay away. Keep those filthy paws away from me."

Caleb chuckled as Poppy blissfully ignored her admonitions.

"I said stop it, right now!" Having Caleb witness her lack of control over Poppy lent a sharpness to her voice.

But Poppy seemed to think her skirt-swishing was all part of some game. As she tried to side-step away from his eager advances, she slipped on the wet grass with a startled squeak.

Caleb shot forward, wrapping one arm around her while he held on to the rug beater with the other.

Elthia had a split second to react to the heat of his body, the heart-accelerating jolt of his embrace. Then her attention was diverted by the sight of a dearly familiar figure striding around the corner of the house, Keith and Kevin at his heels.

But her delight at seeing her brother turned to confusion. He was bearing down on the two of them with murderous purpose in his entire being. She'd never imagined he'd be this upset about her running away.

"What the devil!" Caleb took a protective stance, pushing her behind him. "State your business, mister."

Elthia tugged on her husband's arm. "Caleb, wait, it's—"

Caleb had half turned to face her when Ry's fist landed solidly on his jaw.

Caleb sat up, trying to clear the stars from his vision and the ringing from his ears.

His attacker reached down and grabbed a fistful of shirt, yanking him to his feet. The stranger's fist was cocked, ready to deliver another blow, but he was hampered by the twins beating on his back and Elthia's white-knuckled grip on his arm. Her insistent demands that Caleb's attacker "Stop it this instant" carried the same note of dogged determination as her earlier pleas with Poppy. And they were having just as much effect.

Worried that the madman would turn on her or the boys, Caleb took advantage of his opponent's distracted state with the same lack of conscience the oaf had displayed earlier. He slammed his fist into the belligerent stranger's jaw with enough force to send him reeling back. Unfortunately, the brute managed to stay on his feet. The twins sprang away with a victorious yell, and Caleb grabbed Elthia's arm, trying to force her behind him again as he braced himself for another attack.

She squirmed out of his grasp just as the stranger doubled his fists. "Get your filthy hands off my sister, you bastard."

Sister! Good Lord, this madman was Elthia's *brother*.

Elthia planted herself between them again. This time Caleb let her. "Ry, I will *not* let you call my husband vile names, and you're going to have to come through me to hit him again."

That halted Elthia's brother in his tracks, his expression of anger now shadowed by dismay. "Husband?" He put an arm around her. "Don't worry, Elly, we'll have it annulled." He shot Caleb a narrow-eyed look. "If I don't make you a widow first."

Caleb's stomach dropped. Elthia's brother was here to take her away from him! All noble thoughts of letting her decide herself whether to stay or go fled. It was too soon; the three months weren't up. He—no, the kids—needed her.

Would she want to leave with her brother? Hell, after the way he'd acted last night, why would she want to stay?

But Elthia pushed away from her brother and rapped her fist against his chest. "Ry, will you climb down off that charging stallion and listen? I don't need rescuing. Caleb didn't force me to marry him; I agreed to do it. I'm happy here."

Caleb's fists unclenched and his chest expanded at her avowal. Taking note of his surroundings again, he realized the backyard was now full of kids. He jerked his head toward the front yard. "All right, the excitement's over. You kids get on back to whatever you were doing and leave us grown-ups to talk."

With dragging feet and over-the-shoulder stares, they obeyed.

Elthia's brother glowered at Caleb as he gave her arm a squeeze. "Look, Elly, you don't have to pretend. If he's got some hold on you, if he's threatened you, or if . . ." Caleb saw his jaw clench tightly. "If he's taken advantage of you, I'll see that he's in no position to be a threat to you ever again."

Elthia reddened, and Caleb felt another stab of guilt. But she rallied quickly, rapping her brother's chest. "You're not listening. *I don't need rescuing.* You owe Caleb an apology."

Ry stiffened. "Apology! Elly, why are you defending this clod? Good Lord, he was attacking you when I arrived."

Apparently Elthia wasn't the only Sinclare who grew single-minded when you got 'em riled.

"Attacking me?" Elthia looked like she'd just been told it was going to snow today. "I don't know what you think you saw, but I slipped on the wet grass. Caleb tried to catch me."

Caleb almost felt sorry for the fellow. It must have looked ugly, with him holding Elthia with one hand and the rug beater with the other. Couldn't much blame him for the heated reaction. But Lord help Caleb if Elthia remembered she was mad at him too. He wasn't sure he could face down both of these Sinclares.

Caleb stuck out a hand, deciding the least he could do was try to smooth things over. "Seems we got off to a poor start. My name's Caleb Tanner. Welcome to our home."

Ry studied the extended hand for several heartbeats. A firm nudge from Elthia finally prompted him to take it. "Sorry if I read things wrong." He sounded as if he wasn't sure he had.

"Understandable." Caleb moved to Elthia's side and put an arm around her shoulders. "I'm just glad to see Elthia's family feels so protective of her. She never has been very clear on just what kind of story she gave you folks for her trip here."

"No need to go into that now," Elthia intervened. "We should get you two inside and see to your lips. You're bleeding like schoolyard bullies who just got a taste of their own medicine."

She linked elbows with them and moved to the house. "That was awfully sweet of you to charge to my rescue, Ry," she said, and Caleb hid a smile as he saw his new brother-in-law wince.

"I guess you heard all the fuss," she continued. "But I was just trying to keep Poppy from getting my skirts dirty."

"Poppy! What's that noisy lap toy got to do with this?"

Caleb's estimation of Ry rose considerably as he noted the contempt in his voice and wrinkled nose.

Elthia lifted her chin. "Really, to listen to you two go on, you'd think Poppy was a nuisance rather than part of the family."

Ry's gaze met Caleb's over Elthia's head. A flash of kinship passed between them without a word ever being uttered.

Maybe he wouldn't have both Sinclares on his back after all.

Elthia breathed a sigh of relief as they entered the kitchen. The tension had eased, and chances for another round of fireworks seemed remote now. But she needed time alone with Ry before he and Caleb became *too* friendly.

She grabbed a couple of cloths from the cabinet, wet them, and handed one to each wounded warrior. She looked at Caleb's lip first, making sure the cut wasn't too deep.

From the corner of her eye, she saw the way Ry watched

them, though she couldn't tell what he was thinking. How in the world would she ever be able to explain it all to him?

"Need any help?" she asked.

Ry waved her aside. "It's nothing but a little cut. I can take care of it."

She smiled and reached over to give his hand a squeeze. "In case I haven't said so yet, it's good to see you."

Ry started to return her smile, then stopped and grabbed her wrist. Gently he turned her hand, palm up, and studied it. He met first her gaze and then Caleb's. "Calluses, Elly?"

Earlier they'd had a taste of the fiery side of Ry. It was rare that he ever let go of his control in such an explosive manner. This steely, dangerous tone was a tool he employed more readily and with great effect when he had a battle to fight.

Dear Lord, how could she keep him from saying something that would clue Caleb in to the extent of the Sinclare family fortune? This wasn't how she wanted Caleb to find out, especially while there was still this unfinished business between them.

She sensed Caleb move behind her. Before he could say anything, she spoke up. "Yes, calluses. I'm part of this family, and I've been earning my keep."

Ry's gaze speared her. "And just how have you done that?"

She snatched her hand back and glared at her brother. "Not very well, I'm sorry to say. I lend a hand with the cooking and cleaning and whatever else I can, but just about every one of the children is better at it than I am."

Caleb stepped up and put an arm around her. "Elthia's doing just fine. She's getting better at the household chores every day, and I doubt there's anyone better at taking care of kids."

Ry raised his brow again. "I see."

Elthia saw the thoughtful gleam in her brother's eye and decided the time for their private chat had come.

She turned to face Caleb, reluctantly stepping away from the protection of his arm. "Your clothes are all wet and dirty from your fall. Why don't you run upstairs and change? Ry and I can do a bit of catching up while we wait for you."

Caleb frowned, and Elthia thought for a moment he'd refuse to go. But at last he nodded. "All right." Then, as he moved to the door, he caught Ry's gaze. "I won't be but a few minutes."

The words had the ring of a warning to them.

Ry answered with a you-don't-worry-me smile.

Elthia picked up the cloths and moved to the sink. She could feel her brother's eyes boring into her back. "What happened to your plans?" she asked, breaking the silence. "I thought you were supposed to be in New York for another week."

"I was," he answered, gently but firmly turning her to face him. "Then I got a telegram from a friend telling me my sister had disappeared and her reputation was being shredded." He shrugged, still watching her with that see-through-to-your-soul look. "I thought it best I come home and sort it all out."

"Oh, Ry, I'm so sorry." Elthia accepted another brick of guilt into her already full wagon. "I didn't mean to interfere with your new project. I know how important it is to you."

He shrugged again. "No real harm done. The work'll wait. No project is more important than making sure you're okay."

"If you're trying to make me cry, you're doing a fine job of it." She heard Caleb descend the stairs. "Ry, listen, this is important to me. Caleb has no idea how wealthy our family is. And I want it to stay that way for now. Please."

There was no time for her brother to answer before Caleb stepped back into the room.

"Well," Ry said, "now that your husband's back, let's all sit down and have a little chat, shall we?"

Chapter Nineteen

Caleb planted himself on the sofa next to Elthia, offering Ry a seat across from them. He held her hand in a manner designed to let her brother know he'd have to fight to take her from him.

Elthia's brother leaned back, looking for all the world as if he was merely making a social call. "Let's start at the beginning, shall we? Elly, you can begin with why and how you come to be here. And don't try to tell me you were intending to marry this man all along. You left me a note, remember?"

Caleb felt Elthia fidget beside him. Glancing at her, he was surprised by her guilty-schoolgirl expression.

"It's partly your fault." She sent Ry a mulish look. "You said Father would never abandon the idea of finding me a husband unless I proved I had a bit of backbone and independence."

Caleb frowned. What was this about finding her a husband?

Elthia's brother tilted his head. "*I* said that?"

She nodded primly. "It's what you implied."

"And you took that to mean you should travel hundreds of miles alone, without a word to anyone about where you'd gone."

Caleb sat up straighter. She'd done *what?*

Elthia shifted. "Not exactly. I mean, I hadn't intended to

travel so far, but when I looked at the positions Mrs. Pembroke had open, this was the only one that fit. And I had to do something right away, while you and Father were out of town."

She lifted her chin. "And I wasn't supposed to be alone. Mrs. Pembroke said there'd be another girl traveling with me. But she had to pull out at the last minute."

Caleb was stunned. "Hold it. Are you saying that you really *did* run away? *No one* knew where you'd gone off to?" His blood ran cold, thinking what could have happened to her.

Elthia shot him an I-thought-you-were-on-my-side look. "Mrs. Pembroke knew where I was going. And I left a note for Ry. He just wasn't supposed to find it for another few weeks." She shot an accusatory glance at her brother, as if this was his fault.

Ry, however, seemed unmoved. "And just how long after you arrived did you discover this wasn't a teaching job after all?"

Elthia stared at her lap. "The evening of the first day."

Ry's gaze shifted to Caleb with steely purpose. "And just what happened then?"

Caleb felt a noose tighten about his neck. "If you truly *did* think this was a teaching job, how do you explain the contract?"

Elthia looked up, her expression hurt. "I *told* you that's what I came for. And I still can't explain about the contract."

"What contract?" Ry asked, reclaiming their attention.

"The placement contract I signed," Elthia explained. "I read it carefully, Ry, and I swear it was for a governess post. But when I got here, both our copies had become marriage contracts." She wrinkled her nose. "It's as if it was done by magic."

Ry shook his head. "Not magic, Elly, sleight of hand. How many copies of the contract did you sign?"

"Four."

"And did you read all four of them?"

"Why, no. Mrs. Pembroke remembered the other copies at the last minute, and there were so many other things to do, I just—"

Caleb's groan brought her up short. She looked from Caleb to Ry, then back again. "You mean she tricked me? But why?"

Ry's jaw tightened. "I can shed light on that part of the story. Louella Pembroke has nursed a grudge against the Sinclares for longer than you and I've been around. Seems she had aspirations of marrying Father. She went so far as to try to force his hand by setting up a compromising situation. Unluckily for her, her plan only served to make her look foolish."

Ry pointed to her with a fond smile. "You look a lot like Mother, you know. When you asked her for help with this scheme of yours, she must have seen it as a way to get her revenge on Father."

Elthia frowned. "But I still don't understand. How did she think tricking me this way would get back at Father?"

Ry's face hardened. "She tricked you into signing a marriage contract, then sent you alone to the back of beyond, where there was no one who would protect you. Learning you'd been put in such a situation would have been enough to break Father's heart."

He leaned forward. "But she didn't stop there. Once you left town, she began spreading rumors, hinting you'd run off to marry a stranger because you were carrying Baxter's child."

Caleb surged to his feet. How dare anyone spread vicious gossip about his wife! "She said *what!* By God, woman or no, if I ever lay my hands on this low-down, scheming, backbiting—"

"It's not true." Elthia's whisper halted his ranting.

The white-faced, wounded look on her face dug the spurs into all his protective urges. "Of course, it's not!" he responded gruffly, dropping back down beside her and taking her hand.

Her smile of gratitude made him feel ten feet tall.

"Of course not," Ry agreed. Caleb caught his glance and wasn't fooled by the bland expression. Elthia's brother was a keenly observant man. Refusing to be intimidated, Caleb reached a hand around her, resting it possessively on her shoulder.

Ry flashed Caleb a smile reminiscent of a hungry wolf's before turning to Elthia. "Back to my question. What happened when you discovered why you were *really* here?"

Elthia shifted, casting Caleb a quick, uneasy glance. He wasn't feeling any too comfortable with that question himself.

"Well," she began, "of course I was shocked and confused, especially when I pulled out the contract and it wasn't what I remembered. And Caleb was as surprised by the mix-up as I was."

"I'm sure he was."

Caleb suppressed a wince at Ry's words. Damn! How could a man make such an agreeable sentence sound so menacing. The look he shot Caleb was pointed enough to draw blood.

Ry turned back to Elthia, and Caleb twisted his neck slightly to release some of the tension in his muscles.

"And then what?"

"Well, then, we discussed options. Caleb explained he needed a wife so he could adopt his orphaned nieces and nephews."

Her face lit up. "You must meet them, Ry, two girls and four boys. The responsibility is a bit overwhelming, but they're so wonderful. I won't pretend they think of me as a mother, but I'm their aunt, and I think they're starting to accept me as part of the family. Can you imagine me raising a houseful of children?"

Her brother's smile warmed. There was no doubt he cared a great deal for his sister. "Yes, I believe I can."

Then, as if giving up on getting a straight answer from Elthia, Ry turned to Caleb. "So you two just talked it over and decided to go ahead with the wedding, is that it?"

Caleb met his gaze without flinching. "Pretty much."

"And of course you didn't coerce my sister? You *did* give her the choice to leave if she wanted to?"

Before Caleb could answer, Elthia leaned forward. "Oh, for goodness sake, Ry, I told you I agreed to this, didn't I? Do you think I wanted to run back home and let you and Father know I'd failed at this too?"

Caleb stiffened. Was their marriage just some tool for her to use to beat her father at his own game?

Although she addressed her brother, Elthia turned to Caleb, her expression seeking understanding. "At least the Tanners want *me*. Who my family is or what my faults are were neither enticements nor handicaps. They actually *needed* me. Right then, freckles, lapdog and all, I was their only hope."

She turned back to her brother. "That's why I agreed to do it. And nothing that's happened since has made me regret it."

Caleb wasn't sure how he felt at that moment. There was

relief that she'd entered into this bargain willingly, hope that she might actually *want* to stay, and a jab of disappointment that her reasons were so unrelated to him personally.

And now, a new puzzle, What sort of family were the Sinclares that she'd think men would seek her hand just to be linked to them?

Caleb decided he'd had enough. "Well, now, it looks like we've got all that settled." He raised a brow toward Elthia's brother. "Unless you have any more questions for us?"

Ry responded with an ambivalent smile. "Not right now." Then he turned to Elthia. "Why don't you introduce me to the children? I met a few of them when I arrived, but I was in too big a hurry to . . ." His lips quirked in a half smile. "To discover the source of your distress to wait for introductions."

Elthia nodded and stood. She linked her arm through her brother's. "I hope you plan to stay for a nice, long visit. You and Caleb got off to a poor start, but I just know if you spent a little time together you'd learn to really like each other."

Seeing the like-hell expression flash across Ry's face, Caleb doubted it very much.

The next morning Elthia sat on the porch swing, helping Zoe shell butter beans. Her efforts were not as practiced as Zoe's, but she was proud of the fact that she no longer had to concentrate quite so hard on getting it just right.

Caleb had headed for his workshop after breakfast, but Ry lounged on the steps nearby, no doubt keeping an eye on her.

It worried her that she and Caleb still hadn't settled matters. Much as she longed to confront her husband to find out what his true feelings about her were, she was also just the tiniest bit afraid of what he'd say.

Besides, she wouldn't do anything while Ry was around. He was uncomfortably perceptive, not to mention very big-brother protective. If he suspected things weren't as they should be, or learned of the unconventional bargain she'd made, he might try to haul her back home, whether she wanted to go or not.

And she definitely wasn't ready to leave Texas yet. After she and Caleb talked . . . well, she'd just have to see.

As she worked, she watched her brother interact comfortably with the six youngsters who were all trying to get to know their newly discovered Uncle Ry better. Not for the first time, she thought what a shame it was Ry'd never found a woman to marry. He'd make such a wonderful father. As good a father as Caleb.

A buggy turning up the drive caught everyone's attention. Elthia shaded her eyes, trying to identify the visitor. Catching sight of a bright yellow shawl, she set her bowl aside with a smile. "Peter, please let your uncle know Granny's here."

Ry caught her gaze with a raised eyebrow. "Granny?"

"Oh, she's not a relative," Elthia answered as they stepped off the porch. "Everyone just calls her that." She flashed him a grin. "I can't wait 'til she meets you."

They'd reached the buggy, so Ry didn't have time to question her further. Instead he turned to help Granny climb down.

"Thankee, son," Granny said as he steadied her. Then she flashed him what Elthia could only describe as a coy smile. "My, but ain't you a handsome one."

It seemed her brother had made another conquest. "Granny, I'd like you to meet my brother, Ryland Sinclare. Ry, this is Miss Odella Mae Picket, a neighbor and friend."

Ry bowed. "It's a pleasure to meet you, Miss Picket."

To Elthia's surprise, the older woman didn't ask Ry to call her Granny. Instead, she rapped his arm playfully. "Such a fine gentleman." She offered him her elbow. "If you'd be so kind as to help me to the porch, I'd like to sit and visit a spell."

"Of course." Ry tucked Granny's arm in his with a smile and escorted her across the yard as if they were in a grand ballroom.

After he seated her on the swing, Granny patted the spot beside her. "Sit yourself down so we can have us a little chat."

"It would be my honor, ma'am."

Elthia sat in the rocking chair, smiling as her brother stretched his arm along the back of the swing. He complimented Granny on her colorful shawl, and the woman actually preened.

"Hello, Granny." Caleb stepped onto the porch. "You're looking in fine fettle this morning."

Granny turned her smile from Ry to Caleb. "There you are," she said, thumping her cane on the porch as if she'd been looking for him since she'd arrived. "I'm spreading the word.

There's a barn raising at Billy Hagar's starting day after tomorrow."

Caleb leaned against a support post. "So, he finally got his land cleared and all his supplies in."

Granny nodded. "Yep. Everything's ready."

Elthia looked from Caleb to Granny. "What's a barn raising?"

Granny stared at her as if she'd asked what color the sky was. "Don't they have barn raisings where you come from?"

When Elthia shook her head, Granny turned to Ry as if for confirmation. Ry merely shrugged, his disarming smile admitting that he didn't know any more than Elthia did about the subject.

"Well, land sakes." Granny shook her head. "Don't folks back East believe in helping each other out?"

Elthia spread her hands. "Well, of course, but—"

"I see." Granny patted Ry's knee for good measure. "You folks just have different customs. Well, a barn raising is just what it sounds like. A man gets ready to build a new barn, and his neighbors pitch in. That way you get the thing built in just a few days." She pointed her cane at Caleb. "Your man is always sought after for these things. He's right handy with a hammer."

Elthia smiled. "So I've noticed."

Granny rested her hands on top of her stick and stared imperiously at Caleb. "So, can Billy count on you to be there?"

Caleb nodded. "Tell him I'll bring my own tools."

Foxberry's matriarch turned to Elthia. "What about you?"

"Me?" Elthia straightened. "I'd like to help, of course, but I don't really think I'd be much use building a barn."

Granny cackled. "Don't be silly, child. We leave the hammering to the menfolk. Us ladies help in other ways. We prepare meals, carry around the water bucket, doctor cuts and scrapes, and anything else to make the workers' jobs easier."

"Well, if you think I could be of some help . . ." Elthia glanced uncertainly toward Caleb.

But Granny spoke up before he could. "That's settled then." She turned to Ry. "What about you? With those broad shoulders of yours, I'll bet you're right handy with a hammer yourself."

Ry shook his head. "Sorry, ma'am. I just came here to check

222

on Elly. There's pressing business I left waiting for me in New York. I'm afraid I'll be starting back tomorrow."

Granny sighed. "Now that's a sure 'nuff shame." She turned to Caleb as she opened the strings to her handbag. "This letter came for you. Hiram asked me to deliver it when I came by."

"Thanks." After a quick glance at the envelope, he nodded and stuck it in his pocket. "It's from Annie, my sister."

Elthia wondered if Caleb and his sister were as close as she and Ry were. This was the second letter he'd gotten from Annie since she'd arrived in Texas, so they obviously kept in touch.

It would be interesting to meet his siblings, her in-laws, someday. Then, remembering the unsettled issues between them, she wondered if she'd be here long enough to have that chance.

Caleb waited until he was alone to open the letter. He imagined his sisters were eager to hear how the marriage was working out. Unfolding the single sheet, he propped his elbows on the scarred worktable and began to read.

Dear Caleb,

We've found the solution! Aunt Dorothy's mother died last week. I know it sounds unfeeling to rejoice, but the dear woman had suffered for so long, even Aunt Dorothy acknowledges it was a blessing for her to go on to her reward. Anyway, that leaves Aunt Dorothy alone. She's looking forward to filling her house with the children. I know she's getting on in years, but she's healthy and spry, and Cousin Jeremy lives close by with his family if she should need help occasionally.

I know you're likely already married, and Liz and I feel awful about the sacrifice you had to make. Surely there's some way you can get out of it, have it annulled or something. I bet Judge Walters would help, since he knows the circumstances. Then you can go back to your life the way it was before.

Let us know what we can do to help you work everything out.

Love,
Annie

Well, this was certainly an unexpected turn of events. Funny, he wasn't the least bit tempted. It wasn't just because of Elthia, he told himself. Even without her, he would fight to keep the kids. He was part of a real family again, by God, and he aimed to keep it that way. The thought of returning to his former footloose lifestyle held no appeal for him at all.

He'd write Annie right this minute and tell her that, much as he appreciated her efforts and concern, it was time she accepted that he was going to see this through his way.

Though he'd never admit it to Elthia, Caleb was quite ready to see Ry leave the next day. It had been a *very* long two days.

Having Elthia's big brother watch him with looks that alternated between I-can-see-through-your-walls perception, what-are-you-not-telling-me suspicion, and that's-my-sister-you're-touching glares made it hard for him to relax.

Though Elthia's hopeful prediction that the men would become friends hadn't quite panned out, Caleb had formed a grudging respect for his brother-in-law. After all, they did share a common bond in their concern for Elthia's well-being.

After Ry had gathered his things together, he asked for Caleb's help getting his horse saddled. Ry's friendly tone didn't lull Caleb into thinking he was only looking for the pleasure of his company. Having Elthia's lip-chewing gaze follow them out of the house only reinforced the feeling.

Caleb watched Ry lead his horse from the paddock into the barn. Then he leaned against one of the stalls as Elthia's brother threw the saddle on the animal's back.

After all, they both knew Ry didn't really need any help.

Tightening the cinch, Ry cut Caleb a sideways look. "Thanks for the hospitality of these past few days, Tanner. Especially after the rather . . . extreme way I introduced myself."

Caleb shrugged. "Can't really fault you for looking out for your sister. And Elthia's family is always welcome in our home."

Ry moved to the other side of his horse. "Elly's changed in a lot of little ways since she left home. I'm not sure I approve of all of them."

Caleb refused to be intimidated. Besides, Ry's veiled reference reminded him of the questions he had about the Sinclare family. He'd asked Elthia about it again last night, but again she'd managed to avoid answering him. Maybe her brother would be more forthcoming.

"Tell me," he asked, "what sort of life did Elthia lead before she came here?"

"Didn't she tell you?"

Caleb shrugged. "I know the Sinclares are well-off. And I know she never had to do a lick of housework 'til she came here. What I don't know is just how rich that family of yours is."

Ry turned his attention back to his saddle. "And would that knowledge change the situation any?"

Why the devil couldn't he get a straight answer for once? What were they hiding? "Well, I reckon that all depends on what the answer turns out to be," he drawled.

Ry gave him a considering look, then patted his horse. "I'd better let Elly answer any questions you have about our family." He smiled. "Maybe she knows what she's doing after all."

It wasn't an answer, but at least it had a friendly ring.

Before Caleb could return the smile, though, Ry's eyes narrowed with deadly intent. "But I give you fair warning: If you do anything to make her unhappy, if you so much as bring a lump to her throat, I'll be back. And next time I won't stop with one punch."

Chapter Twenty

Elthia paced across the parlor, straightening bric-a-brac as she went. It was time she and Caleb had a talk about what had occurred that night in the barn, and his aloofness afterwards.

So why was she hiding in here?

Because she was a coward, that's why. Caleb had gone into Foxberry shortly after Ry'd left, but he was back now. She should just seek him out, confront him with her concerns, and find out what he was thinking, what he was feeling.

Had that night made a difference to him at all? Or was she still no more than someone to help with the children? Someone to satisfy a condition of the adoption? Someone he would take to his bed simply because random fate had saddled him with her?

Elthia tossed back her head. It was past time they talked.

She tracked him down in his workshop. He was working on a cradle, and the sight pierced her with longing. How she'd love to see him bend over their own baby there. Could he possibly want a child of his own when he had six in his care already?

Her hand moved to her stomach. Was it possible that even now a new life grew there? Would he welcome the child if it did?

Caleb finally spied her. "Come on in." His smile was wary, as if he wasn't quite sure what to expect from her.

Elthia moved next to the cradle, across from him. "I thought maybe this would be a good time for the two of us to talk."

"About what?"

Rather than answer his question, she ran a finger along the headboard of the cradle. "This is beautiful work."

"Thanks." His stiffness disappeared, if it had been there at all. "Sam Powell asked me to make it. From the looks of his wife last Sunday, they'll be needing it soon."

Elthia felt a sharp stab of jealousy for the Powells. "What about you?" she asked before she could stop herself. "Do you plan to have children of your own someday?"

He gave her a long, thoughtful look before turning back to his work. "I have a house full of young'uns now." His tone was thoughtful. "Don't you think I should be content with that?"

Was he being deliberately evasive? "I didn't ask you what *I* thought. I asked what *you* want."

Caleb's hand caressed the wood as he polished the headboard. "I suppose every man wants to see part of himself live on in a new generation," he mused, "wants to hold a new life in his hand, knowing he played a part in bringing that life into the world."

Then he gave her a sideways look. "What about you? You content looking after other people's kids, or do you have a hankering to have some of your own one day?"

She turned toward his worktable. Taking time to choose her words, she arranged his brushes, then fingered an awl, studying it intently. "I've always dreamed of having a houseful."

"You have that here."

Elthia's frustration rose. They might as well be talking of the weather for all the emotion he revealed. She turned, leaning against the worktable. "And I love each one of them as if they were my own. But that doesn't mean there isn't room for more."

"True." He looked up, and her gaze was trapped by the fire in his. "You do realize you could already be carrying my child?"

She felt her cheeks warm again as she nodded. Her hand fluttered toward her stomach, but she caught herself in mid-gesture this time, and gripped the edge of the table.

His gaze probed deeper. "Would you be sorry?"

"No!" The word exploded from her, and she pushed away from the table, clasping her hands in front of her.

"Even though it would erase any chance you might have of obtaining an annulment?" he pressed.

Elthia crossed to a rocking horse in the far corner. She felt Caleb's gaze bore into her as she set the wooden steed in motion. "I believe our case for an annulment *has* been erased, regardless. I'm staying." There; she'd said it.

As the silence drew out, her hands clenched on the rocking horse. Why didn't he say anything? Dear God, please—

She jumped at the touch of his hands on her shoulders. How had he moved so quietly? His breath stirred her hair, sending shivers coursing through her. She ached to have him hold her more intimately, to hear him speak of passion, of commitment.

"I'm sorry if you have regrets," he whispered huskily. "But I can't find it in myself to apologize for what passed between us, especially if it means you'll stay."

"I don't have regrets, Caleb, and I never wanted an apology." She turned, ready to confront him as she'd planned earlier. But the fire in his eyes burned her words away. His hands caressed her arms, and the yearning she'd bottled up inside began to expand, seeping its way through her. *Please, kiss me till my toes curl.*

He traced the line of her jaw with an index finger, keeping his gaze focused on his finger. "*No* regrets? Not even for that fine life in your daddy's home you'd be leaving behind?"

"Of course not." *Not if I believed you could truly love me.*

His touch made it difficult to concentrate on his words.

He removed her glasses, and her surroundings receded into a soft blur. But she had no trouble seeing his face clearly.

"Such beautiful eyes," he said, reaching up to brush some hair from her brow. "Hidden treasures of rare beauty."

She placed her hands on his chest. The thought that there was something they needed to discuss, some unfinished business between them, niggled at her. But she couldn't quite remember what at the moment—and right now it just didn't seem to matter. If he didn't kiss her soon, she'd likely die from the yearning. Her tongue darted out to lick her suddenly dry lips.

The motion drew Caleb's gaze. His eyes darkened to a rich coffee color. With a throaty, hungry sound, he lowered his head and captured her lips, giving her the kiss she'd yearned for. His hands cupped her bottom. Her fingers tangled in his hair.

He tasted her neck, starting below her ear and blazing a sensuous trail of kisses to the pulse point at the base of her throat. Elthia squirmed against him, pressing closer, trying to ease the insistent tingling in her body by contact with his. His hand snaked between them, moving to the buttons on her bodice.

Yes, oh yes. Eager to feel his flesh on hers, Elthia reached for the buttons of his shirt.

". . . 'thia. Aunt 'thia."

Why was Caleb calling her *aunt?*

Caleb's hands stilled and his head lifted away from hers.

"Aunt 'thia, where are you?"

Merciful heavens, it was Josie! What had they been thinking? It was the middle of the day, for goodness sake, and they were in the workshop. Elthia frantically rebuttoned her bodice. How could they have lost all sense of propriety this way?

Caleb handed her her glasses with a crooked smile and tapped the end of her nose regretfully. "We'll finish this later," he whispered, giving her a look that curled her toes as effectively as one of his kisses. By the time Josie stuck her head in the doorway, he was back at his workbench.

"Uncle Caleb," Josie asked, "have you seen—" She halted as Elthia stepped forward. "Oh, there you are."

Elthia smiled at the girl, studiously avoiding Caleb's gaze. "What's the matter? Do you need my help with something?"

Josie nodded vigorously. "It's Poppy. He got his head stuck in a jar. Keith and Kevin want to bust the jar open, but I told them they better wait till we asked you what to do."

"Oh, no." Elthia's heart lurched as she turned to Caleb.

He stood at once. "Where's the little beast?" he asked. At the same time he placed a comforting hand on Elthia's shoulder.

"Alex has him right now." She turned to Elthia. "Don't you

worry none. Alex won't let them do anything to hurt your puppy."

Elthia smiled for the girl's benefit as she hurried toward the house, Caleb right at her side.

They found Alex sitting on the steps, gently soothing a feebly struggling Poppy. The other children stood around, making sympathetic noises or offering advice. Keith held a hammer.

Elthia sat beside Alex, and he transferred the whimpering ball of fur from his lap to hers. She stroked her pitifully limp pet, frightened by his unnatural lethargy. She felt so helpless.

Caleb took Alex's seat, and she turned to him, trying to keep her voice steady. "We've got to help him before he suffocates."

"Let me have him." Caleb took Poppy from her. "And he's not going to suffocate." He inserted his pinky between the dog's neck and the jar rim. "See, there's lots of room for air to get in. We just need to keep him calm 'til we get this thing off."

She pushed her glasses up. "So you *can* get it off?"

He nodded confidently. "Sure. If his head can go in, it can come out." Then he turned. "Zoe, fetch me a spoonful of lard. Keith, put the hammer away. You're making Aunt Elthia nervous."

For once, Elthia was grateful for his take-charge attitude. His calm assurance that this was nothing more than a minor irritation comforted her as nothing else would have.

While they waited for Zoe, Caleb turned his attention to the remaining children. "Who wants to explain how this happened?"

"It was Keith and Kevin's fault," Josie volunteered.

"It was not!" Kevin denied, rounding on his little sister. "And you're just an old tattle baby."

"Am not!"

"Are too!"

"That's enough!" Caleb intervened. "Now, Kevin, why don't you explain what happened."

Kevin scuffed a toe in the dirt, avoiding both Caleb's and Elthia's gazes. "Well, there was a dab of jelly left in the jar, and Zoe told me and Keith we could finish it off. She run us out of the kitchen so she could sweep. So we came out here."

"And?" Caleb's tone demanded a prompt reply.

"We shared it with Poppy. And he liked it, a lot. We were gonna pick up the jar, honest, but Josie found a big ol' toad frog she wanted to show us. When we came back, Poppy had his head in, licking the bottom." Kevin turned to his sister. "So it was really Josie's fault."

"Was not!"

"Was—"

"I said enough of that."

Elthia noted again how well Caleb balanced discipline and fairness with the children. He was a good father, so comfortable in that role. How comfortable was he in the role of husband?

Caleb turned as Zoe rushed up. "Just right." He quickly applied liberal amounts of the lard to the jar and Poppy's neck and head.

With a firm, gentle tug, the dog finally came free. "Here." He plopped Poppy on Elthia's lap. "Take your sticky mutt. I'm going to clean up, and I'd suggest you do the same with him, if you don't want a bigger, smellier mess on your hands later."

Elthia let Poppy lick her chin, enjoying his tail-wagging revival. She smiled up at Caleb. "Thank you. It was wonderful of you to rescue Poppy, especially knowing how you feel about him."

Caleb flashed her that crooked smile and stood a bit taller. Then he shrugged and waved off her thanks. "Just see if you can keep that mud-colored pooch out of mischief for a while."

Elthia nodded meekly as she stood, but there was a smile on her lips. Lately, Caleb seemed to have a harder time mustering much conviction in his complaints against Poppy. Did she dare hope that was in part due to his feelings for her?

A few minutes later they stood in the bathhouse, Caleb washing his lard-coated hands and Elthia bathing a now frisky Poppy.

Caleb grimaced as he dried his hands. "Seems the biggest part of that pint-sized terror is his voice. Hope you get him clean before you go deaf."

Elthia grinned. "Not going to let this 'pint-sized terror' run you off, are you?"

Caleb only rolled his eyes and continued out the door.

She lathered and rinsed Poppy three times before she decided he was clean enough. As she dried her pet, she thought of all the different sides of Caleb she'd seen today.

Wary but determined as he left the house with Ry, sensuously tender as he kissed her, caring as he dealt with Poppy and the children, sidestepping her thanks once the crisis was resolved, and playfully teasing a few minutes ago as he left the bathhouse.

He was the kind of man who would keep a woman on her toes, who would never be boring, and who would draw out the best in the people in his life. And he wanted *her*.

True, he'd had little choice in the beginning. But lately she'd begun to see signs that he wasn't unhappy with that choice.

She hadn't gotten an answer yet as to what had bothered him that night in the barn, but she wasn't as worried about it now. He'd likely felt some misguided guilt, no doubt believing he'd taken advantage of her. Hopefully, she'd made it clear today that he had nothing to feel guilty about.

She hummed a light tune. Here, in this rustic community, she'd finally found her place. A place in life that offered her something more than a role as the clumsy little bluestocking, accepted by her circle only because she was a Sinclare heiress. *Here* she was a wife and a mother figure, accepted and valued for what she brought to the family as an individual.

It was a heady feeling.

Then she sobered. He wanted her, but he didn't love her. Was it selfish of her to want it all?

Maybe she should start by showing him how truly committed she was to staying. She'd hand over the contract, the one detailing their intent to annul the marriage. Such a gesture would no doubt erase any lingering doubts he might have.

Climbing the stairs, she smiled, imagining the look on Caleb's face when she handed it to him. Of course, being Caleb, he'd pretend it wasn't anything significant. But there'd be that warmth in his gaze that would tell her his true feelings.

Or so she hoped.

Elthia opened the lid of her trunk. She lifted out the blankets and pillows, smoothing the bed linens absently. Would she be sleeping in her alcove tonight, or was it time to join her husband on that wickedly large bed across the room?

Just the thought of the sensuous pleasures they could share

there set her face flaming and her skin tingling. Should she wait for an invitation or dare she invite herself? What reaction would she get if he found her there waiting for him tonight?

Elthia shivered pleasurably, then turned back to dig through her trunk. Where was it? It should be right under her books.

Elthia took everything out of the trunk, one item at a time. She opened every book, fanning the pages to see if it had somehow found its way between the covers. Then she methodically sorted through the whole pile again, holding her panic at bay. Surely it was here; she'd just overlooked it, was all.

Finally she stared at the bottom of the empty trunk, feeling the same emptiness creep into her soul.

It wasn't here. And Caleb was the only other person who even knew the document existed.

When had he taken it? Had he waited until after they were safely wed? Did he worry she couldn't be trusted not to use it against him, or had he never planned to let her get an annulment?

She wasn't the kind of woman men fell in love with.

How could she have forgotten that hard-learned lesson so quickly? What a self-deceiving fool she'd been, seeing softer emotions where none existed.

Her dreams of someday claiming Caleb's love crumbled like a sand castle at full tide. This betrayal was a hundred times more painful than the one Baxter had dealt her. That had merely been a blow to her pride; this one sliced open her heart.

Elthia sat on her heels, jabbing her glasses up, trying to push back the hurt at the same time.

A rush of anger came to her rescue. He had no right to go through her things and steal what he'd agreed to leave in her keeping. As far as she was concerned, everything had changed.

This time she wouldn't take the coward's way out, as she'd done with Baxter. This time she would confront the Judas, face him with her knowledge of his betrayal.

A part of her hoped he'd show remorse, would protest that his feelings had changed and ask her forgiveness. But she ruthlessly squelched that thought, telling herself it was just such optimism that led to the kind of heartache she was feeling right now.

Caleb sat in his office, the invoices he'd planned to review lying ignored on his desk.

She wanted to stay. It's what he'd hoped for since he'd stopped her from running away that morning in the barn.

He didn't need to feel guilty any more. She'd made it plain she didn't regret the loss of her virginity. In fact, she seemed happy and eager to make their marriage permanent.

Everything seemed to be working out perfectly.

He still suspected she was hiding something about her background from him. When he'd mailed off that letter to Annie today, he'd also sent a telegram to a friend who knew how to make discreet inquiries into this sort of thing.

But he no longer cared what secrets were uncovered. What did her past life matter, so long as she was happy in this one?

His thoughts drifted to their exchange in his workshop this afternoon. Dear God, she was so sweet and warm and *right* in his arms. If they hadn't been interrupted, there was no telling how far their passions would have taken them.

Later, on the porch, when she'd looked at him with gratitude and admiration, he'd felt like a storybook hero. Right then he would have tackled any problem, braved any danger for her.

A movement near the door caught his eye. Elthia stood in the doorway, watching him. He sprang to his feet as he took in her strained expression.

"What is it?" He moved toward her. "Is something wrong with one of the kids?" Then Caleb halted as he noticed her subtle stiffening and withdrawal from him. What was going on here?

"Where is it?" Her voice and expression were strained.

"Where's what?"

"Our annulment agreement."

Why had she been looking for that thing? And so what if it was lost? She'd said she wanted to stay. He tried to make sense of it as he watched her fists turn white-knuckled at her sides.

"It's not in my trunk." Her control cracked, but she took a deep breath and started again. "Did you take it because you didn't trust me not to use it against you, or did you have no intention of living up to it from the very beginning?"

Surely she didn't mean that? "Whoa there. Are you saying you think I *stole* that hangman's noose you had me sign?"

Her expression wavered for a second; then she squared her shoulders again. "Do you want me to believe you didn't? That contract didn't move by itself, and no one else knew it existed."

Dammit, she was calling him a thief and a liar. He'd been a fool to think she'd be different, would stand by him no matter what. He fought the pain of her accusation with anger. "Listen Miss High-and-mighty, you can just believe whatever you want. But I don't steal and I don't lie."

He marched to his desk, grabbed a pen, and scratched words out for several minutes. Once done, he snatched up the paper and pinned her with a glare. "This ought to give you something to hold over my head again. I just hope it keeps you warm at night. And see if you can keep a firmer hold on it this time."

He left the room without a backwards glance. A few seconds later, Elthia heard the back door open and then slam shut. Slowly she focused on the piece of paper he'd thrust at her.

I, Caleb Tanner, swear by all that I hold dear that I will release Elthia Sinclare Tanner from all obligations of marriage to me just as soon as I can do so without endangering my chances to adopt my six nieces and nephews.

His signature, scrawled across the bottom in large angry letters, mutely admonished her.

Chapter Twenty-one

Elthia rolled on her side and punched the pillow a couple of times, trying to fluff it into a more comfortable arrangement. Never had the chaise seemed so confining and uncomfortable. There was no question now of her joining Caleb in the big bed across the room.

If he ever came up to lie in it.

Where was he? He'd insisted everyone go to bed early, reminding them that they'd be leaving at sunup for the barn raising tomorrow. But he himself had stayed downstairs.

What was he doing? Whittling in the moonlight again? Or was he planning to sleep in the parlor tonight?

The way he'd avoided her all afternoon, and the icy politeness he'd treated her with in front of the children, had made it clear that the last thing he wanted was to be alone with her.

What was she supposed to make of the contract he'd scratched out? She could still see the look on his face, the intense anger that had to be a mask for something else. Was it guilt, or the hurt of an innocent man whose honor had been questioned?

Had she been wrong? Had she let Baxter's duplicity color her judgment? Caleb wasn't Baxter, wasn't even close to the same.

But who else would have a reason to take it? It had to have been Caleb.

Elthia had no opportunity to speak to Caleb alone the next morning. Though he chatted easily enough with the children during the thirty-minute ride to the Hagars' place, he had not a word, not a smile, not even a glance to spare for her. Elthia devoutly hoped none of the children noticed the tension simmering between the adults.

To her surprise, they weren't the first arrivals. Granny was there, as was Mrs. Johnston and her husband.

Caleb quickly strapped on his worn carpenter's belt, grabbed his tool box, and set to work. Elthia wasn't given time to brood, though. Granny introduced her to Sally Hagar, the farmer's shy young wife, then put her to work.

Within a half hour, another fifteen men had arrived, four with families. Peter and two older boys joined the men at work.

Elthia started off helping cook but at Granny's suggestion turned to keeping the younger children entertained and out of the men's way. That kept her outdoors, which was fine with her.

Though Caleb was by no means the oldest or brawniest of the workers, it soon became obvious to Elthia that the others deferred to him in dozens of subtle ways. Granny hadn't exaggerated when she said his skill was highly respected. Elthia felt a quiet sense of pride for him warm her from the inside out.

Then she remembered the breach between them, and her spirits fell again.

Elthia took a turn at passing the water bucket and ladle among the workers. All of them greeted her with a smile and a word of thanks—all except Caleb. Not that he was rude. He did thank her, but there was no warmth in his tone and ice in his gaze. It was as if he was the injured party, not her.

The men broke from their efforts when the sun reached its peak. They ate the lunch the women had prepared, then relaxed for another hour, sitting out the hottest part of the day.

Caleb sat apart from the others, lounging with his back against a tree and his hat pulled over his eyes. Whether he just rested or actually slept, it was evident he didn't want company.

Once they started back to work, the men kept at it until near dusk. Elthia was amazed by how much they'd accomplished in just one day. The walls were nearly finished and the roof was framed.

After a quick supper and promises from some, including Caleb, to return tomorrow, everyone began gathering tools and children.

Somehow, in the midst of all the activity, Elthia found herself alone with Granny for a few minutes.

"That man of yours is one hard worker," the older lady observed, waving a hand in Caleb's direction.

Elthia nodded, taking pride in the accomplishments of "her man." "Yes, ma'am, that he is."

"I reckon you done a good day's work yourself here, gal."

Elthia's face warmed at the praise. "Why, thank you, Granny."

Granny's cane thumped the ground resoundingly. "So why are you two walking around with chins low enough to bump your knees?"

This time Elthia's face warmed for an entirely different reason. Had they been so obvious? "Why, I don't—"

Granny raised a hand imperiously. "Tell me to mind my own business if you want, but don't go telling me there's nothing wrong. I may be old, but I ain't blind. Both of you look like grounded birds, wounded and missing the heights."

Elthia managed a weak smile. "Mind your own business, Granny," she said softly.

Their gazes held for an endless moment; then Granny shook her head. "I said you could tell me to mind my own business right enough, but I never said I'd listen." She patted Elthia's arm. "All married couples have problems from time to time. The best way to work through them is to always listen to your heart. And never, ever, let your pride get between you and your mate."

Elthia nodded, swallowing past the lump that had suddenly formed in her throat. "I'll keep that in mind."

Granny patted her arm. "It'll work out, don't you worry none. You two have something worth fightin' for."

"You coming?"

Elthia turned to see Caleb standing a few feet away, Josie's hand in his. The picture they made symbolized love, family, trust, acceptance—everything she desired for herself.

Her chest constricting painfully, she nodded and followed them to the buckboard. As Caleb handed her up, she tried a let's-call-a-truce smile. "Thank you," she said.

But he merely nodded and turned to lift Josie up.

The ride home passed quietly. Josie nodded off, her head cradled in Elthia's lap. Caleb and Peter were visibly tired. The rest of them, when they spoke at all, did so in whispers.

When they pulled into the yard, Caleb sent Peter to the bathhouse while he and Alex unhitched the wagon. Elthia carried Josie inside, then helped with the evening chores.

She couldn't take it anymore. She and Caleb had to talk, had to work through the feelings of betrayal. Being physically near, yet emotionally distant, hurt too much.

After putting the children to bed, Elthia turned to the master bedroom. Her hopes of working things out tonight, though, were dashed when she stepped inside. Caleb was already asleep.

She climbed into her sterile bed and listened to his even breathing across the room. Granny had said to listen to her heart. Despite the fact that logic dictated that only Caleb had the knowledge or motive to take that contract, her heart insisted he would never have done something so underhanded.

Suddenly, her doubts disappeared. He hadn't taken it. It was as simple as that. Tomorrow she would apologize.

But would that be enough to set things right?

Elthia woke to the sound of someone calling her name.

"Aunt 'thia," Josie repeated, a whiny, hoarse quality to her usually soft voice.

Elthia sat up as she noted the unhealthy flush coloring the little girl's face. "What is it, darling?"

Josie climbed up on Elthia's lap. "I don't feel so good."

A quick check of the child's forehead confirmed that Josie had a fever, albeit a mild one. "I tell you what," Elthia said, using her I've-got-a-treat-for-you voice. "Why don't you lay in my bed while I get dressed? Then I'll fix you up a nice spot in the parlor and get you something to drink."

Josie nodded, but she watched Elthia dress with troubled eyes. Finally she blurted, "Are y'all gonna leave me by myself when you go back to the barn raisin'?"

Elthia hugged the child. "Of course not, sweetie. I'm going to stay right here with you, all day." Elthia reached down to pick her up, and Josie trustingly lifted her arms, wrapping them around Elthia's neck.

After Elthia made Josie comfortable on the sofa, she hurried to the kitchen, where she met Caleb coming in from the barn with two large pails of milk in hand.

He raised an eyebrow. "You're up extra early this morning."

"Josie's sick."

He set the pails down, his expression immediately registering concern. It made his indifference toward her all the more evident. "What is it? Not a relapse of the measles, I hope?"

She almost reached out a hand to reassure him, but the fear of rebuff held her back. "No; at least I don't think so. She's just feeling out of sorts and is running a slight fever. I don't think it's serious, but she should probably stay in bed today."

Caleb nodded. "There's no need for any of you to come today anyway. With luck, we'll finish right after lunch. Whatever's left, Billy can easily finish on his own."

He moved toward the hall. "Is she still in her room?"

Elthia tried to gather her courage. She had to face him with her apology this morning, before he left. "No, she's in the parlor. I promised her a glass of something cold to drink."

She entered the parlor a few minutes later to find Josie seated on Caleb's lap.

"And here's Aunt Elthia with your water," he said, kissing the top of his niece's head. He settled her back down and stood. "I'll check on you when I get back this afternoon. Now, you rest up and do just what Aunt Elthia says so you can get all better."

At least he still trusted her with the children.

Josie smiled and nodded. Caleb gave her head one last tousle, then turned to Elthia, the warmth in his smile cooling immediately. Lord, but she did miss his smiles. Even irritation or anger would be preferable to this cold, emotionless regard.

Elthia handed Josie the glass and followed Caleb into the hall. She took a deep breath and touched his arm. "If you have a minute, I'd like to speak with you before you leave." She smiled, hoping to see some softening in return.

But Caleb's expression didn't change. He glanced at her hand on his arm as if she'd presumed an intimacy she hadn't earned.

Elthia drew her hand back, feeling the heat rise in her cheeks. Would she ever be able to get past this wall he'd erected? The one she'd helped him fortify?

"Is there some kind of emergency, some problem with the kids I need to know about?"

"No, but—"

"Well then, sorry, but I want to get going while it's still early." He shrugged. "It'll have to wait 'til I get back."

Elthia nodded mutely and watched him leave. Somehow, she had to make him listen. But even then, would he forgive her?

By the time Caleb returned, Elthia had armed herself with a steely resolve. He *was* going to listen to her apology, if she had to tie him to one of his rocking horses to make him do it.

After that, if he still insisted on treating her as if she was to be merely tolerated, then she would have to decide whether or not she still wanted to stay beyond the original three-month agreement. Already this morning, one dream, one she'd barely been aware she'd harbored, had proved a mere illusion.

She confronted him while he was still unhitching the wagon.

He spared her a brief glance. "How's Josie feeling?"

"She's all better now," she said with a smile. "It's amazing how quickly these things come and go in children her age." She paused. "Can I help you with that?"

Caleb didn't bother to look up. "No thanks."

She crossed her arms over her chest, hugging herself the way she wanted him to hug her. "We need to talk."

He tipped his hat back, meeting her gaze. "I've noticed you seem to be right fond of that phrase. And it usually means you have a bone to pick with me." He released the horses. "Now, I'm tired, I'm busy, and I need a bath. What do you say we save this little talk for later?" Without giving her a chance to

241

respond, he turned and led the horses toward the water trough.

Elthia had a very unladylike urge to fling a rock at him. How dare he walk away from her again! She might have wronged him, but by George, he still owed her a chance to apologize.

Well, she'd had enough of his snubs. She'd make very sure he couldn't turn his back and walk away from her next time.

Elthia stood outside the bathhouse. The only sounds coming from inside were soft sloshing noises. He was in the tub, then.

As she reached for the knob, Elthia's courage ebbed. Then she rallied. This was all his fault. He'd forced her to pick a time and place where he couldn't walk away from her.

This time he *would* hear her out.

She grabbed the knob and shoved open the door.

"Whoever it is, go away," he called from behind the screen. "And shut the door; you're letting a draft in."

Elthia carefully closed the door behind her. "That better?"

The sloshing and splashing halted. "Elthia? What the devil are you doing in here? I'm in the middle of my bath, woman."

He was clearly irritated by the intrusion, but then, she hadn't expected to be welcomed with open arms. At least she had succeeded in eliciting some kind of emotion. "I know."

The watery noises resumed. Elthia pictured him rubbing a sudsy cloth across his broad, bare chest. She swallowed hard and almost missed his next words.

"Well, whatever you need, take care of it quickly, please."

Inhaling deeply, she forced herself to cross the room. The loud tapping of her heels on the tiled floor marked her progress. By the time she'd crossed halfway, his movements ceased again.

"Hey now, what are you up to?"

It took every bit of courage Elthia had to take the final step past the screen. "I told you, we need to talk."

A quick, sweeping look gave her a view of wet, bare muscles that heated her cheeks and set her pulse racing. He drew his knees up, whether in deference to her sensibilities or his own, she wasn't sure. She locked her gaze with his, refusing to expand her view to anything lower than the tip of his jutted chin.

"Of all the mule-headed, single-minded females." His glare

could have blistered ice. "I said we'd talk later. Right now I'm trying to take a bath."

She crossed her arms. "And I've decided that now *is* later."

His eyes narrowed. "*You* decided?" With a defiant look, he leaned back against the side of the opulent marble tub and stretched his legs out to their full length. "All right, talk."

Elthia stoically kept her gaze locked with his. "First, I want to apologize for accusing you of stealing. I was wrong."

Caleb's temper rose. So, Lady Privilege had found that misbegotten scrap, had she? Probably tucked away in a book or an unnoticed corner of her trunk. Was her apology supposed to make everything okay again? Well, the hell it would. It didn't pay to trust people. Why did he have to keep relearning that lesson?

"Next time," he said, adding a cold edge to his tone, "make sure you look a bit harder before you accuse people of stealing."

Elthia shook her head, and he was cynically amused to see that she rigidly focused on his chin. "No, that isn't . . . I didn't find the contract."

He sat up straighter. What game was she playing now? "You mean you discovered someone else took it?"

She shook her head again. "You don't understand. I mean, I guess someone else must have, but I haven't discovered who."

"Then why the devil did you just apologize?"

"Because I know you didn't do it." She raised a hand, her expression almost pleading. "I just know."

He wasn't ready to trust her yet. "How touching. You just suddenly decided I wasn't a thief and liar after all."

"I deserve that. I should have believed you from the outset, should never have considered the possibility that you would act dishonorably. And I guess I would have if I'd concentrated more on what I know of you and less on my own flaws and insecurities."

Despite his resolve to hold on to his anger, Caleb was intrigued by the vulnerable determination of her expression. "I think you're gonna have to explain that last bit to me, darlin'," he drawled, trying to make light of his interest.

Her arms crossed over her chest again, but this time it

seemed more a defensive gesture. Her expression closed; then she sighed, gave a short nod, and dropped her hands. "You've asked about my life in Terrelmore. Well, besides the fact that we're rather well-to-do, my father is an important, very influential man. That means the Sinclares are prominent in the community."

She paced, tracing a design on the screen one minute, fussily straightening towels the next. Caleb resisted the urge to prompt her. Whatever she had to say, she would say it in her own time.

"With my bookish tendencies and lack of interest in social affairs, I'm an oddity among my peers," she continued. "I've had my share of suitors, but it was always plain it was a tie to the Sinclares they courted, not me. Until I met Baxter."

Caleb felt a stirring of jealousy at the mention of her former fiancé. Had she loved the man? And why should he care?

"I met Baxter at a library, of all places. I had picked up a book on astronomy. Far from thinking it odd for a lady to be reading about such a subject, he seemed interested in my opinions."

Her wistful look fed his jealousy.

She moved a bar of soap from one shelf to the next. "We met at the library twice more before he learned who my father was. But rather than increase his interest, it seemed to put him off."

Her gaze met his again. "I'd never met a man who was interested in me rather than my family connections before."

Caleb wished he was close enough to remove her glasses. He needed to see her eyes.

She turned away with a shrug. "Two months later we were engaged. I was flattered that such a handsome, intelligent gentleman would want *me*. I even convinced myself I loved him."

Caleb's jealousy eased. She'd been flattered, not in love. He rested his elbows on the edge of the tub near where she paced.

"Then, two weeks before the wedding, I committed a grave sin. I eavesdropped on Baxter and two of his friends. I hoped to hear him say something nice about me. Such vanity!"

He caught a glimpse of her expression before she ducked her head again, and knew this next would be difficult for her.

"They were discussing his successful wooing of the 'funny

little heiress.' He explained how my dowry and expectations made up for all my unladylike qualities." Her expression twisted. "And even if I turned out to be the cold fish he suspected, it wasn't like he couldn't seek his pleasures elsewhere."

It said something for her distress that she didn't hear him climb out of the tub.

She gave a brittle laugh. "I was too much of a coward, too concerned for the scrap of pride that I still clung to, to let anyone know I'd overheard that conversation."

Caleb grabbed a towel, knotting it around his waist the way he'd like to knot it around the neck of that son-of-a-bitch Baxter.

She was still talking, making fluttering movements with her hands. "Instead, I simply told him I'd changed my mind, that I'd decided married life was not for me."

Caleb slipped his arms around her.

After an initial start, Elthia relaxed. She placed her hands on his and leaned back. "I'm sorry I doubted you. You're not like Baxter. Even when we disagreed, you were always honest."

As he nuzzled her neck, his conscience jabbed at him. That wasn't entirely true. "Baxter is a fool. His loss is my gain."

She turned to face him, staying within the circle of his arms. "Does this mean you forgive me?"

She looked so vulnerable, so worried. Did his forgiveness mean so much? He removed her glasses and set them aside. "Does this answer your question?" He kissed her fiercely, hungrily. He wanted to leave no doubt just how much he desired her.

By the time they separated, she was breathless and flushed. She blinked up at him with a bemused smile. "Oh."

Then she took in the state of his undress, and a fetching flush flooded her cheeks. "Oh," she repeated, her gaze flying back up to his chin. She cleared her throat. "I suppose I should let you get back to your bath."

"Excellent idea." His hands caressed the sides of her breasts. "Care to join me? There's plenty of room, and I could use some help with my back." His body was already responding to the thought of having her wet and naked in that tub with him.

Her cheeks were flaming now. "I can't."

Caleb frowned. "Can't? If you're afraid one of the children will walk in on us, I can lock—"

"No, it's not that."

Was she shocked by his suggestion? Did she need the cover of darkness to let loose her inhibitions? He could be patient.

He placed a finger under her chin. "If you just don't want to, say so." His body screamed for release, but he wouldn't force something on her that she wasn't comfortable with.

She shook her head. "No, it's not that."

Then what? He stiffened. Had he read too much into her confession? Did she feel some lingering distrust after all?

Elthia reached for her glasses. "It has to do with the other thing I need to tell you." She finally faced him again. "I discovered this morning that I'm not carrying a child."

A keen sense of disappointment sliced through Caleb. He felt a sudden urgency to see her ripen with his child, to see her cradling his baby in her arms.

Then he realized the other implication of what she'd said. Damn! She'd begun her monthly cycle. Of all the inconvenient—

The sight of her lip-chewing dismay brought him back to his senses. He kissed the tip of her nose. "Then we'll just have to save that little treat for another time."

"You're not upset?"

"Upset you're not with child?" He flashed his best attempt at a leer. "All I can say to that is, we'll just have to keep trying 'til we get it right. Upset you won't be joining me in the bath? Disappointed is a better word."

He pulled her to him for another resounding kiss, then swatted her on her bottom. "Now go on so I can finish my bath." *Go, before I lose what little control I have left.*

"But don't you want to heat up some more water? What's in the tub is bound to have grown cold by now."

Caleb turned her toward the door with a crooked smile. "Believe me, the temperature will be just right."

That night, Elthia had just stepped behind the screen to prepare for bed when she heard the bedroom door open. She knew before he said a word that it was Caleb and not one of the children. "You're ready for bed early tonight," she called as she stepped out of her dress.

"You could say that."

The smile in his voice imbued the words with meaning that heated her cheeks. The sound of him undressing set her stomach fluttering. If only she hadn't started her cycle this morning—would he have invited her to share his bed?

She slipped the satiny shift over her head and heard the creek of his mattress. She imagined him slipping naked beneath the covers. Perhaps, in a few more days, she could join him—

"Elthia."

She stilled. "Yes?"

"Are *you* ready for bed yet?"

Something in his tone set her flesh to tingling. "Uh-huh."

"Then how about a good-night kiss?"

A good-night kiss? Her heart raced at the thought. Something to warm her before she slipped into her lonely bed, something to sweeten her dreams.

"I'd like that." She stepped from behind the screen.

Caleb sat up, his back propped by a pillow. The covers were drawn to his waist, leaving him splendidly bare above. But it was his heated, anticipatory expression that held her attention. His gaze slowly devoured her, taking in every inch of her, from head to toe. She felt as if her gown was transparent, nonexistent.

At last his gaze met hers again and she relaxed, reading approval and something more in his expression. "Well," he said, his smile taking on a hint of challenge, "what are you waiting for? Haven't changed your mind, have you?"

Tossing her head, she returned his smile. Giving his bare torso the same heated perusal he'd given her, she sashayed across the room. "Not at all. Just taking a minute to enjoy the view."

When she reached the side of the bed, she lifted her face for the promised kiss. Instead, he plucked the glasses from her nose and set them aside. Turning back, he stroked her cheek. "There now," he whispered huskily. "Much better."

The kiss he gave her lasted only a few seconds, before he leaned back with a frown. "This isn't working."

Had she done something wrong? "What is it?"

He shifted and patted the space beside him. "You'll have to climb up here so I can hold you proper. In fact, I believe I'm going to insist you start spending all your nights up here."

Elthia hesitated, torn between the desire to do as he asked and the knowledge that tonight was not the night for them to give way to their passions. Had he forgotten her condition?

His expression softened, and he reached for her hand. "Don't worry, sweetheart. Heaven knows the way you look standing there right now, you could tempt a saint. But trust me. I won't do any more than kiss and hold you tonight."

Biting back a sob of joy, Elthia realized that he had really and truly forgiven her. Shedding her inhibitions, she scrambled up into Caleb's enormous bed and flung herself into his arms.

Settling into his embrace, she felt a stirring of hope that perhaps, someday, she'd win his love as well.

Chapter Twenty-two

Elthia awoke slowly the next morning, relishing memories of the night before.

After that wonderfully hot, frustratingly short kiss, he'd wrapped an arm around her and drawn her head to his chest. She'd fallen asleep to the lullaby of his heartbeat. And when she'd awakened during the night, she'd still been wrapped in his arms.

But not any longer.

Elthia came fully awake as she realized she was alone in bed. She sat up and spied Caleb across the room, buttoning his shirt. Remembering his moodiness after that other special night, she shivered and hugged her knees. Was this something she'd have to look forward to after every intimate interlude?

But when he looked up, the smile on his face was warm and intimate. "Good morning, sleepyhead. Miss me already?"

She pushed away her gloomy thoughts and made a face at him. "It's not even light outside yet. Why are you up so early?"

He shook his head in mock despair. "Haven't made a morning person out of you yet, have I?" Crossing the room, he kissed her forehead. "Go back to sleep. The kids won't be up for a while yet. I'm just trying to get a head start on my chores. The barn raising put me a little behind."

She propped her chin on her knees. "Caleb?"

"Hmmm." He picked up his boot and sat back on the bed.

"I've been thinking." She ignored his eye-rolling groan. "Now that we're agreed you didn't take the contract, we have a puzzle on our hands."

He shoved his left foot into a boot, giving her a sideways glance. "You mean, what actually happened to it?"

She nodded. "Exactly."

He pulled on his other boot, then turned to face her. "You're absolutely certain you didn't just misplace the blasted thing?"

"Absolutely."

He rubbed his chin thoughtfully, then snapped his fingers. "I'll bet your mutt got hold of the thing and carried it off."

She rapped his shoulder. "He did not! Poppy might be capable of such a thing," she conceded, "but there's no way he could have gotten to it. It was in the bottom of my trunk."

He shrugged. "Well, it's bound to show up. And there'll be a perfectly innocent explanation for how it got misplaced."

Why wouldn't he take her concerns seriously? Was it because he still believed she'd just been careless? Or was it because he didn't want to share his thoughts, his own worries with her?

Caleb caressed her cheek with the back of a hand. "Stop worrying. I can't imagine one of the kids digging through your things, and no one else had access or reason." He crossed the room to pick up his hat. "I plan to deliver the Powells' cradle today. If you need anything from town, just make me a list."

Elthia watched him leave, not at all reassured by his words. But he was right, worrying wouldn't do her a bit of good. She threw off the covers. Maybe she'd try her hand at getting breakfast ready on her own this morning.

That challenge seemed a less frustrating pursuit than dwelling on the workings of Caleb's mind.

Breakfast was a mixed success, much like her marriage. The eggs and potatoes were cooked to everyone's satisfaction. The bacon, however, was overdone, and the biscuits were too heavy. But she received compliments for her efforts, and there were very few scraps left over. Maybe there was hope for her yet.

Elthia left the kitchen chores to the girls. She had a pile of mending to see to. When she entered the parlor, though, the clutter left over from Josie's bout as a patient caught her eye.

Humming softly, she gathered up the books and set them back on the shelves. Then she picked up the picture Josie had painted of a dog sniffing at a ladybug. Smiling, she put it aside to show Caleb, then collected the art supplies and headed upstairs.

As she lifted the lid of her trunk to put the paints away, she remembered something that set her back on her heels.

She'd sent Peter up here, just before Caleb's birthday, to fetch this same box of paints. It was right after that that he'd resumed his surly attitude. If Peter had found the contract, it would explain a lot.

Poor Peter. Reading that contract must have been a shock. He'd already believed Caleb didn't want him, and now he'd learned she apparently only planned to stay for a short while.

No wonder he was walking around with a chip on his shoulder.

How could they undo this? How could they make Peter believe they did love and want him and his brothers and sisters?

She would discuss it with Caleb. Perhaps between them they could figure out the best course of action.

Caleb watched his nephew fidget uncomfortably. He obviously knew that there was something serious afoot.

Caleb and Elthia had decided the workshop would afford them the most privacy. Peter sat on one side of the workbench, Caleb on the other. Elthia perched on a low stool at the end of the bench, within an arm's reach of either of them.

Earlier, they had agreed she would speak first, so now she cleared her throat. "Peter, do you remember when Poppy got hold of one of the birthday banners we made for your uncle?"

Peter's wariness increased. "Yes, ma'am."

"I sent you upstairs to get the art supplies from my trunk while I cleaned up the mess. Remember?"

Peter nodded.

"Did you happen to see a piece of paper while you were in

my trunk, a contract of sorts between your Uncle Caleb and myself?"

Peter's nostrils flared, and he struck an angry, defensive pose. "What are you accusing me of? Stealing?"

Caleb leaned forward, trying to divert the boy's choler. "No one's accusing you, son. Aunt Elthia just asked a question."

"I ain't your son!"

Caleb winced at the anger in those telling words. It was a slap-in-the-face rejection. Did Peter actually hate him?

Peter scraped his chair back, facing Caleb with red-faced contempt. "Yes, I saw it. It was stuck to the paint box, and I had to pry it off. I took it, too, if that's what this is all about. What does it matter anyway? It only proves that she doesn't want us any more than you do."

A soft protest escaped Elthia. "Oh, Peter, that's not true."

The boy's hands fisted at his sides. "You lied. You told me you married Uncle Caleb willingly, that you two worked everything out." His lips curled. "You worked everything out, all right. You're just planning to stay around long enough to make the judge think we have a real family here, then you're gonna leave us."

Caleb watched Elthia flinch. She reached for Peter's hand. The boy didn't relax, but at least he didn't push her away.

"No, I won't," she said firmly. "I love all of you too much to bear even the thought of leaving."

When Peter remained stubbornly silent, she pushed on. "I made your uncle sign that piece of paper because I was angry that he seemed to be having things all his way. And because I was afraid I couldn't measure up to life here. It was cowardly, but I wanted a way to leave on my terms if it came to that."

Caleb admired her honesty with the boy, especially when she did it at the expense of her own dignity.

"That's all changed now," Elthia continued. "I think it changed the minute I said my wedding vows. I *want* to stay, to be a part of this family. I don't want that contract back. If you haven't already destroyed it, you can tear it up. I'm staying."

Caleb never tired of hearing those words. Maybe someday he could truly believe them.

Peter shrugged. "It doesn't matter. Uncle Caleb doesn't really want us either."

Caleb straightened. It was his turn. "There has never been a doubt of my wanting to have you and the others with me."

"I heard you!" Peter, his eyes blazing, shook off Elthia's hand. "You were arguing with Aunt Liz and Aunt Annie, telling them they weren't being fair, that you couldn't do it." His chin jutted out. "You gonna deny it?"

Caleb could see the boy's hurt through his anger. How would he ever straighten out the mess he'd made of things?

"No, I don't deny it. But there were reasons why I said what I did, reasons that had nothing to do with how I felt about you kids. But those reasons don't matter anymore. I really want to see us build a family here."

Peter remained unmoved. "What were the reasons?"

Caleb raked a hand through his hair. Peter was just too young to deal with such sordidness. "I can't tell you."

"I don't believe you! You're lying about wanting us. Well, I'm the oldest member of *my* family, and that gives me the right to decide what's best for us. And I don't think you're it."

"Peter!" Elthia's exclamation echoed in the ensuing silence.

Peter jerked away from her outstretched hand. "If you're done with me, I promised Zoe I'd help water the garden." He turned and exited the workshop without waiting for a response.

Familiar feelings of inadequacy clawed Caleb. "He hates me."

Elthia rested a hand on his shoulder. "No, he doesn't. He's just hurt and confused. Give him time; he'll come around."

Caleb stared at the empty doorway. "I hope you're right." But he wasn't so sure.

Elthia circled around to face him. "Caleb?"

"Yes?" When she didn't respond, he lifted his gaze to hers.

She quit worrying her lip. "Are you sure you couldn't share your reasons with Peter? I mean, no matter how bad, usually the truth is easier to deal with than the things we imagine."

Caleb pulled her down beside him. "Peter didn't quite get it right. I was arguing with my sisters because they wanted to take in all the kids between them except Josie. Josie was to be sent seventy miles away to our Aunt Dorothy. I dug in my heels and told 'em I wouldn't let Josie be sent off alone."

His jaw tightened. Just thinking about his sweetpea being made to feel like a cast-off raised his hackles.

Not to mention the dark memories it revived.

Elthia's brow furrowed. "But Josie is such a sweet child."

Caleb tried to explain. "It's not that they don't *want* her. They just felt she'd be better off somewhere else." How best to say this? "I mentioned once that Josie isn't really a sister to the other five."

Elthia nodded. "I remember. But she is your other brother's child. She'd be just as much your sisters' niece as Zoe."

"Yes, but there's something you don't know, and neither does Peter." He paused. How would a woman raised as she'd been view this? Would she still see Josie in the same light? "Josie's parents were never married."

Elthia blinked. "Oh."

Then she straightened. "That's not Josie's fault. I can't believe your sisters would hold it against her."

She'd surprised him again. "They don't," he answered, squeezing her hand. "But there are others who would. We tried to keep it quiet, but somehow word got out after Tim died. Already the word *bastard* was being whispered."

He spread his hands. "Once gossip like that gets started, you can't stop it. That's why my sisters thought it best she get a fresh start somewhere far away from the talk."

He rubbed his neck. "And I agreed with them. I just didn't want Josie sent into exile. At the time, Aunt Dorothy was caring for her invalid mother, so one child was all she could take. Annie and Liz had deep roots in Harvestown—it would have been hard for either of them to pick up and move."

Caleb shrugged. "My sisters thought I was crazy when I said I'd give it a shot. No one, including me, knew if I'd be able to do it. I'd never been responsible for even one kid before, and I didn't have a wife to give 'em the mothering they needed." He met her gaze. "But I had to try to keep them all together."

Elthia stroked his cheek. "You're a good man, Caleb Tanner. The children are lucky to have you. And so am I."

He captured her hand and kissed it. "Thanks. But I don't think Peter agrees."

"He will eventually." She drew back, her expression suddenly sober. "But I think you should consider telling him the story you just told me. He has a right to know."

"When he's older. I don't think he's ready right now."

She looked prepared to argue, then caught herself. "I'm not sure I agree, but I'll defer to your judgment, at least for now."

He raised a brow. "For now?"

She smiled sweetly. "I'll let you know if I change my mind."

Caleb drew her onto his lap. "You, my dear, are getting much too sassy." Then he kissed her, quite thoroughly. When he set her on her feet, he had to force himself to release her.

The next few days couldn't pass fast enough.

Grinning at her bemused expression, he swatted her bottom and pointed toward the door. "Off with you, woman. I've work to do and you're too tempting a distraction for my peace of mind."

She flashed him a saucy smile, then turned and sashayed out.

Caleb shifted in his seat as he watched the seductively feminine swaying of her hips. It was *definitely* going to be a long couple of days.

His wife was one special lady. Dare he hope that this time, this *woman,* would be different? Had he found someone who wouldn't leave or send him away?

Then he sobered. That kind of thinking was dangerous, would gouge chinks in the protective walls he'd built. After all, much as she said she'd stay, their last ruckus had started because she thought she'd lost the annulment contract.

No, he'd just take things as they came. He planned to enjoy their time together to the fullest. If she stayed past three months, so much the better. If not . . . well, he'd be ready for it.

Elthia had mulled over their discussion for the past hour and had arrived at a decision. Caleb had been wrong; he needed to put things right between himself and Peter before the boy took his hurt and anger out in a destructive way.

She had to convince Caleb of that, and the sooner the better. When he stepped through the back door, she was ready. "Caleb?"

He gave a mock-groan. "Don't tell me—we need to talk."

"Well, yes. But this really is important."

"Naturally. Come on, we can talk in my office." He ushered her into the room ahead of him. "Now," he said, stepping around his desk, "what is the current crisis?"

Was he mocking her? Elthia decided to ignore it if he was. "It's Peter. I think you should talk to him now rather than waiting."

Caleb's light mood disappeared. "What happened to your deferring to my judgment?"

"Just hear me out. You said Peter is too young, but I think you're wrong. When I look at Peter I see a youth approaching manhood."

She saw Caleb's frown and tried again. "He worked beside you at the barn raising. Would you say he did a man's work?"

"Well, I suppose. But that—"

"There, you see? He'll be a man before you know it. Do you want him to hear about this from you, or from someone else?"

He waved a hand impatiently. "No one here knows—"

"You said yourself, this kind of thing has a way of getting out. Why take the chance? Surely you're not afraid it'll make him love Josie any less if he knows."

"Of course not."

"Good. Then you'll talk to him?"

He gave an exasperated sigh. "Elthia . . ."

She placed a hand on his. "Caleb, he's angry and hurting. He thinks you don't want him, or don't trust him. Hearing the truth, even something like this, will make him feel better."

Elthia mentally held her breath. Had she pushed too hard? Would he think her an interfering busybody?

Finally he nodded. Leaning back, he slid a hand through his hair. "Perhaps you're right."

She relaxed. He did understand. "So you'll talk to him?"

"Yes. Just as soon as I get back from town."

He obviously didn't feel the same urgency over this that she did. Should she push again or be satisfied with his decision?

Caleb sighed. "Something tells me that's not good enough." He moved around to her side of the desk and took her hand. "I'll go find him right now. Feel better?"

She nodded. "Did I mention what a good man you are, Caleb Tanner?"

He shot her a cocky grin. "Yes, but I don't mind hearing it again."

Caleb stepped outside and called to Peter. He put an arm around the boy's stiff shoulders. "Did I ever show you the swimming hole I played in when I was a kid?"

Elthia stood in the doorway, watching them disappear into the woods, praying they could work this out between them.

"Aunt 'thia, Aunt 'thia. Somebody's coming."

Elthia set her mending aside. "All right, I'm coming. Maybe it's your Uncle Caleb." It was too soon for him to be back from town, though. He'd only been gone for twenty minutes.

"No, no. Come see."

Elthia stepped out on the front porch and shaded her eyes. Sure enough, a delivery wagon was plodding up the drive.

Of course! She'd all but forgotten the special order she'd made just before Caleb's birthday.

Oh, dear, and she'd never gotten around to telling Caleb. Well, no sense worrying now. He might be irritated, but she couldn't imagine him staying angry for long.

By the time the wagon pulled up to the house, the children were making extravagant guesses as to what might be contained in the huge crate lashed down in back.

Even Peter was showing interest. His surly belligerence had disappeared since he returned from his walk with Caleb. It had been replaced by a sober, heavy mood that she suspected was due to both guilt over his prior attitude and worry about Josie.

Caleb had said when it was all over they shook hands and agreed to stand together to take care of the family. Peter had declared that anyone who so much as whispered hurtful things about his baby sister would have to deal with her big brother.

Elthia smiled and stepped from the porch as she heard Zoe's excited squeal. The contents of the crate had been discovered.

Chapter Twenty-three

Caleb held the reins loosely as he fingered the telegram he'd picked up on his way through town.

Her family was well-to-do, she'd said.

Her father was prominent, she'd said.

Why the devil hadn't she just told him the truth? Why hide this from him? According to the telegram, her father could buy one or more small countries without blinking an eye. The man had the ear of those in the highest circles. Elthia's family home was a mansion that would rival Europe's finer palaces. And this man had no idea his baby girl had been coerced into marrying an itinerant carpenter with a ragtag passel of kids.

No wonder she'd seemed so shocked at the thought of marrying him. Lady Privilege—he'd had no idea how appropriate that nickname was. She'd been bred to take her place among the world's elite. Not to cook his meals and do his laundry.

What had he done?

No matter what she said about her desire to stay now, he *had* bullied her into marrying him to start with. Not only that, he'd deliberately set out to trap her into staying. How long before she began to tire of the relative drudgery of life here, began to resent him for tying her to him?

No matter how hard he worked, he'd never be able to give

her the kind of life she was used to, the kind of life she deserved. Damn! Even if she never voiced a word of complaint, could *he* live with the knowledge of what he'd asked her to give up?

By the time Caleb neared home he was in a foul mood. Having to maneuver his buckboard around a passing delivery wagon that insisted on taking up much of the road didn't cheer him up any.

When he turned up the drive, he wondered where the kids were. Usually they were outside playing at this time of day. But not even Elthia's yipping lapdog was around to broadcast his arrival.

Caleb took care of the horse and wagon, then headed for the house. He paused on the front porch. Was that music he heard?

He tromped to the parlor and halted in the doorway. What had been a small open space between the sitting area and the library had been expanded and filled with an impressive new piano.

Damnation! So, Lady Privilege had already gotten tired of living on his earnings and decided to turn into Lady Bountiful, had she? Well, if she thought she could just waltz in here and start throwing her daddy's money around like leaves in a windstorm, she was about to learn different.

Elthia looked up. At least some of what he felt must have been reflected in his face because her smile faltered and a hand fluttered to her chest. The kids spied him then, and he was immediately surrounded by young bodies.

"Look, Uncle Caleb, a piano."

"A big ol' wagon brought it."

"Did you hear Zoe playing?"

"Aunt 'thia says she's gonna teach me how to play, too."

The exclamations came all at once, and Caleb wasn't sure who said what. He was aware, though, that Zoe had stopped playing as soon as the commotion started.

Joy had transformed his solemn, sad-eyed niece into the spirited, pretty girl she'd been before her parents' death. With a guilty stab, he remembered Elthia trying to tell him how much music meant to Zoe. He just hadn't been listening close enough.

Ignoring Elthia for the moment, he smiled down at his niece. "That was mighty pretty, Zoe. You got your momma's touch."

Zoe's cheeks pinkened. "Thank you. Isn't it beautiful?" She stroked the polished wood surface reverently. "It's even grander than the one we had in Indiana. And Aunt Elthia says I can play on it every day if I want to, after my chores are done."

Caleb felt the jaws of the trap snap shut. Much as he wanted to demand that Elthia send the piano back where it came from, he couldn't deny Zoe the pleasure she obviously derived from it. "Well now, I reckon we could all benefit from the sound of music floating through this house. Especially when it sounds as pretty as it did just now."

Zoe popped up and gave him a fierce hug. "Oh, thank you, Uncle Caleb. I promise to do my chores better'n ever."

"I don't doubt it for a minute, sweetheart. Now, you play us another tune while I talk to your Aunt Elthia for a spell."

He turned to his lip-biting wife. "Let's go to my office. As you like to say, we need to talk." Taking her elbow, he led her from the room.

As soon as they shut the office door, Elthia made a grab for the conversational reins. "I'm sorry I didn't mention the piano to you. It was supposed to be a surprise for the children, but I really did intend to tell you about it before it arrived. It's just that, with everything else going on . . . Anyway, Zoe really did need this. It'll make all the difference for her."

He let her chattering die down and the silence hang before he spoke. "Are there any other surprises you should let me know about? You going to purchase a zoo for Alex? Build Peter his own workshop? Bring a circus to town for Josie and the twins?"

Elthia tossed her head. "There's no need for such sarcasm. Of course, I'm not going to do any of those things."

"And why not? I'm sure the cost would only be pocket change for the daughter of Rupert Sinclare."

She stiffened. "What do you mean?"

He pulled the telegram from his pocket and passed it across the desk to her. "This is what I mean. Why the blue blazes didn't you tell me about the mansion, and the army of servants, your daddy's obscene wealth, and all the rest that goes with it?"

Elthia barely glanced at the telegram. Indignation blazed on her face. "Did you actually have me investigated?"

Caleb ignored the twinge of guilt at her words and dredged back up his own righteous irritation. "You're dad-gum right I did. I sure wasn't getting any straight answers from you. And that's another thing; why all the secrecy?"

"Because," she said through clenched teeth, "I wanted you to get to know me as an individual, not as the daughter of the esteemed Rupert Sinclare, or as a bottomless pot of gold." She poked a finger at his chest. "And another thing: I'll have you know I will spend my money how and where I please, including occasional gifts for the children. But don't worry; I'll scratch you off my gift list if it makes you uncomfortable to be there." And with that she flounced out of the room.

Caleb leaned back in his chair, wondering how this interview had ended with her sounding like the injured party.

Elthia stepped outside, hoping the fresh air would cool her anger. How *dare* he have her investigated? She would have told him the truth eventually. Now she'd never get that chance.

She checked a moment when she realized Peter sat on the steps, a knife and chunk of wood in his hands.

He stared up at her with a wrinkled brow. "Are you okay?"

She nodded, managing a smile. "I'm fine. I just thought I'd come out here and sit for a spell. It was getting a bit warm in the house." That was true enough.

Peter nodded and resumed his efforts. Elthia sat beside him. He didn't seem to be carving anything recognizable. His vigorous, jerky movements seemed more of an attack against the wood than a shaping of it. A pile of shavings decorated the ground at his feet, testimony to the intensity of his efforts.

"What are you making?" she asked after a long silence.

Peter shrugged. "I don't know. Sometimes I just like the feel of the wood and knife in my hands. It helps me think."

Her smile warmed. "You sound like your Uncle Caleb."

Elthia thought she detected signs that he was pleased by the comparison. "I want to share a secret," she said, hugging her knees. "I'm glad you took that contract from my trunk."

He paused in mid-stroke, the blade of the knife still buried beneath a curl of wood. "You are? Why?"

"Well, you see, at first I thought your Uncle Caleb took it."

Peter finished pulling his knife across the wood. "So that's why you two were out of sorts with each other the last few days."

"Uh-huh. It forced us to work through some things we needed to get straight. I think—no, I know—we're better off for it. It might never have happened, or at least not for a long while, if you hadn't set this in motion." *Though it seems we still have a few things to work out. Like why he won't open up to me more.*

"I'm glad I helped." Peter didn't meet her gaze. Instead, he eyed the last cut he'd made, blowing to clear the sawdust.

Elthia's nose twitched as she tried not to sneeze. "Of course, there's another reason," she said, once she could speak.

"Another reason?" He kept his gaze focused on his handiwork.

"It allowed you and your Uncle Caleb to clear the air between you." She risked placing a hand on the boy's knee, hoping he wouldn't shake it off. "Now you know you can count on us to be there when you need us. We can put all the distrust and blame aside, and work to make this group of Tanners a real family."

And they would succeed, she silently vowed. They had to. She wouldn't let anything tear this family apart now that she'd staked her claim on it, found her place at its heart.

Elthia gradually became aware that something was wrong. She felt Peter's tension, the tautness of his muscles, the rigidity of his control. What was bothering the boy?

He raised his head, and she was shocked at the depth of anguish reflected in his eyes. "I've done something terrible."

She took the wood and knife from him and gripped his hands. "Whatever it is, your uncle and I will help you fix it."

Peter shook his head. "You don't understand, you *can't* fix this."

She gave his hands a gentle squeeze. "Why don't you just tell me what happened, and then we'll see?"

Peter nodded and took a deep breath. "I was so mad when I found that contract, so angry with how unfair it all was. Uncle

Caleb had been forced to give up his traveling life, and you'd been forced to marry a man you didn't want, all because of us. I just figured we'd be better off with Aunt Liz and Aunt Annie."

Elthia felt the first prickling of real alarm. What was he saying? What in the world had he done?

Peter squared his shoulders, bracing himself. "So I sent it to Judge Walters and told him I didn't think he should leave us with you two, that I wanted to go back to Harvestown."

No! Elthia's gut clenched. She had to talk to Caleb, had to hear him tell her they could fix this.

Judge Walters had that damning contract. What would he do? Surely if they explained . . . He seemed a fair, reasonable man.

Please God, let him give them another chance.

Peter's face crumpled, and she tried to pull herself back together as the little-boy side of him surfaced. He needed her the way she needed Caleb.

"I didn't know about it not being good for Josie to go back." His tone and expression pleaded with her to understand. "Or how much Uncle Caleb really wanted us. I just thought that, even if the aunts weren't wild about having us, at least we wouldn't feel like we'd ruined their lives if we went to live with them."

"Oh, Peter, you must never let yourself believe you're a burden to us. We love you boys and your sisters."

"I should have told Uncle Caleb right away, after we had our talk this morning. But I couldn't make myself do it." His Adam's apple bobbed. "Do you think, if I explained to the judge that it was all a big mistake, and that I really do want to stay with you now, that it'll fix things?" he asked.

Elthia struggled to tamp down her own panic. Peter needed reassurances, and her mental hand-wringing wasn't helping. "I don't know, but we'll think of something. Let's go talk to your uncle." She gave Peter's hand another squeeze as she stood, and managed what she hoped was a convincing smile. "Don't worry; we'll work it out."

But as Elthia turned toward the house, she gave in to her own doubts and fears, saying a silent, fervent prayer that it *would* work out. Caleb had tried to explain to her how that contract could be used against them, but she'd insisted he sign it anyway. How would she ever be able to live with herself if it was used to tear this family apart? How would Caleb ever be able to look at her with anything other than contempt?

Predictably, they found Caleb in his workshop. "We need to talk," she announced as she ushered Peter in ahead of her.

He still had that glower of irritation, but to her relief, he let go of it as soon as he saw Peter was with her. "What is it? Has something happened?"

Elthia gently pushed Peter into the chair across from Caleb. "Go ahead," she encouraged. "Tell him what you told me. It'll be all right."

Caleb gave Peter his full attention as the boy repeated his story. Only a slight tightening of his jaw betrayed what he might be feeling as he listened.

"I see," Caleb said, leaning back when Peter reached the end of his tale. "First thing we need to know is when."

"Sir?"

"When did you send the letter?" he elaborated.

Elthia was impressed by Caleb's calm demeanor. She could feel her own stomach churn with nervous concerns.

Peter frowned in concentration. "Let's see; I sent it on that trip to town just after your birthday."

Caleb nodded. "That puts it at a little over a week. So, we can expect a visit from Judge Walters any day now."

Elthia's breath caught. Oh, dear God, there was so little time to prepare, to figure out how to fight this.

"I'm really sorry, Uncle Caleb. Can we set it all right?"

Caleb moved around the table, giving Elthia's arm a squeeze as he moved past her. She took some comfort in the gesture. He seemed to have put his previous irritation with her behind him.

He placed a hand on the boy's shoulder. "We're gonna try. And remember, no matter what happens, you did what you thought was right, and there's no need to ever hang your head for that."

Peter sat a little straighter, though he didn't look any happier. "Yes, sir. And thank you, sir."

Caleb flashed a reassuring smile. "Now, I think there are

some chores waiting for you. And get rid of the long face. You don't want to worry the others, do you?"

Once Peter was gone, Caleb raked a hand through his hair. He picked up a small dowel and idly tapped it against the tabletop.

Elthia, unwilling to be shut out, placed both hands on the table and leaned forward. "Well, how do we fix this?"

Caleb stilled his fidgeting, looking as if he'd forgotten she was there. He shrugged. "Not a lot we can do. Just hope the judge gives us a chance to explain. Then we tell the truth and trust his sense of what's right to decide him in our favor."

Elthia plopped down in the seat Peter had vacated. She tried to match his air of calm, but it was no use. "I'm scared," she admitted in a voice that cracked slightly.

Caleb sat beside her, drawing her to his side. "I know." He didn't say anything else, merely tucked her head under his chin and held her close.

She drew comfort from his nearness, from his quiet sharing of her fears. She nestled against him, inhaling his earthy scent, absorbing his seductive warmth. But it didn't chase away her worries. "I don't like simply waiting for the ax to fall. Isn't there *something* we can do?"

Caleb kissed the top of her head and stood. "Just don't try mopping the kitchen floor in the next day or two."

She made a face at him, knowing he was trying to lighten the mood. But she knew her effort wasn't any more convincing than his had been. Realizing he wanted some time alone, she stood. "I guess I'll go see about supper."

Caleb nodded absently and went back to work. Elthia felt a sliver of resentment for his seeming detachment. Keeping this family together was every bit as important to him as it was to her; she'd bet her life on it. But he hadn't said one word about his own concerns, not even after she'd admitted hers. Would he ever trust her enough to share his deeper thoughts and feelings?

Too much had happened too fast; so many emotional highs and lows to face in the past twenty-four hours. She wasn't sure she could face this new crisis as stoically as he seemed to.

As she crossed the room, her stomach pitched and everything seemed to shift slightly out of focus. She placed a hand on the doorframe, suddenly needing its support.

Caleb's arm slipped around her waist. "Are you all right?" His words, warm and full of concern, steadied her. They *could* get through this, as long as they held together.

She met his gaze with a smile. "I'm fine. Just a touch of this Texas heat getting the best of me."

Her words only seemed to etch the worry lines deeper in his brow, so she reached down for the hand at her waist and gave it a squeeze. "Honestly, I'm okay. Just worried."

Caleb stared at their linked hands, lightly stroking her palm with his thumb. Enjoying the moment of closeness, Elthia stood quietly and allowed her gaze to follow his.

Her acquaintances back East would be aghast at the state of her hands. No longer soft and white, they were tanned from the sun and had roughened from her efforts to learn cooking and cleaning skills. She felt a stab of pride at the sight, viewing it as a medal earned on the battlefield of domestic training.

Finally, Caleb looked up. "Don't worry. I'll make sure this all works out for the best."

His confident words and tone should have reassured her.

So why did she suddenly have this nagging feeling that something wasn't quite right?

Caleb sat on the porch, whittling by moonlight. The house was quiet. He imagined even Elthia had gone to sleep by now.

The last letter he'd received from Annie, creased and wrinkled, lay on the step beside him. Next to it lay the telegram he'd received today. He refused to look at them, to face their mute calls for him to "do the right thing." Not that his ignoring them mattered. He knew the contents by heart now.

Annie's letter made it clear he was no longer the only choice for the kids. And after today it had become painfully clear he might not be their best choice, either.

Peter had felt unwanted. If not for Elthia, he might still feel that way. And once this latest disaster had run its course, the boy would likely feel some guilt for it as well.

Zoe had mourned the loss of her piano along with that of her parents but had been too guilty about her "selfishness" to say so. Again, it had been Elthia who'd seen and answered the need.

And he'd damned sure messed up Elthia's life. He wasn't her only choice or her best choice—hell, he hadn't been her choice at all. She didn't belong here. If the telegram he got today hadn't been proof enough of that, there was the way she'd almost swooned from the heat earlier, and the chapped skin and calluses on hands that were silky soft and flawless only weeks ago.

He couldn't ask her to stay here. And without her, he couldn't keep the children. Not just because of Judge Walters's edict, but because he'd proven himself incompetent.

His sisters had been right—he had no business thinking he could take on six kids and a stranger for a wife all at once. It was time he let go of his selfish desire to create a family for himself and let these people he cared so much about get on with the rest of their lives.

Only problem was, Elthia and the kids were good, honorable people. They wouldn't give up on this family easily, even if it was in their best interest to do it.

So it was gonna be up to him.

Caleb's knife slipped and sliced his thumb. It stung, but it wasn't deep. He watched the blood well up.

One drop, then two more, fell to the ground at his feet.

Like teardrops.

Chapter Twenty-four

"Uncle Caleb! Aunt Elthia!"

Caleb looked up from his coffee as Peter appeared in the kitchen doorway, breathless and white-faced. So, it was time.

Before he could move, Elthia stepped forward, drying her hands on her apron. "What is it? What's happened?"

Peter looked from her to Caleb and back again. "A buggy just turned up the drive. I think it's Judge Walters."

Elthia and Peter both turned to Caleb with identically worried expressions on their faces.

He set down his cup and stood, giving them both his best everything's-gonna-be-all-right smile. It wouldn't do for them to see how sick he felt inside, how hard he battled the part of himself that pleaded and railed against what he was about to do.

This was it. Time to face the music. He kept the smile firmly in place as he turned them with a hand on their shoulders. "Then let's go out to meet him, what do you say?"

They reached their visitor just as he pulled the horse to a stop. Peter rushed up to take the reins.

"Thank you." The judge stepped down, turning to Peter. "I received your letter."

Elthia's hand slipped into Caleb's, and he gave it a reassuring squeeze. Would she hate him for what he was about to do, or be relieved that he'd found her a way out?

Peter nodded. "Thank you for coming, sir. But I've changed my mind. I don't want to go back to Harvestown any more."

Caleb stiffened as the judge turned a suspicious eye his way. Did the man actually think he would coerce the boy?

Judge Walters turned back to Peter. "Well now, that's a very different story than the one you put in your letter."

Peter's hold on the reins turned white-knuckled. "I know, and I'm very sorry, sir. But please, you gotta believe me. I want to stay here with Uncle Caleb and Aunt Elthia. We all do."

The judge's expression didn't betray his thoughts. "I'm sorry, Peter, but this isn't your decision to make."

The whipped-puppy look on Peter's face fanned Caleb's guilt.

"Take care of the judge's buggy, Peter," he said, placing a reassuring hand on his nephew's shoulder. Then he turned to their visitor. "Shall we move to the parlor, Judge?"

Once in the parlor, they sat as they had once before, with Elthia and Caleb side by side and the judge across from them.

Elthia slipped her hand into the crook of Caleb's arm, and he patted it. Would this be the last time she'd reach for him? "All right," he said. "Let's get to this, shall we?"

The judge nodded. "I take it you already know why I'm here?"

Caleb nodded. "Yes. Peter told us yesterday that he sent the annulment agreement to you."

One grizzled brow went up. "You don't deny that you planned to go your separate ways once you'd won custody of the children?"

He met the judge's gaze evenly. Could he go through with this? "No, I don't deny it."

Elthia made a sound of protest. "But—"

Caleb hushed her with another squeeze of her hand. *Forgive me, darling.* "None of this was Elthia's idea," he told the judge. "I sort of backed her into a corner."

Judge Walters looked from one to the other of them. "You do know that, given such blatant intent to circumvent the spirit of the law, I can hardly approve the adoption."

"But you can't—"

This time, thankfully, it was the judge who interrupted Elthia's protest with a raised hand. "Now, if somehow you could convince me that you have decided to honor your marriage vows and can provide the kind of home these children need, then perhaps we could work this out. I'd have to put you on probation, of course. I wouldn't be able to finalize the adoption in three months. I'd watch how things worked out, maybe for a year or so."

Elthia leaned forward eagerly. "Oh, sir, that is *so* generous of you. And we have changed, you'll see. Caleb and I do want to stay married, to build a life for ourselves and the children."

Her words painted an achingly tempting picture. They stabbed at him, drove daggers into his determination to do the right thing. He had to drag deep into his resolve to force out the next words with any amount of conviction. "No we haven't."

Elthia pulled her hand away. "Caleb? What are you saying?"

Her withdrawal hurt, even more than he'd expected. He deliberately added a conspiratorial, we've-been-found-out edge to his smile. "No more games, sweetheart. We gave it our best shot, but we both know you don't belong here. I appreciate your willingness to stick it out for three months, but I can't ask you to do it for a year." It was difficult not to flinch from the hurt reflected in her expression. "Besides, I'm beginning to think I'm not cut out to be a father," he added for good measure.

"That's ridiculous!"

Her immediate jump to his defense almost brought a smile to Caleb's face. Loyal, even in the face of her confusion.

Then she sat back and stared at him as if trying to see through to his soul. "Why are you doing this? Don't you realize how much we all need you?"

You don't need me, Elthia. Nobody does.

Caleb shrugged. "You'll survive just fine without me." *But how will I fare without you?*

Their gazes locked and her silent plea demanded that he explain. But he also saw trust there, a trust he was about to betray.

The sound of the judge clearing his throat brought a reprieve. "I'm not sure what's going on," he said, "though I have my suspicions. However, Mr. Tanner, you leave me no choice. Your request for adoption is denied and the children will be removed from your custody."

"No."

The sob in Elthia's voice stabbed at Caleb. His arms ached to pull her close, to comfort her, to stroke away her pain.

He surged to his feet. He had to draw this nightmare to a close, had to get out of here before she laid his defenses bare. "How much time do we have?"

Elthia stared at him in confusion and disbelief.

Don't hate me, he silently pleaded. *I'm doing this for you. Someday you'll see it was the right thing.*

"You've got until day after tomorrow," the judge answered. "That'll give me time to make all the arrangements for transportation and accommodations."

Caleb nodded. "My Aunt Dorothy's circumstances have changed. I believe she's willing to take them all now."

"I won't be making any hasty decisions about adoption, but that may work until I do." Judge Walters stood. "I guess I'd better head into town and see about finding a room."

Elthia stood as well. "We'd be glad to have you stay here with us, sir. There's plenty of room."

Caleb wanted to applaud her for showing such grace, such generosity, in the midst of her confusion and dismay. Would he ever find another such woman? Hell, who was he trying to fool—there wouldn't be any other woman for him.

Judge Walters shook his head. "Thank you, Mrs. Tanner, but I think it best if I stay in town. I'll need to be close to the telegraph and the livery. Besides, you'll want some privacy as you get the children prepared to move again."

Caleb grabbed the chance to end this. "I'll see you out." He turned to Elthia, stealing himself to meet her gaze. "Perhaps you'd better gather up the children so we can talk to them."

She narrowed her eyes. "You and I are going to talk first."

Caleb gave a short nod. Might as well get it over with. "I'll be back in a minute." It wasn't a conversation he looked forward to. She knew him too well. Facing her questions and accusations would be worse than confronting the children.

He bolstered his flagging resolve as he and the judge stepped outside. He *was* doing the right thing. Even though it

271

hurt like hell to see the betrayed look on her face, she would be better off in the long run; they all would.

Judge Walters was the first to break the silence. "I hope you know what you're doing, son."

So do I. Caleb jammed his hands in his pockets. "I'm just facing facts, Judge. I'm not the right man for the job."

"I don't think your wife would agree with you there."

Caleb flashed him a self-mocking smile, handing the judge the reins as he settled in his seat. "She will soon enough."

Judge Walters merely shook his head. "Remember, pride makes for a cold bedfellow. It does little to ease a man's soul or raise his spirits on a lonely night."

Caleb raked a hand through his hair as he watched the wagon move away. Was the judge trying to say he *wanted* him to keep the children? Wasn't he supposed to be looking after their best interests? Hadn't he read that annulment contract or heard what Caleb had forced himself to say there in the parlor?

Caleb turned to face the house. Elthia was waiting for him inside. For a second he contemplated turning toward his workshop and shutting the door on all of this.

With a sigh, he moved to the front porch.

He'd have to face her and the children, have to live through two days of questions, accusations, and hurt looks.

Then they would all be gone and the true hell would begin.

Elthia paced between the sofas and the piano. Why had he done this? He still cared about her and the children, she knew down to the core of her being that he did. What had happened to make him do this?

It wasn't the conversation with Peter. That had only seemed to make him more determined than ever to keep them together. So what had happened since—

The telegram.

He'd learned about her father's wealth and, predictably, it hadn't sat well with him. Was that what this was all about? Surely he wouldn't react so drastically to what was, after all, an unrelated bit of information.

Would he?

The creak of the screen door halted her pacing. She listened to his measured footsteps in the hall, forcing herself to wait. When he finally stepped into the parlor, her heart missed a beat. Dear God, she loved him. Really and truly, till-death-do-us-part loved him. Why hadn't she realized that before now? She couldn't let him send her away without a fight.

His expression was wary, ready for combat. Well, she wasn't about to disappoint him. "You lied to me," she accused.

She could tell by the way his brows drew down that she'd not only surprised him but got his back up. Good! "You said you'd make sure this all worked out for the best. That was a lie."

He paused, still several feet away from her. "That all depends on how you look at it, I suppose."

"How *dare* you say such a thing! This is *not* best for all of us. What about those promises you made to me, promises that the two of us were going to make this marriage, this family, work?"

His jaw tightened almost imperceptibly. "I shouldn't have spoken before I thought this all the way through. I just realized this arrangement wasn't working after all."

"This *arrangement?*" She couldn't believe he was being so casual. "This is a *family,* Caleb, and you had no right to make such a decision without consulting the rest of us."

Plowing his hair with his fingers, he didn't quite meet her gaze. "Blast it, Elthia, just let it be! What's done is done."

Just as she'd thought. He wasn't any more happy about this than she was. She took a step forward. "Does your finding out about my father's money have anything to do with this?"

"Don't be ridiculous."

She took another step, bringing her within touching distance. And, heaven help her, she did want to touch him, wanted him to touch her. "That's not an answer."

His hands fisted at his sides. "You don't belong here, Elthia," he said, his voice harsh. "You never did. Go back to your fancy house and your army of servants."

No! He didn't mean that. She couldn't have made such a mistake. He needed her, cared for her; she knew he did. How could she not belong here—she was his wife.

His lips twisted cynically. "You chose the wrong man again, sweetheart. Perhaps you'll have better luck next time."

Almost of its own accord, her hand flew up and slapped him across the cheek. Shocked by what she'd done, Elthia raised a fist to her mouth and stared in horror at the flaming handprint forming on his face. "I'm sorry; I didn't mean . . ."

This time his expression softened into that sweet, crooked smile that could set her stomach to fluttering. Now it only twisted the knife of his rejection more cruelly. "Don't worry. I imagine I deserved that."

Unable to suppress a sob, Elthia turned and fled the room without another word.

Elthia stood beside the wagon as Caleb loaded the last of her trunks. She took a last look around the place that had come to feel so much like home. Dear God, she was going to miss it here.

Already the place looked emptier, sadder. The children had left an hour ago, tucked securely in the private coach the judge had hired for the six-hour ride to the train station. The good-byes had been heart-wrenching. Josie cried openly, and the others looked like they wanted to. Watching the carriage pull away, she experienced the same wretched, this-can't-be-happening grief as she had at her mother's funeral.

Judge Walters had offered to give her a ride in their coach, but she'd declined. Putting the children through one such farewell was hard enough; she didn't have the heart to put them through another one. Besides, she wanted more time with Caleb.

She'd shed more tears these past two days than she'd thought a body could produce. They'd soaked her pillows at night and trickled down her cheeks as she watched the children leave. Her throat was scratchy and raw from the sobs she'd already choked out and from the need to release more. But she wouldn't cry again, not in front of Caleb. She'd save any tears she had left for the long ride ahead of her.

She would be returning to Maryland a very different person from the one who'd set out for a small adventure not so long ago.

"That's it." Caleb's words drew her attention back to the present. "I guess we're ready to go now."

He moved to help her climb into the wagon, but she

stopped him with a raised hand. There was still a chance for them, she thought desperately. She just had to make him see how wrong his thinking was. "Before we go, I want to say one more thing."

He rubbed the back of his neck. "Elthia, we've already—"

"No! You're going to hear me out if I have to stand here all day." She tightened her hold on Poppy's basket and tilted her chin up at him.

With a sigh, he nodded.

Elthia said a silent prayer, knowing it was important she get the words just right. "Last night I figured out why you're acting this way, deliberately pushing me and the children away."

His raised eyebrows told her she had his attention.

"People have been leaving you all your life," she began, "and it's made you believe that they always will. So you made the first move this time. After we're gone, you're going to say this was just one more example."

The tic under his eye told her that she'd been right; the stubborn thrust of his jaw told her it didn't matter.

He opened his mouth to protest, but she held up her hand, determined to get through to him. "Let me finish. You're wrong. I would never have left you. So long as I felt I had your love and your trust, I would have had everything I ever wanted, ever dreamed of, right here."

She pushed at her glasses, convinced now that she was right. "But you won't believe that, so yes, I'm leaving. Not because there's no room in my life for you like with your family all those years ago. Not for another man, like with your fiancée. Not even because you don't have money to hire servants and buy me the fine clothes you seem to think I crave."

She poked a finger at his chest. "I'm leaving because you're not man enough to open yourself to unconditional love. The kind of love I'd give everything I own to share with you."

His Adam's apple bobbed once, but he gave no other indication that he'd understood any of what she'd said.

After another moment of resounding silence, Elthia sighed and felt her shoulders droop. She'd failed. She'd handed him her heart and he'd refused to take it. There was nothing left to do but say good-bye. Turning, she placed Poppy's basket under the seat, careful to make sure the cloth covering stayed in place.

She wouldn't get down on her knees and beg.

No, that was a lie. If she thought it would make a difference, she might even do that. But it was up to him now.

Climbing up beside her, Caleb picked up the reins, though he didn't immediately set the buckboard in motion. "Elthia . . ." he said, keeping his eyes focused straight ahead.

"Yes?" Her heart skipped a beat. Had she finally gotten through to him? Was he ready to see that he'd made a mistake?

"I just want you to know, I'm still willing to support you when you get ready to seek an annulment or divorce."

Elthia's spirits plummeted again. Did he really care so little for what she and the children wanted? "I've told you before, an annulment is out of the question now. Our lovemaking may have meant nothing to you, but it meant a great deal to me, and I will not demean its significance by denying it took place." The memory of that blissful night tingled through her. It was impossible to think of sharing such intimacies with another. How could she bear to never feel such passionate magic again?

She tossed her head, feeling a spark of anger at his readiness to dismiss all they'd shared. "If you want to be free of our marriage, *you'll* have to be the one to seek the divorce."

Was that a gleam of pleasure she saw in his eyes? Or only wishful thinking on her part?

They made the entire trip to Whistling Oak without exchanging another word. The only sounds to mark their passage were the clopping of the horses' hooves on the hard-packed earth, the jingling of the harness, and the occasional trill or insect hum along the roadside. Caleb remained as stiff and unrelenting as the wagon seat. Elthia felt little pieces of her soul dropping in the dust behind her like a trail of breadcrumbs. She was actually glad to see the station come into view, even though it meant the final good-byes were upon them.

While Caleb unloaded her things, Elthia stepped inside to pay her fare. Surprisingly, Mr. Josiah no longer intimidated her. She even exchanged a few easy pleasantries with him as they conducted their business.

Then it was time to go. Caleb silently took her hand and

tucked it in his arm as he led her to the waiting coach. Was this the last time she'd feel his touch? She paused with one foot poised on the mounting block and turned back to him.

Please, please, she silently begged, *tell me it was a mistake. Ask me to stay.* But he remained silent, and her last flicker of hope drowned in the tears she withheld.

Swallowing past the lump in her throat, she managed to speak without her voice breaking. "Remember, you hold the key to both of our happiness. You just have to find the courage to use it."

He squeezed her hand. "Good-bye, Elthia. Be happy."

She shook her head, refusing to let those insistent tears fall just yet. Her eyes devoured him, trying to memorize every nuance of his make-up. Would she ever see him again?

"I left something for you in the kitchen," she said as steadily as she could. "You'll need to check on it as soon as you get home. Promise me."

He kissed her hand. "I promise."

Caleb watched her step into the coach and felt a moment of panic. His hand reached up to draw her back. Fortunately, she didn't see the gesture. By the time she turned back around, sitting primly with Poppy's basket on her lap, he had himself under control again. Then he saw the trace of moisture welling in her eyes and had to fight the urge one more time to haul her out of that damned carriage and kiss her senseless.

She was his! How could he bear to let her go?

But instead he said good-bye, drawing out this one last glimpse of her as long as he could. Then, with a nod and a wave, he stepped back and slammed the carriage door closed a bit more forcefully than necessary. He watched the stage move away until it topped a hill and dipped out of sight.

Telling the kids good-bye had been difficult, but this was a thousand times worse. He'd come to care for her more than he'd realized, more than he could ever have imagined. Pulling his hat down low on his forehead, he turned back to his wagon.

Alone again. Alone again. The refrain echoed singsong style through his mind, taunting him all the way home. He pulled into the yard feeling very much like his six-year-old self, arriving for the first time. Only now there wasn't even an Aunt Cora waiting to greet him.

Caleb tended to the horses and buckboard, avoiding the house for as long as possible. Things were too quiet, too empty. And everywhere he looked were reminders of the children and Elthia. He needed to keep busy.

He left the barn and was halfway to his workshop when he remembered his promise to Elthia. She'd left something in the kitchen for him, had she? He smiled, wondering if she'd tried her hand at baking again. He had to admit, her efforts had shown signs of improvement lately.

Caleb stepped into the kitchen and pulled up short. There, with his water dish tipped over and his leash wrapped in intricate patterns around chair legs, sat a woeful-looking Poppy.

What the devil had Elthia been up to? She knew how much he despised the mutt. If she thought he'd come running after her to return that pint-sized fleabag . . .

Caleb unhooked his hairy nemesis from the tangled leash. Then he absently scooped him up as he sat on the floor, propping his back against the counter.

The dog wagged his tail unenthusiastically and whimpered.

"I know, I miss her too." Caleb petted Poppy's head, only to discover he found some comfort in the gesture as well.

He paused at that thought. Just as if she stood whispering it in his ear, he knew that's what she'd intended. She'd known how empty and alone the place would be for him, and had offered the only companionship she could, her cherished pet.

Caleb pressed his head back against the counter and his shoulders shook as he finally gave in to the painful emotions that had buffeted his defenses for the past two days.

Chapter Twenty-five

"I hear her brother had to all but drag her here tonight."

Elthia stiffened and backed deeper into the shallow alcove. That would teach her to act the coward. She'd slipped into this shadowy sanctuary for a short respite from the stares of her acquaintances. Now she was trapped, an unwilling eavesdropper to yet another rehashing of the latest gossip to hit Terrelmore.

"Well, can you blame her?" another voice chimed in. "Imagine having to face everyone after what happened. I mean, of course her father *said* she'd known this Tanner fellow for some time, but everyone knows she signed up as a mail-order bride. Can you imagine! First being jilted, then this."

Elthia's hands fisted against her taffeta gown. They were saying *Baxter* jilted *her*. She supposed no one could believe a little oddity like Elthia Sinclare would turn away such a catch.

"It must be just too embarrassing," someone agreed. "I'm surprised Ry could persuade her to show her face at all."

"I hear her father tried to talk her into filing for a divorce and she flatly refused."

"A divorce?" Elthia heard the arch smile in the speaker's voice. "Does that means an annulment is out of the question?"

Elthia recalled just *why* an annulment was indeed out of the

279

question, and a frisson of heat rippled through her.

Sly giggles played counterpoint to the strains of a waltz coming from the ballroom proper. Then one of the speakers picked up the thread of the conversation. "I wonder what this Tanner is like? I mean, he *does* live out in Texas. How terrible for her if he was some oafish farmer or brute of a backwoodsman."

Elthia bit her tongue to keep from setting them straight. It would have been wasted effort anyway. These superficial debutantes would never appreciate a hardworking, honorable man like the one she'd married, the one who'd sent her away.

"Whoever he was, apparently he didn't appreciate our Elly's charms any more than Baxter did."

The words sliced through Elthia. She hugged herself tightly as the gossipers shared another round of titters.

"Now, now, we shouldn't speak so meanly of the poor dear." The speaker's dramatic sigh grated on Elthia's thinly held control. "Elly is such a sweet thing. It's not her fault she has none of her sister's looks and none of her brother's charm."

"At least Ry is making certain his friends keep her dance card full. She's so lucky to have such a brother."

Amid a chorus of sighs and praises for Ry's many attributes, the gaggle finally drifted away.

Elthia forced herself to step back into the glittery lights of the elegant ballroom. Those "ladies" were just gossipy featherbrains, but their words hurt all the same.

It was just so absolutely unfair. They'd been wrong—about Baxter breaking off the engagement, about the kind of man Caleb was, and even about Ry having to drag her here.

In fact, she had insisted on coming. For the two months she'd been back in Terrelmore, her family had tried to shield her from gossip. Lately, though, she'd begun to feel like a prisoner and a coward. So she'd decided it was time to face everyone, stare down their scandalized whispers and raised brows.

But to be *pitied*—and by those cats—it was almost too much to bear. She'd have to endure it, though, until she could decently take her leave. She refused to turn tail and run away.

An agonizingly long hour later, the first of the guests began taking their leave, and Elthia decided she'd had enough. Catching Ry's gaze, she signaled that she was ready to go.

When she was finally seated across from him in the carriage, she slumped back against the plush brocade seat.

Ry eyed her with brotherly concern, loosening a neckcloth that was still crisp and white after hours of dancing. "I'm proud of how you handled yourself. I'd say it went well."

She grimaced, knowing her hair had long ago slipped into disarray and that her sash drooped as forlornly as her spirits. "It was torture. You know I dislike balls. This one didn't change my mind any. But thank you for keeping me supplied with partners. I only hope I didn't mangle any toes in the process."

Ry flashed her one of those smiles that always set the ladies fluttering around him. "You are a graceful dancer and you know it. I didn't have to bribe anyone to ask you to dance."

"Just give a few pointed nudges?"

He shrugged, not bothering to deny anything.

Elthia stretched her neck, trying to ease the tension from her muscles. It was wonderful to have Ry around, but lately she'd wondered if she was being fair to him. "Aren't you supposed to be in Boston?" she asked.

His smile turned teasing. "Tired of my company already?"

She wrinkled her nose. "You know better than that. I'm very grateful that you want to stand by me, but you don't have to make it your life's work." She picked at a bit of thread on the seat cushion. "Another scandal will rear its head soon, and all of this will be treated like yesterday's news."

But not by her.

Elthia straightened as she noticed Ry staring at her with those devilish eyes of his. She tried not to fidget. Surely she just imagined the assessing gleam in his eye. He *couldn't* know.

"I don't think so," he said finally.

"What do you mean? Of course the talk will die—"

"When are you going to tell him, Elly?"

Trying desperately to avoid her brother's probing, Elthia attempted a guileless expression. *Keep talking. He doesn't know, he's just being annoyingly inscrutable again.* "I haven't the least idea what you're going on about. We were discussing your trip to Boston, remember?"

Ry leaned forward. "What we were discussing is just when you are planning to tell Caleb he's going to be a father?"

Elthia felt the blood drain from her face. Impossible! She

hadn't told anyone, and it didn't show yet. "How did you know?"

Ry grinned. "I didn't, until just now."

She tried to dredge up some anger for her oh-so-clever brother but felt only relief to have someone share her secret.

"He doesn't know yet, does he?"

She shook her head. "I only realized myself a few days ago." Because she hadn't missed her monthly flow, she'd been slow to realize the truth. But Dr. Driscoll had confirmed it for her. Apparently it was rare but not unheard of for a woman to continue with a weak monthly cycle through at least the early part of her confinement. She was indeed carrying Caleb's child.

Ry leaned forward and closed his hands over hers. "You have to tell him. No matter what he's done, he has a right to know."

Elthia nodded. "I know. Just not yet."

He raised a sympathetic brow. "Still hoping he'll come to his senses?"

She nodded again and, to her horror, felt a tear trickle down her cheek. "Oh, Ry, what'll I do if he never comes for me?"

Ry shifted to her side and offered his shoulder. "Don't worry, Elly," he said as he wrapped an arm around her. "If he cares for you as much as he seemed to when I visited you, he won't be able to stay away much longer."

Caleb nearly dropped the pail of milk he carried as Poppy ran helter-skelter in his path. Regaining his balance, he eyed the dog irritably, grumbling out a bad-tempered "Watch it, mutt."

Poppy paused, looked up at him with tail-wagging bliss, then picked back up in his excited chase after God only knew what.

Caleb plodded on toward the house, deciding it wouldn't have mattered if he'd spilled the whole damn pail. He really should sell the milk cows. The barn cat, Poppy, and he together didn't drink enough milk to justify the expense of keeping the beasts.

He entered the kitchen and set the pail on the counter. Catching sight of his reflection in the window above the sink, he winced. He hadn't shaved this morning, and truth to tell, he wasn't sure he'd shaved yesterday either. What was the point?

The kitchen was a mess. Zoe and Elthia would have his hide if they could see it. The sound of their feminine grousing would be music to his ears. How long had it been? Nine weeks? Ten?

An eternity.

With a growl, he stalked out. Forget breakfast—he wasn't hungry anyway. He needed to focus on something besides memories.

But the memories followed him into the workshop. Images of Elthia, standing with her hands on her hips, issuing her we've-got-to-talk ultimatum. Images of her examining the rocking horses, an expression of delight on her face. Images of her flushed and mussed, her kiss-swollen lips smiling at him seductively.

It was actually a relief when he heard a carriage pull into the yard. Granny Picket had taken to coming by once a week. Bless the old busybody, she spent as much time calling him a pigheaded fool of a man without the sense God gave a toad as she did making sure he ate right and generally took care of himself.

But when Caleb stepped out of his workshop, it wasn't Granny he saw, but Elthia's brother. Ry was making a beeline toward the house, but he altered his course when he caught sight of Caleb.

What was *he* doing here? Caleb's heart gave a sickening lurch. Had something happened to Elthia?

"There you are, Tanner." Ry stopped a few feet away and began to roll up one of his sleeves.

Caleb bypassed the greetings as well. "Is Elthia all right?"

"I'm surprised you care." Ry started on his other sleeve.

Caleb frowned. "Look, Sinclare, we may not be together anymore, but let's get one thing straight: I still care about Elthia. Now I'm gonna ask again: Is she okay?"

Ry returned his glare. "No, you bastard, she's not okay. Her heart's broken. She's lost her ability to smile."

Caleb relaxed slightly. She *was* all right then. And he was selfish enough to be glad she missed him. "I'm sorry. But—"

"No excuses." Ry's tone was silky and dangerous. "I told you what I'd do if you did anything to hurt her. Remember?"

He remembered. The significance of Ry's sleeve-rolling action finally sank in. "What I did, I did for her own good."

"Well now, it seems we don't share the same view when it comes to Elly's good. I suggest you prepare to defend yourself."

Caleb held a hand up. "I've no beef to pick with you."

"Too bad."

"Have it your way." Caleb did some sleeve-rolling of his own. If the man insisted on a fight, so be it. He'd felt like pounding on something besides his woodworking projects for several days now. "You have no idea what you're asking for."

Ry's smile turned feral. "I'm going to beat you to a bloody pulp for what you did to Elly. Then, when I get back, I'm going to do everything in my power to convince her to forget you and look for a more worthy man."

Caleb raised his fists, more than ready for a brawl. "Come on, Sinclare. I'm looking forward to seeing if rich boys bleed as easily as the rest of us do."

Ten minutes later, both men sat on the ground, panting and nursing bloodied faces and knuckles. Caleb tasted salty grit on his tongue, along with the metallic tang of blood.

Poppy chose the momentary lull to investigate, yipping as he advanced and retreated between the two men.

Ry used a sleeve to dab at his bloody lip. "How'd you end up with the furry nuisance?"

"Elthia left him as a going-away present." Caleb worked his jaw, deciding it wasn't broken after all.

Ry's wolfish smile returned. "Poetic justice."

"She meant it kindly." He wouldn't let even her brother speak ill of her. Caleb absently scratched the tail-wagging mutt behind the ears. The fight had released some of the tension that had been building inside him since he'd sent Elthia away.

Ry gave a bark of laughter, followed by a wince of pain. "Knowing my sister, I wouldn't be too sure of that."

Caleb shared a grin with him, then sobered. "She really is okay?" He hungered for *any* news of her.

Lowering his arm, Ry sobered. "Physically, yes."

Caleb nodded, hiding his disappointment when Elthia's brother didn't elaborate. Uncomfortable under Ry's scrutiny, he changed the subject. "For a rich boy, you throw a mean left hook."

Ry's mocking grin returned. "For a lout, you weren't doing so bad yourself."

Flexing his hands, Caleb winced at the angry protest of his knuckles. "Seems we're pretty evenly matched," he mused.

"Are you suggesting a truce?"

"I have a bottle of whiskey inside." Caleb hauled himself up, surprised to find he wasn't at all eager to send Ry away. It gave him a connection to Elthia of sorts. "Strictly for medicinal purposes, you understand. But this seems to qualify."

Ry levered himself up as well. "Lead on," he said heartily, clapping Caleb on the back hard enough to make him stumble.

Caleb's glare was met with spread hands and a cheerfully uttered "Sorry." Deciding to accept the apology, Caleb moved on.

They were each nursing a second glass of whiskey when Ry leaned across the desk and finally broke the brooding silence. "All right, woodcarver. Let's have it."

Caleb paused with his glass halfway to his lips. The way Ry'd said *woodcarver*, the arrogant greenhorn might as well have said *jackass*. But Caleb refused to be baited. "Have what?"

"Your excuses." Ry pointed with his glass. "It's obvious you still care for Elly. And it seems she still wants you—why is beyond me. So why the devil did you send her away?"

Caleb set his glass down and twisted it between his hands. "What did she tell you?" he asked without looking up.

"To mind my own business."

Caleb smiled. That was his Elthia. "Seems good advice."

"Shall we step back outside, woodcarver?"

There was that dig again. Again he ignored it. "Look, Elthia has no business out here. You should know that better than anyone. She shouldn't have to sweat over household chores, or deny herself the little gewgaws that catch her eye simply because such purchases don't fit my budget."

"And did she complain about those things?"

Caleb shrugged. "No. But in time she would've resented it."

"Didn't know you counted seeing into the future as one of your talents."

"Cut the sarcasm," Caleb growled. Why was Ry being so ornery? Surely he could see that Caleb had done the right thing?

Caleb downed another gulp of whiskey. "We both know she deserves more than I could ever give her."

"Shouldn't you let her decide that?"

"I thought we made it clear this was none of your business."

"I'm making it my business." Ry leaned forward. "Because I don't really believe you do have her best interests at heart."

Caleb slammed his glass down, ignoring the liquid that sloshed onto his desk. If this blasted rich boy was so set on starting another fight, Caleb might just accommodate him. "What's that supposed to mean?"

"It means that if you really cared as much about her as you claim, you'd find a compromise you could both live with."

"Compromise?"

"You didn't even try to work something out, did you? Tell me, woodcarver, do you enjoy the role of martyr so much you're willing to destroy her happiness to pursue it?"

"You don't know what you're talking about." Dammit, did Ry think he was *enjoying* this hell he'd built himself?

"Don't I? Well, from where I'm sitting, it looks like you're a damn sight more interested in seeing Elly get the life you think she deserves than the life that would make her happy."

Caleb felt the first twinges of doubt. The man could be an arrogant bastard, but there was no doubt he was protective of his sister. "You really think she would be better off here?"

"The point is, *she* thinks she would." Ry grimaced. "Elly isn't always as discriminating as she should be when she gives away a piece of her heart."

Caleb resolutely tamped down the hope Ry's words inspired. "Even if you're right, it's too late to do anything now."

"I didn't have you pegged for a quitter, woodcarver."

At the contempt in Ry's voice, Caleb came out of his chair, bracing his fists against the desk. "I've had just about all the jibes and sneers I'm gonna take, rich boy."

Ry didn't seem overly concerned. "Is that a fact?"

"Yeah, that's a fact." Caleb sat, deciding he'd had enough whiskey. When had he last eaten? "You saying it's not too late?" That flicker of hope had more spunk than he thought.

Ry shrugged. "Only one way to find out. Come back with me."

Caleb straightened. The surge of desire to see her again nearly unmanned him. "You can't be serious."

Ry's brow arched in challenge. "Afraid to face her?"

More afraid than I've ever been before in my life. "Of course not. But—"

"Then what's the problem?"

Caleb stroked his jaw, and he decided it was time for a shave. His spirits rose. "I suppose a visit wouldn't hurt. After all, I can return her mutt to her."

Chapter Twenty-six

Bored to the point of tears, Elthia stood near a window in Sinclare Hall's music room, arranging flowers in a large crystal vase. Seems she often found herself near the point of tears these days.

When she'd first moved back here, she shocked the kitchen staff by announcing she wanted to learn all about preparing meals. She'd not only needed the distraction but was determined to be armed with new domestic skills when she returned to Texas.

When working in the kitchen left her feeling queasy, she had resolutely turned to learning other domestic skills. She'd hounded Mrs. McGinty, the housekeeper, asking questions on everything from how best to polish woodwork to how to starch lace doilies. Yesterday the stoically patient housekeeper had suggested Elthia take over the flower arranging.

This morning Elthia had finally decided to face the truth: Caleb wouldn't be coming for her. Tonight she'd write him a letter and tell him about the baby. She wouldn't be able to hide her condition much longer, and he deserved to know before anyone else. It was bad enough Ry had already guessed.

Her hand fluttered to her abdomen. "Don't worry, little one," she whispered, "we *will* work this out. And whether your father and I are together or not, you'll always know you are loved."

Elthia added a final rose to the arrangement and winced when a thorn pricked her. She put the finger in her mouth, stepping back to study her work.

She'd told her brother to stop worrying about her and return to Boston, but she was almost sorry he'd taken her advice. Her father was off on another business trip, and the house seemed empty without him and Ry.

"There you are."

Elthia spun around. "Ry! What are you doing back so soon? I thought—" She halted when she saw who he'd brought with him.

"Hello, sweetheart."

There was that wonderfully toe-curling, endearingly vulnerable crooked smile that had haunted her dreams for weeks.

This had been a mistake.

Caleb had known it from the moment he saw the lush, well-tended grounds. The mansion itself looked big enough to house every man, woman, and child in Foxberry, with room to spare. The princesses in those fairy tales she'd told the kids didn't have palaces so fine.

He should have told Ry to turn around and bring him back to the rail station right then. But he hadn't been able to resist the temptation to see her. After all, he'd come this far.

God help him, there she stood, even more tempting than he remembered. She glowed with health—no trace of the pining Ry had mentioned. If she lacked something in spirit, it was compensated for by a newly acquired confidence.

Seeing her again brought home to him the fact that he'd never met a woman to match his Elthia. And he didn't expect to meet another like her again. With painful certainty he knew that the long, lonely hell he'd lived through these past months just foretold his future without her.

There was no getting around it. Here, in this setting, she *was* a fairy-tale princess. His own role was closer to that of a peasant laborer than a Prince Charming.

Trying to maintain a relaxed pose, Caleb forced himself not to fidget with the hat he held. Ry had been wrong; there was no possible compromise for them. He'd never fit in her world, and she deserved so much more than life in his. If he could make it through this visit without getting down on his knees and begging her to return to Texas, he could go home with his pride intact.

But not his heart.

"Caleb!"

Breathless joy, rebuke, uncertainty—how had she managed to pack such a wealth of conflicting emotions in that one word?

She spared a quick glance at Ry, and her expressive face registered accusation, question, and maybe a touch of gratitude. Then all of her attention focused back on him.

They stood less than twelve feet apart, yet, like their first night together, it was an impossible distance to bridge.

An insistent tug on his wrist broke the spell. Remembering his supposed reason for coming, he took firmer hold of the leash. "I'm here to return your hairy menace. I couldn't stand the sight of all his moping for you." He let Poppy drag him forward.

Elthia stooped to welcome her pet. The pea-brained mutt greeted her with all the noisy, tail-wagging enthusiasm Caleb didn't dare show. He actually envied the little beast when Elthia let him cover her chin with wet kisses.

"Oooh, yes, all right. Good boy, Poppy. I missed you too." She stood, clutching Poppy at shoulder level. "And is bringing Poppy here the *only* reason you had for coming?"

Not by a long shot. I'd storm castles, fight fearsome ogres, just for the chance to get a glimpse of you. He managed a shrug. "Mostly." Caleb dusted his hat brim, avoiding her gaze. "I also wanted to see if there were any papers you wanted me to sign."

"I see." Her expression turned brittle. "I told you before, I will not pursue legal action."

Caleb stared, at a loss for what to say next. He shouldn't have come. How could he survive another parting?

Ry placed a hand on each of their shoulders. "Well, now that that's out of the way, why don't you take your husband out on the terrace. I'll ask Mrs. McGinty to find us some refreshments."

Elthia gave Caleb a pointed look. "Perhaps our *guest* would prefer to go upstairs and freshen up after his trip."

So, she'd relegated him to the status of guest, had she? "Not at all," Caleb said in a sudden fit of contrariness. "Let's have a look at this terrace of yours."

Elthia bit her lip and pushed at her glasses. Then she tossed her head. "Very well, this way."

He followed her through a pair of tall glass doors, deciding it was still fun to watch her get riled up. And a riled Elthia was definitely easier for him to face than a hurt one.

She sat on a wrought-iron chair as if it were a throne, tucking the dog regally on her lap.

Caleb indolently hitched up his hip on the low terrace wall.

"How was your trip?" she asked primly.

He picked a bit of lint from his pants leg. "Uneventful." *Endlessly long, knowing you were there at the end.*

"And are you planning to stay long?"

"I'll be heading back tomorrow." He wasn't sure he could take being in the same house with her for even that long, knowing she was forbidden fruit.

Elthia smiled politely. "A shame you won't have more time to rest." Was it wishful thinking, or did he sense disappointment beneath that polite hostess demeanor?

She looked down at her four-legged lap-warmer. "I got a letter from Zoe this week."

He should have known she'd keep in touch with the kids. "I guess they're settling in with Aunt Dorothy okay."

"So it seems. Zoe writes that your aunt is teaching her to play the church organ, and there are neighbors close by who have children for the younger ones to play with."

"Sounds ideal." It was what he'd hoped for. Wasn't it?

Elthia frowned accusingly at him. "She also says she misses Texas and wishes we were all back together again."

Ry joined them, inadvertently rescuing Caleb. "Mrs. McGinty's promised to send out some of her spiced raspberry tart. And she's having a room made ready for you now, woodcarver."

Caleb wasn't fooled by Ry's smile. He'd tolerate Caleb only so long as he thought it in his sister's best interest to do so.

Ry turned to Elthia. "And don't worry; I told the servants to put him over in the south wing, so you won't bump into each other if you happen to want a late-night stroll."

Elthia lowered her head to check on Poppy, but not before Caleb saw the red creep into her cheeks. Damn his brother-in-law for that perverse sense of humor.

Ry looked from Caleb to Elthia's bent head. "You know," he mused, "since Caleb's only going to be here for the one day, we ought to take him on a tour of the place. Maybe we could even sail out to the island this afternoon."

Caleb raised his eyebrows. "So you have your own island too?"

Elthia's head snapped up. "Actually, we have several." Her expression challenged him to make something of it. "Ry is referring to a small one in a lake on this property."

She turned to her brother. "I'm sure Caleb would prefer to do something less tiring than hike across the island. A quiet evening close to the house might be more appropriate."

Ry cast Caleb a challenging look. "That true, woodcarver? You prefer a tame walk in the garden to a trip to our island?"

Caleb didn't like Ry's attitude, but the arrogant bastard had his uses. Any activity that included Mr. Rich Boy was guaranteed to keep things from heating up between himself and Elthia.

"I'm game," he said with a shrug.

Elthia flashed them an I'm-only-doing-this-because-I-have-to smile. "Then a trip to the island for the three of us it is."

Caleb slipped from his perch. "In that case, I think I *will* go up to my room for a bit."

Ry's wry grin mocked him for the coward he was. "Not a fan of raspberry tarts, are you?"

Caleb shook his head. "Just need to change out of these traveling clothes and clean up a little."

Ry leaned back. "Elly, why don't you show your husband to his room? The Green Room, I believe."

Elthia didn't look any too pleased with her brother. "I think maybe—" She flashed a relieved smile as a footman appeared carrying a crystal pitcher and glasses. "Oh, Jeffrey," she said, "would you please show Mr. Tanner to his room?"

Jeffrey set the tray on the table and bowed. "Of course, madam." He turned to Caleb. "If you'll follow me, sir."

Something More

Her shoulders slumped as Caleb disappeared inside. Where was the arrogant, take-charge, no-time-for-small-talk man she'd married? More importantly, where was the warm, tender lover? Had he really only come to deliver Poppy? Didn't he have any feeling left for her?

He'd looked so strong and wonderful and *right* when he walked in. It had taken all her self-control not to dive into his arms. If only he'd given the slightest hint she'd be welcome there.

Needing a target, she rounded on her brother. "You forced him to come here, didn't you?"

Ry held up his palms. "Surely you know the woodcarver better than that."

"But his coming here *was* your suggestion, wasn't it?"

"The point is," Ry said, sidestepping her question, "your Romeo is here now. So when are you going to tell him?"

She fidgeted with Poppy's collar. "He isn't leaving until tomorrow." A part of her refused to abandon hope. She met Ry's knowing look. "I *will* tell him before he leaves. I just need to do it in my own time."

Ry stood and kissed her cheek. "Don't worry, Elly; I have faith in you and your woodcarver. I have a feeling you *will* get this business settled, one way or the other, before he leaves."

Caleb helped Elthia climb onto the small pier while Ry tied up the boat. When she stumbled and landed against his chest, his body responded immediately. Their gazes locked; then Elthia abruptly pushed herself away.

She marched to the shore, and Caleb frowned at her hasty retreat. Ry had led him to believe she still wanted him, but she sure hadn't been pleased by that near-embrace. Had seeing him in her home made her finally realize her mistake?

"There's a great view from the top of that rise," Ry said. "It's an easy twenty-minute walk if you're up to it, woodcarver."

Caleb bared his teeth in an almost-smile. "Lead on."

As they started off, Ry assumed the role of guide. He kept up a steady stream of chatter, pointing out places of interest and giving an uninterested Caleb a history lesson on the region.

Ry also kept himself physically between Caleb and Elthia.

293

Each time Caleb moved to help Elthia over a rough patch or move a branch from her path, Ry was there, a half step ahead of him.

Caleb had wanted someone around to keep things from heating up. So why, after the first five minutes, did he want to grab Ry by the collar and hang him from the nearest tree branch?

They came to a shallow creek, and again, Elthia's brother offered her his arm before Caleb could step forward.

Ry glanced solicitously over his shoulder. "It's only a few inches deep. You won't even get your shoes wet if you use the stepping stones. Just follow Elly and me."

Mumbling curses under his breath, Caleb let them get a short lead before he stepped onto the first of the rocks protruding from the water. While not deep, the stream was at least twelve feet wide. Ry and Elthia had reached the halfway point when Ry's foot slipped and landed with a splash in the gurgling water.

Ry had half turned, and Caleb took a great deal of pleasure from the disgruntled look on his usually cool brother-in-law's face. Too bad it was only his foot that got a dunking.

Then his smile fled as he realized Elthia was floundering. Ry's stumble had overset her balance as well. Ry grabbed her hands but only succeeded in easing her fall, not preventing it. With a startled squeak and a loud splash, she landed on her rump.

Ry leaned down. "Elly, are you all right?"

Caleb charged forward. "Out of the way, rich boy. I think she's had enough of your help."

Ry released Elthia's hand. "Now look here, woodcarver—"

"No, you look here. I've had just about—"

Elthia's palm slapped the water. "Will you stop acting like two dogs arguing over a bone and help me up?"

Caleb took her left arm while Ry stepped around to take her right. They exchanged glares over Elthia's head but succeeded in getting her upright without further incident.

"Are you sure you're okay?" Caleb checked the hand he was holding for cuts and worriedly eyed her stance for steadiness.

"Yes, yes, I'm fine." Elthia wrinkled her nose. "Just uncomfortable. Wet skirts are not only extremely unpleasant, they're heavy as well."

Ry's brow creased. "I really am sorry, Elly. Look, why don't I take you to the cabin? We can light a fire and you can slip out of that soggy skirt till it dries."

He turned to Caleb. "The cabin's just beyond that stand of trees. While I make Elly comfortable, you go back down to the boat. There's a blanket stored—"

"Hold on." Caleb placed a possessive arm around Elthia's shoulder. "Since you're more familiar with the island and the boat, I think it makes more sense for you to fetch the blanket and for me to escort Elthia to this cabin of yours."

Ry waved impatiently. "You don't know the way to the cabin."

"Oh, for goodness sake." Elthia's hands fisted on her hips. "Ry, I'm sure there's something in the cabin I can use."

But her brother shook his head. "I don't know. We haven't been up there in a while. Better get the one from the boat, just to be safe."

"Well, you just go ahead and fetch it." Caleb squeezed Elthia's arm. "And don't worry; Elthia can show me the way."

Ry frowned suspiciously. "What do you think, Elly? Should I entrust you to his keeping for a few minutes?"

Elthia rolled her eyes. "Oh, for pity's sake, Ry, stop baiting him. You know I'll be okay with Caleb. Just hurry with that blanket so I can change out of these sopping clothes."

Ry held up his hands in surrender. "All right. I guess, since I caused this little disaster, I should pay the forfeit." He glared at Caleb. "Make sure you watch your step, woodcarver."

"Your concern is touching." Caleb flashed him a toothy grin.

With a sour look, Ry headed back down the path they'd just climbed.

Caleb grinned. It felt good to get the better of his brother-in-law for once. Then he caught sight of Elthia, shaking her skirts and studiously avoiding his gaze. His grin faded.

Damn! He'd just maneuvered himself into spending time alone with her, the very thing he'd sworn to avoid at all costs. Well, there was nothing for it now. He'd just have to keep them both too busy to dwell on memories. That shouldn't be any more difficult than, say, sprouting wings and flying to the moon.

"So," he said heartily, "which way is this cabin of yours?"

Elthia met his gaze for a moment, then pointed to her left. "The path through that stand of firs takes you right to it."

He tucked her arm in his, trying not to think about the more intimate contact he wanted. "Let's go, then."

They walked in silence, keeping their eyes focused on the trail. Here beneath the trees, they were out of the glare of the sun. The insect drone and occasional small-animal-skittering noises were almost drowned out by the squishing of water-logged shoes and the leaf-rustling drag of Elthia's soggy skirts.

Caleb's respect for Elthia climbed as she marched on without complaint. He knew how uncomfortable her wet clothes must be.

The heated touch of her hand on his arm, however, engendered a totaly different kind of emotion. When she preceded him on a narrow part of the trail, he drank in the sight of her regal carriage and swaying hips. When she hiked her skirts up to step over a log, he swallowed hard, forcing his hands to stay at his sides. But the toughest test of his control was her repeated brushing and bumping against him. Her feet seemed determined to catch on every vine or root that dared encroach on the trail.

By the time they reached the cabin, Caleb was in dire need of a long dip in a snow-fed pond. Too bad it was still summer.

"Here it is," she announced unnecessarily.

The cabin was a small, snugly built log structure, with a cedar shingle roof and a stone chimney protruding from the back. Because Ry had mentioned they hadn't been here in a while, Caleb had expected it to show signs of neglect.

He should have known better. Apparently the Sinclares had servants enough to take care of even this place. Everything looked well maintained and neat as a pin, even to the expertly pruned rose bushes flanking the south wall.

Caleb opened the door and ushered Elthia inside. When he followed her, he found himself in a comfortably furnished, one-room abode. There was a kitchen area on one end, a sleeping area on the other, and a fireplace and comfortable seating in the middle. This little cabin, set aside for the occasional Sinclare outing, was better than some homes he'd visited.

That reminder effectively cooled his ardor.

Elthia moved toward the sleeping alcove. "Looks like Ry's hiking back to the boat for nothing. There are lots of clean sheets and blankets here, same as always."

Served Rich Boy right.

Then Caleb saw her hand move to the buttons of her bodice, and he suddenly found it hard to breathe normally. Abruptly, he turned toward the hearth. "I'll get a fire started."

But it was no use. Even with his back turned, his imagination fed him pictures of her undressing, and his memory taunted him with images of what her sweet, trim body looked like under those layers of clothing.

Elthia stared in frustration at Caleb's back. Nothing she'd tried had had any effect on him, not even when she'd shamelessly flashed a bit of leg. She knew she wasn't the kind of woman who captured men's fancies, but she'd hoped Caleb's affections had been engaged enough to lend a certain allure to her actions.

She might as well face facts: He just wasn't interested. Had he ever been?

Elthia stepped out of her dress and petticoats. With a hand on the ties of her undergarments, she glanced self-consciously toward Caleb. But he was still bent over the fireplace. From the sounds of his muffled mutterings she deduced that he was having trouble getting the fire started.

She shed the rest of her clothes and reached for a sheet. Before she wound the cloth around herself, though, she rubbed her stomach. *Don't worry*, she silently assured her unborn child, *your daddy and I will work this out, one way or the other*.

With deft movements, she wrapped the sheet around her body, leaving her arms and shoulders free but covering everything from that point down. After checking to make sure the drape of the makeshift gown hid the slight but telling bulge of her tummy, Elthia tilted her chin and crossed the room.

Caleb's back stiffened as soon as she stepped from the alcove. So, he wasn't as unaware as he'd pretended. With a smile, Elthia lifted a loop of rope from a peg on the wall. She turned to find Caleb, still on one knee, watching her. *Ogling* might be more accurate. She suddenly felt a surge of hope.

When he saw what she held, his gaze quickly flew up to meet hers. "What's that for?" he asked warily.

"I was hoping you could rig a line near the hearth to hang my clothes on. If you're finished fiddling with the fire, that is?"

Caleb nodded and stood. "Of course." He crossed the room and took the rope from her outstretched hands.

Her sheet threatened to slip and she hitched it back up. Caleb's gaze shifted to the exposed part of her chest, but with visible effort, he focused back on her face.

"Thanks," she said with a bright smile. "Do you need help?"

"Help?"

She tried not to grin at the blank look on his face. "Stringing the line," she explained patiently.

"No." He cleared his throat. "No, I can handle it. You just get your clothes gathered up."

"All right."

Elthia collected her wet garments and then watched as Caleb stood on a chair and tied the rope to a couple of rafters. Then she handed the articles up to him, one at a time, to arrange over the line. When she handed up the first of her lacy undergarments he stiffened and hesitated, as if she were handing him a snake.

"Is something the matter?" she asked sweetly.

He met her gaze, and a touch of red crept into his cheeks. "Uh, no, I was just wondering what was keeping your brother." He snatched the garment from her and slapped it on the line.

"I'm sure he'll be here soon."

"Yes, well . . ." Caleb looked around the cabin, then back at her. "In the meantime, I think I'll bring in some extra firewood."

Elthia nodded toward the back door. "There should be some already cut and stacked right out there."

"Mind if I take a little look around while I'm outside?"

Elthia shrugged. "Help yourself."

Once he left, she began to pace. If the last few minutes were any indication, Caleb still felt at least some physical attraction to her. But was that all he felt?

Something More

Enough with the games, the teasing. She had to know if there was something more, something worth fighting to hold on to. As soon as Ry showed up, she'd ask him to go away again for thirty minutes or so. Of course, getting Ry to leave wasn't going to be her problem; getting Caleb to stay was.

Her pacing took her to the kitchen area. She halted as she spied a picnic basket. It had probably been left here from a previous outing. What caught her eye, though, was the neck of an unopened wine bottle protruding from the cover.

Would it help to put Caleb in a more relaxed frame of mind? She pulled the basket toward her, frowning at the weight. There was more in here than a forgotten bottle of wine. Elthia lifted the lid to find it packed full with all manner of items, from cheese and bread to teacakes and cold ham, all of it quite fresh.

Comprehension slowly dawned. She heard the door open behind her. Taking a deep breath, she turned to face Caleb.

He set a load of firewood beside the hearth, then turned to her. "I didn't see any sign of your brother yet. I wonder if—"

Something in her expression must have caught his attention. "What's wrong?"

Elthia shoved up her glasses and quit worrying at her lower lip. "We've been set up. Ry's not coming back."

Chapter Twenty-seven

"What do you mean, not coming back?"

Elthia winced, and Caleb realized he'd spoken louder than he'd intended. But his gut clenched at the thought of having to stay here alone with her much longer without being able to touch her.

"I just found this." Elthia carried a picnic basket to the table and lifted the lid.

He glanced at the wealth of food, then back at her. "So, your brother had a meal sent on ahead. That doesn't mean—"

"There are only two wine glasses."

Caleb poked around in the basket. She was right. And only two sets of dinnerware. But it didn't have to mean what she thought it did, he rationalized desperately. "You're jumping—"

She stared at him with relentless assurance. "I know Ry."

Caleb clenched his jaw. There *had* to be another explanation. But his gut agreed he'd been outmaneuvered.

With a sigh, Elthia waved toward the back door. "There are rungs on the north wall. You can use them to climb up to the roof. Ry and I used to do that when we were children. It gives you a good view of the jetty where we tied the sailboat."

Without a word Caleb turned and stalked out the door. He climbed up to the roof already knowing what he would see.

Gazing at the spot where the boat should have been, he let out a string of curses. Elthia's brother would be wise to keep his distance for a while if he wanted to retain all of his teeth and mobility.

Caleb raked a hand through his hair. What in the hell was he supposed to do now? There was no way he could spend a night alone with her in that cabin without going stark, staring mad. Or begging her to come back to Texas with him.

He turned and started down the ladder. Tempting as the idea was, he couldn't spend the night up here. Reaching the ground, he shoved the door open. "Ry had this planned from the start."

Elthia nodded. "So it seems."

"Even to dunking you in the stream." He shut the door behind him with a little more force than was necessary, but much less than he'd use on Rich Boy next time he saw him.

Elthia nodded again. "Now I know why he seemed to be both breaking my fall and tripping me up at the same time."

Caleb crossed the room with long, angry strides and propped both fists on the table. God, what he wouldn't give for something to pound on right now. "That brother of yours has a rotten sense of humor."

Elthia held up a hand. "I had nothing to do with this." She lifted her chin. "But I'm not terribly upset that he did it."

Caleb's irritation changed to wariness. Oh Lord, she was going to start in on him now. The last thing he needed was to point-blank face her recriminations and questions. He rubbed the back of his neck, searching his mind for something to deflect her obvious determination. "I don't suppose there's another boat?"

"Not even a dinghy."

She didn't seem bothered by the situation. And that glint of determination was still there. It didn't bode well for his already nonexistent peace of mind.

"How long do you figure it'll be before he sends someone back for us?" he asked, trying not to sound desperate.

Shrugging, Elthia waved to the hamper. "Judging by this, and knowing my brother, I don't expect to see anyone until morning."

She winced as he bit off a curse he couldn't quite swallow

Then she sat up straighter and commandeered his gaze with her own. "Caleb, we need to talk."

He smothered a groan. Deciding he'd have to bluster his way through, he smiled. "I've sort of missed hearing you say that."

Actually, that much was true.

He took a chair and leaned back, tilting it up on its two back legs. "So, what do we talk about this time?"

"Do you love me?" she blurted out.

The front legs of his chair landed on the floor with a thud. Damnation! She didn't intend to beat around the bush any. How the devil was he supposed to answer that?

From the appalled look on her face, he guessed that wasn't what she'd intended to say. "Now what sort of fool question is that?" he asked, hoping she'd back down.

Seeing her shift in her chair, Caleb felt a spark of hope that she'd lost her nerve. He couldn't let her continue this line of discussion. It would only hurt both of them.

But he wasn't to be let off so lightly. That stubborn expression he knew so well returned.

She hitched her wrap up a bit higher and tucked a stray tendril back behind her ear. "To be fair, I should tell you that I love you. I love you and I want to spend the rest of my life with you. I no longer feel whole without you."

Caleb's heart expanded until it threatened to cut off his breathing. She loved him! Her words carried him to the mountaintop of joy and the pit of despair at the same time. How could he take such a precious gift and use it to trap her in a life that would burden her?

But she wasn't through. She clasped her hands on the table in front of her and frowned at him. "I believe I have the right to know how you feel about me, about us. How you *truly* feel."

Caleb shoved his chair back and stood. He paced halfway across the room before he spoke. How could he make her see that he was acting in her best interests? It wasn't what *he* wanted. If only . . . "Blast it all, Elthia, it's not as simple as that."

"Yes, it is." He heard the conviction in her voice, the driving need to hear his answer. "Either you feel the same way or you don't. I'm willing to fight everyone and everything, including you, to find a way to pull our family back together. But not if

I thought I would be forcing something on you that you don't really desire. Again, I need to know how you *truly feel.*"

Did she know she was asking him to lay his soul bare, to open a door he could never step through? If he ever said the words, it would all be over.

He turned to her, his face set, trying to find the words to make her quit pushing. "Elthia, it's no good. I can't offer you this kind of life. I can't even offer you something close."

"Did I ever ask you to?"

He clenched his fists at his sides, forcing himself to say part of what he felt. "No, but what do you think it does to a man's pride to know he's forced someone he . . . he cares about, to give up so much?" Elthia moved to his side, and he forced himself not to reach for her.

She met his gaze, her expression earnest, searching. "Caleb, you have no need to feel any guilt. It's not what I'd be giving up that matters, it's what I'd be gaining. A sense of purpose, of making a difference, of belonging. The love of a husband and children. A home where *I* am the domestic center."

When she placed a hand on his arm he almost flinched. He was that sensitive to her touch now.

"I've never felt happier, more at *home,* than I did those last few weeks in Texas," she continued. "That's something you can't put a price on. It means more to me than all my father's money."

Oh, God, she was so sweet, so giving. He raised a hand to brush the side of her face. What she offered was so tempting, he almost gave in. Then his fingers curled and he drew back. He had to stand firm! "You don't understand. There's more to it."

She looked ready to stomp her foot. "Then tell me, so I'll understand," she commanded impatiently.

She was forcing him to pull out the rest of his miserable failings and hang them up for her to see. Why couldn't she just accept his words at face value? "That time we spent together proved that I'm not cut out to be a father."

She had a curious reaction to his words. Her hand flew to her waist, and a lost look crossed her face. But immediately her mood shifted. Dropping her hand, she raised her chin.

"That's ridiculous. You were a *wonderful* father to the children."

His determined champion—always so quick to jump to his defense. If only . . .

Caleb sighed. "No, *you* were a wonderful mother. I completely missed the signals Peter and Zoe were sending. If not for you, they'd still be miserable."

Elthia placed both hands on her hips, then had to raise one quickly to catch her makeshift gown as it threatened to slip. But her glare held. "Caleb Tanner, that is the most self-centered, pitiful bit of drivel I've ever heard in my life."

Her attack caught him off guard. "What—"

She poked a finger at his chest with her free hand. "Are you ready to give up simply because you aren't all-knowing and all-seeing? For goodness sake, so I uncovered those problems before you did. That's why God set it up so most children have two parents, so one can catch what the other one misses."

He backed up a step, then two, trying to avoid her jabbing finger. He hadn't seen her this riled up in some time.

She followed him, step for step. "What about the times you were there first? Should I feel bad because I failed them?"

What the hell was she talking about? "When—"

"Like knowing Alex needed those cages without him having to tell you. Like staying up nights with the children when they had the measles. Like the way you worked so hard to make Peter feel wanted and needed."

How could she compare such everyday things with the others? "But—"

She forced him another step back as she pressed her next point with another finger to his chest. "And let's not forget the fact that you battled your sisters and the courts in order to keep the children together. You even went so far as to accept a bride, sight unseen, so you could safeguard the arrangement and the children could have a mother."

He stepped back again, this time smack into the wet clothes strung on the line behind him. His arms flailed as he attempted to untangle himself and keep track of Elthia at the same time. So much for him taking back control of this conversation.

She pushed on, ignoring his clumsy stumblings. "That's the kind of father you are, Caleb Tanner. And that's the kind of father I want my children to have. I think it's downright arrogant and conceited to expect perfection of yourself, which is what you'd have if you asked for more of yourself."

Caleb finally shook off the clinging bits of feminine apparel and stared at the vengeful goddess bearing down on him. What she was saying—did she really believe it? Could she possibly be seeing things more objectively than he did?

Dear God, was there really a chance . . .

She followed him past the barrier of wet clothes. Shaking her head, she offered a sympathetic smile. "Oh, Caleb, is that why you sent us away, because you're not perfect?"

He was breathing hard, as if he'd run uphill. He wanted so badly to believe her, to greedily grasp the gift she offered him.

She placed a finger to his lips to still his next words. "I don't want perfection, Caleb. I want you."

As if her finger had been a mighty battering ram, he felt the shell around his defenses fracture. With a groan, he pulled her to him, burying his face in her hair. "God help me, sweetheart, I know I don't deserve you, but I can't fight you anymore."

He reveled in the feel of his arms around her, in the silky touch of her hair on his cheek for a few glorious minutes. Then she pulled back enough to see his face.

With a vulnerable, I-have-to-know-no-matter-what expression, she met his gaze. "You never answered my question."

He smiled tenderly and reached up to remove her glasses. Setting them aside, he brushed the hair away from her face. "I have loved you since that morning you faced me in the barn, alone, scared, and wonderfully brave, refusing to back down." Saying the words aloud was more liberating and satisfying than he'd imagined it could be. Why had he ever hesitated?

Elthia threw herself back in his arms, but not before he saw a suspicious trace of moisture in her eyes. "Oh, Caleb. Then you'll take me back with you?"

He squeezed her tight, never wanting to let her go again. "I dare anyone to try to stop me."

She sought his gaze. "If my money is a problem, I'll give it away, or put it in trust for the children, or whatever else you like."

Lord above, but he did love her. He'd been a selfish brute to make her feel such a sacrifice was necessary. He kissed the tip of her nose. "I don't think we need to do anything quite so drastic. As long as you're willing to live day to day off my earnings, I can live with you occasionally doing something special for the children or yourself." He gave her a rueful grin. "If we live off your inheritance I might feel like people thought I married you for your wealth."

He took a deep breath, deciding he needed to go a step further. He owed her that and more. "But you should spend your money however you see fit. You might even want to hire someone to help with the housework a couple of days a week."

Eyes shining, Elthia pulled his head down for a quick kiss. "You *are* a good man, Caleb Tanner."

Happy that he'd pleased her, Caleb gave her a squeeze. "I think we can do better than that."

He lowered his head for another kiss, one he was prepared to make much more satisfying than the tame one she'd just given him. Elthia's arms snaked around his neck. She went deliciously limp in his arms, melting against him in a way that set his pulse racing and his body into an agony of anticipation. She was pliant, she was passionate, and she was his.

He lifted her and carried her across the room, continuing the kiss, even when he set her on the bed. His lips moved lower as he reached for the knotted end of the sheet at her bodice.

"Wait." She pushed his hand away and struggled to sit up.

Caleb clamped down hard on his control. "What is it?" Did she no longer desire his touch?

She fiddled with her hair, tucking it nervously behind an ear. "Before we . . . well, before we go any further, there's something I have to tell you."

So there *was* something wrong. He braced himself for another rejection. "I'm listening."

His self-assured, forthright wife suddenly looked shy and uncertain. "I . . . we . . . Oh, Caleb, we're going to have a baby."

After a second of blank incomprehension, a blaze of pure joy shot through Caleb.

Elthia breathed a sigh of relief. There was no mistaking the fact that Caleb welcomed the news.

"Are you sure?" he asked, as if afraid to believe her. "I mean, before you left, you said—"

"I know. But I was wrong. Dr. Driscoll confirmed it. He tells me that occasionally a woman continues with a weak monthly cycle through the early part of her confinement."

Caleb ran a hand through his hair. "We're going to have a baby." Then his face split in a broad grin. "We're going to have a baby!" he repeated, giving her an exultant hug.

He pulled back, his expression almost comically aghast. "I'm sorry. Did I hurt you?"

Elthia laughed. It would be a long six months if he was going to treat her like she was breakable. "Just because I'm carrying our child doesn't mean I've suddenly turned to glass."

A troubled look crossed Caleb's face. But it was there and gone in a matter of seconds. As if forcing something unpleasant aside, he reached out to hug her again.

She held him back, determined he would not return to shutting her out now that he'd finally let her in. "What's the matter?"

He cocked a brow. "Nothing's the matter. I just thought I'd try to steal another kiss."

But she wasn't buying it. He had to learn to trust her with the bad news as well as the good. "Don't do this, Caleb. Something's bothering you. Tell me what it is, or tell me to mind my own business, but don't lie to me."

He studied her face a moment, then nodded. "All right, no more secrets. The thought just crossed my mind that perhaps this bit of news had something to do with your eagerness to come back to Texas with me." He flashed an unconcerned smile that she saw straight through. "Not that it would change anything," he assured her. "You're coming with me, regardless."

Furious, Elthia drew back, grabbed a pillow, and swung it at him as hard as she could. "You are, without a doubt, the most hardheaded man I have ever come across. This baby has nothing to do with my wanting to be with you."

He raised an arm, deflecting a second blow. He grabbed the pillow from her and tossed it aside. "Now, sweet-heart—"

She glared. "Don't you 'Now, sweetheart' me." She touched

a finger to the bridge of her nose, shoving up glasses that were no longer there. She was thankful that he'd finally trusted her enough to speak of his feelings but was appalled at what those feelings revealed. How could she get through to him?

"Think about it," she said. "I already have your name, so there would be no real social stigma. I'm surrounded by a family who is more than willing to rally round and help me raise this child. I have access to the best doctors in the country." She tossed her head. "So why would I need to be with you?"

He winced. Good! Maybe he'd gotten her point after all.

"Why? No reason." She allowed irritation to color her every word and movement. "Other than the fact that I love you." She poked his chest indignantly. "That I loved you before I ever discovered I was going to have a baby, and that I will never be whole again without you."

He shifted closer, but she held him off with angrily narrowed eyes. "And if you *ever* see fit to question the truth of that again, I *will* sic Poppy on you."

Her words broke down the last of the wall he'd so carefully erected around his heart. There was no way, looking at her now, that he could doubt the genuineness of her outrage, the honesty of her love. He wanted to shout his joy to the world.

But first there were ruffled feathers to soothe. He flashed another smile, this one absolutely genuine. "You sure are pretty when you get riled."

An unforgiving *harrumph* was his only answer.

He toyed with a corner of her sheet, feathering it against her ankle. "You're not gonna stay mad at me long, are you?"

Her eyes flickered down to his hands. "And why shouldn't I?"

He released the sheet and began massaging her foot, giving special attention to the sensitive arch. "Well, sweetheart, it's not that I don't deserve for you to be riled at me, but I was just thinking what a shame it would be for us to waste tonight."

He smiled as he noticed her smother a half-formed sigh. She was enjoying his touch. Well, there was more where that came from. His hands shifted to her other foot.

"After all," he continued, "your brother went to all the trouble of leaving us alone for the night, the least we could do is make the best of it. We'll be heading out tomorrow, and we're not likely to find much in the way of privacy or comfort until we get back to Foxberry." He shrugged. "And since we have to go to Indiana first, that's liable to be a while."

Her gaze snapped to his at that. "Oh, Caleb, do you really think we can get the children back?"

He slid over beside her, putting an arm around her shoulders. "If we have to camp on Judge Walters's doorstep for a month, we'll make him listen. We won't return to Texas without our family."

He brushed her temple, smiling at her shivery response. "But for tonight, we have other things to occupy us."

She turned in his arms, and Caleb's mouth met hers with a hunger and urgency that would not be denied.

As he laid her back against the pillows, he said a silent prayer of thanks for this second chance at happiness, and for the stubborn woman who had fought for him to see and grasp it.

She'd said she wanted to feel loved and needed, to feel like she'd made a difference. Well, she was, and she had.

And he'd ask for nothing more than to spend the rest of his life proving to her just how much.

Epilogue

Caleb climbed up the stairs, careful to avoid the creaky tread near the top. Elthia'd been after him to fix it for weeks now. Maybe he'd get to it tomorrow.

It was late. Most of the house was quiet and dark. Caleb opened the door of his bedroom, smiling at the picture that greeted him.

Elthia sat in the rocking chair he'd finished for her three days before little Grace was born. The baby, now two weeks old, lay at her mother's breast, sleepily suckling.

As he slipped inside and quietly closed the door, Elthia looked up and smiled. She placed a finger to her lips as he approached. By the time he was close enough to put a hand on her shoulder, Grace, with a final smack of her lips, settled back in the crook of her mother's arm, sound asleep.

Caleb picked up his daughter, awed once again by the perfection of her tiny features. She had her mother's red hair and violet eyes, but the nose and chin were pure Tanner.

Grace stirred for a minute, and he gently jiggled her in his arms as he carried her to the bassinet, situated near the chaise.

Elthia slipped up beside him as he straightened, and they stood there a minute, each with an arm around the other, staring at the newest Tanner.

When Elthia yawned, Caleb smiled and picked her up. "Come on, sweetheart, you've had a long day."

She wrapped her arms around his neck and snuggled up to his chest. "But a marvelous one. Oh, Caleb, I can hardly believe they're finally all ours."

Judge Walters had delivered the papers today that made the adoptions final. Caleb and Elthia had invited their neighbors and friends for a grand picnic party to not only celebrate the occasion but to introduce Grace to the community.

He was now the father of not only infant Grace but her six cousins as well. With Elthia by his side, a man couldn't ask for a finer family.

As Caleb climbed into bed beside his sleepy-eyed wife, he said a silent prayer of thanks for all his blessings, the chief of which was the woman at his side. His sweet, opinionated, saucy angel of a wife had helped him finally find that something more he'd been searching for all his life.

Winnie Griggs — What Matters Most

Reed Wilder journeys to Far Enough, Texas, in search of a fallen woman. He finds an angel. Barely reaching five feet two inches, the petite brunette helps to defend him against two ruffians and then treats his wounds with a gentleness that makes him long to uncover all her secrets. But she only has to reveal her name and he knows his lovely rescuer is not an innocent woman, but the deceitful opportunist who preyed on his brother. Reed prides himself on his logic and control, but both desert him when he gazes into Lucy's warm brown eyes. He has only one option: to discover the truth behind those enticing lips he longs to sample.

_4829-9 $4.99 US/$5.99 CAN

Lady
Gypsy
Pam Crooks

When an exotic Gypsy with flowing red tresses steals Reese Carrison's prized stallion, he gallops after her — straight into a tornado. It is not the twister that threatens to ravage him, though, but the woman who tames his horse. For in the eye of the storm, her soothing touch incites a whirlwind of passion he is helpless to resist. Liza longs only to escape the hated world of the non-Gypsy — the Gaje. Instead she finds herself wrapped in the sheltering embrace of a powerful Gajo man — a man who incites traitorous desires. A man whose sensuality strips away her defenses and whose caresses touch down on her heart, leaving in their wake not destruction, but love. A love that says she belongs in his arms, a love that makes her his Lady Gypsy.

___4911-2 $4.99 US/$5.99 CAN

WYOMING WILDFLOWER
PAM CROOKS

Armed with an arsenal of book knowledge on ranching, Sonnie returns to the Rocking M Ranch determined to prove that despite her sex she can be the son her father has always wanted. Lance Harmon has beaten her to the punch, though. She rides in on her high horse, determined to unseat him. But Lance knows Sonnie toppled him years ago, for he has always been head over heels in love with the rancher's youngest daughter. And yet, he plans to chase her away. Trouble on the range demands it. Sonnie doesn't shy away when danger comes rustling through, though, proving to Lance that the one thing that means more to him than the only home he's ever known, is the only woman he's ever loved, his . . . Wyoming Wildflower.

___4843-4 $4.99 US/$5.99 CAN

Alicia's Song

SUSAN PLUNKETT

For Alicia James, something is missing. Her childhood romance hadn't ended the way she dreamed, and she is wary of trying again. Still, she finds solace in her sisters and in the fact that her career is inspiring. And together with those sisters, Alicia finds a magic in song that seems almost able to carry away her woes.

In fact, singing carries Alicia away—from her home in modern-day Wyoming to Alaska, a century before her own. There she finds a sexy, dark-haired gentleman with an angelic child just crying out for guidance. And Alicia is everything this pair desperately needs. Suddenly it seems as if life is reaching out and giving Alicia the chance to create a beautiful music she's never been able to make with her sisters—all she needs is the courage to sing her part.

___52434-1 $4.99 US/$5.99 CAN

Dorchester Publishing Co., Inc.
P.O. Box 6640
Wayne, PA 19087-8640

Please add $1.75 for shipping and handling for the first book and $.50 for each book thereafter. NY, NYC, and PA residents, please add appropriate sales tax. No cash, stamps, or C.O.D.s. All orders shipped within 6 weeks via postal service book rate. Canadian orders require $2.00 extra postage and must be paid in U.S. dollars through a U.S. banking facility.

Name_____
Address_____
City_____State_____Zip_____
I have enclosed $_____ in payment for the checked book(s).
Payment <u>must</u> accompany all orders. ❏ Please send a free catalog.
        CHECK OUT OUR WEBSITE! www.dorchesterpub.com

Susan Plunkett

Bethany's Song

For Bethany James, freedom comes in the form of the River of Time, sweeping her away from her old life to 1895. But on awakening in Juneau, Alaska, Bethany discovers a whole new batch of problems. For one thing, she has been separated from her sisters—the only ones with whom she shares perfect harmony. And the widowed mine-owner who finds her— Matthew Gray—is hardly someone with whom she expects to connect. Yet struggling to survive, drawing on every skill she possesses, the violet-eyed beauty finds herself growing into a stronger person. She is learning to trust, learning to love. And in helping Matt do the same, Bethany realizes the laments of the past are only too soon made the sweet strains of happiness.

___52463-5 $5.50 US/$6.50 CAN

Dorchester Publishing Co., Inc.
P.O. Box 6640
Wayne, PA 19087-8640

Please add $2.50 for shipping and handling for the first book and $.75 for each book thereafter. NY and PA residents, please add appropriate sales tax. No cash, stamps, or C.O.D.s. All orders shipped within 6 weeks via postal service book rate.
Canadian orders require $2.00 extra postage and must be paid in
U.S. dollars through a U.S. banking facility.

Name_____
Address_____
City_____ State_____ Zip_____
I have enclosed $_____ in payment for the checked book(s).
Payment <u>must</u> accompany all orders. ☐Please send a free catalog.
CHECK OUT OUR WEBSITE! www.dorchesterpub.com

Lori Morgan

Autumn Star

Morgan Caine rescues Lacey Ashton from a couple of pawing ruffians, feeds her dinner, and gives her a place to sleep. He is arrogant, bossy, and the most captivating man she has ever met. He claims she will never survive the wilds of the Washington Territory. But Lacey sets out to prove she not only belongs in the untamed land, she belongs in Morgan's arms.

Morgan is completely disarmed by Lacey's innocence and optimism. Like an autumn breeze, she caresses his body, refreshes his soul, invigorates his heart. At last, the hardened lawman longs to trade vengeance for a future filled with happiness—to reach for the stars and claim the woman of his dreams.

___4892-2 $4.99 US/$5.99 CAN

MOONBOW IN THE *Mist*

DIA HUNTER

Leaning out to peek at a flat boat poling up the Cumberland River, Naomi Romans falls flat on her face. Cradled in Shaw Larson's strong arms and staring up into the river peddler's pretty yellow-green eyes, Naomi finds everything changed . . . even herself. The fall brought her memories *back*. She isn't Naomi; she is Prima Powell, the missing daughter of a New York millionaire. Bedeviled by a pair of raccoons, befuddled by two years of lost memories, and bedazzled by Shaw's gentlest touch, Naomi is certain: she is the girl who went stumbling off so long to find moonbows in the mist . . . and now she's found something even better.

___4891-4 $5.50 US/$6.50 CAN